TROUBLE IN THE WIND

BOOK THREE OF THE PHASES OF MARS

Edited by
Chris Kennedy and James Young

Theogony Books
Virginia Beach, VA

Chris Kennedy/Theogony Books
2052 Bierce Dr., Virginia Beach, VA 23454
http://chriskennedypublishing.com/

Publisher's Note: This is a work of fiction. Names, characters, places, and incidents are a product of the author's imagination. Locales and public names are sometimes used for atmospheric purposes. Any resemblance to actual people, living or dead, or to businesses, companies, events, institutions, or locales is completely coincidental.

Trouble in the Wind/Chris Kennedy and James Young -- 1st ed.
ISBN 978-1950420759

For all who have gone off to war to protect the ones they loved…
and never returned.

Preface by Christopher G. Nuttall

"We hope that you, instead of thinking to influence us by saying that you did not join the [Spartans], although their colonists, or that you have done us no wrong, will aim at what is feasible, holding in view the real sentiments of us both; since you know as well as we do that right, as the world goes, is only in question between equals in power, while the strong do what they can and the weak suffer what they must."

Thucydides

Does might make right?

If you ask that question of just about anyone, in this day and age, they will say *no*. Being stronger doesn't confer righteousness. But that answer is itself a product of the modern age. Our ancestors from just about every civilisation throughout history would have argued that might *did* make right, at least as long as *they* were the mighty ones. It is only comparatively recently that we have started to question the morality of empires and suchlike, although—a cynic might argue—that such questioning has not led to restorative justice. How can it?

Regardless of the morality of 'might makes right,' it must be noted that might does tend to define what *happens*. The Romans destroyed Carthage, put bluntly, because they won the trial of strength. Genghis Khan rampaged through China because there was no one who could stop him. Islam dominates the Middle East because the early Muslims were stronger than their rivals; Islam didn't take Europe because the early Europeans were stronger than the would-be invaders. The Conquistadors invaded and held Mexico because they were stronger, even when they were grossly outnumbered. And so on. Wars, as Elizabeth the First opinioned, are chancy things. Moderation in war is imbecility, stated Admiral Jackie Fisher (who never actually commanded a fleet in battle), but so too is triggering an unrestricted war you might lose. Just ask the Confederate States or the National Socialist Workers Party.

So why, you might ask, do I mention this in connection with alternate history?

The vast majority of alternate historical writings, be they everything from novels to timelines and detailed essays, are linked—directly or indirectly—to war. This can happen directly, in a story following a battle that was won in one timeline but lost in another, or indirectly, in a story set in a world created by a changed battle. *SS-GB*, for example, flows from a battle—the invasion of Britain in 1940—that never took place in *our* world, for better or worse. (You can get an interesting little flame war going on any alternate history discussion board over the odds of a Nazi victory.) *Fox on the Rhine*, by contrast, follows Rommel and Patton in France as the after-effects of Hitler's early death (in 1944) start to take shape. And indeed, you can have a neat little series of events flowing from a previous change in the timeline. In one world, where the US wins the Civil War, Lieutenant Colonel George Custer rides to his death at Little Big Horn. In another world (*How Few Remain*), where the CSA became independent, Confederate troops prevent Custer from chasing Sitting Bull and Crazy Horse into Confederate territory…ironically saving Custer's life, although Custer has no way to know he should be grateful.

Many of these stories follow new weapons, either invented ahead of time (antitank bazooka-type weapons in Poland) or brought back in time by Alien Space Bats. They ask questions about what would happen if those weapons were deployed, how they would change the war and, perhaps most importantly, how they'd be countered. What would become of the Panzers if they faced Polish and French soldiers with portable antitank weapons that actually *worked*? Others follow wars and campaigns that simply never happened, from analysing the likely course of Britain joining the American Civil War (on either side) to the logistical problems facing a Russian army as it tried to turn the Great Game—an Anglo-Russian Cold War—into a *real* war by invading British India through Afghanistan. There will always be plenty of scope for armchair generals in alternate history.

But most of these stories, the best of them, focus on the men doing the fighting.

It is a fundamental truth that, if you wish to influence events on the ground, you must put boots—i.e. soldiers—on it. This is not something that pleases modern-day politicians and senior officers. Many of the former recoil in horror at the thought of a single casualty; many of the latter are convinced that advanced weapons, from airpower and drones to cyber and space-based warfare, will allow the West (i.e. America) to emerge victorious without risking a single life. This is, unfortunately, untrue. On one hand, such weapons have almost always proved overrated even when the commanders are allowed their head; on the other, the high cost in civilian lives and the simple fact that bombing is *rarely* enough to force a state to change its course, means that such attacks are often nothing more than expensive ways of doing nothing. (On the plus side, concern for civilian lives—even *enemy* civilians—is yet another sign of moral superiority.)

Men on the ground have no illusions about the world. Combat has a habit of reducing ambiguity, of reducing complex issues to a simple trial of strength. God is on the side of the big battalions, as the saying goes, although the 'big battalions' may be technologically more advanced rather than simply more numerous. Soldiers on the ground cannot allow themselves the luxury of believing fancy theories about war, not when everything depends on them emerging victorious. They study everything from logistics—an army cannot move or fight without food, fuel, and ammunition—to new technologies and tactics. But, in the end, it all comes down to the facts on the ground. And they are determined by the soldiers.

Alternate history shows us how a handful of men—soldiers, sailors, or airmen—can change the course of history. If the Prussians had acted differently at Waterloo, would Napoleon have won the battle? Or, if the British had lost *their* section of the battle, would it be Prussia and Russia that determined the fate of post-Waterloo France? Or, if Stonewall Jackson hadn't rallied the troops during the Battle of Bull Run, would the North have won the American Civil War within a year? If British and French troops hadn't made their stand at Calais, would Hitler's panzers have reached Dunkirk in time to destroy the BEF?

It is often difficult to determine precisely *what* was the driving factor. Good leadership is one, ranging from daring and brilliant commanding officers to men who have access to a superior military-political playbook. Technology is another, from a handful of relatively small advantages to weapons an order of magnitude more powerful and capable then the threats they faced. And there is training and morale, as history shows us; outnumbered, but better-trained soldiers can defeat a force that is simply not ready for combat.

But all of this rests on the men on the ground, the rough men who—as George Orwell put it—stand ready to do violence on our behalf. It is these men who make the decisions that change the course of history.

The stories in this volume are all glimpses of worlds that might have been, of battles and campaigns that went the other way...if they were fought at all. They are stories of brave men and cowards, of heroes standing against overwhelming odds and poor bastards being used as pawns by distant politicians. But they are also a reminder of just how fragile our world is, how little guarantee there is of our future safety...

...And, perhaps most importantly of all, just how different the world could be.

Christopher G. Nuttall

Edinburgh, United Kingdom, 2019

Contents

The Sting Of Fate by William Alan Webb 13

To Save The Republic by Sarah A. Hoyt 51

Here Must We Hold by Rob Howell 77

The Heretic by Monalisa Foster 111

Secondhand Empires by Brad R. Torgersen 139

A Shot Heard 'Round The World by Kevin J.
Anderson & Kevin Ikenberry 173

Marching Through by David Weber 207

To The Rescue by S.M. Stirling 233

The Blubber Battle: The First Falklands Campaign
by Joelle Presby & Patrick Doyle 257

Drang Nach Osten (Drive To The East) by
Christopher G. Nuttall 287

Fighting Spirit by Philip S. Bolger 311

An Orderly Withdrawal by Taylor Anderson 347

Mr. Dewey's Tank Corps by James Young 385

Soldiers Of The Republic by Justin Watson 425

Unintended Consequences by Peter Grant 461

Nemo Me Impune Lacessit by Jan Niemczyk 499

* * * * *

The Sting of Fate by William Alan Webb

Near the Aufidus River, Apuilia, Italy

9:17 pm, 1 August 216 B.C. (537th year since Rome's founding)

Flaring oil lamps cast puddles of light throughout the great tent as Hannibal Barca reclined on a couch, looted from the same Roman house as the peach he was eating. Thick juice trickled into his beard. The sugar in the fruit attracted flies but few places had more flies than Africa and Spain, where he had grown up. Nor did they bother his cavalry generals, Hanno, his eldest sister's son, and Hasdrubal, Hannibal's brother, who lay on couches of their own. Together the three Carthaginians stared at a captured Roman deserter who knelt before them with his head down.

"Why did leave you Roman service?" Hannibal asked in stilted, thickly accented Latin.

The Roman soldier lifted his head and glanced around, as if he didn't understand the question. Hannibal rubbed the leather patch over his left eye. After crossing the Appenine Mountains his army slogged through a huge swamp that took many days to cross, during which Hannibal's left eye became infected. Since then, he had lived with a painful and incessant itching under the eye patch. As he always did Hannibal found a way to turn that to his advantage, developing an unnerving one-eyed glare which he cast now on the Roman. He waited and waited for an answer to his question, but when none came he called on his translator.

"The Roman understood me," he said to his companions in Punic, their native language. "He thinks to play a game with me."

"He picked the wrong lion to taunt," Hasdrubal said.

The Greek slave he had captured came closer. His name was Ecthes, and he was fluent in five languages. Hannibal was only partially joking when he said that Ecthes might be the most valuable property they had looted in Italy.

"Ask him why he deserted," Hannibal said, again in Punic.

Ecthes did as he was told, listened to the answer and then turned back to Hannibal.

"He says the Roman generals are confident they will crush your army, but the men believe otherwise. They believe that the great Hannibal cannot be defeated by any army. Some of his fellow *hastatis* say that Hannibal is favored by the gods, while others say he is a curse from the gods. All would flee if they could, but only he found the chance."

"Ask him who commands the legions tomorrow."

After translating Hannibal's question, and the Roman deserter's answer, Ecthes turned again to his master.

"Today the consul in command was Lucius Aemilius Paullus, so tomorrow it will be Gaius Terentius Varro."

"Good," Hannibal said. "Tell him he's doing well."

Ecthes did so.

"Ask him how many legions I face."

After the usual delay Ecthes gave the reply. "You face sixteen legions general, eight Roman and eight auxiliary. He says all but five thousand are infantry and the rest are cavalry."

"Excellent. Thank him for me."

Once that was done, Hannibal leaned forward and spoke slowly in Latin to be sure he was understood. "Peius tantum Romano meritus civis Romanus." *The only thing worse than a Roman, is a Roman deserter.*

* * *

Guards dragged the Roman outside. Hannibal ignored his screams for mercy, which did not last long. In the middle of crying his children's names the voice stopped, doubtless because the executioners' blade sliced through his neck.

"Did we learn anything from the Roman dog?" Hasdrubal asked, still reclining on his couch.

"I'd say we did," answered Hanno. "If the legions are as frightened of you as the Roman said, Hannibal, we need only pressure them hard and they will break."

Hannibal swung his legs over the couch's side and stood. At the center of the tent stood a large sandbox measuring four feet square, constructed from stout oak. When it was first erected two days before, water had been poured over the sand so it could easily be formed into a diorama of the potential battle site.

On what served as the southern side ran a channel that represented the Aufidus River. Opposite that was a mound in the shape of the hills on the northern flank, while the space in between was relatively flat. Small cut-stone blocks lay piled at either end. Scratched into the surface of one heap of stones was a curved line with the open side facing left, the Punic symbol for the Latin letter R, short for *Rumi*, the Carthaginian word for Rome. The opposing stones had *Hannibal* etched into their surface, since many ethnic peoples made up the Carthaginian Army.

Ecthes stood silent in one corner as Hannibal stared at the sandbox, alternately combing his beard and rubbing the patch over his ruined eye. Minutes passed but no one spoke. They were all used to the ritual; it was how Hannibal planned his battles, and woe unto anyone who broke his concentration.

No Carthaginian held love for any Roman, but Hannibal hated them with a passion none of his countrymen could understand. At nine years old, he had promised his father, who despised the Romans above all others, that he would never stop fighting them. His stated goal in invading Italy was to liberate Rome's allies from Roman domination, not to wage genocidal war on the Roman people.

That was a lie.

"Send for my brother Mago," he said, without specifying to whom he spoke. There was no need; Ecthes knew Hannibal spoke to him. He, in turn, relayed the order to someone outside the tent. Five minutes later, Hannibal and Hasdrubal's younger brother, Mago, stepped into the tent, saw his brother studying the sandbox, and kept quiet.

"Now that we are all here, let me reveal tomorrow's battle plan," Hannibal finally said. The other three men stepped beside their commander but remained silent. They had done this many times over the years.

"We captured a Roman, Mago, and he told us more than he'd intended. He verified that Varro is in command tomorrow, and Varro *will* give battle. The Roman officers are confident of victory, but he said the soldiers are not…" He turned to Hanno and the young cavalry commander knew that a question was coming. "Did you believe him, nephew?"

Reading Hannibal's expressions had been difficult when he had two eyes, but now, with one of them covered by a large patch, it was damned near impossible. Nor was there any pattern to what answers he wanted.

"I did believe him."

Hannibal nodded as if agreeing, and then grinned. "He lied. The Romans believe they will crush us, and therein is the seed of our victory. He claimed they field sixteen legions and that I do believe."

Hannibal looked at the sand table before continuing.

"That puts their number double our own. Moreover, all of their infantry are heavy while many of our troops are not well armored or armed. Our sole numerical advantage is in our cavalry, if you believe his number of five thousand, and I do not."

Hannibal gave Hanno and Hasdrubal that studious look they knew so well.

"It must be higher, but the Romans discount the value of cavalry anyway. Even with equal numbers we must overcome them. When all things are considered, if I were in Varro's place I would expect to destroy this army on the morrow, there is no sane reason to see another outcome. And that is why we will be victorious."

There were grins at that statement and Hannibal's confidence.

"Our formation will be that of the bull's horns, in a crescent like this."

Picking up some of the square stones, Hannibal placed them in an arc with the open side facing away from the Roman side of the sandbox.

"Mago, you and I will be in the center. For my plan to work, the center must hold, but that is where we will place our weakest troops, the Spaniards, Celts, and Gauls."

Hannibal saw Mago's consternation and continued, still smiling.

"They are also most likely to break, so we will put a single line of Africans behind them, but it will mostly be up to us, you and I, my brother, to keep the men standing in place and fighting. Inevitably they will be driven backward, but this must happen slowly. Varro will see us falling back and will commit his reserves to break our line. If that happens, if we cannot hold in the center, then total defeat will quickly follow."

Mago nodded, and Hannibal turned to the other two.

"This moment, when the Romans commit their reserves, will be the crucial moment. If we give ground only slowly, then the Romans will fight their way into a sack, with our wings outflanking them. This is where I will have the Africans, because they are veterans and will not attack until I give them the order."

Hannibal checked to make sure both of his generals had registered his emphasis.

"Discipline here is the key. Hasdrubal, relate this plan to Carthalo. You, Carthalo, and Hanno must be the ones to deliver the killing blow. By the moment that the Roman reserves join the battle, both of you *must* have driven the Roman cavalry from the field. Regardless of the cost, your cavalry must win those fights. Hasdrubal, you will be our left wing with the heavy cavalry, which number how many now?"

"About three thousand," Hannibal's wiry brother said.

"Less than before…why so few?"

"I left a screen near Cannae, as you said to do for warning if the Romans tried to recapture their grain stores."

"You did the right thing. If the battle turns on those men then we have lost anyway. Hanno, you and the Numidians will be on our right. If Varro splits his cavalry equally to both flanks, which he will, then you will outnumber your enemy, perhaps by as many as two to one. Chase them from the field but offer no pursuit."

Hanno nodded grimly, studying the battle map.

"Once you are certain they cannot come back to the fight, you must fall on the Roman's rear, but only after they have committed their reserves. Is that clear? Their reserves must be in the fight. If all goes well and Melqart smiles on us, they will be surrounded, and their very numbers will restrict their movement."

Hannibal paused for effect.

"Does anyone see a flaw in this plan that I may have over-looked?"

I want honest answers, Hannibal thought, looking at his gathered subordinates. *Mindless obedience just leads to a mindless death.* He did not punish men for questioning his plans, so when none of his closest advisors spoke up, he knew they truly agreed with him.

"Then sleep now. Tomorrow we make history."

* * *

Main Roman Camp

Cannae

5:31 A.M., 2 August

Turning his head this way and that, Gaius Terentius Varro used the mirror held by a slave to tuck every curl of his black hair into place. His breastplate, greaves, and helmet reflected candle light so brightly as to make them appear as lamps.

"Mars himself could not look more like a warrior," quipped Gnaeus Servilius Geminus. "And after today he may have competition as the God of War."

"I would never seek to displace great Mars," Varro answered. "But if the people wished to build a temple for me I would not oppose them."

Servilius laughed. "And would no doubt be glad to pay for it, too. So you think the Carthaginian will fight?"

"Where such men as this Hannibal is concerned, who can say for certain? I can only pray he is so foolish, but we should know soon."

As if cued onto a stage, the tent flap opened, and a tall man walked in wearing the accoutrements of a general. High cheeks and a taut face leant themselves to the perpetual scowl he wore.

"Salve, Lucius!" Varro cried, turning to embrace the man. It irritated him to use Paullus' praenomen, his first name, since that suggested friendship, but he needed his fellow consul's support on that most auspicious day. "How fares my fellow consul on this most glorious of days?"

"Salve, Gaius." He nodded toward Servilius. "Salve, Gnaeus. So you mean to fight?"

"You allow no moss to grow between your toes, do you Lucius?" Varro chuckled. "If the Carthaginian will face me, yes I will fight him, yes, yes, yes!"

"If he stands his ground it's because he has a plan to defeat us, on ground of his choosing," Lucius said bluntly.

"Or he's a fool, since only a fool would invade Italy without the support of a fleet. Today I will crush his army and trundle him through the streets of Rome in chains."

"That's what Scipio thought, and Longus, and Flaminius," Lucius responded, his voice rising. "I have to urge caution!"

"Tell me, Lucius," said Servilius. "What do you think the men would say if we retreated in the face of an army we outnumbered?"

"Since when do the *hastati* determine strategy?" Paullus bit out.

Varro's mask of conciliation began to slip. His eyes narrowed, and his smile vanished.

"Fabius is no longer dictator, and you know why as well as I do," Varro said, his own anger starting to creep into his voice. "Rome will not tolerate any more inaction."

"*Rome* is not here; *we* are," Paullus said, his eyes narrow.

"There are more than eighty senators in this army, more than half what is needed for a quorum. They know, like you and I do, that we lost a great deal of stores when Hannibal captured Cannae. To make up for that loss we can still harvest the Apuilan fields, but only if they are under our control. So if we do not fight, the Senate will find somebody else who will."

"It's not fighting that I object to," Paullus replied. "It's losing." With that he turned and stalked out.

* * *

The Main Roman Camp near Cannae

6:13 a.m.

August 2

Mists rising from the Aufidus River drifted over what would be the day's battlefield. The distant Carthaginian camp was still obscured by darkness and fog, but the eastern sky promised dawn's light would soon chase away both.

Several hundred Senators and their kind stood near Varro's tent, waiting for the day's commander to emerge and give them their orders. In this way they could share in the glory of victory. Paullus made his way through them without too many comments. His fellow patricians knew him well enough to leave him alone when he scowled as he did then. Making his way through the bustle of the Roman camp he climbed one of the camp's towers for a look at the ground Varro proposed to fight on. He had seen it before but wanted to evaluate it again. After a few minutes, though, he came to the same conclusion as before.

This terrain favors the Carthaginians, Paullus thought.

The battle would be fought between the river and the line of hills. Even though his perch at the larger camp stood at the far western side of the soon-to-be contested ground, his view from above allowed for him to better understand the ground.

The Romans would be attacking up a slope. It was not steep, but it did not have to be. It was nearly four miles to the enemy's camp outside the town of Cannae, and Hannibal wouldn't be stupid enough to march far away from that fall back position, thereby shortening the Roman's march. The attack wouldn't be directly toward the Carthaginian camp and likely wouldn't be longer than half of four miles. Two miles wasn't so far, and the hill wasn't a hard climb, but together they would take away some of the Romans' leg strength.

From up that high he could also see something else he had missed the previous afternoon when he first saw the ground. The area between the river and the hills angled inward, toward each other. In other words, the further the Romans advanced the more compressed their lines would become. Room for maneuver would become more restricted. Once again, like the upward incline, it was not a major Carthaginian advantage, just another small one. And yet when combined...Paullus could almost see the coming disaster unfolding before his eyes.

Then he felt something crawling on the back of his right hand; a wasp. Red, black, and yellow, it moved across his skin slowly and Paullus could see its stinger held aloft. If it stung him the hand would swell to three or four times its normal size and he would be unable to hold the reins of a horse, much less wield his sword. Other wasps had emerged with the rising sun and flew around his head, but he remained motionless. Then it fluttered its wings and flew away. Paullus descended the ladder with all due haste.

* * *

Large Roman Camp
6:36 a.m.
August 2

When Varro's *adiutor*, his adjutant, Aurelius, entered the tent, he was chewing his favorite breakfast of dense wheat bread with honey and dates. Honey stuck to the backs of his fingers and around his mouth. Servilius had already finished his meal and rinsed his fingers in a bowl over to one side.

"What news, Aurelius?" asked Varro after swallowing a last bite.

"Congratulations, consul! The enemy takes the field."

"Does he?" Grinning, he raised his eyebrows in a triumphant expression as he turned to Servilius. "Let us go show this Carthaginian fool his mistake, eh friend Gnaeus?"

"Lead me, Gaius, and I shall follow."

Unlike most Roman politicians, Varro and Servilius really were friends, and not falsely polite.

The commander's tent was pitched on a large wooden platform, from which two steps led down to the level of the camp. Servilius exited first and called his fellow Senators, *equites,* and other commanders to gather round to hear the words of the consul in command. Paullus joined them but stood to one side.

One by one, Varro handed out the assignments based on who supported him and who did not. Servilius got the plum assignment, overall command of the infantry attacking the Carthaginian center, with some of Varro's closest friends serving under him. Paullus got command of the cavalry on the Roman left, while Varro rode with the cavalry on the right. When he had finished dispensing orders, Paullus spoke up.

"Are the formations subject to change when we see Hannibal's deployment?"

Like most successful Roman politicians, Varro could show hatred with his eyes while the rest of his face smiled.

"I think you have the situation backward, friend Lucius. It is Hannibal who must adjust to *us!*"

Laughter drowned out further objections and a buzzing wasp distracted him anyway; the damned things were everywhere. Disgusted with the complacency of his fellow consul, Paullus called for his horse. When the animal was brought forth, one of his slaves put an angled table with two steps next to the horse, which he used to climb into the saddle. Behind him, Paullus heard a few snickers. A proper Roman general was supposed to step on the back of a kneeling *hastati* instead of using a step ladder. There was even a protocol for how the *hastati* was chosen for the duty.

Paullus' staff joined him without speaking. By now, the younger officers had learned when the taciturn consul did not want intrusions on his thoughts, so as he rode out of the camp gate to cross the river, the only sounds were those of clanking equipment and hooves hammering at sparse summer grass.

* * *

The Roman Left Wing
7:46 a.m.
August 2

Sunshine now bathed the grassland, and Paullus had to admit that in its full deployment, the Roman Army appeared unstoppable. The glittering of sunlight off more than fifty thousand men made it seem like Sol Invictus himself led the Romans into battle. Overcome with pride at being consul for a Republic strong enough to field such a host, for the moment Paullus forgot his misgivings.

Maybe Varro is right, Paullus thought. *Maybe Hannibal should be adjusting his battle plan.*

The Roman *maniples* deployed in the standard checkerboard formation, drawn up in three lines. The *hastati*, the youngest and least experienced men with the lightest armor, occupied the front lines. Next came the *principes*, men between 26 and 35 years of age and then, finally, came the *trairii*, the oldest, most experienced and heavily armed men in the legion. For this battle the numbers of the *hastati* and *principes maniples* had been increased from 120 to 160 men, and those of the *triarii* from 60 to 80. The first two lines of men carried short throwing spears, *pilums*, two per man, while the *triarii* carried the older, longer spear called the *hasta*.

It was a sight unequaled in all of Rome's long military history, especially compared to the rag-tag appearance of the Carthaginian Army. Paullus knew that Hannibal's force numbered at most 50,000 men, while the Romans had almost 90,000, the largest force Rome had ever put in the field. Directly opposite him were the Numidian light cavalry, whose fearsome reputation had become well known throughout Italy. To make things worse, even a cursory inspection showed his force was badly outnumbered.

Numbers aren't everything, of course, for we are equites, Paullus thought. The Roman heavy cavalry, protected by armor and shields, could slice the Numidians apart with their heavy sword at close range. If the Numidians tried to stay out of reach, the quivers which hung from their saddles held three or four *akontes* throwing spears apiece. The Romans also picked large horses with great strength and stamina, while the Numidians' smaller mounts had no armor. Although the Numidians' skill with their javelins was legendary, in a pitched battle, Paullus knew his men had the advantage.

As the minutes ticked by, Paullus wondered what the delay could be. Even so early in the day, the sun was brutal to men wearing armor and to horses bearing riders, and the longer it took, the more advantage it would be to Hannibal. Could it be that Varro had come to his senses and was showing caution? Then he heard a commotion behind him and saw the *equites* making room for a messenger on horseback.

"Consul General Lucius Aemilius Paullus, where is Consul General Lucius Aemilius Paullus?" the man cried.

Paullus raised his arm and waved. "Over here."

Once beside him the rider saluted and took a moment to catch his breath. "Consul, General Varro has been injured. He asks that you meet with him in his tent at the larger camp."

Paullus asked no questions. He knew from the man's look there was more to the story than he wanted to say among so many listeners. Leaving specific orders not to attack until his return, Paullus rode off behind the messenger. When they were out of earshot, he caught up to the messenger and faced him.

"Tell me what has happened."

"Consul General Varro suffered a terrible accident while mounting his horse."

"Futuo." Fuck. "Give me all the details."

"The general stood beside his horse, patting it, before he stepped on a man's back to jump up to its back. It seems that some honey on his hand from breakfast rubbed off on the horse, which attracted wasps. When he tried to climb into the saddle they stung the beast, throwing the general to the ground with his leg stuck under him. When they lifted him, bone protruded from the skin in three places."

"Please Jupiter that he live," Paullus said. With that, he urged the horse into a gallop.

* * *

Behind the Carthaginian Center Lines
9:02 a.m.
August 2

Hannibal sat atop his favorite white Spanish stallion, Zinnridi, directly behind the center of the Carthaginian infantry, where he had stationed his allied and mercenary swordsmen. They were mostly Spanish, but with large numbers of Celts, Gauls, and even some Italians disaffected with Rome. Near him were the commanders of his various units and his advisors, including his younger brother Mago.

Hannibal's army was like an extension of his own being, and he could feel the anxiety building within the men. They were fierce and skilled warriors, but they did not have the iron discipline of the Roman legions. A bloody fight did not bother them, but standing idle while waiting for a fight did. Nobody had expected the Romans to deploy in force and then wait.

"What are they doing?" asked one of his infantry captains, a man named Gisgo.

Hannibal laughed, knowing that all of his men watched him for his reaction to events. He never lied to them, so if he was not worried, they need not be either. And when he found something funny, so did they.

"They are afraid," he said.

"There are a lot of them."

"It is true, their number seems more than all the stars in the sky. Yet they lack one important thing that is needed for victory…" On the horse beside him, Mago smiled; he'd heard the joke before.

"What is that, general?"

"In all of their vast host there is not one man named Gisgo."

Gisgo's men laughed and pushed him good-naturedly, and for a moment, the tension dissipated. But Hannibal had commanded too many battles to think it would last. Mago motioned him to move away from others.

"What do you really think they're doing?"

"I do not think there is cause to fret, my brother. I suspect that Paullus has counseled caution, and Varro must make it appear that he is considering his fellow consuls' opinion. Or perhaps their fool general thinks that standing in this heat affects our men more than it does theirs."

Mago laughed at that. "Most of our men are from Africa or Spain! This feels like winter to them. But what if they do not attack? What do we do then?"

"That is an easy question, brother. We think of a new way to destroy them."

* * *

Varro's Bedside, Main Roman Camp
9:10 a.m.
August 2

Along with Paullus, Aurelius, and two Senators, the only other person beside Varro's bed was his physician. Slaves stood in the corners, as always. The other commanders had gathered outside the tent, below the steps, to await news of the commanding general. Paullus had left Servilius in charge of the legions in case Hannibal attacked.

Varro moaned in his sleep. Sweat poured off his face, and you didn't need to be a doctor to know that his gray pallor meant he was in grave danger.

"I gave him the most powerful sedative that I know of," the doctor said, scratching his well-trimmed beard. "He needs surgery but I'm not a surgeon. I will set the leg and close the wounds as best I can."

"I have to formally ask this question, Doctor," Paullus said. "Will Consul Varro be able to return to his duties as commander of this army?"

"Consul Varro may never wake up, Consul Paullus," the doctor said, regarding Paullus as if the latter were insane. "And if he does, he certainly will be in no condition to command an army, not for many months."

"Heed me as the senior senator present," said one of the two Senators, a bent, white-haired man from a famous Patrician family named Marcus Horatius Pulvillus. The other Senator was his brother Publius. Pulvillus looked almost comical in armor that once fit him but was now much too large for a withered old man.

"It is my opinion that until the Senate either decides whether the fallen consul can finish his duties or appoints a replacement to finish out his term, you are in sole command of this army. What are you orders, General?"

Paullus physically sagged under the weight of his new responsibility, but while he was a more cautious commander than Varro, he was still a Roman. From his earliest days the aggression expected of a Roman in war had been inculcated into his very being. And commanding the army was something he already did, every other day.

"You are correct, Marcus, this is my burden now. Aurelius, send word to each legion that I want to see the *tribuni militum* (tribunes of the soldiers) at a council of war in my tent. Marcus Horatius, would you and Publius attend as representatives of the Senate?"

"We can attend as observing Senators."

"That will be fine. Also Aurelius, summon Gaius Sempronius Blaesus and Tiberius Sempronius Blaesus. Bid them make haste."

"What do you want with the Sempronii?" Marcus Horatius said, either unable or unwilling to keep a hint of contempt out of his voice.

"Come now, Marcus," Paullus said, actually smiling. In the insular world of the Roman Senate, everyone knew every feud among every patrician family, and that of the Sempronii and the Horatii had been going on for centuries. "On a day such as today we are all Romans."

* * *

The Main Roman Camp
9:54 a.m.
August 2

More than thirty men crowded into Paullus' tent, which was even more crowded with comfort items than Varro's. As the day heated up, the air inside the square enclosed space became stale and hot. Slaves poured wine and brought small loaves and olives for anyone who might be hungry. Although taller than most of them already, Paullus stood on a chair so he could be heard by all.

"Gentlemen, with one exception I do not intend to vary far from the battle plan of my fallen fellow consul. The army is already deployed to carry out that plan and to redeploy now would be to invite disaster—"

"Then we had better be about marching soon," cried out one of the Tribunes. "The men are baking out there."

Paullus eyed him. The Tribune was correct, but no Roman senator liked being interrupted. "I am well aware of the condition of the men, Tribune...?"

"Marcus Minucius Augurinus."

"My remarks will be brief, Tribune Marcus Minucius Augurinus," Paullus continued, his tone making it clear he would brook no more interruptions. "The decision of how I will vary from the plan of Varro shall be made on the field, at the moment I decide. Hannibal has prepared a plan to defeat us, and I wish to give him a chance to put that plan into motion. Then I will decide how to proceed. I know that many of you think him a toothless lion unable to withstand the might of Rome, yet three times has he beaten us, and severely mauled two consular armies. The very numbers we put on the field today stand as a testament to his generalship. I will not underestimate him."

"Fabius Maximus is not the dictator anymore!" yelled another tribune.

"I go to kill our enemy," Paullus said in a vicious tone that at once expressed outrage and implied the speaker was being cowardly. "Not to be killed by him. However, if any of you will not follow my directives once battle is joined, then say so now, to my face, as is wont for a true Roman. Does anyone wish to speak now?"

The senators appeared more amused than intimidated, but Paullus knew they heard this sort of thing all the time during debates in the Senate. It was the tribunes to which he aimed the words. Although *equites* themselves, they were young and hot-headed. The silence indicated none were so foolish as to openly challenge him, however.

"Very well, then. From this point forward any disobedience will be considered by me to be treason in battle, and I will act accordingly. One change I *am* going to make now is this...Varro designated ten thousand men to guard this camp, most of them *triarii*. I believe that to be excessive. I therefore order all but twenty-five *maniples* containing the oldest men to cross the river and take up position behind the other camp. If needed to defend this camp, they should see the enemy coming and have time to recross the river, or they can act as a last reserve, if needed. Does anyone have questions or comments?"

"Why not send those *mainples* against Hannibal's camp?" asked Tribune Marcus Minucius Augurinus. "Would that not force him to split his forces?"

The question betrayed the speaker's inexperience and impetuosity, which allowed Paullus to adopt a condescending smile.

"Hannibal will have planned for such a move, as would any competent general. Also, *triarii* are not meant for such an independent move, they have not the stamina of younger men. What they have is experience at killing. That makes them ideal camp guards, or on the battlefield a force to deliver the final blow to an enemy. Now the day grows long and our men grow tired. The time for battle has come."

* * *

Behind the Carthaginian Center

10:48 a.m.

August 2

Never one to ignore the needs of his men, Hannibal had ordered carts from the supply train brought forward loaded with barrels of water, which the teamsters then carried down the lines to allow the men a drink. As he mulled allowing them to rest in place and having a light meal brought forward, distant trumpets cancelled those plans.

"It took the Romans a long time to grow a pair of balls," Mago said.

Hannibal laughed and patted his brother's shoulder. "Thank you, Mago, now I know what to say to the men."

With the slightest pressure from his knees, Hannibal turned Zinnridi and cantered until he reached the rear of Hasdrubal's heavy cavalry on the far left. Drawing his sword he rode behind his men, repeating the same lines every so often.

"The Romans finally grew balls, men, now let's castrate them!"

* * *

The Battlefield Near Cannae

10:52 a.m.

August 2

Under a cerulean sky clear of clouds, the sun climbed toward its zenith. Seated atop a well-muscled Cappodocian stallion, Paullus gave command of the cavalry to two Senators with extensive combat experience and took up position beside Servilius at the rear of the assembled legions. Although tradition dictated the commanding general should command the right wing cavalry, no cowardice attached itself to watching the progress of the battle from behind. Unsure of what Hannibal had planned, Paullus wanted the clearest possible view of the battle's progress.

Officers surrounded them both, including the young up and coming Publius Cornelius Scipio, an officer acknowledged by all to have a great career ahead. Scipio had saved his father during the Battle of Ticinus by charging through a horde of enemies surrounding the fallen consul and then cutting the way out for both of them. Recognizing his energy and leadership, Paullus put him in charge of the seven thousand *triarii* in deep reserve behind the smaller camp north of the river. Scipio did not like being removed from the battle line but did as he was told.

The Romans advanced at a moderate rate, as was usual, and were preceded by unarmored skirmishers carrying spears and swords. In front of the Carthaginian Army came archers and the famed Baeleric Island slingers, while the infantry came forward slower than the Romans. The two sides' skirmishers drew first blood as they fought each other, with the main purpose of each side being to keep the enemy missile throwers away from their main force of infantry. As the two armies closed on each other they mashed the bodies of the fallen skirmishers into a bloody paste.

Paullus had the equivalent of fourteen legions available for battle, after deducting the ten thousand men guarding the two camps. He sent eight of those legions forward in the initial assault, so that the numbers engaged for each side were about the same. Four more he kept in close reserve three hundred yards behind his position. But the last two he had lie down in the grass behind the four standing reserve legions. It was a trick Hannibal himself had used at the Battle of Lake Trasimene. With the ground quickly being trampled into dust, which rose like a brown fog over the field, he counted on Hannibal not seeing those last two legions, or Scipio's *manipels* now repositioned behind the smaller camp.

"I must admit that I did not expect you to fight on this day," Servilius said.

"Whatever plans Hannibal has made for today he cannot now change. That is how we shall crush him."

* * *

Behind the Carthaginian Center
11:00 a.m.
August 2

Arrayed behind Hannibal, Mago, and their officers were five signal flag men, holding long poles on which various colored standards could be raised. At Hannibal's signal, two men raised large square red panels, which meant attack. On both wings, the cavalry began to move, the heavy Spanish and Celtic horsemen on the left and the light Numidians on the right.

"What is the key to our victory today, Hannibal?" said Mago.

"Victory or defeat is up to us, brother. God has given no man a greater spur to victory than contempt for death."

"Are you saying I shouldn't be afraid?"

"Are you?"

Mago grinned, as he so often did. "If I was, I surely would not tell you."

"There is no advantage to fear, it only leeches courage."

"So you know our path to victory?"

"If one does not exist, I will make one."

* * *

Behind the Roman Center

11:32 a.m.

August 2

Paullus and Servilius watched the battle unfold with differing emotions. Servilius largely ignored the cavalry fight on the flanks and concentrated on the infantry attacks, which he nominally commanded, although at Paullus' insistence, Servilius had become his de facto deputy. Paullus tried to see everything at once, and to understand exactly what Hannibal had in mind. Many scoffed at such a thoroughly un-Roman viewpoint, but Paullus ignored them.

The cavalry engaged first. On Rome's right flank the roughly equal numbers of cavalry slammed into each other at the full gallop. Men and horses tumbled under the feet of those behind, spears gutted riders and lifted them from the saddle, and lines of battle disintegrated in a chaotic mass. Squeezed between the river on one side and the massed infantry on the other, some of the cavalry of both sides dismounted and fought on foot.

Across the battlefield on the Roman left flank, despite a two-to-one numerical disadvantage, the Romans fought the vaunted Numidians to a standstill. The restricted conditions of the terrain prevented the faster, more agile Numidians from exploiting their advantages.

When fifty feet separated the two armies in the center, both sides threw spears into the packed ranks of their enemy, after which the two opposing masses of infantry slammed into each other like rutting bucks. A great metallic clash echoed over the field as sword met sword and the first cries of dying men signaled the beginning of an orgy of death. The Romans were better trained and equipped than the Spanish, Gallic, and Celtic soldiers in Hannibal's center, even the *hastati* in the first line of Roman maniples. With their inferior numbers Hannibal's lines were also thin.

The shape of the Carthaginian formation wasn't immediately visible to any of the Roman commanders. As more and more Roman maniples engaged the enemy they pressed inward toward the center, becoming tighter and closer together. Room for maneuver lessened. But the sheer weight of the Roman attack drove the Carthaginian center backward in a step-by-step, hard fighting retreat. The further they advanced, however, the Romans became hampered by the need for stepping over corpses and writhing men at their feet, a hindrance the Carthaginian center did not have.

Regardless, it was not long before Servilius thought the battle won. As the advance seemed on the verge of breaking the enemy lines he ordered the reserves into the fight.

"How many general?" said one of his officers.

"All of them."

But before the man could turn his mount and ride back to the reserve legions one hundred yards to their rear, Paullus called out to him.

"Hold a moment." Leaning forward he pitched his voice low, so only Servilius could hear him. "Leave the two legions I have hidden in the grass."

Servilius' squint was obvious even under his helmet. "That is not our best move, Lucius. Their center is cracking, we should commit our full weight now to destroy them. Once that breaks the battle is won. That is what Varro would have done…it is what Rome demands!"

Paullus looked away, thinking. *That is what Varro would have done…' That was it! That was Hannibal's trap.*

"No, send four legions in now, and hurry." Before Servilius could protest further he turned to another young officer. "Ride now to Scipio, bid him to bring his *triarii* hence at double speed. Hurry!"

"What are you doing, Paullus?" Servilius demanded. "You are leaving our camp under-guarded!"

But Paullus paid no attention. Instead he stared toward the battle raging five hundred yards to his front.

"I am not Varro, Hannibal," he said to no one in particular. "I see your trap, but will you see mine?"

* * *

At the Center of the Fighting
11:56 a.m.
August 2

Like strings of red pearls, long ropes of blood crisscrossed Hannibal's arms and armor. Dirt, gore, and blood made a sticky paste in his sandals. A glancing blow dented the brim of his Thracian helmet, while a second strike cut the left side of his face and caved in the leaf-shaped cheek protector.

He fought dismounted among his troops, as always. Mago had disappeared somewhere to Hannibal's right to stiffen that wavering flank. As overall commander, he stepped back several times and mounted Zinnridi to see over the battle lines. That's when he saw the Roman reserves marching into the fray.

Finally! Hannibal thought. *The climax is at hand!*

He could hear the ongoing cavalry battle, but dust and raging combat prevented him from making out any details. The Carthaginian general drank from the waterskin hanging from his saddle.

Melqart, he thought, speaking to the Protector of Carthage and patron diety of the Barcid family, *grant me victory this day.* Then he rode behind the battle lines shouting encouragement. Seeing his men waver again under the impact of the Roman reserves, he dismounted and rejoined the fight.

* * *

Behind the Roman Center

12:09 p.m.

August 2

Servilius had no intention of missing out on the glory of fighting in Rome's crushing victory over the despised Carthaginians. It was from such deeds that consulships were forged. Along with his staff, he personally led the reserves into battle. But instead of joining him, as Servilius urged, Paullus retreated with a few retainers to where the last two legions lay hidden.

By now the Carthaginian center had been pushed far back, while their flanks remained in place. The effect was that the further the Romans pushed into the center, the closer they came to being outflanked. Paullus saw Hannibal's plan in every detail now. His army was fighting on three sides, and unless they could break the Carthaginian center once and for all they might be surrounded. The junior officers surrounding him saw it too, and urged commitment of the last reserves. Paullus did not respond.

Within minutes of the four reserve legions pushing into the center, his right flank began to crumble as the Allied cavalry fled the field, closely followed by the remnants of the Roman cavalry.

"Be ready!" he cried, an order that was passed to the men lying in the grass. They did not stand yet but could be in battle formations within seconds. Instead of following the panic-stricken Roman cavalry, however, the Carthaginian heavy cavalry turned behind the Roman lines and rode all the way to the other side of the field, where the Numidians still fought the Roman cavalry on the left flank. Such a move could only have been planned prior to the battle.

Even though heavily outnumbered, the Romans had fought the Numidians to a standstill, but thousands more Carthaginian heavy cavalry turned the tide immediately. Like the right flank, the cavalry on the left fled the field in panic.

Then Hannibal's trap closed.

The Carthaginian Army still had about nine thousand men on horseback, and as Paullus watched, they attacked the Roman infantry from behind, thereby closing the trap. The Romans were now surrounded on all four sides.

* * *

At the Carthaginian Center
12:22 p.m.
August 2

In places, the Carthaginian center was only two men deep and fatigue began to set in. As Hannibal watched, two of his men fell simultaneously, leaving a hole in the front line for the Romans to pour through. If they could push through in strength, the battle was lost, so he personally filled the gap, stabbing one Roman in the groin and another in the side. Then some Spaniards pushed him to safety and filled the gap.

Once again mounting Zinnridi, Hannibal could see his cavalry in the rear of a huge, writhing mass of Romans, who were pressed so close together they couldn't fight, or even turn around. The battle had become a slaughter, exactly as he'd planned.

* * *

Behind the Roman Center
12:27 p.m.
August 2

The last reserve legions were on their feet and being organized by their centurions into battle formations. Hoofbeats alerted Paullus to turn in his saddle as young Scipio rode toward him. Before Scipio could speak, Paullus called out his orders.

"Post your men on the left flank and take to battle at the double step! Hurry, every minute is costing Roman blood."

With a whoop of joy, Scipio whirled and joined the column of marching *triarii*.

The two reserve legions formed up beside each other when Scipio's men moved up beside them. Drawing his sword, Paullus pointed it toward the battle. Turning to the two legions assembled behind him, he yelled, "Follow me!" Closing on Scipio's right, they effectively formed a three-legion-wide marching juggernaut.

* * *

The Carthaginian Center

12:42 p.m.

August 2

H annibal's sword point slid across the Romans' *pectorale*, his heart guard, punctured his right shoulder and sent blood running down his side. The man fell, and Hannibal stepped back, searching for another enemy to kill. Coated head to toe in mud and blood, at that instant, he first noticed men fleeing on his army's right flank. At the same time, his brother Hasbrudal rode toward him with his horse's mouth flecked with foam.

"We are undone!" Hasdrubal said. "The Romans have broken our line!"

Hannibal grabbed the horses' reins and tried to calm the heaving animal. Hot breath snorted from its nostrils and across his arm.

"Calm down, brother. Tell me exactly what has happened."

Hasdrubal nodded and gulped a few breaths. "Your plan worked to perfection. We defeated their cavalry and rather than chase them, we rode to the aid of the Numidians. Between Hanno's men and mine, we crushed the Roman's on our right flank and then attacked their infantry from the rear. We cut them down like ripe wheat until three new legions marched into *our* rear. I tried to fend them off but it was hopeless. They have turned both our flanks! We must retreat now, Hannibal, while we still can!"

With his one good eye Hannibal saw men running for their lives, first by ones and twos, and then whole groups. Mounting Zinnridi again he looked for some part of the line that still held around which he could rally his men, but saw none.

"Hannibal! We must go!"

"Where is Mago?"

"I do not know!"

"He was on my right the last time I saw him, over there, rallying some Gauls."

Hasdrubal turned in the saddle to look where his brother pointed, but all he could see was Romans chopping their way through the Carthaginian line.

"Mago is smart, he will meet us at camp. Now let us go and organize the defense."

With the nearest Romans no more than fifty feet away, Hannibal looked over what was left of his army. The remnants of the cavalry had already cut their way out and left the field, galloping for the main Carthaginian camp across the river. Across the line, Allied infantry soldiers had thrown away their weapons and run for their lives. But a large part of his army fought on, regardless of how hopeless the situation. They likely realized that capture meant slavery or death.

"Hasdrubal, go to the camp! Prepare it for defense. I'm staying here to organize a fighting retreat. We will meet back at camp."

"In this hour of our greatest trial you cannot be selfish! The army is lost, Hannibal, but without you the war is lost!"

There was no escaping his brother's logic. Dying on the battlefield would uphold his personal honor, but without Hannibal driving the war forward, the Senate in Carthage would make peace. While breath yet remained in his body he could not allow that. So, with his mind made up, Hannibal turned Zinnridi to the east and followed Hasdrubal back to their camp.

* * *

The Main Roman Camp
8:34 a.m.
August 3

Well wishers came until late in the night, bringing wine and rare delicacies to share with their victorious commander, Consul Lucius Amelius Paullus. More than eighty Senators had accompanied the army to Cannae, along with many of their sons and even a few grandsons. A few had died in the fighting and a few more had been wounded, but all the survivors who could walk came by Paullus' tent to offer congratulations. The worst blow came when Paullus heard that young Scipio had fallen while leading his legion of *triarii*.

Despite a raging hangover, Paullus crawled out of bed, donned his uniform, and did what victors were supposed to do; see to his army. After a quick visit to Varro's bedside, where the doctors told him they'd set the leg and kept their patient asleep so he could use his strength to fight off infection, Paullus drained two cups of watered wine and forced down some bread. He performed a short ceremony of thanksgiving to Mars, God of War, and then another to Jupiter Optimus Maximus. Then, surrounded by three hundred Roman cavalry who survived the fight, he went out to survey the battlefield and decide his next move. Riding toward him came Servilius.

"Ave, Lucius!"

Paullus waved for him to lower his voice.

"Salve, Gnaeus."

"Victor's head?" Servilius said, smirking.

"That, or I angered the gods."

"We all know *that* cannot be the reason, unless the Carthaginian gods are having their vengeance. Alone of all of us you, discerned the enemy's trap. Had we committed all of the reserves the entire army would have been trapped. I recommended it, and Varro would have done it. I congratulate you, Lucius."

The proper Roman response was to show humility, and no Senator personified the Roman outlook on life more than Lucius Amellius Paullus.

"Jupiter granted me one day of insight greater than is normal."

"It is certainly not hard to see his hand in keeping Varro from having command on the fateful day."

"Gaius may have won a more complete victory than I did. Perhaps the the Senate will honor me with a triumph, at which time it might be proper to again explore the hand of the gods in yesterday's events. Let us speak no more of it now. What news of our enemy?"

"Hannibal fled with perhaps six thousand cavalry. No man claims to know his destination and that is probably true. I doubt that Hannibal knows. He rode north but that could be to deceive us."

"What were our losses?"

"Aurelius has the exact numbers, but I believe we lost about two thousand auxiliary infantry and eight hundred Romans. The cavalry lost some seven hundred men and another four hundred auxiliary."

"Close to four thousand then."

Servilius nodded. "A few enemy infantry may have escaped into the countryside but more than twenty-five thousand fell and so far we have captured thirteen thousand, including at their camp."

"Food stores?"

"It appears they tried to burn whatever they had in their camp but failed. The warehouses at Cannae are untouched. By any measure, it is a complete victory. And I hope that you found my service worthy of praise."

The question contained far more innuendo than an outsider might have known, but Paullus was not an outsider. He understood perfectly the real question that Servilius asked and, in asking it, the implied promise that went along with a *yes* answer.

"I know you preferred Varro as your commander, Gnaeus, but without your wisdom our victory would have been far more difficult. Should the Senate reward me with a triumph, it would be my honor if you would agree to ride at the head of the infantry."

"I would be proud to do so, Lucius, and rest assured that I shall champion the cause for you to be so rewarded to the Senate."

* * *

Epilogue

Off the Coast of Southern Italy
6:27 p.m.
August 9

As the old Greek-style *lembus* galley set course to the south, the small port city of Locri receded to little more than a dark strip on the horizon. The captain's sidelong glances and squinted eyes betrayed his suspicions about the identity of his passengers, but Hannibal did not care. With forty of his best remaining cavalry men on board he doubted the man would be brave enough to try and collect the reward for the Carthaginians' head. The captain might understand Punic, though, so as they sat on the starboard gunnels Hannibal and Hasdrubal kept their voices low.

"We have escaped for the moment, Hannibal, but they will be coming after you."

"Yes, they will."

"You cannot count on aid from the Senate, either. Some of them hate our family more than they do the Romans."

"I know."

"Then what are your plans?"

Hannibal patted his brother's shoulder and stared into the halo of the setting sun.

"My plans have not changed. Nor have I abandoned my promise to our father."

* * * * *

William Alan Webb Bio

As a West Tennessee native raised in the 60s and 70s, and born into a family with a long tradition of military service, it should be no surprise that the three chief influences on Bill's life have been military history, science fiction and fantasy and the natural world. In 1972 he won the Tennessee State High School Dual Chess Championship, and spent every waking moment playing board games, role-playing games, and naval miniatures. College featured dual concentrations in History and English. Everything after that is anti-climax, except for wife, kids, published books and all that kind of stuff.

Website: www.thelastbrigade.com

Facebook page:

https://www.facebook.com/keepyouupallnightbooks

# # # #

To Save the Republic
by Sarah A. Hoyt

Gaius Terencius Varro woke up muttering obscenities undirected and unfocused. The words dropped from his lips half-growled, "Faex! Cane! Deodamnatus! Irrumator!"

Coming fully awake on the hard, uncovered couch, Gaius wondered precisely about whom or to whom he was speaking. After a few moments' contemplation, he was bereft of response, unless it were "himself." Still fighting off the last vestiges of unconsciousness, he turned over and looked up at the ceilings of this provincial house which his seventy bodyguards had commandeered for him and tried to force his mind to function. That process, strangely, was easier attempted than done. Above him, there were squares of wood that someone had tried to form into a ceiling and paint into a contrivance of marble. The contrivance didn't work, and there was a corner where water had leaked in, having poured past a hole in the roof.

It was the home of some local grandee, whose name Terencius neither knew nor cared.

There was something like fear rising up in him like gorge, but more importantly, there was self-disgust and self-hatred.

I ran, he thought. *Like a hare, I ran from the field of battle.* Before he'd succumbed to exhaustion there had been reports from that field, brought to him by a late-following member of his retinue. The pride of Rome lay dead by the river Aufidius. The crows and wild boars would feast well tonight on noble Roman flesh, and forty thousand Roman mothers would mourn their sons. And all of them, all of them would heap their abuse on the head of Terencius Varro, the butcher's son who had become consul.

Only a week before, he had been proud of his ascent, happy as Consul of Rome, proud of his role, standing as equal of Lucius Aemilius Paullus, man of noble blood, one of the Cornelii. And now...

Of course, Terencius had been sick of the war of harassment Fabius had led against the Carthaginian for two years, ever since cursed Hannibal had crossed to the Italian peninsula with his following of mongrels and the freakish elephants of war.

The elephants hadn't lasted long, even if long enough to cause damage to the Roman cavalry whose horses hated the very smell of the beasts. But they had—Terencius had thought—left a stamp of fear on the psyche of Romans, perhaps on their very soul.

What else explained the attacks and retreats, the ambushes and small fights with Hannibal over these two years, the vile, petty confrontations that were as drains to Roman pride?

He and Paullus had thought so. He and Paullus, in concerted, intent talk, in the discussions prior to their standing for consul, in their decision of what to do instead.

He and Paullus. They had agreed that Rome needed to stand up and provoke a manly battle with the Punic invader, and wipe him from Italy, remove the blot of spit from the Republic's face. Or perish of the shame.

He and Paullus.

But Paullus was dead and, at any rate, his family would never let any of the blame fall on his noble shoulders.

Which left Varro to bear the blame.

* * *

Rome had never raised a prouder army. And Varro was proud of it. It had been his—and Paullus'—impassioned speeches that had caused so many it enlist. It was all due to their eloquence, begging the people of Rome to have a care of their reputation, of their standing as the military power in Italy, lest they be seen as weak, their city as easily invaded and subjected to attack after attack by every passing barbarian until they collapsed.

The citizens had responded to the call. Many men had enlisted. The core of the force were blooded veterans, legionnaires remaining from the two legions Publius Scipio had salvaged from the defeat at Trebia. They'd been passed on to Germinus and then transferred to Fabius Maximus.

They had spent two years harassing and chasing—and losing—Hannibal. They'd been repeatedly ambushed by the Gauls. They'd been nearly destroyed under Minucius. And as proud fighting men, they were sick and tired of this constant retreating and fruitless chase.

Hannibal didn't fight like a man, but like a boy or a woman, playing games of deception and retreat, of ambush and then disappearing, like a creature without honor.

Which left those chasing him feeling twice as humiliated in defeat. Sure, those two legions had been augmented and rebuilt after each loss, but the core of it remembered the humiliation, and the betrayal. They knew with whom they were dealing. This force had then been augmented by a fresh recruitment of men equally tired of watching their city humiliated, even if they hadn't been on the front lines themselves.

And all of them agreed with Verro.

Verro remembered the pounding heart, the exhilaration of the moment.

For if there was no greater honor than to be born a Roman citizen, the honor must be greater still when the city elected one to defend her. When the city reposed its pride and its confidence in you.

And the confidence had been as massive as the force raised, the largest force ever raised by Rome: eighty thousand men on foot, alone.

Varro and Paullus commanded double armies each. Four legions apiece, plus equivalent allied units. In all, eight legions and eight alae. In effect, a quadruple consular army.

The night before they'd left Rome, after the festivities with which Rome had toasted its valiant defenders, a doubt had assailed Varro.

Not a strong doubt, precisely, but a slight niggling problem.

He was, after all, the son of a butcher. He'd seen his father's servants handle herds brought in from the countryside for slaughtering, and as such he knew there was a number beyond which a group of any animal—and humans were after all animals, even if reasoning ones—became impossible to handle, impossible to cause to learn to act in concert.

He'd seen the handlers of large herds break them in smaller groups to bring them in safely. And a thought assailed him that perhaps this massive army they had raised—a proof that the people of Rome agreed with Varro and Paullus that it was time to fight without subterfuge—was too large a herd, too difficult to cause to move cohesively as though controlled by a single mind. As good armies must be to prevail.

They were reclining at table at Paullus' home, and Varro—always conscious that he'd trained under Paullus and always was—and always would be—in some measure junior to this man of noble ancestry and education—cleared his throat and said, "Do you believe we can manage to make them fight together, as a unit?"

Paullus had grinned. "Undoubtedly. Surely, though the new recruits have only fought together for a very few months, we are all Romans. Every man has been trained in the virtues of the republic and the art of war from birth. Else, they would not be Romans but mewling barbarians. And besides, Varro, the core of our forces is experienced. And we've worked together before. We know how to coordinate our forces."

Varro had swallowed down his doubts with a handful of olives and the excellent wine that Paullus had provided.

The next morning had proved both exhilarating and terrifying. Both the doubts and the pride, the certainty and the prickling questions had warred in his mind as they left Rome.

The dust cloud that surrounded his and the Paullus' cavalry wings was normal. The cavalry was in fact only about six thousand strong, a little light for an army of this sort.

And the dust was about normal for cavalry on the move.

But behind them came a veritable dust cloud, a lower but palpable haze thrown by the sheer massive numbers of foot soldiers on the move and their supply transport. The supply transport, alone, must be far more than normal to feed such an army.

They'd left Rome's stores depleted, and even so, they left their mark on the countryside as they moved slowly—large forces can't move any other way—southeast towards the flatlands of the Adriatic coast.

Though Paullus and Varro had agreed to trade off command every other day in the traditional manner—a tradition lately violated by Fabius, not for the best as his results had proven, it did not matter. Both agreed. It was imperative that they avoid the kind of ambush that had been laid for Flaminius and his army at Lake Trasimene.

Flaminus had allowed himself to be enraged by Hannibal's destruction of the countryside. That was no surprise. Any man of honor would, since Hannibal's widespread destruction of the area that Flaminus had sworn to protect meant that he despised both Rome and—personally—Flaminus. It was like being harassed by dogs, or set about by unruly street urchins. To endure it meant that a man lost all his pride.

But he should still have been more wary. As it was, Flaminus had not thought that Hannibal, being a desert barbarian and as such a man without honor, would not hesitate to create an ambush.

As the Carthaginian had, near Lake Trasimene.

Hannibal had set up his troops, throughout the night, carefully disposing them for battle in such a way that he would have full view of Flaminus—or anyone really—when he and his troops entered the Northern defile. He put the Iberian and Africans that constituted his heavy infantry on a slight elevation, from which they had ample room to charge down on the head of the Roman column from the left flank. He'd had his Gallic infantry and cavalry well concealed in the hills in the depth of the wooded valley from which the Romans must enter, so they could rush down and close the entrance, blocking all retreat. Then he put his light troops on the heights, at intervals, overlooking the valley, with orders to stay hidden.

The night before battle, he ordered a few of his scouts to light fires on the hills of Tuoro, some distance away, to make Flaminus think that the Carthaginians were still far away.

Knowing that Flaminus would be hot on intemperate pursuit, Hannibal camped where anyone entering the valley would see him.

As Flaminus hurried to close with Hannibal, the Carthaginian cavalry and infantry swept down from their concealed positions in the surrounding hills, and blocked the road. The Romans had no time to draw into battle array and instead fought a hand to hand combat with open order.

And thus at Trasimene, Hannibal ambushed Flaminus and killed fifteen thousand Romans, half the force, who had either died in battle or drowned in the lake trying to escape that way.

Flaminus himself had died, slain by Ducarius, the Gaul.

Flaminus' defeat had caused such a panic in Rome that Quintus Fabius Maximus, Verrucosus, the cautious Fabius, had been elected dictator by the Roman Assembly. And he'd initiated a year of cautious war, utterly failing to destroy Hannibal while suffering a great many defeats at the Punic invader's hands.

Oh, none as bad as the defeat at Lake Trasimene, but none of them painless either. It was how the legions had been whittled down to a remnant.

Which was why it was imperative that they now face Hannibal as men, and put an end to his provocations. And they would.

But they were aware that while it shouldn't be possible for an entire army like Hannibal's to perform ambushes like a little force, it was obvious they would. They had at Trasimene.

Therefore Varro and Paullus agreed.

"I have reports," Paullus said, during one of their rests in the march. "That the cursed invader's army is camped at Cannae, on the River Aufidius, waiting for us."

And Varro, who had been raised in the best traditions of Rome, but had seen his father dicker with farmers and shepherds, and had perhaps a little more insight into the mind of men for whom honor was secondary to victory, had said, "Let us not trust those reports. Remember the fires he burned on the Tuoro hills. For all we know these troops massed by the Aufidius are some local shepherds kidnapped and dressed like his fighters. If we rush to meet them, we will doubtlessly find our rear attacked and destroyed, our camp followers and supplies annihilated, without our fighting men being able to defend them. And then we'll face having to proceed or retreat on an empty belly and with no support. I don't believe we can do that. Not while Hannibal's cursed raiders nibble at our flanks."

And so they distrusted the reports and wended slowly through, keeping their eye open for ambushes.

Their slow progress had its inconveniences, just as their size had its problems.

The slow progress allowed for transgressions against locals. Though it was Varro's well thought out opinion that any peasant who didn't guard his daughter—or for that matter his handsome son—when that mass of fighting men tore through, it was also his ultimate responsibility to—at least—receive the report of how the various commanders had dealt with transgressions against the local populace from theft to rape to murder.

The problem being that Italy wasn't Roman. While each of the cities and tribes had an alliance with Rome and took a subordinate role to the city, and had treatises of mutual protection and support, they weren't Rome. They had their own traditions, their own beliefs, and often their not so deeply buried hostility to the city that had defeated them or their ancestors. Any fresh violation of local rights and norms might cause a city to rebel, something perilous at this juncture.

Worse, any provocation might cause a significant number of inhabitants of a city that was still ostensibly loyal to Rome and afraid of Rome's retaliation to either carry intelligence to Hannibal or to collaborate with him in one of his cursed ambushes or deceptions. Fortunately, they had taken on in this force an unusually high number of legion commanders, and the men were usually blooded, if not of sufficient social influence to deal with contretemps. Why, a full third of the Senate of Rome had joined the army, and the rest of them had family in the army. That, by itself, provided plenty of influential people to diffuse the situation.

Though the thought itself annoyed Varro, being that he was not one of the influential people, it seemed to him it was a matter of no consequence. His sons would be. And their sons after them. It was a matter of advancing the family, and himself—as ancestor—would reap the reward due to his sacrifices to obtain that advancement.

For him to undermine the system would mean only that there was nothing for his sons to attain.

As for their size, while it forced them to go slow, Varro knew well enough that in past engagements with the cunning Hannibal, by the time the Roman forces had broken through his center, it was too late, and their cavalry had been destroyed.

* * *

"**M**aster," a voice from the door. "There is a man to see you."

Looking up, Varro saw Calvus. Calvus was one of his bodyguards, a huge man with a shaved head. He was also the son of a family who had served Varro's family since either of the two families could remember. "Master" here referred both to rank and to the relationship that had existed between the two as long as they could remember.

When Varro had been teased by older boys for his family's late-arrival to wealth, Calvus had interposed his bulk and often brought the jeering to sudden silence.

"Yes?" Varro said, and sat up, rearranging his tunic. He didn't remember stripping off his armor or even his helmet, but here he was, barefoot and in a house tunic. And remembering, as through a fog what Calvus had said, he queried, "A man?"

Calvus appeared to struggle for words. "A...foreigner."

Since to Calvus a foreigner could be anyone, from a local of this village to a Greek, Varro was not sure what that meant. He had a sudden misgiving that it was Hannibal himself, come to bid for surrender. But that was ridiculous. It wasn't to Varro that Hannibal would come for surrender or to dictate terms. And in fact it was highly unlikely that Hannibal even knew that Varro was still alive.

Varro was unsure how many days it had been since the battle. It seemed to him he'd slept a very long time. Perhaps longer than a day. Or perhaps it was their journey that had taken very long.

He remembered his wing of the cavalry stampeding in a panic, carrying him with them. The shame of it burned in him. They had sworn an oath, the first time that such was done by Romans before battle. Everyone had sworn that they would not, "Abandon their ranks for flight or fear, but only to take up or seek a weapon, with which to smite an enemy or save a fellow citizen."

He had broken the Oath. He was forsworn. "Bring the stranger in," he said. "But you and Servius come in with him, and keep watch, lest he strike."

Calvus left to return seconds later with the man. Varro sat up straighter. The man was—this was not even surprising—a Carthaginian. This was easy to tell at a glance, though he wore a tunic that would pass unnoticed on any peasant in this region, only his cloak giving away that he was a man of some substance. It was the sum of the parts that made it obvious. He was lighter-built and more dark-skinned than most Romans, but the most important thing about him was that he did not move like a Roman. There was something of the merchant in a foreign port to him. Sure, assured enough not to be trifled with, but glancing sidelong and in an easy way of shrugging the shoulder and sidling, as though to project an impression of amiability and accommodation.

The Phonecians were, after all, a merchant race, and lacked the sturdy assurance of the Roman farmer.

"Milord Varro," he said and smiled, and nodded. And Varro, who was not a lord, nor a nobleman of any kind, hardened his heart against him. Or tried to. The thing with flattery was, of course, that it worked. It was hard not to let oneself fly into sympathy with someone who flattered one so outrageously.

"I am Abibaal," the stranger said. "And I come to you with a message from our great commander, Barca."

Varro experienced a visceral response to Hannibal's name, and he started to get up from his couch and order the stranger away, before he thought better of it. He sat down again, but spoke, his voice rough and gruff but, he hoped, decisive. "I want no messages from your master. Nor do I wish to surrender. I am a Roman citizen, I. I have my pride."

"No one is asking your surrender, Consul," Abibaal said, and again, there was the sliding smile, and the bow, as though he had never thought of such a monstrosity. "Terms will be sent to Rome, but we're told that Rome will surely refuse."

The Phoenician paused for barely a second before continuing.

"It is rather that we thought, given your loss, you might not be comfortably received in Rome again."

"And what business of that is yours?" Varro snapped.

"I will be honest with you." Here a trace of accent showed in Abibaal's excellent Latin, giving him something of a sibilant tone. "Any commander bringing such a defeat back to Phoenicia and having lost upon a single battle most of the nobility of his city would surely be crucified as an example of what happens to those who lose."

Varro narrowed his eyes at the man. Before he could shape his mouth to protest, his guest continued.

"Now, that might not happen in Rome, but surely there will be penalties for such a loss, and we're informed that you're not of such high birth that you have a large family to protect you from such penalties."

Damn you, Varro thought.

"More than others, we know that they are unjust. We know your entourage near-kidnapped you away from the battle front, and that if it were not for them, you'd have fought and died there, like the noble Paullus."

This man's insolence angers me, Varro thought, beginning to move his arm and signal the Phoenician be executed. His visitor continued as if he did not notice, shifting his eyes to meet Calvus' as he continued.

"But since you're here, and Rome might think that you turned and ran, surely Rome, who mourns their lost sons now, will soon turn to punish those responsible."

The 'to include your entourage' did not need to be spoken for Varro to recognize the veiled threat. His hand fell limply to his side, the signal to slay the Phoenician ungiven.

"You must see that you are at risk, and mighty Hannibal Barca has sent me to offer you safe conduct to our ranks, where you'll be protected and a noble counselor."

In no way will I turn traitor, Varro thought angrily.

In his rage, Varro didn't remember what he said, precisely. He gathered later that he actually hadn't told his servants to throw the man out and whip him to death, though the image had been in his mind so strong, he would have sworn an oath that he had.

Apparently the Carthaginian smiled and left, ahead of the servants who would have thrown him out, somehow seeming to go of his own volition. This had the effect of making Varro's attendants into an escort, rather than those who expelled him. Varro was well aware of what *that* would seem like to external observers.

* * *

Insulted, wounded, it took Varro quite a while in solitude to contemplate the strange encounter.

When he did, he found that instead of anger, he felt a

strange ambivalence, as though the ground had turned slippery under his foot or as though he'd put his foot down on a stair expecting to find a step and found instead nothingness and howling wind.

Which in a way described the whole battle of Cannae.

* * *

They'd been so sure that their numbers would have them. And in retrospect, Hannibal hadn't done any of the things he'd done before. No hiding on the hills. No lighting of false fires. Nothing fanciful or difficult. Nothing that would make it justifiable for them to be so utterly defeated.

It was only after the report of what had actually happened came to him that Varro built together, in his head, the image of the strategy the Phoenician had employed.

It had been deceptive, since that seemed to be the trend of the man's mind. It was well know that men didn't change their mode of thinking, however much their circumstances might change. And it had been cunning, since Hannibal was in fact a shrewd general, as well as anything else. Faced with a force twice the size of his own, he had perforce used tactics to overcome the disadvantage.

The tactics used were a thing of beauty and elegant. In the past his center had always held, while his wings mauled at the Roman wings, until it was impossible for those to go to the rescue of the center.

But now, now that Rome had beefed up its army, so they could penetrate through the well-defended center of the Hannibal's army, so they could in fact use their massive numbers as a ram and bowl over all opposition, Hannibal had made that center very weak, staffed with the poor soldiers of Iberia, the Gallic Celts, who would break and run at the slightest push.

His cavalry took up positions on the far left and right wings. When fully assembled, the Carthaginian line must have looked— Varro could see it in his mind—like a crescent that bulged in the middle.

Hannibal had put his stronger troops, the Libyans, at the edges of his formation. As the Roman infantry advanced into the pocket created by the retreating Gauls and Spaniards, they were enclosed by the stronger, and still fresh troops at the perimeters, who then blocked all escape. With no way to avoid entrapment, and the sheer number of the Roman infantry making it impossible to move, the battlefield had become a killing field, and the killing was the Carthaginians to do. For the Romans—or for most Romans—it remained only surrender or dying.

His spies had brought back the accounts of those for whom surrender was anathema.

"They died screaming, Master," one informant had said. "Their tendons cut, they died begging that the Carthaginians cut their veins and thus end their suffering."

"Master, some say that a great many dug holes and plunged their heads into them, so as to suffocate," was the tale brought any another.

In Varro's mind, the proud army marched, all smiles, leaving Rome amid prayers and song. The fine flower of Roman nobility, many more influential than he was. Many more much better born, belonging to old clans and older families.

And then he saw it in his mind's eye as it turned to a killing field, the flies buzzing in the heat of August and landing on the unseeing eyes of the blood-and-vomit covered corpses.

"You can smell the field from miles away, Master."

* * *

Varro sent Calvus to Rome, and Calvus brought word back. When news of the battle—and word of the immense losses—had filtered back, people had taken to the streets screaming the name of kinsmen they presumed lost. Public lamentation had been violent. An envoy had been sent to the oracle at Delphi to find out what it meant. Meanwhile, human sacrifices had been made for the protection of Rome. Human sacrifices on the mountain of Jove. Something not done since remote antiquity, something they were used to considering a mark of barbarism.

Varro was thinking of this, of the hysteria that must be sweeping to Rome to create so uncharacteristic a response, when Calvus came in to the darkened chamber where his master had taken to sitting with a jar of wine in contemplation. Contemplating his lost honor and the fact that, as an oath breaker he would bring not fortune and fame to his family, but a great stain. A stain which his children would have to expunge before they could attain any honors of their own. Or perhaps his grandchildren.

My name will not be mentioned by any that come from me for a generation, Varro thought. *Indeed, I am almost certain it will become an epithet in all of Rome.*

"What is it, Calvus?" Varro asked, his words slightly slurred.

"Master, there is a man to see you."

"If it is the Carthegenian—"

"No, master. A Spartan."

"A Spartan, here? What does he wish?"

"To speak with you, master."

Varro sat up straight. "Very well, same as before. Send him in, but do come you and Servius and keep me company while he is present, lest he decide to attack."

Calvus bowed and left.

Moments later a man entered. He looked quite different from the Carthagenian. This was an older man, more experienced—it was obvious—in both life and battle. His scarred hide spoke of wounds and fights, and his dark eyes had depths that were hard to pin down exactly. If Varro had been asked, he'd have said the man looked amused.

When he opened his mouth, he spoke in clear Greek, "Consul, I come to make you an offer."

"If you've come to scare me with tales for children, of how Rome is going to crucify me—"

"No. Rome is unlikely to crucify you, Consul. We know better than that. Abibaal is young and not very experienced in the ways of Rome," the Spartan replied evenly.

Varro snorted.

"I beg you to believe that he was not saying what he said at the instigation of Hannibal Barca, who is no fool," the Spartan continued. "Abibaal was charged with bringing you a message that you could find not only safety but honor on our side, that we understand what happened, and none of us thinks that you betrayed your men or your co-consul."

"Safety and honor from tricksters."

The man looked surprised and wounded.

"I am Spartan," he said. "We are not tricksters. If I were not here as an envoy I might have to demand satisfaction for such an insult."

"No, not the Spartans, the Phoenicians," Varro protested.

"Ah. Their ways are not ours, Consul. That is the difference between a warrior race, or, in the case of the Romans, a race of honest farmers, and merchants like the Phoenicians. They are not as blunt or honest as we are."

The Spartan's expression was briefly distasteful, as that of a man who had found a weevil in his fruit.

"Or at least that is not how they present, since they often have to wheedle, to deal, and there is some deception involved in business dealing," the battered warrior continued. "But you know, it doesn't make them necessarily fundamentally dishonest. I've been with them but not of them for over a year now. I've taught Barca his Greek, and yet, I assure you, he's fulfilled his promises to me."

Varro's eyes narrowed. He gestured for the Spartan to continue.

"What you must think of when it comes to a deal with them is whether you're a competitor, which you are as the commander of an opposing army, or an associate, an ally," the Spartan patiently explained. "If you're the commander of an opposing army they'll treat you as though you were a competitor in business. There is no trick they won't use to get the best of you and to win over you."

Varro's nostrils flared at that thought, his anger rising even as the Spartan sought to placate it.

"But if you're an associate, an ally, they will be true to their word and keep it as though bound by the most stringent honor. You see, it is known in business that if you don't treat your partners well, they will not trust you and will therefore then turn on you at a crucial moment."

The Spartan spread his hands plaintively.

"If the Carthaginians—if Hannibal Barca himself—gave you protection and position with him and his people, you could trust him onto death, if it came to that. He would never be forsworn."

This brought up the uncomfortable prickle of guilt again, in the back of Varro's mind, because he had in fact broken his oath. At the same time, Varro realized he had gone down quite a wrong side spur in his protests. He'd never meant to say that he wouldn't trust Hannibal. His objection to going over to the other side was quite of a different order.

"Forget what I said," he said. "I am tired and have not slept much. I meant only to say that I'd never betray Rome. My duty, sworn, is to defend Rome from her enemies, not to make common cause with them."

"Of course," the man said. "And I understand that, but what you must ask yourself is whether it is most effective to make cause with the Carthaginians in order to defend Rome."

Varro cast a suspicious glance to the jar of wine in the corner. It wasn't particularly strong wine, and he'd added plenty of water to it, so surely he wasn't dreaming this conversation and its peculiar lack of logic, was he?

"You speak nonsense."

"Do I? As I told you, I am Spartan. My name is Sosylus. And I am fascinated with history."

Sosylus gestured at his clothing.

"I am Spartan, a warrior," he said. "As you probably know from Greek history, Spartans and Athenians have warred much. And my city started out proud and rough, a city of warriors. Each boy was brought up to be a warrior. There were no shirkers among us."

The Greek gave a smile that softened his sharp features and at the same time made Varro aware that he knew the irony of what came next.

"And no historians either. I doubt if I'd have made it in the old days, as I was weakly when I was born, and would likely have been cast from the sacred hill by my father, to dash my brains at the bottom."

Another barbaric process, Varro thought.

"But still that was what my people were, a strong and proud people, until we were invaded. You probably have heard—hasn't every educated Roman—of the three hundred who defended the mountain pass, so their very sacrifice to the gods of war, their courage, would rouse the rest of Greece to defense. And it did. It worked. Or did it? Eventually the Persians conquered us, anyway. And changed us. And, yes, we changed them."

Sosylus paused, taking a swig from the waterskin at his waist.

"The truth is, though, that by that time we were already changing. The reason that the three hundred needed to make their final stand is that Sparta had already lost its appetite for war. It didn't rush to meet the enemy. It spoke big words but tried to temporize."

Varro thought again of Fabius Maximus.

"And in time, it got conquered. And in time it fell. In time all of Greece fell. Yes, and to everyone." He paused a moment. "I bet you any of my ancestors, brought forward to see what the city has become, would be horrified and feel that the sacrifice was for naught."

"So?"

"So, what do you think of Rome, you, Varro, the butcher's son, who, through wealth and your own brains were elevated to Consul and commanded the greatest army the city has assembled."

"Rome is the best city in the world," Varro spat angrily. "It is the only one where men are men and don't grovel at the foot of a king."

"Ah. But they do grovel at the foot of their noblemen. Their great families, their gens, all of it counts, doesn't it? How many times did people throw in your face that you were plebian born, and not even a landowner, but the son of a butcher."

Varro shrugged.

"It is always hard for the first one who places his foot upon the ladder of success. It can't be thought—"

"Of course. But how common is your path to success, Varro?" the Spartan interrupted. "If people are all alike, really, in Rome, and if your origin means nothing, if there are no kings, then why is it so difficult? Why aren't there more butcher's sons who ascend to commanders? Why aren't there more in the Senate? And why—and you know this is true—will you be reviled for doing the sensible thing, whether you did it on purpose or not, and escaping a killing trap?"

Varro felt the need to interrupt the man, but bit his tongue.

"Do you think if it had been the noble Paullus who had done so, anyone would have blamed him? Or do you think that anyone will believe you two were united and of a mind, both decided to attack as soon as possible; both agreed to the strategy and the place where the battle would happen?"

The Spartan gestured at Varro.

"Or will they blame you, Varro, while enshrining Paullus' memory because the Cornelians will not have it otherwise? Will they say you attacked without his agreement, perhaps even without informing him, simply so they can hold him blameless?"

"That would be difficult," Varro said. "Both of us spoke before the Senate and the people of Rome, both of us said our strategy was the same."

"Rome is performing human sacrifices," Sosylus said, "and has sent to foreign oracles for solace. Do you believe they will remember what they do not wish to remember?"

"But why would Hannibal want me to turn? Or need me? Myself and my seventy body guards are as nothing before his troops and his advisors, even foreign ones such as you," Varros said.

"Ah, but you are a Consul of Rome," Sosylus replied smoothly. "You see, if Hannibal is to do more than simply harass the country-side in Italy, he must get more troops and more support from the Assembly of Carthage. And there are too many people in it who hate the Barcas and their vendetta against Rome. Now, after Cannae, many of the local tribes have come to pledge their loyalty to Hannibal, but he doesn't know how to deal with them, and they don't seem to trust him very much. Now, if a consul of Rome itself were at her side—"

Varro wanted to Sosylus to be gone, to be thrown out, as he had told his servants that Abibaal should be thrown out—even if not whipped to death—but something stayed him. He turned to Calvus.

"See this man, Sosylus, gets a room, and bring him back when I tell you."

If Sosylus saw his position as hostage, he did not show it, nor react. He smiled and bowed, both looking oddly with his craggy and scarred countenance, and he followed Calvus out of the room.

* * *

Varro paced. He paced the small room with the leaking ceiling and the pitted mosaics underfoot, and he tried not even to think of the man to whom it belonged, and where he might be, and what he might think of the Romans who had commandeered his house.

The truth was that Rome saw itself still as a small and rural city, where her sturdy sons defended her with valor on the battlefield.

But Rome had become far more than that. Its webs of alliance and influence, of fear and trade, permeated the entire Italian peninsula. This was why Hannibal had managed to hurt her without ever coming within sight of the city.

And therein lay the problem. More and more, the lands outside Rome were not honest farms, worked by families and those connected to the family. They were vast estates, worked by slaves for the benefit of landlords who could not be called farmers.

People like the Cornelians didn't dirty their hands with any work. And they did despise those who did, no matter how far they reached from their humble origins.

Which—

Which meant Rome was changing.

Varro was not stupid; quite the opposite. He could see the time coming when Hannibal was defeated. He needed someone to convince the Assembly in Carthage to give him support. If that didn't happen, he'd run out of men and support.

And it was unlikely the revolting tribes of Italy would be able to form a cohesive bond and help the invader.

But if he had Varro...

If Varro helped, yes, Hannibal would win. But Hannibal could not run home any more than he could manage to weld the tribes into an alliance.

He was a good general, but, ultimately, a desert raider. He wouldn't be able to think long term.

Sooner or later he'd die. Probably not naturally, and Varro would not need to instigate it. And then Varro would have power. Power to weld the republic back into the honest thing it was meant to be. To get rid of wealth-and-blood proud noblemen and create a strong republic where all men would be equal.

His path was now clear. He'd betray the republic, in order to save it and make it what it should be.

He walked to the door, his step firm. "Calvus, send for Sosylus, the Spartan."

* * * * *

Sarah A. Hoyt Bio

Sarah A. Hoyt was born in Portugal and lives in Colorado. Along the way she's published over 32 books (around there anyway. She keeps forgetting some every time she counts) she admits to and a round dozen she doesn't. She also managed to raise two sons, and a countless number of cats. When not writing at speed, she does furniture refinishing or reads history. She was a finalist for the Mythopoeic award with her first book, and has won the Prometheus and the Dragon. To learn more about Sarah and read samples of her work, visit http://sarahahoyt.com.

# # # # #

Here Must We Hold
by Rob Howell

Frost filled the courtyard of Abingdon Abbey as a golden dawn promised the best of days. Crisp and cool with brilliant orange, yellow, and crimson leaves on the trees. The archivist of the abbey, cloak tightly held around himself, breath coming out in clouds, rushed across the frosted grass as quickly as his crutch would allow. He entered the scriptorium, sighing with relief when he saw his assistant had already arrived. A fire burned in the hearth, and the boy was lighting the last set of candles.

"Bless you, lad." The archivist went to the fire and warmed his hands. "How much progress have you made on the copy for Peterborough?"

"All the way through Alfred's death."

"Excellent." The archivist moved to the assistant's desk and looked at the parchment. "This is well done."

"My letters are wretched, brother," protested the young man.

"You're already much better than I was at your age."

"Perhaps." The assistant glanced at the crutch and then at the scribe's gnarled fingers. "But then, I hadn't—"

"My gifts?"

"Your...gifts?" The assistant blinked. "But your hands? Your leg?"

"It is true my fingers ache more than you're ever likely to know, and it would be nice to walk as I once did." He shook his head. "But they are gifts nonetheless. The Lord granted them to me so I would never forget."

The assistant blinked again.

The archivist smiled. "It's of no moment now. You must continue your work. Make sure to copy that section on Aethelflaed. I'm sure the monks in Peterborough don't have it, and few enough remember her these days."

"Yes, brother."

"Good lad." The archivist limped over to the armarium set into a niche in the wall. Inside was a bound codex. He reverently lifted it out and carried it over to his table. Small pieces of parchment, dry and old, fell to the ground despite his care. He then retrieved another codex, this one much newer and set it alongside the first one.

He stared at the older codex for a long moment before slowly turning it to a page. The old parchment cracked. The morning's gloom forced the scribe to squint at the letters. Then he opened the other codex to the corresponding page and compared his previous day's work with the words on the older pages, a difficult, tedious task even in bright light. Painful at the moment.

He sighed in relief after completing the examination. He looked at the next section.

Before continuing, he bowed his head. "Sancte Michael Archangele, defende nos in proelio; contra nequitiam et insidias diaboli esto praesidium." He crossed himself and reached for a quill. He dipped it into the inkpot and started to move it toward the blank page. Then his hand shook, causing an ebon drop to fall to the floor.

Hastily, he pulled the pen back.

No. Not today of all days.

He bowed his head again in prayer, flexing his fingers.

He tried again, but the quiver in his hand made it difficult for him to even fit the tip of the quill into the inkpot.

I must get this right.

He tried again but with no better results.

Maybe it's the cold. Yes, must be the cold.

The scribe reached for his crutch and rose.

His assistant looked up. "Is everything well, brother?"

"It is as God would have it. My task today is one that must be done well and correctly. We all must age, though, and my eyes and hands require me to be patient on a cold, dark morning."

The assistant's eyes flicked to the codex. "You have waited years for this, if it is what I think."

"It is."

"If I may be so bold, I think God will not begrudge you performing the task after Terce."

"Nor do I, lad." He limped over to the abbey's chapel and knelt before the altar. Behind it was an icon of Mary. He bowed to her.

Bless me in this task, Mary. Especially with this *page.*

As had often been the case, he thought he saw her icon smile upon him. He knelt there on the relentless stone floor until Abbot Siward came in hours later to lead the abbey in their mid-morning prayer.

"What is wrong, brother?" asked the abbot.

Startled, the scribe looked over. Stiffly, he pulled himself to his feet. "I apologize, my lord abbot. I needed to pray."

"The Lord will not chastise you for praying, brother," Siward said with a smile. "Nor will I. Is there anything you need?"

"No, lord abbot. I am just old and today's task is too important for me to attempt before the sun warms the scriptorium."

The abbot considered the monk and then smiled again. "Thank you, brother."

"For what?"

"I was debating which psalm to read for Terce. Nothing seemed right. Now, it is clear that God wishes me to read Psalm 143."

The scribe bowed his head and whispered, "You needn't do that one on my account."

"No, I don't. However, I've not read it in some time, and I think it fits. Besides, I know it's special to you, and I would give you all the strength I can today."

"Thank you, my lord abbot."

The other brothers of Abingdon Abbey filed in.

When they had settled, the abbot intoned, "Remember with me, brothers, the wisdom of Psalm 143. 'Blessed be the Lord my God, who teacheth my hands to fight, and my fingers to war...'"

* * *

Wulfstan, son of Ceola, waited for the tide to ebb so blood could flow.

Across Panta Channel, on Northey Island, Danes lined the shore waving axes, swords, and spears, yelling curses mostly carried away by the freshening breeze from the shore. At low tide, a causeway connected Northey Island with the mainland just southeast of the town of Maldon. Northern raiders preferred such islands because they needed only a small guard to protect their ships.

"They say there are nearly a hundred ships," hissed Godric, Odda's son.

"So?"

"That's at least three *thousand* warriors!"

"And there's three thousand fyrd with us, not including our brother thegns and all the house-carls of Essex."

Godric looked in amazement. "They're but farmers. Hardly a byrnie amongst them and all they bear are cheap spearheads on ash-wood poles."

"Then those of us who have taken rings from Byrhtnoth must fight all the better." Wulfstan strode forward to the edge of the causeway, leaving Godric behind.

Byrhtnoth, son of Byhrthelm, Ealdorman of Essex, already waited at the edge. Two hands and more greater than six feet, with hair white as a swan, he looked down at his newest thegn. "Do you think you can hold against them all at the water's edge, boy?"

Wulfstan considered the causeway, then shook his head. "No, lord. I'll need two others."

The ealdorman laughed. "Very well. Aelfhere and Maccus, you stand with the boy."

"As long as he does all the work," said Aelfhere. "I'm too old for this."

"As am I," said Maccus with a matching grin.

One of the Danes, shorter, broader, but with lithe, quick steps moved forward and sent a blast from a horn across the channel. With all eyes upon him, he yelled, "You! The tall one with the white hair. Are you the Byrhtnoth we've heard of?"

The ealdorman stepped to the channel's edge. "I am. And who are you?"

"Olaf, son of Tryggvi, jarl of these men." He gestured at the host behind him. "As you can see, they thirst for the fight." He smiled. "However, if you send us rings of gold and hauberks of steel then we'll see no need for the spear-rush. Indeed, a day as beautiful as this is one for sailing. If you give us these gifts, we'll grant a truce and then enjoy the wind and spray of the sea."

"Of you I've heard, and I've no doubt of your word. Here is my answer." Byrhtnoth grasped his shield and lifted his spear. "Spears of ash we shall give you, and swords of steel as well, yet only their edges and their points. Tell your folk that here stands a good earl with loyal thegns and the fyrd about him. To our king, Aethelred, we have sworn oaths, and this land we shall defend no matter that we may fall."

"So be it. Tell your god when you see him that we gave you a fair chance."

"I shall, when my time truly comes."

The Dane laughed. He turned and said something to the men behind them. Some of them ordered their ranks and moved to their end of the causeway. Inch by inch, the causeway appeared as the tides, inexorably, pulled away.

Wulfstan stepped up, locking shields with Aelfhere on his left and Maccus on his right.

"This'll do." Aelfhere turned to those behind him. "The rest of you fill if we fall, but give us room."

Byrhtnoth began arranging the troops behind them. First, he called forward the few score bowmen at hand.

"Aelfnoth, you command the left. Wulfmaer the right. Leave off until you see any bowmen on their side. We can hold this causeway easily, but not if they start killing us with arrows as we stand. Understand?"

The two thegns nodded.

"Good." The ealdorman turned to the bulk of his men. A score he had already left guarding the horses which had allowed the English to reach Maldon in time. The others he split into three blocks, one to each side and then one, slightly larger, in the center. In the front rank of each block he placed the house-carls, who wore steel armor and bore shields. The fyrd arrayed themselves behind that line, ready to thrust with their spears past the shields. The fyrd may have been farmers and herdsmen, but most had stood in shield walls before.

Yet never against three thousand raiders. Godric was not the only English warrior to wonder at the size of the host before them.

Byrhtnoth marched to each group in turn, giving them all the same message. "Stand firm, lads. They only want plunder and easy wealth, not your steel. They'll run once they see we're true English men." Each sent a cheer following the ealdorman. Then he and his score of personal thegns returned to the area near the causeway to stand behind Wulfstan and the two flanking him.

Byrhtnoth leaned on his spear.

The sun crept higher.

The sea crept lower.

The more impatient of the Danes started splashing over, only to have Olaf snap at them to wait.

So they taunted and insulted the English.

Who just kept waiting.

When the sun reached halfway to its peak, the tide had exposed the causeway, leaving only puddles of water here and there. Olaf motioned, and the Danes marched.

When they were three paces away from the end, the front ranks charged, hoping to overwhelm Wulfstan, Aelfhere, and Maccus.

The three defenders, however, stepped forward in unison at the last moment, and shields crashed together. The front ranks of the Danes stumbled, with those immediately behind colliding into a pile. Wulfstan stabbed down with his sword, spilling the day's first blood.

He stabbed again, this time into an exposed leg, earning a yell. Next to him Aelfhere and Maccus bloodied their weapons as well.

The following ranks pressed in, stepping over their fallen brothers. An axe sliced along the edge of Wulfstan's shield, cutting through the iron binding and carrying a chunk away. Wulfstan twisted back, slashing through the Dane's byrnie. He then stabbed into an exposed flank.

That exposed his own flank, but Aelfhere anticipated the youth's mistake. He stepped forward, interposing his shield and allowing Wulfstan to regain his position.

One of the pile at Wulfstan's feet apparently still lived, for a hand reached out to grasp his ankle. He tried to tug his foot away as another Danish line approached, but the hand held firmly. Desperately, Wulfstan lifted his shield high and chopped down.

A spurt of blood from the wrist rewarded his slash, but the crash on his shield drove him to a knee. He pushed himself up with a thrust at a Dane's belly. His sword slid through iron rings and the Northman stumbled back, grabbing at his entrails.

Another Dane charged in wildly, axe raised high. Maccus simply made a small step and directed him off the causeway. He splashed into the water, spluttering and struggling to gain his feet.

But yet they still came. Wulfstan's limbs tired, and all three of the Byrhtnoth's thegns rasped desperately for breath. Behind them, three more thegns prepared to step in, should they be needed.

By now, the dead and dying Danes provided a grisly breastwork for the defenders, but that slowed not the Northmen. They scrambled over the bodies of their brothers, slashing with axe and sword, stabbing with bright spears.

An axe chopped off most of Aelfhere's shield, but the old warrior returned the favor by breaking the axe's handle. The destruction of shield and axe gave the two warriors a moment to stare at each other, but the moment swiftly ended when another Dane pushed past.

The Northman pressed Aelfhere with his shield, trying to force him back and provide an opening for his fellows behind him. However, the dead and wounded made him place his feet awkwardly. His leg extended, and Wulfstan slashed down. The Dane stumbled, twisting away. Aelfhere finished him off. The man's shield fell to the ground and Aelfhere grabbed it in but a moment.

The attackers paused, gauging anew their options to create a breach. Meanwhile, the defenders leaned back and gasped for breath. Wulfstan heard Byrhtnoth urge the three to step back in favor of fresh replacements, but Maccus snarled back with words Wulfstan could not comprehend. They earned a laugh from Byrhtnoth.

Still gasping, they raised their shields when the Danes stepped forward. This time, a Northman bearing a shield led several clustered spearmen who, instead of charging, reached the edge of the pile and flicked their spear tips at the defenders.

Aelfhere tapped one away with his sword. Maccus tempted one spearman with a target, but slammed his shield on the top of the spear tip and chopped through the spear's shaft.

Two spear points came toward Wulfstan, one from each side. He twisted away from one while at the same time putting his shield in front of the other. However, with the bodies at his feet limiting his steps, the maneuver left him off-balance. The spearman thrust again, hitting Wulfstan's shield. His aching legs could not compensate for the lack of balance, and the thrust made Wulfstan stumble.

Maccus moved his shield to guard Wulfstan's suddenly exposed side from the following thrusts, but in so doing allowed a spear to rake along his sword arm's shoulder. He grunted in pain, but Wulfstan scrambled back into position. Maccus turned back, sword still raised, a scarlet streak running down the iron rings of his byrnie.

A horn blew from amidst the mass of Danes on the causeway. The Danes stepped back and Olaf moved into the gap between the lines.

With a broad smile, he gestured at the pile. "You three have made the Valkyries busy today. I've no doubt they'll lift you on their white horses when your time comes."

"Today is not that day, Dane," snarled Maccus.

"Perhaps." Olaf looked up at the sun. "But the day is not over and we have many hours left before the tide returns."

Byrhtnoth stepped forward. "All the more time for you to sail back to your homes."

The Danish leader laughed. "I had a different thought. Your three champions here have well guarded this causeway. Some score of men and more will dine with Woden tonight. Perhaps, though, you would consider moving back and allowing my brethren to form on your side of the channel. Then we shall see what the Victory-Judge says of our worth."

"Do you doubt the worth of English men?" asked Byrhtnoth. "Are these dead here not enough of an answer?"

"I do not doubt these three men at all. Indeed, should they wish, I would accept them into my hall," Olaf replied easily. "Yet they weary, and I would allow others of my kin a chance to prove themselves."

"They do weary, but instead of allowing you to form up, I could name others to take their place. Eadric, Aelfwine, and Leofsunu are here at hand and none before have doubted their courage."

Olaf looked at the three thegns. Then he stared into Byrhtnoth's eyes. "Of *their* courage I do not doubt."

Byrhtnoth's eyebrows, as white as his hair, lifted. "But you doubt mine?"

"I didn't *say* that." Olaf gestured. "I will say that this causeway is no place for a battle. And it is truly a beautiful day to be on a ship."

The ealdorman considered. "There is wisdom in your words, and I will consider them. I grant you truce to carry your dead and wounded back to the island. When that task is complete, I will give you my answer."

With a grin, Olaf gestured at his men to come forward and carry the bodies away. For Byrhtnoth's part, he ordered Wulfstan and his companions to step back in favor of Eadric and the others.

Cleaning his sword, Aelfhere looked at the ealdorman. "You can't be thinking of accepting the jarl's thought."

"I am, in truth."

"Don't let your pride kill us all," snapped his old comrade. "Ofermode has oft slain many a worthy thegn."

"You think ofermode prompts me to allow them over?"

"Why else? Sure these lads and I slew a score of theirs, but we had every advantage." He gestured to the fyrd lined up around them, eyes all turned their way. "Your fyrd are stout, it is no denying, but they are no match for the Danes."

"You may be right, but I don't know I have any other choice."

"What in God's name are you thinking?"

"You heard the jarl. They could as easily get into their ships and sail anywhere. They've already plundered Ipswich, but there are many other places they could raid. I've sworn to defend all of Essex, and if I have too much pride, such great ofermode, it would not be in keeping my sworn word to Aethelred, son of Edgar."

Aelfhere's eyes narrowed, and he looked back across the channel. The Danes had almost finished retrieving their dead.

Byrhtnoth put a hand on the older thegn's shoulder. "I have the Danes at hand. If I allow them over the causeway, then we'll have them penned in with the channel at their back. They'll *have* to fight through our lines. It will not be easy, but if our hearts are the bolder, then we may stand and have a chance to drive them off." He sighed. "I fear this host, if we don't stop it here, it will come back time and again for our treasure. Nor will any gifts of gold and steel keep them from raiding as they please."

Aelfhere nodded. "For once you have paid the Danegeld…"

"Yes." Byrhtnoth straightened and looked about. "You take the left side."

"My place is in the front," protested Aelfhere.

"Your place *was* in the front. I would have all three of you, who held so strongly, lead the fyrd. They will be the braver for having seen your deeds and even this respite is little enough for you after that slaughter."

Maccus joined them, arm now bandaged. He boasted, "I'm the bravest man here, but I'll admit my arms show some small signs of weariness."

Byrhtnoth laughed. "Then take the right." He gestured the two older warriors off, then leaned down to Wulfstan. "The center I give you, with but these instructions, for you well know all else you'll need."

"Yes, my lord?"

"First, send back to those we left to guard our horses. Tell them to join with the rest of your men. We'll need every spear we can muster, and I can walk back to my hall if needed. If we live."

"And the other?"

He looked across the channel and spoke in a soft voice. "Keep your eyes on Godric and his brothers. We shall need our hearts to stay firm."

"My lord—" protested Wulfstan.

The ealdorman raised his hand. "There is no time for that. You know it as well as I."

After a long moment, the young thegn muttered. "As you command. What if they don't follow my orders?"

"The men around you all saw your deeds on the causeway. If you *lead*, all will follow."

"Except perhaps Godric."

"Yes." Byrhtnoth slipped a ring off his arm. "And if any ask, you may show them this ring of gold. You have my favor, and my thanks."

"Thank you, lord."

Byrhtnoth nodded, then yelled across the channel. "Olaf, son of Tryggvi! I grant you passage. Come quickly. I've got good English beer at my camp and fighting is dry, thirsty work."

Olaf laughed, glancing at Byrhtnoth's dispositions. "You are brave."

"God will preserve us."

"And Woden will preserve us. Perhaps today we'll find out whose god is mightier."

"When the sun sets, all will know what God alone knows now."

Olaf turned and gestured. The Danes crossed the causeway, initially with suspicion, then with confidence. They settled into a line of approximately six hundred abreast, five or six deep. The front ranks stood with shields and glittering swords, those behind with bright axes, and the rear ranks with spears. The line bristled with steel, lust for battle, and the promise of victory.

Ravens, hunger whetted from the fight at the causeway's edge, circled above them all.

Byrhtnoth stepped forward in the hundred paces or so that separated the lines. "Blessed be the Lord my God, who teacheth my hands to fight and my fingers to war! For Essex and Aethelred!"

"For Essex and the king!" shouted the fyrd.

Olaf, in his sardonic way, commanded his line to advance.

Byrhtnoth shouted, "Stand firm, lads! Let them come to us." He and his thegns slid back behind the center group of men. "Wulfstan, keep them in the line and working together. They've got more armor than we do, so we have to keep the Danes as far away as possible."

Wulfstan nodded and stepped into the middle of the ranks. "Kill them as they come! They'll keep coming, climbing their dead, and then we kill more as they stumble!"

The fyrd around him raised a yell. Wulfstan noticed some of the fear in their eyes went away when they remembered his deeds from but an hour before. He glanced at Byrhtnoth, waiting stolidly to advance with his best warriors at the just the right time. Wulfstan's heart soared. He yelled at Olaf, "Come, Northman! Your doom awaits!"

The jarl laughed.

Other Northmen, some fifty or sixty paces away, answered with their own war cries, but the slow, steady pace of the oncoming advance did not change. Stupid warriors charged from fifty paces.

Pity they're not stupid, thought Wulfstan. He paced back and forth amidst his men. "Shields! Keep yourselves locked together. Step into them at my call. That'll toss them off their feet and you can gut them on the ground!"

The shieldmen, all experienced warriors or they would have borne spears with the fyrd, nodded. His words were obvious, basic, but Wulfstan could almost hear them all say, *"Lad's young, but he knows what he's about."* They became perfectly still. Poised.

Behind him, he heard Byrhtnoth command, "Aelfnoth! Wulfmaer! Get your bowmen ready!"

The Danes were now about twenty paces away.

"Bowmen, loose!"

Above Wulfstan came a flight of arrows wobbling in the wind. The Northmen lifted their shields and scornfully blocked the meager volley. They sent their own volley. A few fyrdmen along the English side yelled in pain, but none of the shieldmen.

Fifteen paces.

Another flight of arrows from each side, with much the same result.

At ten paces, the Danes charged with a loud yell.

The fyrd around Wulfstan took a half-step back in fear, but he shouted, "Stand firm!"

For a moment he thought the command failed, but the spearmen stepped forward just in time to support their front line.

The lines crunched together.

Shields crashed.

Swords flashed.

Flights of arrows landed among both sides.

Screams of men and metal followed.

Sprays of mud and blood came in their turn.

Ravens and Valkyries wheeled above, eyeing their harvests.

The press crushed all the warriors together. Some died simply because they couldn't move. They would go to the next world with a memory of steel approaching while they could do nothing. The press held up many who could not stand, but dead or dying, could not yet fall to the ground.

Fortunately, in the rush, Wulfstan had managed to get his shield above his head before the press would have prevented it. "Stand firm," he yelled. He struggled to get his sword above his head as well. "English! Stand firm!" he repeated. He could strike no other blow. He finally succeeded in raising his sword just in time to block an axe from smashing into the fyrdman next to him.

Something slammed into the block of men. Warriors, English and Dane both, swayed, less in control of this sea of flesh and steel than they had been of the tide. The wave knocked some off their feet. A few of those managed to fall under their shield. After the battle, a dozen or so would manage to dig themselves out of the pile.

The rest simply died, trampled underfoot.

Wulfstan stepped on something too soft to be grass. *There's a farmer who's sowing days are done.* He almost giggled, the moment indescribably funny, but he pushed off the flesh beneath to gain an extra hand's-breadth of height. That height allowed him to strike at an axe haft.

His first blow earned little but a Danish curse and an attempt to pull the axe back. The press prevented that attempt, and Wulfstan swung again, this time sending splinters flying. A third time and the shaft cracked.

The Northman dropped the axe. For a moment, it sat on various shoulders, floating, then sinking beneath the surface.

An arrow thumped into Wulfstan's shield. A spear bounced off, careening past him. Warriors near him, on either side, were not so lucky. He could see more arrows rising in the distance. He managed to twist, getting his shield into a better position to ward their steel points. Crashing thumps rewarded his twist, but holding shield and sword above the fray was not without problems. The press and flow wrenched his shoulders back and forth. His muscles, not completely recovered from the fight at the causeway, made their protests known past the fear, mud, and noise.

He pushed the protests down and focused on the front line, now only two ranks away.

"Stand firm!" he yelled again.

Suddenly, the crunch of battle spat Wulfstan out of the press. In front of him a Dane, tossed out of the press in similar fashion, raised his shield and charged. Wulfstan met the charge with his own shield.

Linden wood smashed into linden wood and the two men pushed for any advantage. The Dane stabbed under their shields. Wulfstan rolled to his left and slashed at the Northman's leg, but the Dane blocked it. The pair exchanged blows crashing on each other's shield, moving around the battle as if they were the only ones on the field. The Northman got his feet under him and with a bellow of rage, pushed Wulfstan back a few paces. The Dane charged again. This time, Wulfstan did not meet him squarely but instead stepped to his left, pushing the Dane stumbling past to sprawl on the mud.

Another Dane charged Wulfstan before he could pounce on the first one. This time the thegn stepped to the right. He smashed his pommel into the Northman's nose, splattering both with blood and knocking him back. Wulfstan followed the punch with his blade into the warrior's throat.

For a moment, no one was within five paces and he bent forward to catch his breath. He straightened to see Godric and his brothers in line with a group of fyrdmen. Bodies, English and Dane, ringed them.

They didn't run immediately.

But the look in their eyes told Wulfstan their courage would not hold. Especially since a line of Northmen, shields locked together, stepped toward them. The second rank of the Danes raised their axes and bellowed a war cry as they advanced.

Godric and his brothers wavered.

Wulfstan charged into the flank of the Danish line, knocking several into a pile and stumbling on top of them.

Fortunately, several of the fyrdmen stepped around Godric. They bloodied their spears on axe wielders suddenly without their shield-wall.

Godric and the two other sons of Odda simply watched, amazed.

And, in so doing, allowed Wulfstan to push himself up, stabbing blindly beneath him. An axe slashed toward his helm. He blocked it but it the blow sent him stumbling.

Again, Wyrd favored him. His stumbling brought him next to Godric and his brothers. They had their shields raised, but their eyes remained wide and terrified.

"Fyrd of Essex. Get back into your line!" Wulfstan then hissed at Godric, "Raise your shields, or I shall name you nithing and the scops will sing of your cowardice until the world ends."

Godric hesitated, eyes flicking to his brothers.

"You fight, or I will kill Odda's sons first," continued Wulfstan.

The three brothers flinched, but raised their shields. Wulfstan looked at the fyrd around him, who generally hid grins as they moved into place. He then locked his shield with the others and they advanced into the swirling mass of steel and blood.

A few Danes, startled to see a unit in good order marching at them, backed away in search of allies.

Behind them, not ten paces away, Byrhtnoth and his thegns stood, heavily beset.

"To the ealdorman! To Byrhtnoth!" yelled Wulfstan. His line advanced, but a group of Northmen appeared out of the melee. They smashed their shields into his line, blades slithering past the iron-shod linden.

Wulfstan pushed back, struggling to keep his feet.

One of the fyrdmen supported him and Odda's sons by holding his spear in both hands along their backs, his breath coming out in harsh grunts as he pushed with all his strength. Other fyrdmen slipped their spear tips at any opening they could see.

Danish spearmen returned the favor, stabbing past their front line.

Wulfstan chopped at a spear tip aimed at his face. The Danish shieldman in front of him stuck his leg out in his effort to push through the line. Wulfstan slashed down, turning the Dane's madder-dyed pants more crimson than before.

The shieldman fell to his knee, and suddenly Wulfstan could see his face. He thrust his blade through the Dane's eye and then stepped over him to attack the second line. Inside the preferred range of their axes and spears, the blood of two more Danes reddened his steel.

The Danish line collapsed. Suddenly, Godric and his brothers had openings. They desperately slashed, driving the Northmen in front of them down. Spear tips in eyes and cheeks finished them off.

Wulfstan tried to command them to reform, but his voice caught in his suddenly desert-dry throat. After a moment, he croaked, "Back into a line."

The fyrd, also trying to recover, started to move with limbs clearly leaden. Godric shook his head, mouth open.

"Get into a line!" Wulfstan repeated with a snarl.

Odda's sons, exhausted and terrified, hesitated.

Before Wulfstan could do or say anything, a fyrdman tapped Godric's shoulder with his bloodied spear. "You heard the lad."

While they arranged themselves, Wulfstan looked for the ealdorman. He didn't see him, but then he heard his voice rising over the fray. He advanced his group around another cluster. On the other side, Byrhtnoth stood surrounded by a line of bodies. "Come, my friends! My blade still thirsts!" he yelled.

But his fight had not been completely one-sided. Blood flowed from wounds on Byrhtnoth's arms and a spear point had ripped along his cheek. Wulfstan also saw many friends with whom he'd never again share a meadbench in this world.

Yet he didn't stand alone. Eadric and other thegns remained at his side despite their own wounds. More Danes pressed in. Axes flashed around the ealdorman.

Eadric stepped forward to keep them away from Byrhtnoth, but there were too many. One he warded with his shield, but the blow pushed his shield out of the way and the next blow crashed into his helm. As he fell, Eadric desperately tried to block yet another blow with what strength remained.

It wasn't enough. His blade hit the axe, but without enough power to stop it. However, the head of the axe twisted and instead of chopping through Byrhtnoth's boar-crested helm, the flat of the axe slammed into the ealdorman.

Byrhtnoth fell. The other thegns stepped over him as the Danes pushed to finish him off.

His height and flowing white hair had always proven useful in battles. He had been able to rally his warriors many times, simply by being there. Today, his easily recognizable presence meant many of the English saw him fall, despite all their prayers and blood.

"The ealdorman is down!" yelled one of Godric's brothers. Fear and panic drove him to swing wildly at all around him. Two Danes fell, but so did a fyrdman behind him. The other brother was no better, and he spilled more of both English and Danish blood onto the trampled mud.

Godric echoed the cry, "The ealdorman is down!" He, too, slashed about and warriors of both sides scattered away. He suddenly realized he had a chance to flee.

Wulfstan saw the wild look in the son of Odda's eyes. He stepped forward, punching out with his shield. Godric chopped into it. For a moment, Godric's blade stuck in the wood. Wulfstan's sword, almost before either thegn realized, chopped down, slamming into the mail just above Godric's knee.

The thegn cried and fell to his knees.

His brothers turned their desperate focus on Wulfstan. They struck wildly with their swords.

Wulfstan released his shield and spun away from their blows. He slashed down through the neck and shoulder of one and crunched his blade into the other's helm. The last of Odda's sons fell, but whether dead or simply unconscious, Wulfstan never knew.

He looked down at Godric, sword raised.

"No!" Godric pushed himself to his feet, eyes wide in terror. Wulfstan's sword came down, but to each's surprise, Godric blocked it with his own. "No," he cried again.

"Then follow me to Byrhtnoth!" snarled Wulfstan.

Godric, eyes closed, nodded.

Wulfstan leaned in and hissed, "I'll give you leave to rest when Byrhtnoth is rescued or avenged, not before!"

The terrified thegn didn't do anything.

"Understand?" demanded Wulfstan.

Godric whispered. "Yes, Wulfstan."

"Then make ready." Wulfstan looked about and yelled at all the English in sight. "We go to Byrhtnoth," he declared. "We'll save him or leave our bodies atop his."

A ragged cheer rose, and the English formed up again, this time with Godric at the point. The fyrd followed the limping thegn, and they advanced on the cluster around the ealdorman. The slow pace allowed the English line to not only stay together, but also tighten up. By the time they reached Byrhtnoth, they were as strong a line of shields and spears as ever faced the Danes.

But they also took time, time which the thegns of Byrhtnoth did not have.

Aelfwine had often boasted of his lineage in meadhalls. Many he slew with his spear on that day, but an axe ended his line.

Offa shoved his stern sword into that Dane and rushed into three others. He slew one, wounded another, and then fell as his namesake would have wished, blade to blade with the third.

Dunnere, who had chosen to stay at his farm instead of accepting Byrhtnoth's rings as a thegn, did not flinch. His spear spilled the blood of many Northmen until two northern axes rent him apart.

Above them all was Eadweard, taller even than Byrhtnoth. He broke through an advancing wall of shields. His sword flashed, but in the end the Danes surrounded and overwhelmed him.

Wulfstan cried at each death. Tears ran down his face. He opened his mouth to order the charge, but…

No! We must get there in good order!

So he kept pace with Godric.

Step.

Step.

And then it was time. Wulfstan charged into the Danes. Since he had no shield of his own, he simply rammed his shoulder into the middle of one of the Danish shields. He stabbed into the nose of the Northman to his right, the spun around, his back to the shield.

The eyes of the Dane suddenly next to him suddenly widened, but Wulfstan slashed across his neck.

Then the spears of the fyrd were there.

And, to Wulfstan's surprise, so was the sword of Godric. The hobbled thegn had taken advantage of the hole created by Wulfstan. With the help of the spearmen, they pressed past the line of Danish shields into the axes and spears behind.

Wulfstan fed many more ravens, as did Godric and all of the fyrd. They pushed past the Danish line and there was Byrhtnoth.

He lives!

The ealdorman, clearly dazed, kept trying to rise, but the press around him prevented it. Just as clearly, only the shelter of his few remaining thegns prevented the Northmen from finishing him off.

Wulfstan watched in dismay as three Danish spearmen struck at once and Leofsunu fell, his battered shield rolling away. Into the opening jumped a Dane, who slew the brothers Oswald and Eadwold with his axe. Byrhtwold, their father, avenged his sons. The axeman's head flew away.

But three more followed, axes raised high. Wulfstan rushed them, but before he could reach them, their axes felled the father upon the bodies of his sons. In his rage, Wulfstan slew not only Byrhtwold's killer, but also the other two Northmen.

Byrhtnoth tried to rise, but a new rush pushed Wulfstan back into him, knocking the ealdorman down again.

Wulfstan's blade flashed above them all, sending blood spraying about as he fed raven after raven. However, a Northman's ribs held Wulfstan's sword for just a moment. Not long, but enough to give a Danish spearman his chance. His spear slithered through the fray. Wulfstan never saw the spearpoint before it entered his side.

But Godric did, to his horror and shame.

Then the spearman stepped over Wulfstan's body and aimed at Byrhtnoth, now clear of defenders.

Godric did not hesitate.

He forgot the pain in his knee.

Moved faster than at any point in his life.

And for the first time in his life, Godric, son of Odda, charged into the fray. He gutted the spearman, slew another behind him, and then another. He dropped his shield to push bodies, shield, and broken weapons off his ealdorman.

A shadow loomed over him. Another Dane, axe raised high, stood above. He struck down, and Godric raised his hands desperately.

But the fyrd had followed. A spear struck the Dane's byrnie. It did not penetrate, but it caused his blow to fall awkwardly. Instead of chopping through hands, arms, and helm, the back of the axe merely crunched onto Godric's raised hands.

Byrhtnoth, from a knee, stabbed the Dane. He pushed off Godric's shoulder and rose.

On that cloudy day, all could see his swan-white hair.

As if with one voice, all on the field, English and Dane both, cried, "He lives! Byrhtnoth lives!"

Soon after, a horn blew. The battle halted and everyone looked over. Olaf stood amidst a pile of English dead.

With a small, twisted smile, he yelled over to Byrhtnoth, "I think, perhaps, your god is mightier."

"I think He is." Byrhtnoth looked at the slaughter and the ravens already swooping down. "But there are many here that are dear to me. I would not mind if your god took them to his meadhall for a time that they can boast of their glories."

"The Valkyries bear their souls away as we speak." Olaf looked around. "Where is the one who held the center of the causeway?"

Godric knelt and cradled Wulfstan's body. "He lies here, Northman."

"I hope Woden keeps him until I get there myself. He was a good man."

The thegn nodded, washing Wulfstan's face with his tears. He ignored everything around him until Byrhtnoth came to him.

The ealdorman held out a gold ring. "Godric, your bravery has earned this."

"Mine?" Godric snorted. "I'm the least of men. Nithing, I am. The scops should write of how we forgot the oaths made on golden rings. We would have fled. Would have taken the best horses and run. Wulfstan stopped us."

"If you had fled, many of the fyrd would have followed." Byrhtnoth looked about. "And if that had happened, who knows when England could have stopped Olaf and those who followed him."

"I know. I cared not."

Byrhtnoth sighed, running his hand over his face. "Stay here with Wulfstan. My head hurts, and there is much to do."

"My sword is there." Godric nodded his chin at the blade. "Give it to someone worthy."

"You didn't flee."

"Only because of Wulfstan who would not lie dead in my arms but for my shame," Godric snarled. "And the same for the other brothers I betrayed who lie here."

Byrhtnoth said nothing more, but he picked up Godric's sword and left.

* * *

The sun flowed through the scriptorium now, filling it with heaven's golden light.

The scribe placed the quill down and looked at the

parchment with satisfaction. His letters ran in even rows, all well-formed, and he had not needed to scratch any away to fix a mistake.

He bowed his head again. *Thank you, Mary.* His eyes focused on his fingers, which he suddenly realized ached so much he couldn't open his hands.

A familiar voice spoke in his ear, "The battle is over. You have my leave to rest."

Startled, he looked about, but there was no one in the room but his assistant.

"Do you need something, brother?" he asked.

"Oh, uh—" The archivist shook his head. "I just thought I heard something. No one came in just now, did they?"

A puzzled look crossed his assistant's face. "No, brother."

"Strange. I could have sworn I heard something." His face cleared. "But there is something you could do. Would you please go to the abbot and ask him to join us?"

"Is something wrong?"

"No, lad, but I think he needs to be here."

"As you wish." The assistant placed his quill on his blotter and left.

The archivist stared out the window and watched leaves fall off trees in the breeze, ending their lives in glorious color.

Abbot Siward walked in. "The brother said you wished to see me?"

"I did." The archivist gestured at the codex before him.

The abbot read, "CMXCI. In this year Ipswich was plundered and Siric, Bishop of Canterbury and Aelfeah of Winchester first suggested to pay tribute to the Danish men because of the great destruction they caused on the seacoasts. And in that year Olaf came to Maldon with XCIII ships and there the ealdorman Byrhtnoth came against him with his force, and many men were slain and drowned there on both sides. And there Eadric and Eadweard the Tall were slain and many other thegns loved by the ealdorman. Most dear to Byrhtnoth was Wulfstan, who fell defending his lord. And many ships of the Danes were captured, such that it would be years before they came again."

Siward placed a hand on the archivist's shoulders. "I am glad God chose you to copy our chronicle. It will be a glory to the abbey for many years."

"Thank you, my lord abbot." The scribe gestured at his assistant. "But it will be up to him to continue the work. I beg to be released of this burden. I am no longer capable of doing it properly."

"You have done this task since I was appointed abbot nearly eighteen years ago. Abbot Aethelwine told me you had done the same throughout his time as well." Siward smiled. "God is well-pleased with you."

The archivist stared at his hands. Tears returned, dropping onto fingers that would never untwist again.

The abbot spoke again, but this time the archivist heard a different voice. The same voice from a few moments ago. The same voice that saved him. Wulfstan's voice.

"Godric, ego te absolvo."

* * * * *

Historical Note

On 11 August 991, 93 ships filled with northern warriors decisively defeated the English in the real Battle of Maldon. It's possible the English slew enough Northmen they could hardly crew their ships, but no matter how many they killed it was not enough. After the battle, Archbishop Siric and others suggested to Aethelred II Unraed that he offer the Northmen ten thousand pounds to leave England alone. The king paid, and the Northmen left. As Kipling would lament, though, they returned the year after with those same 93 ships. And the years after.

However, it's easy to understand why the English and others kept paying the Danegeld. The strategic mobility provided by those ships allowed them to attack where the defenses were weakest time and again. Rarely could the defenders bring any significant force to bear. The extant copies of the Anglo-Saxon Chronicle all vary slightly, but they all detail the harm this fleet brought to England for many years to follow after Maldon. The entry at the end of the story, by the way, is a cobbling together of a number of entries from the Chronicles modified to suit my purposes.

A remnant of a poem, *The Battle of Maldon*, provides our best description of the battle. I have adhered as much as possible to the poem with one major change and one significant explanation.

The explanation is a defense of Byrhtnoth. As described in the poem, Wulfstan, Maccus, and Aelfhere hold the causeway so fiercely the Northmen ask the English to permit them to cross. Then the poem says Byrhtnoth allows this because of his "ofermode." This word is a challenging one for scholars, as it only occurs this once in extent Old English documents, but the general accepted meaning is, essentially, "over-proud." In other words, Byrhtnoth allows the Northmen to cross because of his arrogance.

While that interpretation matches the tone of the poem, some scholars have pointed out the strategic opportunity allowing the Northmen to cross provided Byrhtnoth. J.R.R. Tolkien actually discusses the ethics of Byrhtnoth's choice in his alliterative poem *The Homecoming of Beorhtnoth Beorhthelm's Son*. It will come as no surprise that scholars continue to debate both Byrhtnoth's ethics and Tolkien's discussion.

In some ways, though, it's irrelevant why Byrhtnoth made his decision. I prefer the smart theory over the arrogant one for two reasons. The poem describes Byrhtnoth's thegns dying much as I've described them, fighting even though their lord had fallen and the battle was already lost because that's what good, honorable men did. I like the idea of Byrhtnoth being worthy of their loyalty. More importantly to the outcome of the battle, had Byrhtnoth allowed the Northmen to cross out of arrogance, I can't imagine the English would have been as eager to fight.

And that did matter. It is the cracking of their morale that probably decides the battle. In the poem, Godric and his brothers fled after Byrhtnoth fell. Godric actually rode away on the Byrhtnoth's horse. Many Englishmen, seeing what they thought was their ealdorman running away, followed on Godric's heels. Obviously, my major change forces Godric to stay and therefore all the English to stand firm. The slaughter, which was already great, would thus be all the worse.

This outcome might mean the Northmen would have to leave a major portion of their ships. In that case, Aethelred would have faced a weaker fleet in years to come, and he might have succeeded in creating a useful English navy using those ships as its core. He certainly tried to create such a navy, but it was never more than a nuisance to the Northmen. In fact, the Chronicle says his navy did more harm than good.

Aethelred is remembered as an ineffectual king who listened too much to bad advice (Unraed does not mean "unready" but instead "ill-advised"). However, given the strategic challenges facing him, it is difficult to imagine he could do much more than he did. That's a much larger discussion, though.

I'll freely admit even with a significant victory at Maldon the English would have still struggled to keep the Northmen at bay. However, it's a possibility, especially since Olaf Tryggvason converts to Christianity in the two or three years following the battle. I wanted my change to the outcome of the battle to matter, after all.

I should also briefly mention that Psalm 143 is not incorrect. Many of you might know the passage used as coming from Psalm 144, but that is a more modern numbering of the Psalms. These priests would have used the Vulgate, in which case it is called 143.

Finally, it's a shame that all we have is a fragment of the poem. It's powerful, evocative, and worthy of heroes. If I can hope this story will do anything, it's that it encourages you to read the poem someday, if you haven't already done so. The deeds done that day should never be forgotten in the halls of men.

* * *

Rob Howell Bio

Rob Howell is the creator of the Shijuren fantasy setting (www.shijuren.org) and an author in the Four Horsemen Universe (www.mercenaryguild.org). He writes primarily medieval fantasy, space opera, military science fiction, and alternate history.

He is a reformed medieval academic, a former IT professional, and a retired soda jerk.

His parents discovered quickly books were the only way to keep Rob quiet. He latched onto the Hardy Boys series first and then anything he could reach. Without books, it's unlikely all three would have survived.

His latest release in Shijuren is *Where Now the Rider*, the third in the Edward series of swords and sorcery mysteries. The next release in that world is *None Call Me Mother*, the conclusion to the epic fantasy trilogy *The Kreisens*.

You can find him online at: www.robhowell.org, on Amazon at https://www.amazon.com/-/e/B00X95LBB0, and his blog at www.robhowell.org/blog.

# # # # #

The Heretic by

Monalisa Foster

"France will be lost by a woman and shall thereafter be restored by a virgin."

—Marie d'Avignon

I t is a terrible thing to know one's future. To know that one cannot avoid it. To know that even if I could, I would not.

I do not walk my path alone. God has sent me counsel. It is for love of God that I take each inevitable step, knowing where it will lead: to victory; to pain; to lives lost. But also to freedom—not for me, but for France.

In my mind's eye, I see them making the sign they will hold up as they escort me. I cannot read, but I know what they will call me: superstitious; a liar; a seducer of the people; blasphemer; presumptuous, cruel, and braggart; idolater and apostate; invoker of devils.

Heretic.

Even knowing how it will end, I march towards this future of my own free will. I walked the path knowing that I would take an arrow. I walk it again, knowing it will end in fire.

I know it will be worse than anything I can imagine. Worse than the beatings, the arrow to my chest, the wound to my thigh. I know that they will draw it out. There will be no quick release, no snap of the neck as the rope catches my fall.

No mercy.

Only fire.

They will make me live my own Hell because deep in their hearts they know my soul is destined for Heaven.

Do not call me brave. Save that for those who overcome fear. I fear not, for God is with me.

* * *

May 7, 1429

Heart pounding like a drum, Jehanne sat upon her white courser, banner in hand. Made of thick, white satin with golden fringe, it was the finest thing she'd ever called her own. The words "Ihesus Maria" had been embroidered with gold thread. Christ sat between two angels and golden lilies littered the background. She loved it. More than her sword, more than her armor.

Her armor was finely made as well, for it too had to inspire. The Duke of Alençon had made a gift of it. It had taken some time, but she'd gotten used to the yards of linen that she had to be wound into before she could put it on. The fabric's oppressive tightness had become a familiar friend, along with the bruises that came with fighting in armor. After each battle, her whole body was black and blue. But nothing about wearing the armor felt wrong anymore.

Instead, she was filled with the knowledge that no matter what happened, it would be God's will.

Awareness of what she was, what she stood for, and what they saw when they looked at her made her sit that saddle as if she'd been born to it. It was hard to believe that once, not so long ago, she'd been terrified of horses.

Jehanne was no longer alone.

La Hire, with his prickly disposition, was on her right, swearing under his breath because he knew she did not approve of such language. Like her, he had dark eyes and dark hair worn in a casque-cut. One of the few leaders who truly believed in her, he now prayed beside her before each battle, his sonorous voice echoing her own, soft one…

Saint Michael the Archangel, defend us in battle. Be our defense against the wickedness and snares of the Devil. May God rebuke him, we humbly pray, and do thou, O Prince of the heavenly hosts, by the power of God, thrust into hell Satan, and all the evil spirits, who prowl about the world seeking the ruin of souls. Amen.

On her left, Poton. Also dark of eye and hair, he was a minor noble who served as her chief lieutenant and called her an inspiration. He towered over her more than most and ruffled her hair as if she were his page boy.

Next to him, D'Aulon, blue-eyed and light of hair. A skilled archer, he also served as her bodyguard, scribe, and squire. Of the three, he was the youngest, the one that seemed to understand her impatience the most.

They had let her inside their hearts. She could tell by the way they looked at her as if she were an angel. Ears hot with embarrassment, she'd scolded them for it, but it had only made them admire her more.

It is no small thing to be inspiration to so many, La Hire had scolded back. *Perhaps that too is part of your burden, la Pucelle.*

A cloud slid over the sun and spirit—a sense of things gathering and shifting—rose up inside her.

The catapults hurled their first volley. The rocks soared high above her head and crashed against the Tourelle's stone walls.

It had begun.

Ahead of them, men took up their battering rams and ladders. They ran towards the ditch surrounding the fortification. Flaming arrows arced above them, aimed at the Tourelle's wooden doors.

She kicked her horse forward and lifted her chin defiantly as she galloped across the field.

The cavalry thundered around her. Like a tidal wave, they surged forward. She couldn't have stopped them if she'd wanted to. They rode like men who knew their purpose and sacred duty in this world.

Men armed with lances and axes followed the cavalry, adding their voices to those of screaming horses. They pressed around her in air thick with dust and smoke.

And then the sky darkened and rained arrows down on them.

Horses dropped. Men fell by the dozens, their eyes rolled back in their heads. Those not hit pressed forward, eyes wild with vengeance. Lances ran through bodies. Poleaxes split heads. Brains spilled out on the ground.

Jehanne rode into the fray, urging them on, holding her banner high. The tang of saltpeter and gunpowder ignited the fire in her blood. Exhilaration roared through her, a kind of madness that distorted time and sound.

She lost track of La Hire. An arrow passed high over her shoulder—D'Aulon was still behind her, putting his bow to good use. She pulled on the reins, veering left to avoid a lance.

The corner of her eye caught sight of Poton just as an axe went through his horse's leg. The animal screamed as it went down.

Poton went down with it, pinned between the dying beast and the ground. His sword flashed in the sun as steel met steel.

Jehanne dug her spurs into her horse's sides, driving him toward Poton. She raised her standard and brought its sharp end down into the neck of the man attacking Poton.

Momentum carried her forward, the shaft of her standard fighting the pull of bone and sinew as she yanked it free. Twisting around in her saddle, she pulled on the reins.

Poton was alive. He'd lost his helmet but managed to get out from under his dead horse and finished another attacker off with his sword.

A triumphant smile splitting her face, she raised her standard.

It was the look on Poton's face that told her something was wrong. He fought his way towards her, his gaze fixed not on her face as it usually was, but lower.

There was an arrow sticking out of her chest. Hot, thick blood rose in her throat and filled her mouth. The stench of burning oil and flesh filled her nostrils.

Shrieking, her horse reared, pawing the air.

She fell as the clouds turned red and swirls of gray sky twisted into black.

* * *

In the corner of the one-room shack with its thatch roof and rotting beams, an unconscious Jehanne was covered by blankets and pelts.

Hours—had it really been only hours?—ago, Jean had pulled the arrow from her chest and tossed it into the fire. He'd heard thousands of men scream. He'd heard women scream, but for some reason, Jehanne's scream still echoed in his ears like it would never stop.

D'Aulon had bound her wound and forced wine down her throat to ease the pain. She'd slipped into an exhausted sleep.

Jean had then left the shack, leaving the work of taking off her armor to D'Aulon, her squire. The young man had taken it with him when he'd left. He would make sure that it was repaired. They both knew, without the slightest doubt, that as soon as she was conscious again, she'd demand its return. And D'Aulon was nothing but conscientious about his duties.

The shack's wooden door swung open on creaking hinges, letting in a night wind heavy with the stench of death. It stirred the fire and sent ashes upward through the chimney.

"My watch," La Hire said, his voice almost a whisper as he ducked through the too-small door.

Jean shook his head. He'd propped his leg—the one that had gotten itself pinned under his horse—on a chair. His elbow rested on the rough, wooden table, kept company by a jug of wine and a cup with a chipped lip.

"Jean Poton de Xaintrailles," La Hire said, leaning over Jehanne's sleeping form, "do you think you're the only one who cares about her?"

"I haven't finished my wine," Jean said, wrapping his hand around the cup.

La Hire's thick, black eyebrows rose, making the dried blood still clinging to his forehead flake and drift down into his eyes. He swiped at his face, smearing more soot into the gash on his cheek.

"Go. Get some sleep," La Hire said as he crossed over to the table. With bandage-wrapped hands, he raised the jug of wine to his lips and drank deeply.

Jean put his other leg up over the arm of his chair, letting it swing as he slid down into a more comfortable position. He tilted his head back and looked at La Hire through half-closed eyes.

A string of curses poured out of La Hire. Despite the hushed tone, Jehanne stirred and mumbled.

"Heh. Hear that? Even in oblivion, she scolds me," La Hire said proudly as he looked around. The shack was bare. If La Hire wanted to stay, he'd have to find a corner not already claimed by rats and bed down on packed dirt soaked in urine.

"Fine then," La Hire said, "but I'm taking the wine." He grabbed the jug and trudged off. The door swung shut behind him.

Jean opened his eyes and pulled himself up. He rubbed at his throbbing leg. La Hire was right of course. Jean needed to rest, but he knew that he could not. Not this night. Not until he was sure that Jehanne would live.

D'Aulon said she would, but like the rest of them, he was caught in her spell. Her squire would not allow himself to think that she could die. Not again.

When that arrow had hit her, they had thought her dead. Word had spread through the ranks like wildfire. Motivated by revenge, the men had fought harder, taking the Tourelle.

What an incredible revelation that had been.

Jean knew that the men believed that she was a gift from God. He knew that they would follow her into Hell. They loved her fire, her vigor, the way she urged them on, the way she made them believe that they could not be hurt.

He knew that whatever she did, motivated them to do better. What man wanted to be outdone by a strip of a girl who looked all of fourteen, if that?

Yet that same girl, plain and sturdy, had a quality about her, one that must come from God, for somehow she knew what they needed and gave it to them. In its own way, it was genius, and bestowed on a girl who'd been confirmed to be only seventeen. It had to be divinely inspired.

She didn't leave them time to be afraid, to think about what was happening.

She let them believe in prophecy, in God's grace, in themselves. She was a spark of hope in their simple minds. But it was what they needed. Simple people needed simple things they could understand.

The people were, first and foremost, Frenchmen, no matter how simple the Dauphin and his mother-in-law, Yolande of Aragon, thought them. And these peasants and townsmen were tired of having their country stolen from them, whether it was one cow, one sheep, or one coin at a time, or all at once as Isabeau, the Whore Queen had sold so much of France to the English.

None of them were saints. Not the Dauphin. Not Yolande, and not the Duke of Alençon either. Despite their support of Jehanne, her cause was not theirs. She was something to be used for as long as it served them. Jean had been at Court long enough to know how things truly worked.

His gaze fell upon Jehanne's banner, propped up in the corner by the bed. No longer white, it was gray with soot and stained with blood, its edges frayed and heavy with mud.

Her spark, her divine purpose had pulled him in as well. And he liked who he was in her presence. Dared he hope that it lasted beyond the victory that she craved?

"Crown the king," Jehanne murmured.

Always the same words, even now.

Jean swirled the wine in his cup, looking into it as if it held images of his future. It returned only his reflection—a tired man with the pain lines on his face the most prominent of his features. He drained the cup and threw it into the hearth.

It shattered into a hundred pieces. Flames leapt for the shards and consumed them.

And somewhere in the back of Jean's mind, a human sacrifice screamed as she burned.

* * *

May 23, 1430

"How long has it been?" Jehanne asked.

"Three-hundred-and-ten-days, *la Pucelle*," Poton said.

Jehanne shivered, despite the warmth of the night, the sweat-soaked linens under her armor, the black, hooded-cloak over it to make them blend into the night.

Her gaze lingered on the silhouette of his face. Her ears and cheeks burned hot, and she was glad that he could not see her face. On that night when she'd taken an arrow to her chest, when she'd woken to him keeping vigil over her, when he'd blushed at the sight of her, something had woken up inside her. No matter how much she prayed to be relieved of it, her blood stirred at the sound of his voice, at his scent, at his mere presence. Yet not once had he touched her. Nor she him.

"Less than a year, yes?" she asked.

"Ten months and a week," Poton said. "Yes, less than a year."

She offered him a grateful smile. He'd tried to teach her to count, and she had done her best to learn, but the numbers brought her no comfort. To her, each day felt like a lifetime.

The voices had ceased the day that Charles got his crown.

It had been a glorious July day in Reims. After the crowning ceremony, she'd knelt before Charles and called him king for the first time. Joy had filled her. Tears had streamed down her face.

After, she had gone to the chapel to thank God and pray, hoping that the king would join her as had been his custom, but he hadn't, opting instead to celebrate.

At first, she didn't think anything about the silence of the voices. The saints didn't come when called. Saint Michael, Saint Catherine,

Saint Margaret, all made themselves known in their own way, in their own time.

So she'd continued as she had before. Praying. Fighting. Fighting less and less as the king relied more and more on like-minded peers.

The twinge in her thigh where an arrow from a cross-bow had pierced it, reminded her that Paris and September hadn't been that long ago. Even then, the voices had been silent, but she'd not given in to despair. She continued to pray. She'd even confronted the king for not sending her the support he'd promised.

He'd looked at her with contempt and asked her what her counsel—her voices—had been saying, and her face had burned hot with shame. He had been the only one to whom she'd conveyed God's divine message.

Her silence had told him everything he needed to know. The sneer on his face had softened however. In October he'd sent her to Saint-Pierre-le-Moûtier. His army had initially retreated from the heavily fortified town. She'd led a second assault, doing what she always did—urging them on, making them believe that they could not be defeated.

The voices remained silent. Still, she prayed for their counsel.

The following month, the king had sent her to La-Charité-sur-Loire, but again, he'd not sent the support she needed. She'd had to abandon the siege and return, defeated.

After Christmas—despite La-Charité-sur-Loire—Charles VII, had ennobled her and her family, naming them Du Lys. Her family and the people of Domrémy, now exempt from taxation, had rejoiced.

And still, the voices were silent. She prayed for guidance, asking if she'd made a mistake by accepting such Earthly honors. To refuse these honors would insult the king. She'd been at Court long enough now to know that much. And the king did not take insults lightly.

Surely, insulting the king she'd just helped crown was not God's plan. It would undo them both—Charles and her.

For the first time since she was thirteen years old, she felt alone and abandoned. The truce with England left her with little to do and life at Court did not suit her.

When the truce ended she thought the voices would return. They were silent on the way to Compiègne.

They were silent today when she attacked the Burgundian camp just north of Compiègne.

And they were silent now as she and her men retreated as part of the rear guard. The men were silent too, disheartened by another defeat.

Her brother, Pierre, rode at her side, uncharacteristically quiet. Only the horses seemed to have anything to say as they huffed their way through the darkness of a new moon.

Warning snaked through her belly.

The whoosh of an arrow cut the still night air. It was followed by another.

La Hire cursed.

D'Aulon pulled his horse in front of hers and raised his bow. He sent two arrows flying into the darkness before Jehanne had a chance to draw her sword.

Poton's voice rose through the cacophony of panicking horses and men. He urged them forward. Their horses passed her and disappeared into the night. Swords clashed. Groans and screams followed.

Sword held high, Jehanne urged her horse to follow. She brought her sword down, aiming for a Burgundian's thigh. It met its mark, followed by a scream that receded in the darkness. Blood dripped down the sword, snaking into the seams of her armor.

She struck wildly at anyone that came at her. It was like fighting shadows, but her sword struck flesh and metal as often as it missed and cut through air.

Time slowed, muting the clash of metal, the protesting voices of horses, the sickening sounds of arrows and lances piercing flesh. The air filled with the reek of blood and viler things.

Pain bloomed in her hand. Her sword spiraled out of her grip, spinning out of reach. It fell slowly, as if in a dream, disappearing into the dark.

A harsh tug on her hooded cloak pulled her off-balance. Her back hit the ground, jamming her armor into her flesh.

Mounted shadows swarmed around her as hooves stomped.

"Help!" she shouted as she rolled over and pushed up.

"No one left to answer your call," a voice from the dark said.

"Show yourself," Jehanne answered, going for her dagger.

She held her blade high.

Torches flared to life around her. She blinked. Two of the Burgundian horsemen opened up a space to let another rider through. He wore the red lion of the Luxembourgs.

"Surrender or die," the voice said.

His tone clearly said he'd rather she not surrender. But why not just kill her then? Why pretend she had a choice?

Her breath was coming in rasps, her hand shaking around the dagger still held aloft.

Saint Michael, help me…

Silence. It was like a wall around her. Worse than a wall. An oubliette rising around her, brick by brick. She looked up at the cloud-shrouded sky as it pulled away from her, rising out of her reach.

Someone pulled her helmet off. She ducked a punching fist. And then another. One caught on her left temple. The world tilted wildly around her, the oubliette reforming as someone used her voice to whisper, "I surrender."

* * *

December 5, 1430

The golden light of dawn crawled through one of the slits in the walls of Jehanne's cell. It crawled over the stone and mortar, and flowed over the threshes. She closed her eyes.

Light touched her cheek, warm and soothing. It slid down her neck and chest, coming to rest over her heart.

It spoke to her about her service to God. She knew him instantly. Saint Michael. He who was like God. The longer he spoke, about her service, her purpose, the more the light filled her. It spread to her belly until she burned with a fire that did not consume her, but left her feeling like she had been in the terrible presence of God.

She didn't know how long Saint Michael was with her. Time seemed to have no meaning, for while a moment may have passed in her cell, it seemed like she had been basking in his saintly presence for hours.

She opened her eyes. The cell was like a tomb, devoid of color. There was no serenity in this shade of a world. She waited for light and life to return to what everyone else called reality. Slowly, it solidified around her, snatching her back to the here and now which was terrible in the exact opposite of God's terrible presence.

There was a reason she never spoke of her visions, except to the king. And now not even to him. He had not ransomed her. He had abandoned her to a reality made up of a metal bars, chains, and cold stone covered by rotting straw.

A reality made of iron cuffs that bit into her raw wrists and the oozing sores on her ankles.

She scratched at her shaved head and pulled the rough burlap dress farther over her knees. Now that the Saint was gone, the cold of winter slipped under her skin, bit into her flesh, and burrowed into her bones.

The door swung open to admit Sister Marie Mengette. One of the two nuns that de Luxembourg had assigned to guard her, the middle-aged woman had kind blue eyes. She carried a tray with two bowls.

Steam rose from one. Jehanne's mouth watered.

Sister Marie passed the bowl of broth between the bars and carefully slid it toward Jehanne so that it would not spill.

Together, they prayed, thanking God for providing sustenance, for de Luxembourg's mercy, and for deliverance.

"Sister Marie, do you have any word?" Jehanne asked as she brought the bowl of broth to her lips. Bits of pork and carrot floated in the mixture. Her stomach made a loud noise, protesting the slow pace with which it was being fed.

Sister Marie looked over her shoulder. De Luxembourg may be merciful, but he was not stupid. While the nuns had the only key to the door, they did not have the key to her cell. No one but the nuns were allowed into the room, but a guard was always posted just outside, listening.

"No, child. I'm sorry."

Jehanne set the bowl down on the floor.

"You have to eat, child," Sister Marie insisted. She pulled a crust of bread from the folds in her robe and put her hand through the bars.

Jehanne took it and tore off a small piece. She chewed on the burned, stale morsel without tasting it, wishing it was communion bread instead. At least then it would have a purpose.

"My brother, Pierre?" Jehanne asked.

Sister Marie shook her head and said, "You should eat more."

"This is not the sustenance I seek," Jehanne said. One thing that de Luxembourg had not allowed was for her to see a priest. She wanted—needed—to confess. But no men were to be allowed into her prison.

Sister Marie let out a sigh. "You look like a starved dog."

"I was never one for vanity," Jehanne said.

"It's not about vanity, child. But strength. You need your strength."

They'd had this conversation before, almost word by word.

"D'Aulon?" Jehanne asked.

Another shake of the head. And with it, Sister Marie's gaze went meaningfully to the bowl. Jehanne raised it to her lips, sipped, swallowed. One question, one bite or sip, depending on the meal. That was the unspoken deal between them.

"La Hire?"

"From what you told me of him, he's too tough to kill," she said and gestured to the bread.

Jehanne hid a sigh of relief. So La Hire was probably alive. She said a silent prayer as she chewed on the bread.

"Poton?" Jehanne could not keep the tremor out of her voice. It was Poton whose fate worried her the most. Guilt welled up in inside her. Her brother Pierre alone should have held that place of honor in her heart. Instead it was shared by Poton. Jean. She'd never said his given name. Never dared.

A puzzled frown formed on Sister Marie's face, but she did not shake her head.

Jehanne finished her meal.

"Thank you, Sister," she said, pushing the empty bowl towards the bars.

Sister Marie lifted the lid from the second bowl. A pungent scent wafted from it like smoke.

Jehanne's chains made a scraping sound as she dragged them across the floor. If she pulled them taut and if Sister Marie wedged herself in between the bars, she could reach Jehanne's sores.

The salve stung as the nun's gentle fingers spread them atop the abused flesh.

"I asked for linens to bind them," Sister Marie complained. "But they wouldn't let me have them. Said you might use them to hang yourself."

She turned Jehanne's wrists over, pushing the metal cuffs up her arms. "I told them you would never commit such a sin."

Their gazes met for an instant that lingered too long.

Finally, Jehanne shook her head. "I already know my fate, Sister. God has shown me."

With a look of relief, Sister Marie crossed herself and returned to applying the salve.

"I will burn," Jehanne said without emotion.

The nun's shaking hands withdrew. Tears welled up in her eyes as she set the salve aside and covered it with the lid.

She took the rosary off her belt and they knelt in prayer.

Jehanne went along with it, just as she did every day and every night, she on one side of the bars, the nun on the other.

Yet it didn't feel right, not like prayer used to, not like when Saint Michael came to whisper the word of God in her ear.

And while she had just felt his presence, and that of God, there had been no guidance, no counsel.

And Jehanne knew why.

She had let a man into her heart. She may still be *la Pucelle* in body, but not in mind nor spirit. And she didn't know how she could banish Poton from her heart.

* * *

January 5, 1431

The inn outside Beaurevoir Castle had seen better days. Jean had been here once before, years ago. The food was just as bad, the ale just as watered down, but the war had taken its toll on the thatched roof, the door and windows, and the level of service.

He sat against the back wall, with his aching leg propped up on a stool, waiting for the tanned hide that now served as a door to part for his compatriot. Flurries of snow slipped under the gap every time the wind blew. Despite the fire blazing in the hearth, winter seeped in at every opportunity.

After Compiègne, they'd all been ransomed. Jehanne's brother, Pierre, had been sent back to Domrémy. He'd lost the use of his arm and was too ill to protest. Whether he'd made it back home alive was still unknown. La Hire had managed to come through the brief but bloody battle unscathed, merely adding to his collection of scars. D'Aulon, similarly, had survived, uninjured, and been summoned by the king.

When they'd heard that Jehanne had been taken prisoner but not ransomed, they'd raised seven thousand *livres tournois* themselves, given them to D'Aulon to give to the king.

They had yet to hear back. From D'Aulon, or the king, or even Yolande herself. The implications of treachery and political games turned Jean's stomach.

He stared into the mug. A mouse had climbed to the table top and looked eagerly around. Jean took his dagger out, raised it, and brought its point down, pinning the mouse to the table. It didn't even make a squeak.

Hands clapped.

Jean looked up. La Hire was standing in the half-light, wearing a long beard to make him harder to recognize and to hide the new scar he'd earned at Compiègne. It paired well with his scowl.

La Hire reached into the battered leather purse hanging from his belt.

"Get lost," he said to the inn keeper as he tossed a coin at him. "And see we're not disturbed."

The man tucked the coin away and scurried through the make-shift door.

"What news?" Jean asked as he used his foot to shove the stool at La Hire.

The stool creaked as La Hire lowered his bulk onto it.

"She's been moved. To Arras."

Jean snatched the dagger from the back of the mouse's neck, and used the flat of the blade to sweep the carcass to the floor. He used the edge of his cape to clean off the blood and held onto it to hide the shaking of his hands.

"Why? Has her ransom not been paid?"

"It seems that the English are willing to pay more."

Jean swore under his breath. The seven thousand they'd sent with D'Aulon represented everything they'd been able to scrape together, not just from their own estates and relatives, but from the hundreds of men that had contributed what little they had to free *la Pucelle*.

"And there's more," La Hire said, grabbing at the mug of ale and taking a tentative sip which he spit out on the dirt floor. "What pig swill is this?"

Jean shrugged. "What else have you found out?"

"They're bringing in Bishop Cauchon of Beauvois."

"Whatever for?"

"They mean to try her for heresy."

Jean's stomach clenched into a knot. His grip on the dagger tightened.

"What heresy?"

"The English have always called her the Witch of Orleans."

"Cauchon is not the kind to cast her as a witch," Jean said. "English partisan that Cauchon is, he is an educated man, known for his fairness and integrity."

La Hire scoffed. "Well, your fair, educated bishop has already announced that *la Pucelle* must deny her visions and repent. She must say that she was not speaking for God. If she does not, the English will burn her."

A sick feeling overcame Jean. If there was one thing he knew with all his soul, it was that Jehanne believed that she spoke words given to her by God, that she was on a holy mission. And many believed her. Many still believed in the Old Testament's heroines. God had brought about victories through the exploits of girls and women like Judith and Deborah. Even as Jehanne had lost favor with her king, she had not lost favor with the simple people. In fact, the more she fell in the king's eyes, the more she rose in theirs.

By failing to ransom her, the king was making a critical mistake. One that would turn this war from a secular struggle between Burgundians and Armanacs into a religious one. The simple people Charles and his ilk despised cared not for the dynastic squabbles that had decimated France for almost a century. But they would care about *la Pucelle* being sold to their enemies.

"She will never deny her visions," Jean said, his voice shaking. "To do so would reject God. She'd rather burn."

"So, what are we going to do about it?" La Hire asked.

* * *

January 7, 1431

Sister Marie had told Jehanne to prepare herself. The Bishop of Beauvais, a man named Pierre Cauchon had been appointed to try her as a heretic.

She would be taken to Rouen, the seat of the occupational English government. She would no longer enjoy the protection of her ecclesiastical prison with the sisters holding the keys to her cell. Instead, the English would keep her in a secular prison guarded by their own soldiers.

Sister Marie had delivered the news with tear-filled eyes as Jehanne stood before her, statue-still, numb, no longer feeling the cold of the stone under her bare feet.

"I would like to be confessed," Jehanne said, once again. She'd asked for a confessor every day since her capture. It had always been denied.

Once again Sister Marie said, "I will see what I can do," in that tone that said that there was nothing she could do.

"Thank you Sister Marie. For all your kindness."

Sister Marie withdrew and turned the key in the lock.

Jehanne lowered herself into the corner with the fresh threshes.

Saint Michael, please help me.

She pushed the heels of her hands into her eyes.

Her visions had returned, but not in the way she had hoped. They all centered around Jean Porot. Sometimes they were sweet, innocent. Her hand in his. A kiss on the cheek. Her name on his lips. Other times they were more carnal. She knew them to be visions, not dreams, for they didn't occur while she slept. They only came when she was in that other reality, that other world full of warmth and color, where she was unquestionably in the Saint's presence.

"I can't," she whispered.

There was a reason she insisted they call her *la Pucelle*. Not Jehanne. Not D'Arc. Not Du Lys.

The voices, her counsel, had demanded it of her. She had sworn to remain a virgin until the war was won.

As long as it shall please God. The words hit the air like a hammer, ringing around her, echoing off the stone. Saint Michael's voice flowed into Saint Catherine's and then into Saint Margaret's and then back into Michael's again, over and over.

How could they ask this of her? Of all the things she was ready and willing to do, this was not one of them. She'd seen where these things led. She'd seen more bad marriages than good ones. She'd seen the pain of childbirth and the anguish of losing child after child. At Court, she'd seen infidelity, violations of God's laws, the flaunting of vows.

She was not like those people, who could take an oath and not fulfill it. She did not want to be bound by vows of marriage, assuming Poton would even marry her. Nobles didn't marry for love. They married for power, for alliances. She could not bear the thought of being his mistress, of bearing bastards.

No, no, no.

Her work was not yet done. Yes, Charles was king, but the English were still in France. She had so much more to do.

She covered her head with her arms. Sobs tore at her chest until she was wrung out. Her tears flowed down her cheek to be absorbed by the stone.

The visions hit her again and again, whether she closed her eyes or kept them open. It was the worst torment she could imagine.

She'd rather burn.

Jehanne curled up into a tight ball, squeezed her eyes shut, and covered her ears. Inside, she screamed as flames licked at her bare feet, as her flesh swelled and crisped.

No, no, no.

Rough hands clamped over her mouth.

"Quiet, *la Pucelle*, or you will give us away."

She opened her eyes. A priest stood over her, framed in shadow. She'd not heard him come in.

The man behind her lowered his hand and let her go.

She rushed forward, falling at the priest's feet.

"Father, please, I must confess." The words came out in a mad rush, pounding out faster than her heart. "I've had impure thoughts. I've despaired, I've—"

Soldier's boots. With fine spurs.

She backed away, dragging her chains behind her, only to bump into the other man. Her heart was going to bruise itself against her ribs. She couldn't breathe.

"We've come to free you," the voice behind her said.

She whirled around. Poton. In Luxemburg's regalia. The tunic a little tight on his broad frame. The trousers mismatched, but passable in the dark.

Blood rose to her cheeks, her ears. She pushed him away and fell back, tripped by the chains.

He knelt down beside her, working a key into her bonds.

"Hurry up," the priest said. This time she recognized La Hire's deep grumble. He lowered the cowl of his robe. Even with it down, his beard hid so much of his face, her eyes went wide with disbelief.

"How?" she asked as Poton pulled the cuff off her right leg and set to work on the other.

"Didn't give the priest much choice," La Hire said with amusement.

"You threatened a priest? You're impersonating a priest!" Jehanne said.

La Hire shrugged as he stole a glance over his shoulder to the open door.

"Seeing as I'm already going to Hell, what's one more sin?"

She let out a gasp.

"Hurry up, Poton," La Hire said. "We don't have all night."

The cuff fell away from Jehanne's left ankle. Poton took her hands, folding them into his own for just an instant before setting to work on the locks.

Trembling, she held her hands up for him.

"Where'd you get the key?" she asked.

"The good Sister," Poton said, frustration creeping into his voice as he worked the lock.

"Quickly," La Hire urged, as he stuck his head out the door.

Poton's hands were steady, methodical. The locks finally gave way, and the chains rattled to the floor. Jehanne backed away from them as if they were vipers.

Poton took off his cloak and draped it over her shoulders.

"Can you walk? I can carry you."

She pushed herself up on weak legs and lost her balance. Months of being chained to a wall had done nothing for her strength. She ended up in a pile on the floor, surrounded by Poton's cloak.

He scooped her up and hoisted her over his shoulder.

"That's better," La Hire said. "Time to go."

La Hire adjusted the hood of Poton's cloak so it hid her head.

For the first time in months, she was outside the room. She caught a glimpse of the guard and said a prayer for his soul.

Down the spiral stairway they went, their way lit by what must have been a torch held high by La Hire.

"Here, Sister," La Hire said. "The keys."

"Go. Hurry," Sister Marie said.

"Come with us, Sister," La Hire said. "We can protect you as well."

Poton hoisted Jehanne off his shoulder. She landed on wool blankets set atop hay. Poton was already climbing into the back of the wagon and pulled the tarp shut by the time she yanked the hood off.

He pulled her against him and held her tight. His fingertips raked over her scalp. She shivered at the touch.

"What did they do to you?" he asked as his fingers found the scar above her temple, the one she'd gotten when she'd been captured.

The wagon lurched forward.

Jehanne pulled away, drawing the cloak around her and crawled into the opposite corner. She wedged herself in it and anchored her fingers around the wood struts.

The hurt in Poton's eyes was clear as the wagon filled with unearthly light. She squeezed her eyes to shut it out, but it pierced her eyelids.

She raised her palms to her face.

"Make them stop," she cried out. "Jean, please, make them stop."

* * *

J ean scrambled across the cart and clamped his hand over Jehanne's mouth. He pried her hands off the struts and turned her so her back was up against his chest.

He had to keep her quiet or she was going to give them away.

Jehanne struggled in his grasp, but she was weak. He had never seen her so gaunt, her eyes so sunken in. She looked like she had aged a decade.

He snuck a peek through a hole in the planks. La Hire, in his priest's cassock was urging the horses on. Sister Marie sat beside him, under a swaying lamp.

He wished that La Hire would go faster, but understood his caution. A nun and a priest together, driving a wagon at a reasonable speed would not attract unwanted attention. Still, how long before someone realized that the bishop's very valuable prisoner was gone?

He kissed the top of Jehanne's head. "It's all right. It'll be all right."

She continued to struggle for far longer than he thought she'd have the strength for. The rose light of dawn cut through the slats of the wagon before he took his hand from her mouth.

He'd thought her asleep, but she twisted in his grasp. When her eyes opened, they were filled with an unearthly light. The face was the same, but Poton knew that he was not looking at his Jehanne.

"Marry her," Jehanne said, in a voice not her own. It sounded like the voice of a queen.

"Marry her," the voice commanded, "or she will burn."

Jehanne's eyes closed, and she went limp and slumped back into his arms.

Poton trembled as he held her.

Jehanne had always said that the Saints Margaret and Catherine also spoke to her. Jean didn't know which one had just spoken to him, and it didn't matter.

* * *

My escape was attributed to witchcraft and for many months; they scoured the countryside for me. For us.

We stayed ahead of them thanks to my counsel who warned me whenever we were in danger of being discovered.

But it was not without a price. Nothing ever is, after all.

The saints did not cease tormenting me. Even as their counsel guided and saved us, day after day, week after week, every waking moment, every dream was filled with the need for Jean Poton.

On a fine Sunday morning, Jean asked me to marry him. He told me that he understood me well enough to know that I did not want to be a wife or a mother. He told me that he understood how important my virtue, my virginity, were to me. He said he did not expect me to sacrifice them, but that God had commanded him, and his heart demanded that he marry me.

The saints had been cruel to him as well. I had seen signs of it here and there all along, but I'd ignored them in favor of prayer. Nevertheless, no matter how long or how hard or how earnestly I prayed, the answer was always the same.

My work was done.

Charles was king.

Saving France from the English was not my task.

So, I married Jean and on our wedding night, I gave him the most important thing I had left.

A year later, he took me to his home. In that year, I became another woman: Catherine. For my sister who had died before I ever set off to crown the king. For the saint that had been my counsel. No one will ever look at Catherine Poton de Xaintrailles and see Jehanne D'Arc.

Catherine can read and knows her numbers. She has long hair. Her body is that of a woman, not a waif that can fit into a suit of armor. Catherine cannot ride a horse. In fact, she is terrified of them, just as I was before I was commanded to overcome that fear.

And Catherine doesn't hear voices. She has no counsel. She is not overly pious. She does not spend hours in prayer. She does not give advice on military matters. She has no interest in politics and no desire to go to Court or test what must be God's hand at work in that she's not been discovered.

It took me a long time to make peace with this woman I have become. For God had indeed blessed me, with a loving husband who holds to his vows, and most of all, with easy births. A boy we named Pierre, after my brother, who did not survive the wounds he took while fighting at my side. Another we named Michael. A third called Etienne after his "uncle" La Hire. And finally, a daughter—Margaret.

Amongst all of this, both of us, Catherine and Jehanne, have found something most people only dream of: love and happiness.

One night, Saint Michael will appear to me as the angel of death. He will come for me at last and give me a chance at redemption. He will hold in his hands scales perfectly balanced to weight my soul.

It is not as worthy of an offering as the soul of a martyr, but I hope it will be enough.

* * * * *

Monalisa Foster Bio

Monalisa won life's lottery when she escaped communism and became an unhyphenated American citizen. Her works tend to explore themes of freedom, liberty, and personal responsibility. Despite her degree in physics, she's worked in several fields including engineering and medicine. She and her husband (who is a writer-once-removed via their marriage) are living their happily ever after in Texas. Her epic space opera, *Ravages of Honor,* is out now.

Link for author page: https://www.amazon.com/Monalisa-Foster/e/B075Z7SDJ1

# # # # #

Secondhand Empires
by Brad R. Torgersen

"General Chrysoloras?" the young man's voice said softly.

The old figure—slumped in a wooden chair positioned at the small room's single open window—did not react.

"Sir?" the voice said, this time just a bit louder.

"I gave orders that I was not to be disturbed," the figure grunted, still facing away from the door. Birds chirped pleasantly in the cool autumn air outside, though the booming of far-away Ottoman gunpowder cannon belied the peaceful scene.

"I apologize, sir," the young man said, his head bowed respectfully as his shoulders pushed through the partially open doorway. "We all know what your orders were. But something has happened, and I really think you ought to come see for yourself. Emperor Palaiologos's ambassador demands it, in fact."

"Once upon a time *I* was Palaiologos's ambassador," the figure rumbled unhappily.

"Yes sir," the young man said timidly, but still did not withdraw from the room.

The stubs of snuffed candles covered a pewter plate on a small desk, next to a thin bed. Rolls of official parchment were laced into bundles on the desk's surface, and the remnants of a fire glowed weakly in the tiny stone-and-mortar fireplace.

After a pregnant pause, the figure said, "You won't go away without my attendance, will you?"

"I'm sorry sir," the young man said.

The figure sighed as if the weight of the world were upon his shoulders—was it not true, since his mission to the Pope had failed?—and reluctantly stood up. He did not have the clothing nor the bearing of a field commander. As a man of letters, the general was more comfortable among academics than he was among soldiers. But God and fate had placed him in a village on the eastern-most shore of the Black Sea. With five hundred of Palaiologos's men under Chrysoloras's control and strict orders to find an ally. In the most unlikely of places. Right on the Ottoman Turks' proverbial back porch.

"It would be better if we just let Constantinople go," Chrysoloras remarked bleakly, shuffling away from the window on legs which silently complained of too many years spent abroad in the service of the emperor.

"Sedition?" the young man asked, opening the door wide so that his master could pass. Chrysoloras grunted at his aide-de-camp's raised eyebrow.

"Acknowledgment of the obvious," Chrysoloras replied.

The wooden door to the general's meek quarters *thunked* shut solidly. He slowly gathered speed as the muscles of his body loosened with repeated movement. It had been a chill night and a morning without breakfast. The rumbling in the general's stomach reminded him that he'd eaten too little, too often. His coat draped over shoulders which were distinctly bony compared to when he'd first set sail the year before.

At the time, Chrysoloras had told himself it was preferable to being executed. His inability to persuade the Pope—or any of the princes of the West—to aid Emperor Palaiologos against the Ottoman Turks had been the signature defeat of his career. Despite an education and talent in the diplomatic arts, he'd returned home empty-handed. And been promptly dispatched on what he now believed to be a futile diversionary adventure which would probably cost Chrysoloras and the others in his command dearly.

And for what?

Constantinople hadn't been the same since being hollowed out by the Black Death. Coming on the heels of Crusader occupation, the plague had dealt insult to injury, leaving Palaiologos with a capitol more in historical legacy than in function. And the royalty of the West must have known this, too. If once their knights had lusted for glory and conquest at Byzantine expense, now those same Western kingdoms twiddled their fingers dismissively at the exhortations of Palaiologos's representatives. Nobody seemed at all bothered by the idea that a Muslim army would eventually cross the Bosporus.

So why was the Eastern Roman Empire going to spend itself blocking the Ottoman threat for the sake of people who regarded Emperor Palaiologos's plight as a mere bagatelle?

The walkway through the village was narrow and paved with foot-worn cobble. For all Chrysoloras knew, Alexander the Great might have strode this same way once upon a time. How odd—the general thought—that legendary leaders and great nations should all succumb to the one enemy they could never vanquish: time. It had swept away the Athenians and the Spartans and the Romans who came after them, though there were some who still pretended the era of the Caesars had not yet passed.

And one thousand years hence, what future man would go in the spiritual steps of Chrysoloras himself? With a new country's might rising or falling. And would anyone remember what happened here, now, in this anonymous place?

Turning past corners of several squat buildings, Chrysoloras arrived at the portico of the house his men had commandeered for their headquarters. He stopped cold when he spied the strange-looking, armored riders sitting on the backs of somewhat squat, solid-looking horses. The strangers' faces and eyes were not the faces and eyes of the Abkhazi, nor the Kartli, nor the Sassun. Armenians? No, definitely not them, either. The riders seemed to have come from a place far to the east and north of the Caspian Sea. Their skin was dark from living in the sun, and their expression was that of men who had seen a long road filled with much danger and hardship.

The shafts of spears—tipped with wicked points—fluttered colorful streamers, while slightly curved swords were sheathed in similarly curved scabbards. To the untrained eye such warriors might have been mistaken for Turks. But these were clearly not Ottoman sons.

They watched Chrysoloras's arrival in silence.

A different person—Eastern Roman—walked quickly out of the portico and confronted the general.

"Took you long enough," he said curtly.

"Patience, Orrin," the general said. "I'm an old man. You are not."

"Regardless of your age, I'd think the sound of those guns clos-ing across the river would put a spring in your step!"

The young ambassador was adorned in a red velvet doublet, much in the style of his Western counterparts with whom he'd been used to interacting prior to being pushed into this seeming exile with Chrysoloras. His displeasure with the situation had been piped into the general's ears on an almost daily basis for the better part of elev-en months.

"It would seem we have guests, yes?" Chrysoloras said, pointing at the strange men on horseback.

"Guests, indeed," the ambassador said, mocking Chrysoloras's somewhat cavalier tone.

The general sighed.

"Fine, Orrin, I capitulate to your urgency. What's the news, and how does it help or hinder us?"

"Better if you hear it from the Khan's envoy himself," the em-peror's ambassador said stiffly, beckoning for Chrysoloras to follow the ambassador back the way he'd come.

"These are not Tamerlane's men, are they?" Chrysoloras said, feeling a hot shock run up and down his spine. If the Ottoman threat was not bad enough, there was the Tumurid threat too. Chrysoloras's men were technically on Timuran soil, though the villagers hadn't expressed any allegiance to any particular sovereign.

"No, and that's the vexing part," the ambassador said, leading both Chrysoloras and his aide-de-camp through a dingy hallway to a larger banquet hall which had been cleared of dining furniture and now served as the Byzantine garrison's main audience chamber. Guards to either side of the doorway stiffened at Chrysoloras's entry.

"The general!" shouted one of them, to which every other Byzantine soldier in the room stood quickly to attention.

"As you were," Chrysoloras said, waving away their trained, precise military decorum. He'd never been particularly comfortable with the stiffness of protocol.

At one end of the long table, several men—of the same derivation as the riders—were clustered. They watched Chrysoloras approach, but did not render the same honors as had been done by the Eastern Roman troops.

"You are the commander?" said one of the strangers, in thickly-accented but carefully-pronounced Greek. It had been the tallest of them who'd spoken. His helmet—resting on the table before him—had a prominent crest which differentiated it from the rest.

The general was taken aback.

"I am," Chrysoloras said, also in Greek, feeling an almost electric impulse in his stomach. He'd visited many a Western court and knew the niceties expected therein. But these men were of another breed entirely. The bits of gold affixed to weapons and helmets spoke of rank, but like the men outside, these soldiers had the expressions of people who'd been hardened by a long and terrible journey. How was it possible that this man spoke a language familiar to so few in Chrysoloras's command?

"Missionaries," the dignitary said, by way of explanation. "Languages have always been my fascination, and when I had a chance to learn Greek, I took it. Now, I believe it will serve us both well. My master Jorightu Khan of the Yuan Dynasty seeks to communicate with an officer of Emperor Palaiologos."

"Surely you mean an ambassador," Chrysoloras said, tipping his head in Orrin's direction.

"No," the stranger said. "Diplomats can be too eager to make promises which are never kept. I need a man who can do better."

Orrin's cheeks flared pink. He too spoke Greek, though not nearly as well as Chrysoloras thought the young ambassador should. He was about to retort, but was stopped short by the quick look Chrysoloras gave him. Now was not the time to let one's bruised pride do the talking.

"I am such a man," Chrysoloras said calmly. "Though you will forgive me if I am not familiar with your khan's kingdom specifically."

"You have perhaps heard of Yesuder?" the strange dignitary said.

Chrysoloras stared dumbly for a moment, trying desperately to remember why that name sounded familiar. Then it hit him.

"You've come much farther than I first guessed," Chrysoloras said frankly. "And I am afraid we're in no position to offer you a rich welcome, what with the Turks approach to this village."

"It is because your emperor and my khan share a mutual problem that I have been sent to find you," the austere foreign officer said.

"And by what name shall I know you?" Chrysoloras asked.

"I am General Ulagan. Jorightu Khan sends his salutations to your Emperor Palaiologos."

"We are grateful for the khan's good will," Chrysoloras said. "Can you be more specific about this problem?"

Ulagan snapped his fingers once, and both of the men at his sides set to work unrolling a cloth map illuminated by the morning sunlight filtering down from the hall's upper-level windows. Chrysoloras, the ambassador, and Chrysoloras's aide-de-camp approached. The cloth was silky smooth and fine in appearance, though the geography displayed on it looked very little like anything Chrysoloras had ever seen.

General Ulagan began stabbing his finger at various places, using Mongolian names which Chrysoloras—despite all his training— couldn't begin to understand. Sensing Chrysoloras's confusion, General Ulagan breathed deeply, and snapped his fingers a second time. The map was rolled up as quickly as it had been deployed, and returned to a bamboo-tube receptacle slung by a cord over one of Ulagan's officer's backs.

Ulagan tapped a thumb at his lower lip, thinking.

"Your garrison will soon be overrun," he said.

"I know," Chrysoloras said.

"When news reached me that your emperor had dispatched troops this far east I had assumed he would send a considerably larger force. When the Turks become aware of how few you are, they will send word to their commander, and whatever your emperor hoped to accomplish here will have been for naught."

"I know that too," Chrysoloras replied glumly.

"Why have you not evacuated?"

"To where? There are no ships to carry us away. We were deposited here with the knowledge that we would not have the luxury of retreating. I've devoted the past day to composing several messages of surrender which will—I sincerely hope—spare the lives of most of my remaining men."

"You will be taken as slaves," the general said matter-of-fact.

"Perhaps not."

"Hope is not a strategy," Ulagan said, his expression growing dour.

"I apologize for not being the kind of man you expected," Chrysoloras said. "If it's great tactics and martial knowledge you require, I can't help you. I am an officer by appointment, not experience. I have spent my life learning to use words, as opposed to swords. I can't battle my way to a solution, so I must use the tool God has given me. You've arrived at a bad moment, and may be surrendering with us."

"No," Ulagan said. "We have not ridden across half the world just to be captured by the Muslims."

"*Why* you have come so far, and to what end?"

"First things first," Ulugan replied. "If you can get your men moving, now, my men have a clear route of escape secured."

Chrysoloras raised an eyebrow and looked at the ambassador. The young man's dour expression had instantly transformed into one of astonishment. The general's ordinary instinct would have been to warn the ambassador against making rash decisions. What evidence was there to trust these strangers from the northeast? If Chrysoloras had learned anything in his life, it was to never, ever assume that things could not get worse. Because they could. And would.

But still...Who was to say these Mongolians had not been guided to this specific place at this specific moment, for a work far greater than any Chrysoloras or the young ambassador could comprehend? It was folly to strive against the mind of God. And though Chrysoloras had become a cynic since his failure to sway the Pope, he'd still been praying fervently for a better option.

Chrysoloras turned to face the guards at the doorway. He clapped his hands loudly three times and said, "Inform the captains! Gather every man who can ride or walk, and bring what weapons and provender can be carried!"

* * *

The road north was little more than a cow path which had been recently churned up by Mongolian horse hooves. The prior night's autumn rain had turned things muddy, and it was hard going for both animals and men. Oxen—yoked to carts—trudged tiredly. Men were caked in wet soil up to their waists. Chrysoloras's troops eyed the Mongols suspiciously, while the Mongols themselves barely payed the Byzantine troops any mind. Ulagan's riders sat erect and alert in their saddles, eyeing the trees to both the east and the west. There appeared to be at least twice as many riders as Eastern Roman men walking, and Chrysoloras could hear muttered grumbling among his people who resented the fact. But the captains kept the men in line as they moved up the gentle slope—their pikes and spears braced on their shoulders, forming a lazily wavering forest of wooden shafts rising into the air.

Behind them, the little village slowly shrank in the distance. The Turks would find none of Chrysoloras's men there. The villagers themselves would soon be under new management, and whether or not they would like the Turks any better than they had liked the general's men—and they had not liked Chrysoloras's people much at all—was an open question. Ostensibly, the garrison had been protecting those poor people from the Ottoman threat. But protection and *occupation* could look eerily similar if you were one of the hapless souls forced to watch as one army moved out, while another army moved in.

Chrysoloras rode alongside Ulugan, one officer looking remarkably unlike the other. Ulugan seemed to have been born to the saddle, and rode as if his steed were a part of the man. His helmet gleamed dully in the afternoon sunlight, while his lamellar armor rested easily on what Chrysoloras judged to be a muscular, mature frame. While

Chrysoloras himself was frumpy and hunched, his soiled boots and drab topcoat looking very unlike the finery which typified other generals of the Eastern Roman Empire.

The ambassador rode near the middle of the column, surrounded by his entourage. Whenever Chrysoloras looked at his young counterpart, he noticed the ambassador peering over his shoulder—no doubt pining for the comfort of solid walls. Chrysoloras sympathized. He knew intimately the vulnerable feeling a diplomat experienced out on the open highway. Even being surrounded by men sworn to die to protect you didn't completely assuage the sensation of unease when traveling as an Eastern Roman dignitary on foreign soil.

"Things must be desperate for you to have undertaken such a long journey," Chrysoloras said to his Mongolian counterpart.

"The Yongle emperor of the Ming Dynasty wants us all dead," Ulugan said solemnly. "Our people once ruled China completely to the far eastern sea. But as your own emperor knows too well, change is inevitable. The Yuan were rolled back, like a receding wave on the low tide. We could have united with our brothers of the Golden Horde and fought Yongle, but the Golden Horde wanted nothing to do with a people they considered to be vanquished refugees. So you see, General Chrysoloras, we are not so different. Both of our countries are in severe peril. There is nowhere for the Yuan to go but southwest, and the Muslims are in our way. Including the kingdom of the one you call Tamerlane, though the Timur are our people by blood. And your emperor must keep both Tamerlane and the Turks from taking Constantinople. If you could not find a willing ally to your west, the Yuan are ready and able to answer your call for aid."

Chrysoloras allowed himself a small chuckle.

"Do you mock our offer?" Ulugan asked sharply.

"Not at all," Chrysoloras said, continuing to use Greek, which seemed to be the only language the two generals knew between them.

"Why the amusement?" Ulugan demanded.

"My emperor will no doubt wonder what's to prevent the Yuan from pressing across the Bosporus, assuming the Ottoman Turks can be conquered. Your Khan would ask the same question in Emperor Palaiologos's place, I think. If I can speak plainly—one general to another—the most dangerous enemy is sometimes the friend you have improperly judged."

"That is wisdom," General Ulugan said, nodding his head in agreement. "Very well. Let me explain. Three great seas border the land desired by Jorightu Khan. The Turks occupy the western portion, while the people of Timur occupy the eastern. We Yuan would make it all our own. The people of Timur will become part of us again. But Jorightu Khan desires a friendly Christian neighbor. With Eastern Romans there may be dialogue. The productive establishment of trade. The Ming Dynasty may hate the Yuan, but the Silk Road will roll regardless. Or so Jorightu Khan believes."

"Did you not tell me earlier today that hope is not a strategy?" Chrysoloras said.

Now it was Ulugan who chuckled.

"Words are indeed your weapon," the Mongolian general said. "I have been speared with my own speech! Allow me to say that I cannot question the wisdom of the Khan. Were I in his place I would probably choose a different path. But that is not for me to decide. I have my orders."

"Constantinople is my home," Chrysoloras said. "Part of me wishes greatly for it to be defended at all cost. And yet, another part of me wishes for the Turks to flood into the West. It would serve those kingdoms right for how they have treated the Eastern Roman Empire since the split between Eastern and Western Christendom."

"We are each officers of withered nations," Ulugan said. He leaned to the side and spit into the mud over which his horse traveled.

"Perhaps we can help our respective rulers to make our nations great again?"

Ulugan permitted himself a smile for the first time.

"It would make my heart glad, to die in the service of a strong Yuan country."

"I can persuade my emperor," Chrysoloras said, "assuming I can reach home again. By land it would take many months. It will be shorter on the Black Sea, assuming I survive to discover passage."

As if on cue, a shout of alarm rose at the top of the column. All heads—Mongolian, and Eastern Roman—jerked forward at the sound.

"We are ambushed!" Ulugan said, baring his teeth in a snarl.

"Captains!" Chrysoloras bellowed. "Make ready to repulse the enemy!"

Latin men swirled among the Mongolian horses as the different ranks jostled to reform toward the threat. The bristling mass of Eastern Roman spearmen rushed forward through the mud, eager to bring their weapons to bear, while archers formed up behind them. General Ulugan barked hard orders in his native language and sent his riders thundering out into the treeline.

"Where are they going?" Chrysoloras asked, his chest heaving as the adrenaline of impending battle flooded his veins.

"They are faster, and can flank the enemy!"

"My own men will engage them head-on. I am afraid we aren't sufficiently numerous to challenge a real army, however."

Chrysoloras—though he didn't have a soldiering bone in his body—urged his horse forward. The cacophony of clashing weapons could be heard up ahead, and soon the screaming of men filled the air. Chrysoloras's bodyguards kept him penned, their own horses pulled in tight to protectively surround the general. His bodyguards' heads swiveled this way and that, looking for any threat. But since the ambush had come from off the road proper, it was difficult to tell how many Ottoman Turks were involved, or if they were even Turks at all. Much was still obscured by the trees.

Several ear-splitting cracks were heard.

"Hand cannon!" Chrysoloras cried.

The ambassador had dropped back and now crowded up next to Chrysoloras. Orrin's eyes looked crazy with fear.

"We will be overrun!" the ambassador wailed.

More ear-splitting cracks.

"We can't go back," Chrysoloras said, his gaze switching from General Ulugan, to the ambassador, and back again.

"Then we must go *through*," the Mongolian officer said with a glint in his eye. Chrysoloras had seen that look on the faces of fighting men before. He grimaced, but nodded his head in approval. The ambassador moaned with horror at the prospect of wading directly into combat, but Chrysoloras's bodyguards readied their swords and spears, while Ulugan barked additional orders in Mongolian—which rallied all the remaining riders into a wedge shape, with both generals and the ambassador at the center. As a whole, the wedge rode hard for the skirmish line which blocked the road ahead. As they approached, Chrysoloras raised himself out of his saddle and bellowed for the Eastern Roman line to break in the center.

Galloping full on, the wedge went directly into the gap.

At almost the same instant, Ulugan's riders—who'd gone both east and west—came out of the trees and ran at the Turks from both directions. Men and horses died as a volley of hand cannon fire brought down several dozen riders. But the strength of so much cavalry was too much for the Turks, all of whom had been on foot. They were blown back by the mounted assault like autumn leaves before a storm. Spear tips, driven by ton after ton of horse mass, punctured even the heaviest Turkish armor. Crossbow bolts sank into the faces, chests, and stomachs of the Turks who remained out of reach of the Mongolian spears. And the Eastern Roman formation regrouped and pressed after the Mongolian horses—laying waste to the broken ranks of Turks who were trying to get back on their feet.

Then, as quickly as the ambush had come, it was done. The combined Mongolian and Eastern Roman force found itself in the clear. Albeit diminished from what they had been before the attack. Scores of horses and men lay in the mud or amongst the trees. Moaning, maimed, and dying. Or dead.

A few Turks fled on foot for the now-distant village.

"We have no time," General Ulugan said, reining in his horse and breathing heavily. His own spear had found its mark no less than three times, and there was blood spattered along one of Ulugan's legs—though not his blood.

"We can carry the badly wounded in the wagons," Chrysoloras implored.

"Do you have room?" Ulugan said doubtfully.

"We will make room!" Chrysoloras said with determination.

"Let it be so," General Ululgan said, and began giving orders to his riders who remained in their saddles.

They set about collecting survivors and putting them into the backs of the carts being pulled by the oxen.

Chrysoloras felt his pulse begin to slow, as the survivors were re-organized, the walking wounded judged fit to march, and weapons or equipment taken from the fallen. Mongolian, Eastern Roman, and Turkish alike. He'd never in his life been that close to an actual fight. The visceral impression it had left on him was like the after-image of a lightning strike, rendering him mildly stunned and unable to shake the quick-seared memory of men vomiting up blood as spears went straight into and through their ribs. Blood so dark it had been almost black. And eyes so wide with shock, the whites had been visible to an absurd degree.

Then Chrysoloras noticed someone was missing.

"Orrin?" he said, turning about in his saddle to look at the faces of the other riders.

The young ambassador was nowhere to be seen.

"Orrin!" Chrysoloras shouted with alarm. Though he'd never considered the young diplomat to be a friend, the ambassador had still been a kindred servant of the emperor, and someone over whom Chrysoloras felt a degree of paternal responsibility.

"There, sir," said Chrysoloras's aide-de-camp, who'd slung an injured arm with a piece of cloth ripped from a dead Turk.

The aide-de-camp's good arm was aimed—finger pointing—at a dead horse still lying in the middle of the muddy road.

General Ulugan rode over to the spot, to peer down at the body.

"The ball appears to have taken the top of your diplomat's head off," he said plainly.

Chrysoloras could not bring himself to go look. He closed his eyes tightly shut and nudged his horse around until it faced north again. Then he opened his eyes, swallowed thickly several times, and sent his horse forward.

Gradually, the column reformed with Chrysoloras and Ulugan at the center. They moved slowly—still encumbered by mud—but made progress steadily until dusk, at which point Ulugan cleared his throat and asked if Chrysoloras was prepared to march into the night.

"I don't think the men nor the animals will stand it," Chrysoloras said.

"It's terrible country for bivouacking," Ulugan remarked.

"Do you really think the Turks will pursue us in the dark?"

"The fact we were ambushed tells me that the Turks were aware of my cavalry during our approach to your garrison headquarters and may have additional formations searching the land for us right now."

"I still wonder how you knew to where to find my headquarters in the first place?" Chrysoloras asked.

"Rumors travel. The same rumors which brought the Turks to the river, also reached me. My horses were faster than Turkish feet. And now we're committed by blood to seeing this alliance through."

"So it would seem," Chrysoloras admitted, thinking of the ambassador, whose death had been as random as any foot soldier's. Was that the fundamental essence of war? To die without a chance to give the moment meaning? There was a coldness to this realization which went far beyond the chill of the night air. No matter how tightly Chrysoloras wrapped his topcoat around himself, he couldn't stop the shivers.

"We go until you think it's appropriate not to go," he said glumly.

They traveled until the horns of the moon showed themselves, then the cohort bedded down for the remainder of the night.

* * *

Per habit, Chrysoloras skipped breakfast. He found General Ulugan breaking camp with his riders, and sought his counterpart's counsel as to their next move.

"It stands to reason that neither the Timurids nor the Turks control the northern shores of the Black Sea," Ulugan said. "If that is your preferred route then we must circle north and west until we find a port with ships capable of ferrying you back to your capitol. I would go with you, then. I will dispatch one of my lieutenants—with the rest of my cohort—to return to our people and share the news that we Yuan and you Eastern Romans are discussing friendship."

"If the Ming Dynasty has closed all of China to you, and the Golden Horde refuses kinship, where are your people now? Are they all living as nomads?"

"Scattered like dandelion seeds across the vastness of the Kazakh wilderness. It's hard there. And the Yuan are strangers to the land. We have been scratching an existence from the mountains for too long. In another generation we could forget ourselves completely, unless we forge a new home elsewhere. My khan believes the three seas will protect us, as they presently protect the Turks."

"Which makes your job of eventually taking the land from the Turks just that much more difficult," Chrysoloras said bluntly.

"We expect Eastern Roman assistance, of course," Ulugan said.

"My emperor's war chests are filled with spider webs these days," Chrysoloras said. "He has spent us to the brink of dissolution to pay for mercenaries who shore up the home guard which watches uneasily over the western shore of the Bosporus. I fear that once the Yuan are deeply involved in the campaign, my emperor may desire to let you and the Turks exhaust one another. Then he tries to take Ottoman lands for himself."

"Palaiologos would be that conniving?" Ulugan said, shocked.

"He is a creature of his court," Chrysoloras said, shrugging. "Is your khan that much different?"

General Ulugan had to think on the matter for a moment.

"No," he finally admitted. "Though I would not dare say such things if I were closer to the khan's throne."

"And you won't catch me uttering a word of this anywhere near Constantinople," Chrysoloras said, smiling.

"We each serve imperfect masters," Ulugan grunted.

"That much is for certain," Chrysoloras agreed.

Before the combined assembly could return to the road, a quick roll of the living and the recent dead had to be performed. For those wounded who'd not lasted the night, there was a hasty burial in soft earth, after which the wagons and oxen were pushing north once again.

Throughout the morning, Ulugan dispatched horse scouts in various directions to discover whether or not any Turkish columns were on the move. He absolutely did not want to be caught surprised a second time. Especially not with news of the limited size of his force having reached the ears of interested Turkish commanders. The next ambush would not be something either the Yuan or the Eastern Romans could simply bull through.

Chrysoloras noticed that some of the ice which had existed between his men and the Yuan had thawed in the wake of the prior day's battle. Which merely confirmed for him a thing which he had long suspected: nothing worked to fasten men together better than shared strife. Even men from very different places and who could not understand a thing each other said without interpretation.

Wounded Yuan warriors rode in the carts alongside wounded Eastern Romans. Water and food were passed around freely. Weapons were examined, compared, changed hands, and then exchanged back again. As if the only thing missing between the two peoples had been a twining moment of suffering, which the ambush had provided. Leading Chrysoloras to privately conclude that the attack—while tragic, especially for the ambassador—had not been so pointless after all. In spite of the lives lost.

Midday saw a fork in the road, and the cohort took the route west. They were still far enough away from the Black Sea that the water was over the horizon, but sea birds occasionally appeared in the air, and before long clouds began to gather for another autumn storm.

Which the Mongol horsemen seemed perfectly used to, while the Eastern Romans groaned audibly at the expectation of rain. The march was hard enough for them without getting drenched in the process. And there was nowhere for them to seek shelter until it was time to bivouac again for the night.

"Too many months with a solid roof over their heads," Chrysoloras admitted as the first droplets of water began to fall from a gray sky.

"Nature is forever the soldier's friend," General Ulugan remarked dryly, putting his palm out to feel the moisture pattering down in tiny droplets.

"It has never been *my* friend," Chrysoloras said, frowning, as he tried for the hundredth time to draw his topcoat around him more tightly.

"Just how *does* a diplomat get assigned a soldier's duties?" Ulugan asked as his horse plodded beside the horse of his counterpart.

"Back home," Chrysoloras replied, "my family has money, friends, and influence. Though I returned from Rome without securing the Pope's—nor any of the other kingdoms'—support, Emperor Palaiologos couldn't just put a noose around my neck without the potential loss of an important family who stands to back him for the duration of the war with the Ottoman Turks. But he couldn't trust me with further diplomatic duties, either. So instead of firing me from the job, he pretended to promote me into another. I was to be made military expeditionary commander to the far side of the Black Sea. It was a position I could not refuse, lest it bring shame and political trouble to my family in turn. So I obeyed as a good servant must obey and went off to endure my punishment. There was little hope of securing a worthwhile alliance in soil so poor as that of Georgia. They have no strength with which to keep Tamerlane at bay, much less Tamerlane and the Turks combined. I have to think we were in fact dropped there as bait, with the Turks as the fish, biting a hook."

"My fathers have soldiered for khans going back to the great Kublai," Ulugan said. "The only time any of us were not riding or marching was when we were making a family—so that more heirs could be bred for service. From the days when I was a boy, the spear and the sword have been my constant companions. I have shed blood time and again for my people. If Jorightu Khan is successful and the Yuan are able to settle in peace in our new homeland, I am not sure what my sons or grandsons will do. Farm? Pick up a trade of some sort? Enlist in the bureaucracy?"

"I am sure there will still be plenty of soldiering to do in the Southern Yuan Dynasty," Chrysoloras remarked.

"True," Ulugan said, then his chin dipped to his chest. "But there are days lately when this life—the choices I've made—make me tired. I would never betray my sworn allegiance to my khan. Absolutely not. But is there another life for me, somewhere else in the world? Another future I might create for my sons?"

"Creating better futures for sons and daughters would seem to be the primary reason why we're both out here—despite it all."

General Ulugan grunted his agreement.

And the rain began to fall more heavily.

* * *

The scout rider returned with bad news.

"How many Turks?" General Chrysoloras asked his counterpart.

"Not Turks this time," General Ulugan said.

"Timurid?" Chrysoloras guessed.

"So it would seem."

"They never bothered my people before, so I wonder why they would go to the trouble now?"

"It's not your people Tamerlane would be concerned with. It's the Yuan. I said it before, the Timur are of our blood. And though many of them—including Tamerlane himself—have given their hearts to the Qran, they are still children of that great empire first established by Genghis Khan. And few hatreds are so strong as those which exist between certain siblings. The Golden Horde rejected us, but don't want war with us. Tamerlane, on the other hand, will see our approach from the northeast as an immediate threat and spare no expense to ensure our failure. The Timur people are not friendly with the Turks, no, but their enmity to the Yuan is deeper than politics. My riders and I are direct evidence, now, that the stories of our migration are to be taken seriously."

A rumble of thunder punctuated Ulugan's final sentence. Rain still fell around them as they huddled beneath a huge tree at yet another fork in the road. All of the men, including their horses, had stopped to get their fill of fresh water in a small, swollen creek that ran parallel to the road and passed over a tiny falls at the fork. At another time, the place would have seemed beautiful. Now it was merely cold and damp, and once the riders and the foot soldiers had taken on as much water as they could handle, the two generals pushed them onward, going northwest.

At nightfall—the men, the horses, the oxen, all exhausted—news came from a different scout that more Timur troops had been spotted probing inland from the Black Sea. As Chrysoloras had said, the Georgians could do little to prevent Timurid armies from roaming freely across and controlling whatever portions of the land Tamerlane saw fit to decree his. And now a Yuan cavalry force was right in the middle of it.

Horse scouts were dispatched throughout the night, with orders to return regular reports.

The situation as it developed by morning was not good.

"They've guessed our objective," Chrysoloras said, worried.

"Perhaps," Ulugan replied. "I still think Tamerlane's men are less concerned with you and your Eastern Romans than they are with me and my horses. If we can reach a port and secure passage to Constantinople, that's one thing. But my cohort will still be vulnerable and under the command of less experienced men than myself. I am loathe to leave them on the shore of the Black Sea in this way. I doubt they can escape to return to the rest of our people."

"What if we were to split up?" Chrysoloras said, using his finger to draw in the wet sand where Ulugan had just been making a crude map with the point of a stick.

"Bad idea," Ulugan said. "Divided, my cavalry stand even less of a chance than if we stick together."

"Sorry," Chrysoloras said, then rubbed out what he'd been drawing and tried again. "Suppose we leave the entirety of the cavalry together, and just you and I try to make it to a safe port? If there's a chance for your cohort to make it back to the Kazakh steppe before the crab's claw of Tamerlane closes, we should afford them that chance. Especially when the Timurid troops don't know our precise position yet."

"And that leaves both you and I completely vulnerable," Ulugan said, frowning. "Besides, what do we do with your infantry? The carts, and the wounded too?"

"Have them all go together. Now. Cut across country if they must. Directly north, and keep on going until they're beyond immediate reach of Timurid troops. Once the cohort are free and clear they can return to your people as time and geography permit."

"Stranding strangers in the midst of still other strangers," Ulugan said, frowning.

"They won't stay strangers forever," Chrysoloras said. "You've watched them as well as I have, the past two days. They don't love each other, to be sure, but they don't hate each other either. They're all fighting men with a common purpose. They will figure it out. Besides, consider it a kind of guarantee. If anything happens to you while we're en route to Constantinople, they're on the hook for it. If anything happens to *them* en route to the Kazakh steppe, you're on the hook for it. If this alliance is going to last, we have to start making it work at lowest echelon, is that not so? No better time than the present. They will have strong reasons to keep working together. And so will we, frankly. Because I will want to see those men eventually returned home."

General Ulugan's expression was one of vexed indecision.

"We have to get them out *now*," Chrysoloras said firmly. "While there's still time for them to depart, and have a chance. Us? We *depend* on that departure to mask our trip to the sea. Tamerlane's army won't be looking for a small group of a few dozen people. They will be looking for a cavalry formation so large that their passing will be unmistakable. So, while the Timurid troops pursue north, we keep going west until we reach the water, and then follow the water along the shore until we get to a port of our liking."

"It will be very hard going," Ulugan said. "Both for them, and for us. With tremendous risk. I will also say that I am unused to taking gambles for which I don't already know enough variables to feel confident of a win."

"If you have a better idea, I am definitely open to hearing it."

General Ulugan opened his mouth to say something, then closed it. He brought his thumb up to his lip and tapped several times—a habit of which Ulugan may or may not have been aware, Chrysoloras thought—and opened his mouth to speak a second time, then closed it once more. Seemingly realizing that anything he were to propose didn't have any less risk associated with it, while the chance of the two generals getting caught and failing to reach Constantinople actually increased.

"Very well, Chrysoloras. In addition to being a lifetime diplomat—who sometimes plays at being a general officer—do you also enjoy games of risk?"

Chrysoloras simply smiled.

Issuing instructions to the Eastern Roman captains proved more complicated. None of them were particularly thrilled with idea of allowing their commander to split off from the main group. Either because some of them suspected they were being abandoned to act as a decoy, or they believed Chrysoloras was dooming himself to near-certain capture and possibly death without their protection. Chrysoloras couldn't be sure. He merely emphasized over and over again that their original mission had been to secure an ally in the fight against the Turks, and now they had such an ally—if only General Ulugan could be delivered to Palaiologos's court, where Chrysoloras would help Ulugan make his appeal before the Eastern Roman throne.

If Ulugan had similar trouble getting his lieutenants to buy into the plan, he didn't say. But before the sun was halfway up the sky all of the Eastern Roman assets—along with the Yuan cavalry—had reformed into a column that headed directly north. There were no maps to tell them what they might face as they tried to get beyond Timur-controlled territory. But when the last horse had vanished out of sight, Chrysoloras breathed a great sigh on their behalf. Then prayed silently in his heart for God to watch over and protect those men—Christian and heathen alike.

* * *

For a full week, Chrysoloras and Ulugan went west until they found the beach, then traced the coast until they spied a significant settlement with fishing boats large enough that one might be hired for a cross-sea voyage.

In terms of money, they were relying entirely on what Chrysoloras had managed to exchange during his time in garrison. Gold and silver remained gold and silver just about anywhere in the world. But using explicitly Eastern Roman coinage for this particular transaction would not be in anyone's interest. So, when they entered the fishing port—this time with identifying weaponry and armor carefully tucked away—they did so as innocuously as possible.

Chrysoloras also knew the local dialect, and was able to translate for the Yuan at each step of the way, though the Yuan themselves got some very odd looks from the Georgian locals who seemed to believe that the Yuan were in fact Timurid, but didn't behave at all like the Timur people typically behaved.

Having at last secured an interested ship's captain, Chrysoloras used up most of the Georgian coin he'd managed to acquire and got the whole group a comfortable set of beds—with a hot meal that night and once again in the morning—before they were due to set sail.

Alas, while men might plan, God tends to laugh.

Soldiers of Tamerlane's army were in the streets the following day.

"This seems to fairly destroy our plan," Ulugan said as he watched Timurid men passing below the window of the second-story lodging where they'd spent their night.

"We can't give up now!" Chrysoloras said, slapping his palm against the wooden window sill.

"If we try to reach the ship, they'll stop us. If the ship tries to launch, again they will stop us. No amount of money will change these facts."

"Are we sure about that?" Chrysoloras asked. "I don't know a constable who can't be bribed, assuming you can pay high enough."

"With what? You already gave most of your coin to the owner of the ship we're commissioning. Do you have the means to bribe every single Timurid man we might see today?"

"Well, what's your alternative?" Chrysoloras asked, echoing himself from a week prior. "If you have a better idea, now's the time to hear it."

The Mongolian general was unable to voice a different plan of action. They couldn't just hide out. They didn't have enough money to keep paying for lodging, and in any case, the officers of Tamerlane's army would be by eventually to inquire about any strangers who might have come to stay in the past few days. At which point, the Georgian proprietor would give up his guests without a fight.

When the group was back on the street, they made as much effort as possible to conceal weapons and put away potentially identifying finery. In those instances when a Timuran troop was seen asking questions, the group sidled into an alley or otherwise backtracked until they could take an alternate route, thus turning a foot walk which should have taken no more than ten minutes into an excruciating ordeal which lasted over an hour.

When they reached the commissioned boat, the captain was seething with anger.

"They've been by to ask about you *three times!*" he hissed between yellow teeth.

"What did you tell them?" General Ulugan asked.

"I told them I haven't seen you at all today and that if you didn't turn up soon, I was going to pocket the commission and refuse the voyage as a matter of principle. You may be paying me, but every hour I am not on the water is also an hour I am not bringing in a catch. We need to go *now* otherwise we're liable to wind up with...oh shit. *Shit.*"

Chrysoloras's hair stood on end when he saw the captain's eyes get big. The whites weren't quite as prominent as those of the men who'd been speared during the Turkish ambush, but they were close.

"What is it?" Chrysoloras hissed to his aide-de-camp. "I don't dare turn around to look!"

"They're coming," the young man—still with his bad arm in a sling—said under his breath.

"How many?" Chrysoloras asked.

"Five. And they're armed. None of them are smiling."

"Quick, everyone aboard," Chrysoloras ordered, then turned his head to look at the side of general Ulugan's face. The Yuan officer seemed to stare at the approaching Timurid men like someone who's seeing a long-lost relative for the first time in his life. There was an eerie familiarity to the Timur people, and yet, they weren't Yuan at all.

Neither Ulugan nor any of his men would stand a chance of fooling the Timur into believing Ulugan and his men were Timur themselves.

"Get ready to push off," Ulugan said to the captain, who continued to stare.

"What? How?!" the captain said, his eyes fixed on the approaching soldiers.

Sensing what was about to happen, Chrysoloras said one final prayer, and then stood face-to-face with the captain on the dock.

"Just get these people to Constantinople," he said. "You've been paid well enough to make a home for yourself in ports other than this one. If something happens to myself or my comrade, be good on your word, and get my men and their companions to their destination."

Both Ulugan and Chrysoloras were facing out to sea, away from approaching danger. Ulugan already had his hand on the curved sword he'd kept concealed beneath baggy clothing.

"Are you at all good with a blade?" Ulugan spat.

"I told you before," Chrysoloras admitted, "I use the tool God gave me."

"Talk isn't going to get us out of this one, I am afraid," Ulugan said.

When the Tumurid men were at the dock's edge, they began to loudly demand things in their own language. Not Georgian, which Chrysoloras would have understood. And not in the languages General Ulugan understood, either.

Chrysoloras suddenly spun around and began walking back down the dock, past the men. As he did, he said very loudly in Greek, "I can't understand a *thing* any of you are saying! This has got to be the *worst* hospitality of *any* seaside resort I've *ever* visited! I mean, the *nerve* of you people!"

Chrysoloras gesticulated with great exaggeration to maximize emphasis on his words—which he knew none of the Timurid troops would understand.

But Chrysoloras certainly got their attention. The lead Timur man spun on his heal and reached out to grab Chrysoloras by the arm.

Which was when General Ulugan did what he'd been waiting to do, and whipped his sword from its scabbard. While the four troops were surrounding their officer and his subject—still talking loudly in a tongue none of them understood, and waving his arms and hands in the air—Ulugan sank his sword into the back of first one, then the next, then the third soldier in turn. *Stab, yank, repeat.* With a most precise, rapid, and clock-like precision. As if he'd practiced the move again, and again, and again.

By the time the third body was toppling, the Timur officer himself had grabbed for his own weapon and opened his mouth to scream for help, when Chrysoloras used a free hand to ball a fist and punch the officer directly in his throat. The man gagged and fell backward, letting go of Chrysoloras's arm, while General Ulugan wrestled with the fourth soldier on the dock.

Chrysoloras looked up at the captain of the boat, who just stood there looking sick.

"Go!" Chrysoloras shouted. "Now!"

The captain blinked several times.

"Please!" Chrysoloras implored him, then turned and tackled the Timur officer as he picked himself up off the ground and began to stagger back toward the street—where several Georgians had gathered to see what all the fuss was about.

Ulugan's sword finished the last soldier with a bloody stroke that opened the man's neck from left ear to right breast. Then Ulugan was chasing after the stumbling officer who had Chrysoloras's arms wrapped around his ankles.

The Yuan officer's blade plunged into the Timur officer's back—in a scene which was sure to repeat itself a thousand times in the future, if the plans Chrysoloras and General Ulugan had hatched came to fruition—and the man was at last down.

But not before one of the Georgian women began to scream at the sight of so much blood, which of course made heads turn up and down the dock proper.

General Ulugan picked Chrysoloras up off the wood and said into his ear, "Are you alright?"

"Fine, I think," Chrysoloras said, and had to avert his eyes from the sight of redness spreading out fantastically from the Timur officer's body.

They each turned to look back at the ship, and realized the captain still hadn't done anything. Looking instantly at each other, then the boat, then back at each other, Ulugan and Chrysoloras bolted to the dock's edge and physically carried the captain across the plank and onto the deck of the boat.

Chrysoloras leaned close and screamed into the captain's ear, *"If this vessel fails to launch they will put your neck on the block, to match ours, now MOVE!"*

That seemed to do the trick.

Before either the Georgian dock patrol or the Timurid troops could muster a response, the fishing boat had separated itself from the dock's cleats and was getting up a triangular sail to begin tacking with the wind, which blew blessedly from inland that morning.

A quarter of an hour later the boat was slashing nicely through the waves of the Black Sea, putting mile after mile of water behind her.

"Have you ever been on a lengthy ocean voyage before?" Chrysoloras asked his counterpart as they both stood at the gunwale, and looked southwest.

"No," Ulugan admitted. "I am hoping sea legs are akin to horseback."

"Interesting analogy. I will hope the same, for your sake. Meanwhile, I look forward to showing you my home."

Chrysoloras placed a hand on General Ulugan's shoulder.

* * * * *

Brad R. Torgersen Bio

Brad R. Torgersen is a multi-award-winning science fiction and fantasy writer whose book, *A Star-Wheeled Sky,* won the 2019 Dragon Award for Best Science Fiction Novel at the 33rd annual DragonCon fan convention in Atlanta, GA. A prolific short fiction author, Torgersen has published stories in numerous anthologies and magazines, to include several Best of Year editions. Brad is named in *Analog* magazine's who's who of top *Analog* authors, alongside venerable writers like Larry Niven, Lois McMaster Bujold, Orson Scott Card, and Robert A. Heinlein. Married for over 25 years, Brad is also a United States Army Reserve Chief Warrant Officer—with multiple deployments to his credit—and currently lives with his wife and daughter in the Mountain West, where they keep a small menagerie of dogs and cats.

# # # # #

A Shot Heard 'Round the World by Kevin J. Anderson & Kevin Ikenberry

Dusk

5 December 1812

Near Smorgon, Russia

Antoine de Montagne nestled his chin against his chest, somewhat into the fold of his officer's coat as the march stopped for the fourth time in the last hour. With his eyes closed, the din of the retreat faded to a soft roar as his desire for warmth and rest overtook his senses. A tight hand grabbed his right arm and jerked him upright.

"Captain de Montagne." The voice was low and firm. "You would do well to keep your bearing."

Montagne blinked and stared into the face of General Caulaincourt, Napoleon's second in command. The man's face contained a tight smile, but his eyes were chips of dull ice. "My apologies, sir."

"Sleep will come for us, Captain. But not quite yet. We have a mission to undertake," Caulaincourt said. He leaned closer. "The Emperor wishes to depart for Paris immediately; within the hour. I have arranged for the Imperial Guard Horse Chasseurs to meet us at the front of the retreat. He will move along the line via sleigh and then east to Ashmiany. As a translator, you will accompany us."

Montagne brightened and felt ashamed for it. There would be warmth and sleep yet. A sleigh would speed him home, and his service could end in dignity rather than mired in the mud with dysentery or some other disease ravaging his body. In his joy, a concerned question formed. "Why not Colonel de Fleur?"

Caulaincourt flashed a thin, vindictive smile. "The Emperor is disappointed with the Russian response to his demands for surrender, and so he wishes his Translator General to suffer a bit for his failures. As you are the only other officer fluent in the Slavic and German dialects he could encounter for the first part of the journey home, he has chosen you to translate for him."

Montagne flushed with pride. "I understand, General. I shall do my best."

"I know you will, Captain de Montagne," Caulaincourt replied. "I will rejoin the Chasseurs, select a guard force for our journey, and will accompany the Emperor as well. You wait here and join the Emperor's sleigh. Leave your horse with one of the lieutenants."

"Yes, sir," Montagne said. "I will collect my things and be ready."

Caulaincourt nodded and turned his eyes to the ragged march. "Tell no one of his plan. The *Grand Armeé* will learn tomorrow."

Montagne squinted. "Sir? The rumor is a *coup d'etat* took place in Paris. They say General de Malet has aspirations for the throne? Is it true, sir?"

Caulaincourt's thin smile broadened slightly. "Nothing travels faster amongst an army than rumor, Antoine. There is business the Emperor alone must attend to, and that is all you need to know. Our very government is at stake. Be ready to leave when the Emperor arrives. He will want to move quickly. There is peril at every turn."

So it is true. Montagne couldn't help but smile at the general's casual use of his first name. *And I must ride with a surly Emperor all the way to Paris.*

"Will you assume command here, sir?"

"No." A quiet storm passed over the general's face. "General Mamet will take command. I shall accompany you in the sleigh once the Chasseurs are briefed and prepared to undertake the escort mission."

Montagne said nothing. There wasn't a proper reply to the general's words any captain could utter. "I shall be ready, sir."

Caulaincourt nudged his horse and moved down the line to the east. Montagne saw him speak with several other officers as he moved forward. Caulaincourt exemplified leadership, and Montagne would have followed him anywhere. For a moment, he wondered if any of the officers whom Caulaincourt spoke to knew of Emperor Napoleon's journey home. A freshening breeze pushed cold air past his tight collar and down under his wool coat, making him shiver. Montagne's saddle bags and bedroll sat astride his horse; he would need nothing else for the journey.

Chin tucked into his collar again, he began to realize that departing with the Emperor might indeed get him home soon. Perhaps even in time for Christmas. What a present that would be! Faint cheers filtered forward from the rear of the formation, and there could be no other explanation than the Emperor passing his troops in review.

Montagne patted the horse's neck and prepared to dismount. The closeness of the cheers caught his attention, and he turned. The small sleigh carrying Emperor Napoleon approached and slowed to greet him as the sporadic musket-fire from the near-constantly harassing Cossacks erupted toward the rear of the march.

Montagne dismounted, collected his bags, and passed the reins to a young, shivering lieutenant before turning toward the Emperor. The twin, black horses of the Emperor's team pulled a rickety wooden sleigh devoid of any of the rich trappings the great man often enjoyed during travel. The driver sat on a pedestal behind the passenger compartment under the light of a single lantern. *Necessity versus comfort.* The front rails of the sleigh came up to Montagne's chest. Above the withers of the two horses was a crook used to hold a bell. It sat curiously empty as he stepped behind the horses toward the passenger compartment.

Montagne saluted crisply and held the pose until Emperor Napoleon glanced at him and gave a half-hearted salute out of annoyance. Montagne felt his legs perceptibly shake. He'd never been in the presence of the Emperor, having only seen the great general and leader from a distance during the marches. His face was calm, almost idyllic, in the midst of the chaotic movement home. Even as the musket-fire from the French infantry roared through the approaching night, the Emperor seemed completely at ease. At his left shoulder sat another captain, wearing the shoulder brocade of a personal aide-de-camp.

Montagne boarded the sleigh and sat in a small, curved portion of the sleigh barely deep enough, or wide enough, for him. Facing the rear, he stared into the faces of Emperor Napoleon, his aide, and the driver perched above them on an elevated seat.

The aide nodded a cool welcome. "You are the translator, yes? Captain de Montagne?"

"That's correct."

Napoleon's eyes flashed to him. "You are fluent in the languages of these heathens?"

"I am, sir," Montagne swallowed. "Russian, German, and several of the Slavic dialects."

The Emperor squinted at him and there was distrust in his voice. "How did you come to this ability?"

"My parents traveled extensively in this region, sir." Montagne replied. "My father is a professor at *École Polytechnique*. He teaches history."

Napoleon harrumphed loudly. "Perhaps I should have had you craft the surrender of Czar Nicholas. A fluent son of a historian might have done a better job. Nicholas might have capitulated instead of refusing."

Montagne met the Emperor's eye, but said nothing in reply, as discretion required. Truth be told, the region surrounding them had never truly been peaceful and likely never would.

A violent flurry of rifle-fire erupted somewhere behind them— sporadic, harassing fire of the Cossacks. The brief attack ended after two methodical volleys from whichever company honored the threat and ended it, as they always did. The harassers vanished into the night.

"Damned Cossacks," Napoleon said. His face screwed up in disgust. "Men without honor never stand and fight."

"Shall I send a messenger, sir?" the aide-de-camp asked.

Napoleon shook his head. "They will fire and flee. Let them go."

With the crack of the driver's whip, the sleigh lurched forward.

The route of march for the *Grand Armeé* wound through deep forests along paths barely wide enough for the army to pass in their standard formation. As such, the Emperor, and his commanders directed the artillery to move forward and set the pace, which in the deepening snow seemed fittingly glacial. Still, the troops cheered their Emperor and he seemed to relish seeing them all again before leaving them in the midst of the brutal Russian winter.

There was no conversation that included Montagne. The aide and Napoleon communicated quietly, reviewing notes and dispatches. The younger captain's black hair came to a point between his eyes and his sullen face bothered Montagne for a reason he couldn't quite identify. Every time the aide's eyes flashed to meet his own, the distrust became palpable. Montagne turned his thoughts to his birth home in the south of France. There were no vicious winters there. He couldn't remember ever seeing his breath in the cold until they'd moved to Paris for his father to join the faculty of *École Polytechnique*. They'd spent two months of every year at their summer home in the hills above Nice. He hadn't visited there for four years or more and the sudden longing for the warm sun and beautiful beaches on the nearby coasts threatened to bring tears to his eyes.

His reverie ended with the sudden stop of the sleigh. He rocked backward, slamming his shoulder blades into the curved railing. Napoleon and his aide pitched forward in their seats. The look on the Emperor's face changed from annoyance to rage. He stood abruptly, casting aside the blanket of furs from across his lap.

Montagne saw the Emperor's eyes flash across the formation and lock onto the nearest officers he could see.

"You! Get your men and push this sleigh. Now!"

A horde of soldiers splashed through the mud and leaned against the sleigh. Montagne stood from his seat, ready to jump out and assist them, but Napoleon barked, "Sit down!" and he sat like a scolded child.

Eventually, with numerous men grunting and pushing, the sleigh cleared the far side of the creek, but did not proceed further. The driver shouted at the soldiers, but to no avail.

Still standing, Napoleon took in the scene. He bellowed at the driver, "Move!"

The driver struggled with the reins. "Sir, we must halt the army. We cannot pass here because of the aid station. The trail is too narrow."

Napoleon surveyed their surroundings and pointed at a sparsely wooded area across the muddy stream where fresh stumps poked through the snow. "There! Take us up that hill and we will go around."

Montagne recognized this place from their march months before. The *Grand Armée*'s supply trains had cleared paths through the forest as they moved and sometimes paralleled the route of march. In this case, they had cut a wagon-width trail through the narrow growth of birch trees to get the supply trains to this particular ford. If memory served him correctly, there would be another cut area on the far side.

The aide turned to him in concern. "Sir, you will be away from the army. We do not know where the trail may lead."

Napoleon gave his aide a dismissive glance and looked at the driver again. "I know *precisely* where that trail leads. Go around the aid station."

The driver shouted commands to the marching army. They milled about and gradually parted to allow the sleigh through. A few soldiers stared at the sleigh with harsh glances while most gawked, wide-eyed at their beloved leader standing in his sleigh and directing them as a conductor would an orchestra. The driver guided the sleigh into the hastily created path, through the creek bed, then successfully onto the other side.

As they climbed the small, sparsely forested hill on the narrow trail, Emperor Napoleon sat down and brought the blankets over himself again. He glanced at his aide. "Ensure the driver understands to find the first cut back to the *Grand Armeé*. We camped in this place on the march to Moscow, and I recall an access on the far side of the clearing where the wagons were able to move around the swollen creek during the summer. Now it is frozen mud. The damned thing slows me down again!"

His aide relayed the instructions to the driver, and Napoleon looked across to Montagne. In the orange light of the solitary lantern above and behind them, his eyes were flinty. "General Caulaincourt informed you of my intent?"

"He did, sir."

Napoleon turned to stare forward. "I cannot fight a war in two places. Therefore, if the Russians do not wish to fight, they are not worth the efforts of our armies. In Paris, I will expunge my detractors, reconvene the government, and we will focus our affairs elsewhere. To hell with this place."

Montagne fought against asking the question on his tongue. With the advance of the *Grand Armeé*, most of Europe had fallen under French rule. Aside from Russia, which Emperor Napoleon had now apparently removed from his aspirations, his only other possible target for conquest would be England. Yet the British were embroiled in an armed dispute with the American colonies, who were allies of the French. The Emperor said no more, instead he closed his eyes and lowered his face into the protective warmth of his collar.

The weather changed and large flakes of snow fell in ethereal curtains. The fresh precipitation muted the sounds of the army behind them as they crested a small hill that led to a clearing. The driver turned to follow the treeline, stark white birches with naked branches. Montagne leaned over the side of the sleigh to peer into the darkness. With the nearest lantern hanging above him, Montagne could see only a few yards in front of the horses. Their steps faltered and slowed. As the crack of the driver's whip sounded, the horses reared and skidded to a halt in the snow, Montagne saw a single, bearded man dressed in heavy furs blocking their path. A Cossack.

He held a rifle in his hands.

* * *

"*Allez!*" the driver called to the man and waved his whip as if to sweep the Cossack from the narrow path. Montagne spun in his seat to peer between the horses at the scene. The lone man did not move. He stood in a narrow space at the edge of a wider clearing. Two trees, barely far apart enough for the sleigh to pass, rose on either side of him.

Again, the driver called and actually cracked the whip over the horses. Unable to move, they whinnied and stamped their hooves only a few feet from the Cossack. Montagne glanced back to the Emperor who sat with his eyes closed as if trying to sleep. The aide looked up from his notes and met Montagne's eyes. After a moment, the aide slid the papers into a case and reached for a pistol tucked into the blankets at his feet. He nodded at Montagne. Taking his cue, Montagne stood in the sleigh and turned to face the Cossack.

"Move," he called to the man in Russian. The Cossack did not move, and he tried again in several dialects, including Latin and Greek. The fur-adorned man remained still, his rifle trained on the driver. He did not even look at Montagne nor did he speak.

In the silence, Montagne heard approaching riders. The team of horses pulling the sleigh startled and quivered in the snow. A thunderous roar of voices screaming something unintelligible raced into the clearing from the right.

More Cossacks!

Montagne ducked down in the sleigh. The aide handed him a pistol and crouched, assuming a protective stance in front of the Emperor. Montagne did the same and watched the Cossacks charge out of the night, directly at them. They raised their voices in an unintelligible scream, and Montagne raised his pistol and trained it on the closest targets.

Steady. Be steady.

The twilight reflected off the low clouds providing just enough light to see dozens of riders waving rifles rode down upon them. He whirled to his left, to the near side of the clearing at the thunderous sound of more horses approaching. Montagne saw the lone man no longer stood before the sleigh and realized what the Cossack had done.

An ambush! Here is where we will die.

The familiar shapes of the Imperial Guard Horse Chasseurs charged into the clearing and raced toward the galloping Cossacks. Several fired rifles from horseback, which were unlikely to hit anything. The Cossacks, however, returned the gesture both at the caval-ry and at the sleigh. Rounds impacted the small sleigh near where he crouched, and Montagne dropped toward the floor next to the aide. Napoleon did not. The Emperor sat rigid in his seat, his eyes follow-ing the attack with a critical gaze.

The Chasseurs met the Cossack charge in the middle of the small clearing. Men on horseback joined in hand-to-hand combat. The guards, swords in hand, hacked and swung at the Cossacks who de-fended themselves with their rifles and what appeared to be axes. Men fell from their horses. More rifle-fire filled the small clearing. Another surge of Cossacks charged into the fray, threatening to overwhelm the small detachment of cavalry; they were closer, and faster, than the first charge. The aide stood, centered his pistol and fired. One of the lead Cossacks tumbled into the snow.

Emboldened, Montagne rose from his crouch and aimed. With the barrel centered on the Cossack closest to them, he squeezed the trigger. In the burst of smoke from the barrel, Montagne expected to see a similar result, but the rider screamed and brandished an axe high above his head as he closed the distance to the sleigh.

Montagne ducked into the sleigh and the aide handed another loaded pistol to him.

"Fire, Montagne! Keep firing!"

He took the weapon, resumed his firing position and felt a strange calm wash over him as he again centered the barrel on the target and fired. The rider tumbled into the snow not forty feet away. He felt the aide tap him on the leg with the other pistol, again loaded and ready to fire.

So fast?

Voices yelled from the forest to his right and snapped his thought off like a dry twig. A regiment of infantry ran up the snow-covered hill and took up firing positions at the edge of the tree line. The driver sat frozen, watching the battle before them. Napoleon's aide sat next to Montagne, his eyes on the dim battlefield.

A volley of rifle fire-tore into the Cossacks. Montagne flinched at the closeness of it all even as he raised a pistol and fired again. This time, the aide joined him. The Cossacks whirled as one and charged down on the exposed infantry, for the moment, forgetting their target. A second volley was fired at almost point-blank range and many Cossacks and their horses crashed into the snow, but not all of them. The maniacal attackers tore into the infantry. Riflemen came up with bayonets and stabbed at them, eventually knocking them from their horses, but not before there were more casualties.

The French Chasseurs circled and regrouped in the center of the clearing and charged toward the Cossacks fighting the exposed infantry. As if in a dream, the cavalry closed the distance at surreal speed. Every weapon was clearly visible, sword or rifle, as they brandished and fired. The Cossacks roared in defiance and whirled against the guards before turning back to the east and galloping for their lives. Some fired over their shoulders in a hopeful attempt to take down one of the guards, but they soon hunched forward on their mounts and ran.

* * *

"Driver!" Napoleon roared as he stood abruptly behind Montagne and the aide. "Move!"

Startled to action, the driver raised his

reins and prepared to snap them across the backs of the team when a single rifle fired from darkness.

BOOM!

Montagne felt the rush of air as a musket ball rocketed through the air past them. He flinched, eyes closed, expecting to feel the impact. A heartbeat passed, then he opened his eyes and turned to the wide-eyed aide. The lone Cossack stepped out from behind a large tree, his musket barrel curling smoke into the night air. It dawned on Montagne that the weapon wasn't pointed at either himself or the aide. Nor had the Emperor been struck.

As one, they looked at the driver on the seat behind the sleigh. The top of the man's head was missing.

Montagne raised his pistol and pointed it at the Cossack as he stepped once more into the narrow path. The Cossack angrily slammed his musket into the snow. He simply stared at the sleigh for a long moment. Montagne hesitated to pull the trigger.

He wishes to die.

"Your army plundered our homes. They drank themselves into a stupor while they burned my family alive in my barn. Imagine losing everything to a people with whom you had no quarrel. You wanted a war but leaders never feel the pain of the innocents who die at their hand. Now, you will understand the toll."

The hair on the back of Montagne's head stood erect as he translated. Napoleon's stern face sneered and his teeth bared. "Get that fucking peasant out of my way! Kill him now!" Napoleon screeched, pointing at the Cossack.

BOOM!

Montagne flinched as the sound seemed to come from extremely close behind them. Napoleon's face grew still and he tucked his right hand inside his jacket in a characteristic gesture. Montagne saw the Emperor look down at his hand. He removed it from the jacket and Montagne saw bright red blood. Napoleon reached for the sleigh's curved railing with suddenly trembling hands.

Beyond the sleigh, the fur-clad shadow fled into the darkness. Montagne turned the pistol on the target, centered, and fired in one smooth movement. The figure fell forward into the snow.

BOOM!

The aide fired his pistol seemingly next to Montagne's ear. He whipped around to see the aide had executed the Cossack, and was now lowering the pistol. There was movement between them. The aide snatched at the Emperor's shoulder but missed. Napoleon pitched forward against the railing of the sleigh and fell forward, tumbling face first into the snow.

"Montagne! Help me!" the aide called as he leapt from the sleigh into the snow.

Montagne knelt in the snow next to the aide. The other captain cradled the Emperor's head across his legs and peered down into his still face. Montagne stared into sightless eyes for a long moment and turned his face up to see Caulaincourt shuffling toward them.

In that moment, words failed him. His ability to translate quickly and correctly vanished. Emotions overwrote his abilities. Mouth agape, he closed it and mentally shook himself to report.

"Sir, the Emperor is dead."

Caulaincourt removed his ornate headgear and placed it over his chest. The man's eyes closed in silent prayer. Montagne tried to pray but could not as the company of infantry swarmed protectively around the sleigh. Several of them moved into the forest and re-trieved the body of the Cossack he'd killed. As they laid the body next to the man, he saw the size difference and felt tears forming in his eyes.

My God. The Emperor is dead and France is in disarray. I failed to protect him.

And I have killed a child.

What have I done?

Montagne closed his own eyes and tucked his chin to his chest. He knew the others would assume his grief for their Emperor, and while some of it certainly was, he felt more for those displaced and affected by war. People whom armies and generals never considered.

Teeth clenched together, Montagne fought for control and when he had it, opened his eyes to find Caulaincourt staring at him. The general's eyes were somber, but focused. He knelt next to Napoleon's body and grasped the dead man's right hand affectionately.

They sat in silence for a moment, eyes on their fallen Emperor until the infantry returned and ringed them with quiet murmurs of shock and dismay. He found his voice. "What should we do, sir?"

Caulaincourt made eye contact with Napoleon's aide-de-camp first. "Load Emperor Napoleon's body into the sleigh. You will proceed to Ashmiany for new horses and provisions. I will meet you there and escort the Emperor's body personally. We will change the horses and proceed with all possible speed to Paris."

The general cleared his throat and spoke in a louder voice.

"Lieutenant Moreau? Summon the commanders to the front of the march immediately. I will meet them there. Have General Mamet report directly to me here. For the rest of you, I am giving you an order you will follow immediately and without fail. Speak not of what has happened here under penalty of death. The army, and the world, cannot know what has taken place until we decide to tell them. Do you understand?"

Amidst the murmurs and quiet assents, the aide replied in a loud, clear voice, "Yes, sir." He got to his feet and called for the infantry to assist him. Caulaincourt stood and motioned for the translator to step to the side.

"You did well, Montagne."

He took a breath and replied slowly. "I killed a child, sir."

Caulaincourt snorted. "That child killed your Emperor. His cowardly action has taken a great man from the field. Without him, France as we know it could crumble. Our enemies could pounce upon us and wipe us from the Earth in the coming days."

The enormity of what he'd seen finally cleared in Montagne's mind. The war in Spain would certainly falter as would the actions of the French fleet. The loss of Napoleon could embolden the British to attempt an invasion of Europe. Given the state of the *Grand Armeé*, there would not be much of a fight. With discord rampant in Paris, and the Emperor dead in the Russian snow, what might happen to the very world around them stunned Montagne to silence.

"We must keep our thoughts present." The general took a deep breath and exhaled a cloud of steam into the frigid night. His normally calm, almost placid face, appeared more troubled than when on the march. "You are fluent in English, as well?"

The question momentarily stunned Montagne. "I am, sir."

Caulaincourt took a moment to assemble his thoughts. He turned to Montagne and pulled him farther from the crowd, his voice low.

Caulaincourt sighed and looked up into the darkness. "A war on two fronts did this. We pushed too far east. Our appetites were too large. Our enemies continue to wear us down from all sides and we cannot maintain constant warfare at sea and all across Europe forever. The toll is too great."

The usually calm, composed general seemed on the edge of either anguished weeping or incalculable rage. Caulaincourt closed his eyes for a couple of seconds. When he opened them, his composure had returned combined with a sureness, a confidence, Montagne hadn't seen before. The general's eyes were clear and bright in the near darkness as he turned back to face Montagne.

"You will escort the body to Ashmiany with me and then you will acquire horses and proceed to Calais will all possible speed."

"Calais?" Montagne blurted. Caulaincourt glared at him and he apologized. "My apologies, sir."

Caulaincourt continued, "You will proceed to London on my personal orders and relay a message to their monarchy directly. I will compose it and you will personally deliver it to King George III, or his Prime Minister, in London. Is that clear?"

Montagne's mind whirled. Was Caulaincourt assuming command of the *Grand Armeé*, or the entire French government? Would he plead for peace? Would he capitulate to the powers that wished the *Grand Armeé* to return to their borders?

He nodded. "Yes, sir. I will proceed directly."

"Meet me at the head of the march in an hour's time, Montagne. Do not be late. The balance of our future depends on you."

* * *

They arrived at Ashmiany shortly before midnight. The French encampment there was small as most of the logistical stores to feed the approaching army pushed to the east ahead of them. The tiny, war-torn village would be glad to see the French retreat. With the army only six hours away now, the tents and wagons would be loaded and gone within a day's time. None too soon for the displaced villagers cowering in their homes.

The aide disappeared to coordinate with those in charge regarding the logistics of the return. Montagne stood by the sleigh, stamping his feet against the cold for a moment before two soldiers arrived to guard the sleigh. Each of the men glanced at the wrapped bundle on the floor of the sleigh for a moment and then took up positions on either side of it, facing away. Satisfied, Montagne moved up a slight incline and found the paddock. A lone sergeant guarded the horses. As he approached, the man stood and saluted.

"I bear a message from General Caulaincourt and require two horses on his orders." Montagne said. For the first time, he was aware of both the placement of his sword and his officer's pistol under his coat as well as the critical nature of his mission.

"Yes, sir," the attendant said and disappeared into the makeshift shack to gather the saddle and tack.

"Where is the quartermaster?"

The sergeant pointed down the incline to the familiar wagon trains. Two privates, likely roused by the sergeant, appeared in the doorway. One was thin and gangly with a speckled complexion, the other portly with dark eyebrows and sullen eyes.

Montagne pointed at the gangly one. "Go to the quartermaster and draw ten days' rations and water."

One private disappeared, and Montagne stared at the other one. "Fetch the horses. The fastest you have."

Suddenly alone outside the paddock, Montagne turned to gaze over the small village which the logistical forces of the *Grand Armeé* called home. Though the hour was late, the village buzzed with activity. Armed men ran from point to point as if preparing a defense. From here, he would press on to Miedniki and on to Vilna. Each had a small French logistical garrison to support the needs of the army as it retreated toward France.

Another sergeant approached and saluted. "Sir, we are preparing for an attack. Local outposts have been harassed by the Cossacks since dusk. It is best you arm yourself and report to headquarters."

Montagne bristled. "I will do no such thing. I am under orders from General Caulaincourt in command of the *Grand Armeé*. As soon as I have a proper mount, I must depart. Prepare your defense, Sergeant. My mission remains unchanged."

The man uttered *"Mon dieu,"* before turning back toward the village and sprinting into the night.

As Montagne stood waiting for his horses, the cold suddenly seeped far inside his coat and shoes. He grew anxious to be off on his mission, and he looked into the paddock several times, until finally the sergeant appeared with his horses. Down the hill, the gangly private and two other figures moved toward him, each carrying a sizable load. They divided the load between the two horses, and when the mounts were ready, Montagne did not hesitate. He swung into the saddle on the black gelding and did not look back as he galloped off for Miedniki.

* * *

Two days west of Vilna, the forests gave way to large expanses of dormant grasslands. Under their intermittent blanket of snow, the fields showed the marks of couriers and small units of the French army along the route of march as they coordinated the retreat of the main effort.

Montagne followed the trail west as fast as his horses could go. Every couple of hours, he dismounted and led them through the fields and occasional stands of forest to rest them and get his own blood flowing. Fatigue tore at him from all sides. Stopping to sleep for any length of time seemed out of the question. Every time he'd come across an encampment, he'd been too awake and refreshed to feel compelled to stop. During the long night, he'd almost fallen from his saddle twice before finding a dilapidated barn. He'd lain down in the old, musty hay for an hour at most before guilt propelled him onto the horses and moving further west.

As he rode, paying attention to the horses and his pace, Montagne's mind tried to grasp the situation. Somewhere to the south, Caulaincourt and the body of the Emperor moved at high speed to Paris. He tapped the reassuring lump under his jacket of the general's note for the British monarchy and resisted, again, the temptation to read it even under the pretense of committing it to memory.

No. Montagne shook off the thought and lowered himself from the saddle to walk alongside the horses for a while. The general trusted me to deliver his message. *I must trust he knows what he is doing.*

He swung his right leg up and over the horse's back as the black gelding flinched backward. Montagne ducked and reversed the movement, reaching his leg toward the ground as the whistling hum of a near-miss shot through the space where he'd been a second before. The crash of a musket firing sounded through the strand of dormant trees he'd been about to enter. His heart racing, Montagne withdrew the pistol from under his coat and visually checked its readiness. Thankful for war horses familiar with the sound of weapons that didn't spook easily, Montagne used them for cover and

looked toward the sound of the shot. In an instant, he saw a silhouetted rider on a pale horse gallop west and away from him.

He stood frozen in the snow for half a minute, trying to calm
both his racing breath and his frantic mind. Had he been followed?
Why would someone shoot at him? As he crossed eastern Europe,
every dark corner of forest and wide-open plain had kept his eyes
darting back and forth except for this one. He'd failed to stay alert
and it almost cost him his life. Montagne rubbed the several days
growth of beard on his chin and closed his tired eyes. He leaned his
forehead against the horse's hide as he fought against the fatigue
threatening to undermine his ability to focus on the work.

The Emperor is dead. The toll has been too great.

You must not fail.

He heard Caulaincourt's voice in his head. The implications of
the general's unread message weren't clear to the translator, but there
were two possibilities he surmised. Surrender to the British demands
and an end to the war in Spain was certainly a possibility, though
Caulaincourt's own feelings about the British matched the fallen
Emperor's own, and that meant surrender was out of the question. If
not surrender, then was the message one of peace? Cooperation?
Something else?

His eyes snapped open. "I have to ride," he said to the wind.
"For France, if not for me."

Survival instincts initiated, Montagne grabbed the lead for his
horse and led the pair as fast as he could run into the protection of
the strand of trees his attacker had vacated. In the dark, cold forest,
Montagne stamped his feet and gazed for several minutes in all directions before climbing back astride his mount and pushing west once
again.

Friendly way stations grew more numerous as he rode, and he traded horses several times in the ensuing days. Yet his own fatigue wore down on him unlike anything he'd ever experienced in his service. The forests and hills of Germany slowly became the rolling terrain of eastern France. At Roubaix, he turned northwest and made for the coast. The grasslands were brown with winter. He thought again of the sun and warmth of the family lands above Nice, and he longed to turn toward Paris and ride further south without looking back.

As he rode, Montagne wondered if Caulaincourt and the other leaders shared his fatigue, and not just with the war, with the struggle and upheaval of his country. He'd been ripped from his chosen studies and placed into the armed service of his country by a man seemingly hell-bent upon destruction at all costs. Emperor Napoleon would be equally celebrated and scorned for centuries to come. The suffering of so many would be forgotten.

Perhaps it's time I leave this all behind. For good.

The enormity of the thought struck him as the pre-dawn twilight spread over the sprawling coastal plain of Calais. Fishing boats crowded the harbor afraid to move into the channel and the constant swarming presence of the English fleet. Montagne believed it would be easy to find a patriotic fisherman to risk delivering him to the British.

At the last post, just as the sun rose to the east, Montagne surrendered his horses and sought out the quartermaster for rations and additional loads for his weapons only to be directed toward a distant, quiet tent. As he approached, Montagne listened to the whisper of caution from his mind and drew his pistol before he stepped inside. A lone, dark figure sat on a stool. He looked up and raised a pistol, pointing it at Montagne's chest. Montagne's own pistol was trained on the young man's smiling face. The two stood for a moment in awkward silence.

The Emperor's aide laughed and spoke in fluent English. "Captain Montagne, I'm afraid I must relieve you of that note. His Majesty will never receive it as long as I live."

Montagne smiled at the man's audacity. "Because of your loyalty to the Emperor?"

"No, my duty to the Crown." The aide stood and stepped closer. "I give you this chance, Montagne. Where is the message?"

"Go to hell," Montagne said and pulled the trigger. He squeezed his eyes shut expecting the report of the aide's pistol pointed at his chest. When it didn't come, Montagne opened his eyes and saw the aide lying on his side grasping for the pistol that had fallen from his grasp. Montagne stepped forward, kicked away the pistol, and knelt.

The aide coughed and blood sprayed from his mouth. Still, the man sneered as he struggled to speak. "France will fall, Montagne."

"Perhaps," Montagne replied. "But not today."

* * *

Finding a boat to traverse the channel took considerable effort. Not many sailors were willing to entertain the certainty of intercept with the British navy even while traveling under a flag of truce. War made cowards of dishonorable men. Montagne, in his addled state, wandered through the docks. Morning should have been a busy time along the docks in the wide, sure harbor, but the vessels remained in their moorings as if frozen. The few fishermen at their boats watched him with uneasy eyes. Most looked away when he acknowledged them with a nod and a hopeful smile. Others turned their backs on him. When they did, he realized how much war had changed him. As a young officer, the idea of a Frenchman turning his back on the army, and a representative of the Emperor himself, would have angered him beyond the edge of reason. But the near-constant warfare had taken too much of a toll on the populace. He understood that toll for the first time in his life. His own commitment to the mission would have waned save for his respect for Caulaincourt and his own dreams of returning home to a land at peace.

An older man with a shock of white hair under a black knit cap merely squinted at Montagne's request. He nodded and pointed at the small, single-masted boat. Before Montagne could even settle himself in the small bow, they were under sail across the placid harbor. Montagne lay in the ship's tiny bow to sleep.

Near noon, a rough hand shook him awake. Montagne sat upright at the whistle of a single cannonball arcing over their heads into the ocean. Over the stern, where the rudder sat unmanned and amidships, a warship approached. Montagne struggled to stand. He waved his arms.

"Sit down," the old man called over his shoulder. "I've hoisted the proper flag. They'll take you aboard, Captain. Just negotiate my freedom."

Montagne looked up at the simple white rectangle floating in the wind where the sails once billowed. As the warship came alongside, he looked up to see British soldiers pointing their rifles at his chest, careful sneers on their faces.

They collected him from the fisherman and roughly hauled him aboard what appeared to be a French-built *Pallas*-class frigate flagged as a British warship. His feet had barely touched the deck when the ship's captain, a pleasant-faced man with dark, windswept hair appeared in front of him.

"You're in quite the mess, sir," he said with a grim smile.

Montagne straightened. "If you'll permit me to come aboard, Captain," he said in fluent, British accented English. "I am carrying a message from General Armand-Augustin-Louis de Caulaincourt, the Commander of the *Grand Armeé*, for the eyes of King George III only."

The ship's captain blinked but said nothing. "Can you elaborate further?"

"I appreciate your discretion, sir. That is a conversation best held in private. Your quarters, perhaps?" Montagne asked.

The captain nodded stiffly. "I am Captain Murray Maxwell of the *Daedalus*."

"Antoine de Montagne, senior translator for General Caulaincourt," Montagne said. He kept his gaze stern as if asking the young captain to say nothing more. "Sir, if you would, please release the fisherman; I traveled under the flag of truce to be here. Your quarrel is not with him or his meager catch."

Captain Maxwell nodded. He turned to a burly sailor with a trimmed beard. "Master-at-arms, release the fisherman. Take Captain de Montagne to my cabin. Post two guards at the door. I shall join him shortly. Mister Mowett? Make sail and continue the trials."

Montagne heard the crew spring to action as he found himself escorted belowdecks to the captain's cabin and an uncertain future. He didn't have to wait long.

The promise of delivering critical intelligence to the Admiralty, and the King himself, kept Maxwell firmly in Montagne's confidence. Upon hearing the news of Emperor Napoloeon's death in Russia,

Maxwell called his sailing master. Maxwell interrupted the sea trials for the newly-commissioned *Daedalus* and reversed course for England with all possible speed, yet he told no one of Montagne's news or mission. The seas were rough during the transit, but Maxwell's treatment of Montagne never deviated from genteel and pleasant. Montagne wondered what the crew discussed in hushed tones as they glanced at him during his time on deck, but no one said anything to him save for the ship's captain.

They anchored in Portsmouth two days later and, circumventing the authority of the port commander, Maxwell arranged a coach and escort for himself and Montagne to London. Montagne had said nothing to anyone besides Maxwell about the demise of Napoleon and it became clear Maxwell understood the information's impact on all of Europe. The young ship's captain climbed aboard the coach to complete the last leg of the journey with Montagne.

* * *

The coach arrived in London in the late afternoon of Christmas Eve. The slushy thoroughfares were crowded as families with children moved from place to place, enjoying the holiday cheer. Montagne thought of his own family in the south of France and his desire to join them as soon as possible. As much as he wanted to believe his time in the army was drawing to a close, and that the constant wars of the Emperor's rule of France would fade into a lasting peace, the churning in his stomach told him that unless a miracle occurred in the next few hours, he was still in the center of an enemy's country and too far from home.

Montagne watched the faces of excited children as the coach made its way to Buckingham Palace. Wearing his British naval uniform, Captain Maxwell swung out of the carriage at the palace gate and spoke to the guards, who in turn dispatched a runner to the palace. Montagne fought crippling anxiety and the fatigue of the previous fortnight as they waited for a response. At last, the *Daedalus*'s captain climbed aboard and the carriage passed through the fortified gates.

Captain Maxwell turned to him, both flushed and relieved. "His Royal Highness, the Admiral of the Fleet and Lord Liverpool, the Prime Minister, are both present, as I'd hoped." Maxwell lowered his voice, as if someone might be eavesdropping. "The Admiral of the Fleet is one of King George's sons. His Majesty has been ill for some time, and Lord Liverpool effectively runs the government and our war efforts. I said nothing of the contents of your message. I merely implied the news would be of critical importance."

"There have been rumors in France for some time regarding your king's health." Montagne smiled. "I am indebted to your trust and courtesy, Captain Maxwell."

The young officer smiled in return. "I hope the larger conflicts between our countries find a peaceful resolution. Without trying to sound naive, I believe you and I could be friends in other circumstances."

"Let us hope that peace comes swiftly."

Once the driver parked the carriage in front of the main palace entrance, they exited together. Several armed guards surrounded them with weapons at the ready. Maxwell stared at the sergeant of the guard in charge who nodded. They were ready to proceed.

Maxwell gestured Montagne forward and fell into step at his right shoulder. "Come, Captain de Montagne." The guards pressed in, accompanying them. Montagne drew a long deep breath and tried to still his thrashing heart. Even after two years in the *Grand Armeé*, during countless actions and marches close to the front with artillery and musket rounds passing overhead, he had never experienced such abject fear.

They will take me and execute me without listening to a word I say. Caulaincourt's message, whatever it is, will be lost and forgotten.

The sudden urge to laugh at the terror in his bones almost overtook his senses as they stepped inside. Entering the ornate palace, Montagne kept his head and eyes forward, refusing to be distracted by the furnishings of King George's residence. The escorts directed them into a wide corridor where two gentlemen stood waiting for them. Both were older, distinguished men wearing powdered wigs. One wore the traditional dark blue dress uniform of an admiral of the Royal Navy and the other a dark, traditional jacket with a ruffled shirt underneath. Both were older, and Montagne noted the powdered wigs they wore likely covered hair of a similar color. The admiral was stout, if not a bit rotund, unlike the sailors of the *Daedalus* and others whom Montagne had observed along the shores of home. This man had likely never seen a posting at sea because of his lineage.

The escorts retreated to a watchful position around the four men. Captain Maxwell clicked his heels together and saluted. Unsure of the customs and courtesies, Montagne nodded and bowed very slightly at the waist to both men.

"Your Highness, Lord Liverpool. I am Captain Murray Maxwell, of His Majesty's Ship *Daedalus*. Allow me to present Captain Antoine de Montagne, translator for General Armand-Augustin-Louis de Caulaincourt, Commander of the *Grand Armeé*."

His Royal Highness, the Admiral of the Fleet, frowned at Montagne. "What news do you have that is so critical to interrupt the preparations for our Christmas celebrations, Captain de Montagne?"

"You said Caulaincourt is in command of your army?" Lord Liverpool questioned immediately. His gaze intensified on Montagne. "I do not understand. Has there been a change in command of the French forces?"

Montagne nodded. "Sir, Emperor Napoleon is dead."

"What?" Lord Liverpool gasped. The men looked at each other.

Montagne met their shocked expressions. "He was killed by Cossack irregular forces outside of Smorgon, Russia, on the fifth of December as the army retreated from Moscow."

The Admiral of the Fleet harrumphed and looked at Lord Liverpool. "This is a ruse."

"Sir, with respect, I was with the Emperor as he died. There was news of a possible *coup d'etat* in Paris. As the Russian campaign stalled and the *Grand Armeé* ran low on provisions, the Emperor ordered our withdrawal. During the retreat, the Emperor told General Caulaincourt he could not govern France from the front and proceeded home. As he started his journey, Cossacks attacked. He was killed in front of his aide-de-camp, General Caulaincourt, and myself. I can personally verify that he is dead."

The Admiral of the Fleet turned to Lord Liverpool and they stared at each other for a moment. His Royal Highness asked, "And what of the aide?"

"He died at the Emperor's side. Only General Caulaincourt and I survived the attack," Montagne lied. Their question had been far from innocuous and confirmed the true identity of the man he'd executed as a spy in Calais.

Liverpool deftly changed the subject. "What is the message General Caulaincourt asked you to deliver to His Majesty? Let us see it."

Montagne reached into his pocket and withdrew the small, wax-sealed roll of paper. "General Caulaincourt was adamant this be seen by King George III or yourself first."

"And Napoleon is really dead?" the Admiral asked again, as if he couldn't believe it.

Montagne nodded. "If all has gone well, General Caulaincourt has returned to Paris. As for the status of the French government, I cannot say."

Lord Liverpool nodded to his counterpart. "As the Prime Minister, I am charged with handling all matters of importance for the Crown while His Majesty is ill. As you are aware, His Royal Highness, the Admiral of the Fleet, is Prince William, the Duke of Clarence. While not the heir to the throne, he will review the note as well. Is this acceptable, Captain de Montagne?"

Montagne considered the situation and knew he had no alternative. "Of course, sir."

Lord Liverpool extended a hand, palm up, to Montagne. "If you please?"

Montagne extended the rolled message to the Prime Minister. Lord Liverpool took the message, broke the wax seal, and unrolled it.

As he read, the older man's mouth fell open slightly. He laughed once, and then again, before almost clutching it to his chest. "General Caulaincourt says he is returning to Paris with the intent of dissolving Emperor Napoleon's government and establishing peace through Europe. He says the Emperor's death at the hands of Cossacks has challenged his own personal convictions for warfare," Liverpool said. "From what I know of the man, I am inclined to believe him."

The Admiral of the Fleet harrumphed again. "We must be careful in our dealings with General Caulaincourt. With the French government in disarray, anything could happen…as we've seen over the last several decades."

"Indeed. However, if this is a legitimate and honorable expression of his intent, there are great possibilities. Has our blockade been established at the American colonies?"

His Royal Highness nodded. "They should be in position. I await the confirming dispatch from Admiral Warren any day now."

Lord Liverpool's eyebrows rose and a hint of a smile played on his lips. "How quickly can you sail a diplomatic mission to Paris?"

"Two days. The family's Christmas celebration must be preserved. I can have a ship dispatched and at the ready." His Royal Highness, the Admiral of the Fleet nodded. Where there had been doubt in his voice before was sudden enthusiasm.

"Begging your pardon, sir," Captain Maxwell spoke. "The *Daedalus* is docked in Portsmouth now and is ready to sail. I would be honored to transport the diplomatic party."

Lord Liverpool brightened. "Done! Captain Montagne? Will you accompany the party and assist with the presentation of terms?"

"Terms?" Montagne squinted and hastily added, "Sir?"

Lord Liverpool nodded and handed the note to His Royal Highness. "General de Caulaincourt has offered, in an attempt at peace, his full cooperation and diplomatic influence. You are aware we are in armed conflict yet again with our former colonies in America?"

Montagne shook his head. "I was only aware of naval actions in the Atlantic, sir."

"Well, we have seen several engagements with the Americans on the ground and they've held a significant advantage. That ends now. Once your navy and logistical support is withdrawn from America, we will see just how much resolve our former subjects have." He smiled again and glanced at His Royal Highness. "We shall recall Lord Wellington from Spain and instruct him to provide a thorough and complete invasion plan for the colonies. By summer, I will walk that ground myself and take their surrender personally. I've heard their capitol city is quite beautiful. Perhaps a proper flag flying over it will complete the scene?"

The Admiral of the Fleet beamed. "Quite right. His Majesty will be most pleased."

Lord Liverpool smiled at Montagne and Johnson. "You've delivered quite the Christmas present, gentlemen. Please join me for Christmas dinner tomorrow. You should have enough time to have your uniform laundered, *Colonel* de Montagne. And, you as well, Captain Maxwell."

Montagne blurted. "I'm sorry, what did you say, sir?"

His Royal Highness turned the message to Montagne, where he read Caulaincourt's flowing script promoting him officially with the duties of Translator General of *la Grand Armeé*. "I take it this is a surprise?"

"Completely, sir."

Lord Liverpool laughed. "A commanding general's staff should always carry appropriate rank for their office, especially when they've performed their duties as honorably as you have. We would never shoot the messenger, Colonel de Montagne, whether it's Christmas or not. I trust you have a family, yes? Tell me about them over a glass of wine, and we'll toast a new peace for Europe and a bright new future."

* * * * *

Kevin J. Anderson Bio

Kevin J. Anderson has written more than 165 books, including 56 national or international bestsellers. He has over 23 million books in print worldwide in thirty languages. He has been nominated for the Nebula Award, Hugo Award, Bram Stoker Award, Shamus Award, and Silver Falchion Award, and has won the Dragon Award, SFX Readers' Choice Award, Golden Duck Award, Scribe Award, and New York Times Notable Book. He also has received the Faust Grand Master Award for Lifetime Achievement.

* * *

Kevin Ikenberry Bio

Kevin's head has been in the clouds since he was old enough to read. Ask him and he'll tell you that he still wants to be an astronaut. A retired Army officer, Kevin has a diverse background in space and space science education. A former manager of the world-renowned U.S. Space Camp program in Huntsville, Alabama and a former executive of two Challenger Learning Centers, Kevin works with space every day and lives in Colorado with his family.

Kevin's bestselling debut science fiction novel, *Sleeper Protocol*, was released by Red Adept Publishing in January 2016 and was a Finalist for the 2017 Colorado Book Award. Publisher's Weekly called it "an emotionally powerful debut." His military science fiction novel *Runs In The Family* was released by Strigidae Publishing in January 2016 and re-released by Theogony books in 2018. *Peacemaker*, Book 6 of the Revelations Cycle, was released in 2017, spawning its own line of books in the Four Horsemen Universe.

\# \# \# \# \#

Marching Through
by David Weber

"I'm sorry, Cump, but it isn't possible."

There was compassion in his brother's tone, Sherman thought, looking out the hotel window at the bustling Cincinnati Street, but not hope.

"John, I understand he's angry. Truly, I do. But this is more than just—"

"Not for him, Cump. And not for Tommy or Aunt Maria. And—I'm sorry—not for me, either."

Sherman turned from the window, lips tight, and his brother looked back steadily.

"You should have gone to London, Cump." John Sherman's voice was flat. "If you had, Ellen—"

He broke off and shook his head sharply.

"Do you think I haven't thought the same thing?" Sherman's tone was tighter than his lips. "Do you think I don't realize everyone in the family must feel the same way? Of course I do! But I can no more undo that than I could ascend bodily into heaven, and it would seem nothing short of that will appease him."

"She was his daughter, Cump!"

"And she was my *wife*!"

"Yes," John grated. "Your *first* wife."

"Damn you, John!" His eyes flashed. "I *loved* her!"

"Then perhaps you should have remembered that before you dragged her off to that hellhole!"

"I dragged her nowhere, John! And it was scarcely a 'hellhole,' for that matter. It was certainly better than California!"

"Yes, and she hated California, too," John said coldly.

"I never asked her to come to Pineville!"

"No? Well you certainly didn't try to *dissuade* her, did you? And it took you little enough time to find solace for your loss, Cump."

Fury flashed through Sherman as that last, deadly sentence struck home. Yet even as it did, the memory burned across his mind once more. The memory of Ellen, feverish, pale-faced, in the fourposter bed. The hushed voices of the doctor and Marie, murmuring in the background, while he held her hand, stroked her forehead.

"Tell Daddy I love him," she'd whispered through cracked lips.

"You can tell him yourself," he'd lied.

"Tell him!" she'd insisted.

"I will," he'd promised. "Now rest."

"I'll have time to rest soon enough."

She'd actually managed a faint smile, and her eyes had moved, seeking Marie as she stood in the doorway, listening intently to Doctor Kennebec's instructions. Then she'd looked back up at him.

"The Church says God's angels are all around us, Cump. I never expected to meet one of them *here*, though."

"I know." He'd stroked her cheek. "Rest."

"I will. I will!" Her voice had been even weaker, and her too-thin fingers had squeezed the hand holding hers. "I'm not frightened,

Cump. Truly. I'm just…so tired." Her eyes had slipped shut. "Tell Daddy," she'd repeated, so faintly now he could barely hear. "Tell Daddy how much I love him."

"I will," he'd repeated. "I will."

And he had, at the funeral, while his father-in-law listened in stony-eyed silence.

It was the last time they'd spoken. He knew now that it would always be the last time they'd spoken. And now, even John…

"I thank you for coming." His voice was colder than ice, and he knew it, but there was nothing he could do about it. It was at least better than seizing his brother by the throat. "I see it was a mistake to call upon you in this matter, however. I assure you, it won't happen again, Sir. Good day!"

He turned back to the window, spine ramrod straight, arms folded across his chest, as he gazed down at the street, wondering if his brother would speak again.

Heels across the floor and a sharply closed door answered the question.

William Tecumseh Sherman's squared, proud shoulders sagged, and he closed his eyes, leaned forward to rest his forehead against the glass.

John didn't understand. He never had. And neither had Ellen. Or her father.

He *had* loved Ellen—he had! But there'd come a time when he had to stand upon his own two feet, and she'd needed to understand that. Or to support him in it, at least. Perhaps she would have, one day…if she'd lived. But she hadn't.

He opened his eyes again, his expression bleak, remembering a nine-year-old whose father had died, leaving a destitute wife and eleven children. Even at nine, he'd been hugely proud of his father— a judge on the Ohio State Supreme Court. A distinguished juror. A man with a glowing future.

Until he died and took his family's entire future with him.

Sherman knew how unspeakably fortunate he and his family had been that his father and Thomas Ewing had been such close friends. And that Ewing had been such a good man. The man had stepped into the hole his father's death had left and taken the entire family under his protective wing.

A powerful man in Whig politics, Thomas Ewing. A profoundly respected jurist; William Henry Harrison's Secretary of the Treasury; the nation's first Secretary of the Interior under Zachary Taylor; Senator from Ohio. He'd been instrumental in securing John Sherman's election to the House of Representatives, and he was one of the men who would be sitting down shortly at what they were already calling the Peace Conference at Willard's Hotel in Washington City in an effort to stave off the Union's collapse. A man Sherman not only sincerely respected but loved and deeply admired. His foster father, the man whose approval mattered to him more than that of anyone else in the universe.

And the man who would never forgive him for his daughter's death. Never understand—never be *willing* to understand—why his son-in-law had preferred Louisiana to London.

I hated banking, he thought now. *I hated it almost as much as I hated the Commissary Service. I know Henry meant it for the best when he offered me the San Francisco office, and I jumped at the chance, but I ought to have known better.*

And John was right about how much Ellen had hated California, too. She'd never wanted to leave Ohio. In fact, she'd returned to Ohio without him for seven months in the middle of his four years in San Francisco. And her parents had insisted that their daughter Lizzie remain with them in Ohio the entire time.

Even from distant California, then, Thomas Ewing's shadow had loomed over his life, and Ellen had never understood—never sympathized, at least—with his need to prove he was more than Thomas's charity ward. His admiration and love for Thomas had been boundless, yet Ellen had never understood how his sense of indebtedness had always colored them both. Never grasped what drove him to prove that he could provide his own family with the financial security of which his father's early death had deprived him as a child. To prove he could do that—could succeed where his own father, through no fault of his own, had failed *him*—without depending on anyone else's largess, however willingly that largess was offered. It was why he'd left the Army in the first place, because an Army officer's peacetime salary was too low to provide that security. It was why he'd gone into banking, despite the fact that he'd never truly had the head—or the heart—for it.

And then the bubble had burst in California. He'd closed the bank there, returned east to run another branch in New York City…only to see that go under, along with its parent bank in St. Louis, in the panic of '57. At thirty-seven, he'd found himself the unemployed father of three, with no prospects in banking in the current climate, and Ellen had been not so secretly pleased. Not that she'd gloated at his misfortune. She would never have done that. Indeed, the true problem was that she'd never seen it *as* misfortune. For her, it had been fate pushing them back to Lancaster and the family she loved, and she'd never truly comprehended how much he hated his dependence on her family and its wealth. She came from that world, she knew he'd been raised in it by her own father, and in her eyes it ought to have been the natural order of things for him as it was for her.

But it hadn't been. And so even as Ellen had rejoiced at the thought of returning to Lancaster, Sherman had sought a different route. Perhaps he couldn't avoid relying upon his foster father's connections, but at least he could try to do it on his own terms. So he'd gone to Kansas, joined the real estate and law firm of his brothers-in-law, Thomas and Hugh. It was still a "family business," but he and Tommy, especially, had always been close...and Leavenworth was over six hundred miles from Lancaster.

But that hadn't worked out, either. The firm had never prospered—in no small part because Tommy had preferred to concentrate on abolitionist politics instead of business in "Bleeding Kansas"—and as it slowly sank into failure, his old, debilitating friend melancholy had visited him again.

He'd grown increasingly desperate. So desperate that he'd even tried to get back into the Army, but there'd been no openings two years ago. So desperate that, despite his pride, he'd been forced back to Lancaster, forced to accept a position managing the Ewing family's coal and saltworks in nearby Chauncey. Only temporarily, of course. Only until Thomas could find something more suitable for him.

Like the position with the London bank.

Ellen had been excited about that. San Francisco was a rude, crude, raw-boned place, unable to challenge Lancaster in her eyes, but London was civilized. The largest city in the entire world. With over three million inhabitants, it was twenty times the size of Cincinnati, Ohio's largest city, and four times the size of even New York. A place with culture and wealth, the beating heart of the largest and most powerful empire in the history of the world.

And one more "new beginning" provided by her family in an occupation he'd come to loathe.

There'd been no escape. However little the opportunity excited him, it had seemed the only one available...until he'd received the letter from Louisiana, at least.

It had come to him from George Graham, a man he'd never met, and it had invited him to consider the post as the first superintendent of the newly organized Louisiana State Seminary of Learning and Military Academy. He'd never heard of the Seminary at that point, either, but he'd jumped at the chance and taken the train to Baton Rouge for a personal interview.

He'd spoken not just with Graham, but also with Paul Hébert, his old classmate from West Point and the past Governor of Louisiana, during whose governorship the Seminary had been established three years before. Graham, the Seminary's board chairman, had spent those three years acquiring funds, finding a campus, and commissioning the first buildings. Now he needed a superintendent, and since he envisioned the Seminary as following in the footsteps of the Virginia Military Institute, he'd clearly needed a military man for the post, so he'd consulted Colonel Don Carlos Buell, under whom he had served in the Mexican-American war, for possible candidates. Buell had written a glowing letter extolling Sherman's qualifications for the position, and Hébert had enthusiastically endorsed Buell's suggestion.

He and Graham had taken to one another immediately. The salary had been less than he would have been paid in London, and Rapides Parish had scarcely been a cultural mecca, but it was also a hundred and fifty miles farther from Lancaster than even Leavenworth had been. Perhaps even more importantly, the glowing terms in which Buell and Hébert had recommended him had come at a time when the black tide of his all-too-frequent bouts of depression had rolled cold and deep. They had reminded him that he *was* a capable man, a man others valued for his own achievements and ability, and the Seminary would inevitably grow. He could place his stamp upon it, build something that was the product of his hands and his heart that, in time, might deserve the respect he craved from Thomas Ewing. Besides, he'd liked Louisiana. There were things he didn't care for about Southerners, but that was true of Northerners, as well. He'd liked and respected the Louisianans, they'd respected him, and he'd accepted the offer on the spot.

Ellen had *not* been pleased when he telegraphed her that he had. She'd had her heart set on London. Besides, like the rest of her family, she had powerful Abolitionist beliefs. She despised slaveowners, and she'd refused even to visit Louisiana.

Despite that, he'd dug into his new duties, and the truth was that however disappointed Ellen might have been, *he* had never been happier, never more aware that he was building something out of his own skill and effort and determination. And his time in Louisiana had brought him back into contact with old comrades from the Army and West Point, not least Hébert, who, along with Graham, had been delighted to give him entrée into the first circles of the state. He'd spent many weekends at the Hébert sugar plantation in Iberville, and renewed his friendship with Hébert's family.

Obviously, that happiness had revealed itself in his letters to Ohio, and almost exactly a year ago today, Ellen had decided to visit Louisiana after all. Officially, she'd come to bring the children to visit him and to see with her own eyes what he was building. Actually, he had known she'd hoped to convince him to give up Louisiana and "come home," but he'd hoped he might be able to convince her to stay in Louisiana, instead.

She had stayed. But not the way he'd hoped.

He opened his eyes again, gazing bleakly down at the busy street.

Typhoid fever.

God knew there were outbreaks enough of it in Ohio, but, of course, none of the Ewings cared about that. Ellen had come to Louisiana to contract it, and that meant *Louisiana* had killed her. It meant Sherman's "stubborn" refusal to "come home" to Ohio had killed her.

It meant *he* had killed her.

Perhaps he had. He sometimes thought that, in the stillness of his own heart. And he knew her death, alone, would have driven a wedge between him and his family and his in-laws. But he hadn't left it there, had he? Oh, no.

They hadn't been there, he thought. Hadn't seen Ellen in that mosquito-netted bed in Iberville, while the Hébert family fought to save her. Like Ellen, the Héberts were devout Roman Catholics.

Their parish priest had visited daily, and Hébert's sister Marie had nursed her through every stage of her illness. Been there every single day. Slept on a cot in the same bedroom at night. Ellen's parents hadn't seen their daughter in the grip of delirium, clinging to Marie Hébert's hand as if to life itself while Marie sat with her, read to her...prayed with her. Hadn't seen Marie fighting every inch of the way, spending her own strength like fire, risking infection daily, *daring* the typhoid to take her as well. She'd poured her *life* into the fight, refused to give up.

And in the end, she'd had to watch as Ellen slipped away from them, into the shadows.

Her parents hadn't seen *any* of that...just as they hadn't heard Marie promise Ellen, promise her through her own tears as the light faded in Ellen's eyes and that emaciated body failed her at last, that she would take care of Ellen's children as if they were her own.

For six weeks, Marie had fought that fight at Ellen's side. She'd nursed her, read to her, sat setting embroidery stitches while Ellen napped fitfully. She'd become closer to her than her own sisters in those six horrible weeks...and she'd sat on the other side of Ellen's bed when it had been his turn to hold her hand, promise her he was there. Promise her he loved her.

And it was Marie who had embraced him through her own tears as Ellen lost her final fight at last. Marie who had—

Another door opened, and his nostrils flared as he turned from the window.

"I'm so sorry, Billy," she said softly.

Ellen, like everyone else in his family, had always called him "Cump." Marie never had. Now she crossed the hotel room to lay a hand on his forearm and stand looking up at him. She wasn't a tall woman, smaller and more fine-boned than Ellen had been, and he saw the tears in her eyes.

"I should have said no," she told him in that same soft, Southern voice. "It was too soon. Of course your family—Ellen's family—sees it that way."

"No." His headshake was firm. "It was what she wanted, too."

"That doesn't mean it was the right thing to do, Billy. And it's not as if Mrs. Ewing couldn't have raised the children without me. In fact, I'm sure that's what Ellen *would* have wanted, if her mind had only been clear."

She was a stubborn woman, Marie, Sherman thought. And she'd always defended the Ewings.

It was a pity none of them had ever so much as spoken to her.

"You may be right," he said now, "but I didn't ask for your hand only because of the children." He took that hand from his arm, raised it to his lips, and kissed it. "I asked for it because I saw you in that sickroom. Because I saw how you fought for her, exposed yourself to the same disease. Because I realized who you *are* and because I realized I loved that person. I wish, with all my heart, that Ellen were still alive, but that was in God's hands, not ours. You know that as well as I do. And I know you understand I truly loved her, and that there's a part of me that feels unspeakably guilty when I admit I love you, too. But I do, Marie. God help me, but I do."

And so do the children, he thought silently. The children she refused to let call her "mother," because she would never, ever, "steal" that title from Ellen. *They love you because you and your family were always there for them while their mother lay dying and I was too lost, too desperately worried about Ellen to be strong for them, too. They don't just love you—they* adore *you...and that's one more reason for Ellen's family to hate you.*

"But it's made such a mess." The tears hovered in her voice, as well, now. "What will you do now, Billy? What will become of us?"

"I don't know," he admitted. "I don't know."

He gathered her in his arms, and she laid her head upon his chest as he stood holding her and stared into the frightening void of the future. And not simply of his own future.

It seemed impossible, as they stood in this hotel room in the heart of the seventh largest city in the entire nation, yet even here, with the sounds of Cincinnati's busy streets coming to them through the closed window, the stink of distant blood was in his nostrils. He could feel it coming, and not all of Cincinnati's industry, all of its optimistic future, could change that.

In three weeks, Abraham Lincoln would take the oath of office as the sixteenth President of the United States, and God only knew what would happen then. But if the Peace Conference in Washington failed—and Sherman saw no way it could succeed—disaster waited for them all. South Carolina, Mississippi, Florida, Alabama, Georgia, Louisiana, and now Texas had already declared their secession from the Union, and other states hovered on the brink. Volunteers were rushing to form regiments, both North and South; arms were being stockpiled; and the first wrong move on the new Lincoln Administration's part would send some, at least, of those other hovering states into secession, as well.

For decades, the Republic had sown the wind. Now harvest time had come, and all across the country men faced the bitter decision. Did their swords belong to their nation...or to their states? Neither the doctrine of secession nor the battle cry of "states' rights" had originated in the South, but the South had embraced both of them ferociously, fanatically, taken them to the deadly height of their logical end, and Lincoln's election had ignited a fuse Sherman feared could lead to only one outcome.

Despite the Abolitionist stance of the Ewings and most of his own siblings—especially John—Sherman found much to admire in the South. And whatever the rights or wrongs of slavery, he fully understood why Southern Whites feared the Blacks who had been held in bondage for so long. The wrongs of the "peculiar institution" might be endless, yet even had the South been prepared to admit them all, it could not have magically erased that fear, and in the present, heated atmosphere—

Thirty years might have passed since Nat Turner's rebellion in Virginia, but the lunatic Brown's attempt to initiate another slave insurrection at Harpers Ferry lay barely sixteen months in the past. Its impact had loomed large on the 1860 elections, and Brown's transformation into a martyr after he'd been hanged had contributed to both Lincoln's election in the North and to the South's fury.

William Tecumseh Sherman had lived in Kansas. He knew the bloody-handed sorts of men who had flocked to both sides of the struggle there. Knew the fanatic stripe of both the pro-abolition and pro-slavery extremists, and Brown—John Brown of Potawatomie—had come from that same frothing cauldron of arson, terror tactics, and murder. If he'd been better than some, he'd been worse than many, and Sherman understood why the South saw him as the terrorist and insurrectionist he'd set out to be at Harpers Ferry. In their eyes, the abolitionists who had transformed him into a martyr and messiah had simply shown their own true colors, proclaimed precisely what they wanted to happen *throughout* the South, and that had become one more faggot to fuel the nation's blazing sectional fury.

Sherman himself believed secession was illegal, but he also doubted that it mattered very much. The American colonies' rebellion against George III had clearly been "illegal"…until it succeeded. As Sir John Harrington had said almost three centuries before, treason "never prospered," because if it did, if it succeeded, then it was no longer treason, and so *successful* session would *become* legal after the fact. He knew too much history to think it could be any other way.

But as a soldier, William Tecumseh Sherman had sworn an oath to "support and defend the Constitution of the United States against all enemies, foreign and domestic," and as a pragmatist, he feared secession's inevitable consequences. The United States of America spanned a continent. He suspected that few in Europe realized what that meant, realized how enormous the United States actually was. Certainly few of the Europeans he'd met had seemed to truly grasp that it was twice as far from New York to San Francisco as from Paris to Saint Petersburg, or that New Orleans lay farther from Chicago than Berlin from Rome. The notion of a single nation—a republic—that size was simply something for which the history of the world offered no basis for comparison.

Ultimately, he knew, as the continent's vast, empty spaces filled, the Union would become the most powerful nation in the world. "Manifest Destiny," Mr. O'Sullivan had called it in the *Morning News* when Texas was annexed, and he'd been right. Nothing could stop that onrushing expansion. It was as inevitable as fate.

Unless…

If secession "prospered," that enormous union would crumble. It would splinter into at least two nations, and quite probably more, because once secession was validated by success, who could stop the process the next time "irreconcilable differences" flared? From one vast, growing nation, it would disintegrate into a patchwork of potentially warring states, like Europe, fighting like snarling dogs over what should have been their common birthright. But how was that to be avoided?

Sherman blamed President Buchanan, in large part, for allowing inflamed passions to drive policy to its present pitch. If he had said, bluntly, that the Federal government would use force to compel obedience to the Constitution and heeded Winfield Scott's advice to increase the strength of the Army and to garrison the Federal posts throughout the South, then at least a line would have been drawn, the grim reality of the options would have been in the open. But instead, Buchanan had allowed partisan interests to block fresh recruitment and done nothing to deploy Federal troops. Only eighteen companies—just *eighteen*, all of them Artillery, out of an Army that numbered a bare 18,000 men—were stationed *anywhere* east of the Mississippi, and he'd done nothing to change that.

His inert response was understandable, perhaps, given his personal sympathy for the South. True, he'd used his final message to Congress, less than two months ago, to deny the legal right of states to secede. But he'd denied it only after enumerating all of the reasons that justified Southern anger…and then gone on to say that "the injured States, after having first used all peaceful and constitutional means to obtain redress," would be justified in "revolutionary resistance"—*extralegal* resistance—to the Government of the Union if that redress was not found.

A more feckless response was impossible to imagine. First he'd infuriated the South by denying the legality of the right to secede it had championed for so long. And then he'd infuriated the *North* by asserting that the South had a *moral* right to do just that...whatever the law might say.

Looking into the future's hollow-skull eyes with bleak honesty, Sherman saw no way any successor—and certainly not one like Lincoln, elected by a simple plurality in a race where no candidate had won a majority of the vote—could recover from the position Buchanan had left him. No way anyone could avert the looming wreck. And that meant that, like all those other men, he, William Sherman, had to decide where his sword belonged.

He had decided. Not without an agonizing internal struggle, but he'd decided. That was why he'd resigned as the Seminary's superintendent last month when the state government demanded the muskets stored in the school's armory. Those muskets were the lawful property of the United States government, which had provided them to the school. He'd had no authority to hand them over to the state. And as he'd said to George Graham in his letter of resignation, "I accepted such position when Louisiana was a state in the Union, and when the motto of this Seminary was inserted in marble over the main door: 'By the liberality of the general government of the United States. The Union—*esto perptua*.'"

Graham had understood. So had Marie. Just as she'd understood why he'd felt compelled to seek an Army commission once more rather than simply stand upon the sidelines. But his efforts had been rejected in a chilly, formal letter "regretting" that "the Department can find no employment for your services at this time."

Now he knew why. His foster father, Thomas Ewing's political allies, even his own brother, had thrown their influence into denying the man they blamed for Ellen Ewing Sherman's death a commission. And there was clearly no hope of changing their minds.

"Billy?"

He looked down as Marie lifted her head from his chest.

"Yes?"

"Billy, what will you decide now?" she asked him softly. "I know you've done what you believed you had to do, and whether or not it's the choice I would prefer you make, I respect you for it. I came with you to Cincinnati, and whither you go, I will go, too, even if that's to Washington City itself. But, Billy, these people..." She shook her head. "These people are not worthy of what you've tried to give them. Of the oath you swore or the service of your sword. They aren't worthy of *you*. Perhaps, someday, they will be again. Perhaps someday they'll understand what they've thrown away. But not today, Billy. Not today. So come home. Come home, where people *do* love you, and let your heart heal."

"Marie, I can't just turn my back—" he began, but she shook her head again.

"I haven't asked you to," she said simply. "I will *never* ask you to take up arms in any cause which is not your own. I will respect your decision, whether it is to remain in Louisiana or to leave her. To serve her if it comes to war, or to give your sword to neither side. Or even to return here and once again seek to give that sword to those people in Washington City and fight *against* Louisiana, should that be what your heart demands. Whatever decision you make, I know it will be one of honor. I will be content with that, whatever it is, and wherever you may go, I will be *proud* to stand beside you. But don't break your heart beating it against the bars while the people who ought to love you lock the door against you. Give them some time to heal, to realize the truth, as well."

He gazed down at her, the sounds of the street coming through the window behind them, and realized she was right in at least one sense. He'd come here, whether he had known it or not, on a fool's errand. There was no commission for him here, no opportunity to serve. And neither was there any way to support his wife and his children when those children's grandfather would use all of his influence to ensure he couldn't.

"Very well, my love," he said finally. "Perhaps you're right. Clearly, any more time here would be wasted. And perhaps some peaceful resolution can be found after all. But if it can't—"

"Hush, Billy." She reached up, placed her fingers across his lips. "I said I'll respect your decision, and I will. Now take me home while you make it."

* * *

"A courier, General."

General William Sherman looked up, then drew rein as the dust-caked courier cantered closer under the hot September sun. The youthful lieutenant reached him and saluted sharply.

"Lieutenant Stevens." Sherman returned the salute with a wry smile. "I almost didn't recognize you under all that dust. I presume you bear word from General Hampton?"

"I do, Sir." The lieutenant opened his dispatch case to extract a sealed message. "This is his formal dispatch, but I was instructed to verbally inform you that Jeffries' Brigade was attacked by enemy cavalry this morning. The attack appears to have been made by local militia and it was repulsed with only light casualties and several prisoners were taken. General Hampton wishes me to assure you that his column's rate of advance will not be retarded."

"I see."

Sherman called up a mental map of his columns' lines of march and nodded to himself. McPherson's defeat at Madison had smashed the last organized army in his path almost two months ago. There'd been a fair amount of skirmishing since then, more of it in Hampton's front than anywhere else, but like this affair, all of it had been fleabite bickering organized out of whatever volunteers might be to hand. Resistance might stiffen if the enemy found a way to free the troop strength to replace McPherson's shattered Army of the West, but with the intensity of the fighting in Virginia…

"Thank you, Lieutenant." He passed the dispatch to his chief of staff. "Please return to General Hampton and inform him that I would have expected no other outcome."

"Yes, Sir!"

The lieutenant saluted again, wheeled his horse, and went dashing back the way he'd come.

"It must be nice to be so full of energy," his chief of staff observed, and Sherman snorted.

"What you mean, James," he said, "is that it must be nice to be so *young*."

"I'd hardly call forty-four 'ancient,' General," Colonel Adcock replied in a dry tone.

"Then you should try experiencing it from *my* side." Sherman shifted in the saddle, and Adcock chuckled.

Sherman lifted his canteen and sipped from it as he watched the long, dusty column march past. Other columns—columns of smoke, not men and horses and guns—rose in the distance. Most came from burning fields or barns, but some streamed up from the fires heating railroad rails before his troops twisted them into "Sherman's neckties" around handy tree trunks to prevent repair crews from simply spiking them back into place. He watched that smoke and his jaw tightened as he remembered his letter to Governor Norton when he'd severed his logistics from the river and set out across Norton's state, foraging his way in a fifty-mile wide swath of destruction through the heart of its cornfields and wheat fields, its pastures and orchards, to sustain his advance.

"War is cruelty," he'd written when Norton had furiously denounced his troops' "looting" and the "savage outrages" along his scorched-earth march. "There is no use trying to reform it; the crueler it is, the sooner it will be over."

That had never meant he *enjoyed* destruction. He hated it. But so long as these people continued to support the armies in the field, they were just as much the enemy as those armies were. And those armies could not survive without the fodder they produced, the horses and mules they raised for the Army, the beeves and hogs they sent forward to feed its soldiers. The enemy's field strength had begun to dwindle as defeat followed defeat, and desertion and draft riots had become an ever-growing problem for him as war weariness cut ever deeper. Yet these rich farms continued to feed and bolster those beleaguered armies and keep them stubbornly fighting. It was time the people of those farms learned the price of supporting a war that dragged on and on, killing men—their own fathers and brothers and sons, as well as their enemies—by the thousand, day after day. He would spare their lives, but he would also teach that lesson to them, however harshly he must. And the instant they were willing to make peace, to end the killing, he would extend a helping hand once more. He knew they would go on hating him until the day he died, whatever he did, but that mattered less than nothing beside duty and the need to *end* this before the entire continent was littered with battlefield graves.

He recapped the canteen and urged his horse back into motion.

"How much longer do you reckon this can go on, Sir?" Adcock asked, as if he'd heard his commander's thoughts, and Sherman turned to cock an eyebrow at him as they rode side-by-side. "It's just that it seems it's already gone on forever," the colonel continued, quietly enough no one else could hear, "and the armies are *still* deadlocked in Virginia."

"They are," Sherman replied after a moment, "and they'll stay that way. But these people have run out of armies to stop us, because they have no one to pull away from the Washington-Richmond fighting. The truth is that the war's already been won in the West, whatever happens in the East. These people may not have realized that yet, and with Washington and Richmond only a hundred miles apart, it's inevitable that all eyes are on the Army of Northern Virginia and the Army of the Potomac. But I expect it's starting to dawn on them that when they lost control of the Mississippi and the Missouri and the Tennessee, that was the beginning of the end. I knew that when we threw them out of Chattanooga. And England and France both declared *their* recognition of the truth when they established their embassies in New Orleans."

"Perhaps so, Sir." Adcock nodded, but his tone was doubtful. "It's just that *they* don't seem to realize that."

"Oh, I expect some of them did realize it even then." Sherman shook his head. "It's not something a fellow finds easy to admit, though, and there are stubborn men on both sides of this war. That's the reason we're out here burning farms and confiscating livestock, Colonel." His expression turned grim. "They won't admit it until they're so thoroughly whupped they have no choice. And then, perhaps, we can get back to rebuilding everything we've had to destroy."

He tapped his temple with one forefinger.

"Inside here, James. Inside here. That's where we have to convince them to cave in…or they have to convince *us*. And unless I'm mistaken, we'll know in about two months which side is going to do just that."

"The election." Adcock grimaced. "You really think that will decide things?"

"I think it almost has to, after four years." Sherman's jaw tightened. "Giving in—or not giving in—always happens in the mind. And unless I miss my guess, General McClellan's already given in."

"Who do you think will win, Sir?

"Everything indicates the vote will be a near run thing, but it's trending against the Administration, I think," Sherman replied. "And if McClellan wins—"

He shrugged, and Adcock nodded as they neared another mile marker.

"I expect all this—" the colonel waved a hand at the marching men, the columns of smoke, the creaking supply wagons of a massive army headed east "— will have a certain influence in the final vote, Sir."

"That's why we're here, James." Sherman's eyes were bleak and dark with regret, but they were also unyielding, and his nostrils flared as he gazed at the signpost. "I never wanted to come home this way, and I'd sooner never see another farm or another town in flames. But that's why we're here. And it's why I've been pushing so hard ever since we left the river. I want this done now, while there's time for the lesson to sink in. If we can show these people—and *ours*— that we can take even their largest cities, we may just give those voters another reason to think *hard* about who's caving in to whom, come election day. So I suppose we'd best be about it."

He touched his horse with a heel, urging it to greater speed, and it sprang into a trot as they passed the signpost.

"CINCINNATI—20 MILES," it said.

* * * * *

Historical Note

The only non-historical character in this short story is Marie, Sherman's second wife, and even she actually existed. She died in infancy, however, so I felt free to appropriate her for the story.

William T. Sherman was a much more complex and "modern" man then I think most people realize. He was deeply opposed to secession and a division of the Union (mostly for reasons I address in the story), but he liked and admired Southerners, and despite the abolitionists in his own family and foster family, he was not utterly opposed to slavery. Few people realize that not only was he the first superintendent of what ultimately became LSU, but that he was also offered a commission in the state militia of Louisiana. He declined the commission, resigned his post, and returned to Ohio, where his foster father (who was also his father-in-law) helped him get the commission he had originally been denied.

One of the ways in which he was a "modern" man was in his approach to warfare. Under the rules of war of the 19th century, his tactics when marching through Georgia were fully justified on the basis that Georgia was a "rebellious province," but it was never his intention simply to punish evil people or inflict unnecessary cruelty. Rather, he felt that the cruelty he was practicing *was* necessary. That it was actually the greater mercy, because it would cripple the South's ability to support its remaining armies and thus end the war—and the killing—and restore the Union in the shortest possible time.

He was a man who believed deeply in personal responsibility, personal honor, and duty to country. He was also a very personally motivated and driven man, however, and I have deliberately placed him in a position where those factors governed his final decision as to where his military skills actually belonged.

Someday, I intend to write the novel of which this short story forms a tiny portion. I suspect that many of my Southern friends will come hunting for me when I do, given how universally beloved Sherman is in the South.

I would point out, however, that he did *not* burn Atlanta. John Bell Hood did that. Just saying.

* * *

David Weber Bio

David Mark Weber is an American science fiction and fantasy author. He was born in Cleveland, Ohio in 1952. Weber and his wife Sharon live in Greenville, South Carolina with their three children and "a passel of dogs."

Previously the owner of a small advertising and public relations agency, Weber now writes science fiction full time.

\# \# \# \# \#

To the Rescue
by S.M. Stirling

"I can see why December isn't prime tourist season in France," Colonel Theodore Roosevelt—junior, and usually known as Ted to his friends—said.

"Yeah, I was expecting beaches and bathing beauties and casinos, sir," McGregor said in his Missouri rasp from the gunner's position below and behind the commander's cupola.

He could see out too, though more narrowly through the telescopic sight of the cannon.

There certainly weren't many girls not over-encumbered with clothing and morals visible on December fifth in this year of not-much-grace nineteen sixteen. Not in this up-country north-central part of France near Nevers, at least. It had been snowing off and on for days, and the temperature was in the twenties in this early morning hour. Surprisingly, that was low enough to be a little chilly even in the usually stuffy engine-heated interior of an armored fighting vehicle, with its stinks of exhaust, hot lubricating oil, sweat and nitro powder. Weather and politics were synchronized this year all over the northern hemisphere, as a wretched autumn that had ruined crops from Kansas to China shaded into record cold, so that the countless refugees trudging the roads and sleeping in ditches could freeze as well as starve.

"And I think there are people here who don't like us, sir," McGregor added.

Roosevelt grinned to himself as something clanged off the turret of his Lobo Mk. I. It was probably shrapnel or a shell fragment, but might be a rock the shelling had kicked up. He pitied the infantry out there. Anything on a battlefield could kill them. There were only a few weapons that could kill a tank, and there weren't very many of them at any one spot. That was the whole point.

The vision blocks of the tank were an improvement on the ones in the Lynx Mk. V armored car he'd been using until recently—tanks were a novelty this year, whereas he'd ridden across the border into Mexico in one of the first experimental armored cars with Pershing in '13—but the view was still limited. Right now, it mostly involved the rest of the 2nd Cavalry (mechanized) HQ company's vehicles spread out over the white-and-black winter fields, and the night-colored poplar-shapes of dirt thrown up by German whizbangs—shells from 77mm field guns.

Each had a bright momentary red spark at its heart, like a malignant evil eye winking at you as the slab-sided mass of riveted armor lurched forward at about twice walking pace. He bared his teeth as one close round made the tank rock as it crested a slight ridge. That jarred his left arm, currently in a sling due to a round even closer than that; the medics had tried to make him head for the rear right away, but there was work to do first.

Time for morphine and convalescence later. That's a keep-their-heads-down barrage. German doctrine tells their infantry to hug the bombardment. They're coming.

The 27th Division had gone into line against the Germans right off the boats and trains; it was an illustration of the difference between even well-equipped and trained green troops and real combat veterans, though they were learning fast—the survivors were, at least, right now how to do a fighting retreat. Time to knock the pursuers back on their heels…

The bombardment moved further south.

Aimed at the 27th…or what's left of it, not us, he thought. *They haven't realized what's coming up on them. The enemy infantry should be in sight soon.*

He could see bodies in the infinitely drab grey-brown-green of modern American field uniforms, and a Lewis-gun team in a crater waiting for the boys in equally inconspicuous *feldgrau*; the colors weren't that different, so the quickest visual recognition signal was the shapes of the helmet, the flared turtle dome of the American model and the coal-scuttle German. The Americans were trying to help the French to dig in and establish their new Loire Front solidly. The storming advance of the Kaiser's legions *had* slowed at least. The new duo of Generals Foch and Lyautey, who were as much government as France had these days, claimed it was because they were getting a grip on things.

Roosevelt's own opinion was that the Germans were slowing down mainly because they were outrunning their supplies, not because of French resistance; bringing anything across the wreckage of the old Western Front and its poisoned remnants had to be a nightmare. And he thought Foch and Lyautey knew it, which was why they were shoveling every French civilian into anything that could cross the Mediterranean and dumping them in French North Africa—newly christened as the National Redoubt.

When the Huns get the railways working again over the old front line it's kitty bar the door, he thought grimly. *Our logistics stink even worse, and we can't improve them by making prisoners repair a rail line and die.*

They'd hit the 27th and its neighbors an almighty knock with their *stosstruppen* and infiltration tactics, which were just as nasty as the reports said, or more so. The only good thing was that they weren't using V-gas anymore, and hadn't since the 6th of October.

That's because they know we captured hundreds of tons of V-gas when we took the U-boats they sent to destroy our east coast cities. They don't want it shot back at them.

V-gas stood for *Vernichtungsgas*, Annihilation Gas. Some were calling it horror-gas; it was fantastically more lethal than chlorine or phosgene or even nitrogen-mustard, some sort of nerve agent so deadly that a tiny dot the size of a period at the end of a sentence on your skin would kill. The Zeppelins had unloaded hundreds of tons of it on the Entente's capital cities, and shells had rained down as much more on trenches, artillery parks and railway junctions from the North Sea to the Swiss frontier. A million troops and three times that number of civilians had died in the course of one day. Indirectly it had killed as many again since then, and the toll wasn't complete. Reports said even Hindenburg and Ludendorff had been surprised— and the Kaiser fainted dead away, not having been told about it before the massacre of his British royal relatives and legions of their subjects.

But they don't know we don't have much horror-gas ready to deploy yet because it's so hard to get it out of the rocket-mortar shells without killing everyone concerned.

Fortunately the American tanks showed two could play at the game of deadly surprises. There was more ringing hail on the armored hull of his beast—the men were calling it the *Lobo*, the wolf, as well as the code-name that had stuck as a descriptor for the type of machine in general. After the Intervention, modern American military jargon was chock-full of bits of Spanish.

The clanging on the hull went on and on, a Maxim gun's distinctive stutter, and 7.92 rounds went peening off the steel in trails of sparks he could see through the vision blocs, enough to mow down a company's worth of men caught in the open. Machine-guns had ruled the Great War's battlefields…until this year.

A ruined stone farmhouse lay ahead, blackened by fire and with its roof caved in, smoke-marks up from all of the windows…but ruins made good strongpoints, and he caught muzzle flashes from a basement window. They might not know what a tank was or what it could do, but they did know it was American—the white star was a giveaway.

"Driver, tank halt. Loader, HE," he said into the speaking-tube.

There were three men in a Lobo Mk. I's turret, and together with the gear they filled the squarish shape—that was one more crewman that his old Lynx armored car had needed in Mexico. A Lynx used a pom-pom firing little shells from a belt as its main armament.

The loader was a weasel-quick, wiry-strong young man named Martinez who swore he was from Laredo, Texas and probably actually hailed from well south of there. Regardless of nationality, Martinez was snake quick as he plucked a 57mm shell out of the rack at the rear of the turret and slammed it into the breech of the six-pounder cannon. One of the privileges of command was picking the best from the replacement pool as the Great War and conscription continued the yearly doubling or tripling the Army had undergone since the plunge into Mexico in 1913. And the—unwritten—policy was to accept Mexican volunteers and provide identity papers to regularize them. He'd noticed Martinez that spring when the first tanks reached them, and he needed to expand the three-man crew of his personal Lynx to five.

Desmond up in the bow geared down and then put the tank into neutral, and Roosevelt jammed his good hand against the front of the cupola as the massive weight surged forward and back and then settled still on its treads. The sheer inertia of these beasts required care.

The British had been working on tanks, too, when London was destroyed on October 6th, though they'd gotten no further than pro-totypes: Their *landships* had been pushed by the head of the Navy, of all things, a man called Churchill who'd fallen from office, gone out as a battalion commander and met a shell almost immediately, which had taken the steam out of it. The two projects even had the same cover story as armored water-tanks, hence the name.

Roosevelt had seen the plans for theirs. There were advantages to the fact that his father was President, and that General Wood, the Chief of the General Staff, was a longstanding friend of the family and honorary uncle. Helped along by the fact that Roosevelt Jr. had won the Medal of Honor during the Mexican Intervention in a way even his father's enemies admitted was fully justified, though they tended to attribute it to both father and son being bloodthirsty mani-acs.

Which is just what you'd expect of hysterical poltroons like William Jennings Bryan and Woodrow Wilson.

The British experimental vehicles were huge rhomboidal mon-sters with the guns in sponsons on the side of an absurdly high hull rather than a turret and no suspension between track and hull at all—possibly because their top speed was about four miles an hour, as opposed to twenty for the Lobo. The American version had tracks running on three two-wheel bogies on each side cushioned by massive springs. It wasn't a soft ride, but it was much better than nothing at keeping you from being battered to death.

"Up! Up!" Martinez shouted as the breechblock clanged shut: which meant *loaded and ready.*

"Target machine gun; ten o'clock, range six hundred, McGregor," Roosevelt said to the gunner. "In that basement window."

"Got it, Colonel," the gunner said, spinning the traversing wheel; they'd been together since '13.

Including that monumental screwup in Durango. By God, just surviving *that was worth a medal! Turning it around...I should have gotten promoted to God, j.g., not just handed the Medal of Honor and a major's bars!*

The turret moved with a whir and clack of manually-driven gears meshing—there was talk of an electric or hydraulic motor, but everything was short and time most of all. McGregor's foot flicked up the guard-bar with a clang and touched the firing pedal.

"On target!"

"Fire!" Roosevelt barked.

One of the things I like about armored cars...and tanks...is that you get to fight personally even if you're a commander...and you're not *being irresponsible.*

Crack on the last syllable of the order, and the six-pounder cannon recoiled like the piston in an engine, just missing the loader as he bent and ducked in drilled reflex.

"Hit! Hit!" McGregor said.

The twenty-six tons of the tank rocked back on its suspension slightly—that was pure Newton, since the shell moved at eighteen hundred feet per second. There was a backflash from the basement window as it exploded within…then a bigger one, with sparks flying out at high speed and a crackling like fireworks on the 4th of July. The noise of the secondary explosions was audible even through the armor and engine-growl. Someone had left a can of belted machine-gun ammunition where they shouldn't, or maybe a crate of grenades.

Or both. Probably both.

Seconds later smoke began drifting up—evidently there was something in there still ready to burn, too.

Then figures in *feldgrau* and coal-scuttle helmets broke free of the re-burning ruined farmhouse. One had a Lewis gun in his arms, and several of the others had Thompsons, unmistakable with the drum magazine; all of them had stick-grenades thrust through loops on their webbing and they were moving in a quick zig-zagging sprint towards a location picked in advance.

Those boys have been to school.

Roosevelt didn't need to say anything; his crew had been ready for survivors to break cover rather than choke or fry.

McGregor cut loose with the coaxial machine-gun, a .50 Browning, and the bow-gunner—an Oklahoman named Albert Drowning Bear—was an artist with the .30 in a ball-mount in front of him. He claimed his name also meant "Chief," which was what everyone called him. He was also a wireless radio enthusiast, which helped since unlike most, this commander's vehicle had a two-way set as of June 15th and he doubled as its operator.

Tracers stabbed at the Germans and dirt spurted up all around them. Several fell, limp or thrashing. Roosevelt felt a cold satisfaction. Germany had attacked America first, and without warning, back at the beginning of October.

Though granted, we were obviously getting ready *to intervene,* Theodore thought. With the Mexican Intervention's demands winding down as the Protectorate turned peaceful, the Army and Navy had both been newly enormous and thoroughly prepared. Even more ominous from the German perspective, the Army had begun to add multiple divisions per month as universal service took hold.

Only inspired work by the US secret services had kept the V-gas strike from killing millions of Americans too. Despite warning and frantic evacuation, over a thousand military and civilians *had* died in Savannah, which was the only port where the U-boat had survived long enough to surface and launch.

So Germans in general had it coming...

The survivors went to ground in an outbuilding and shot back, showing more balls than brains—or just less experience with tanks. A Lewis gun was nearly as portable as a rifle; both sides built their squads around them now.

Dad made our Army adopt the Lewis back in '13, he thought.

The innovative, scientifically-inclined President had had to fire the chief of the Ordnance Department, a reactionary fossil named Crozier, to do it.

Then the Kaiser made the German Army adopt it when he saw that newsreel film of Dad shooting a Lewis from the hip in '13...which was just so absolutely like him, and the Kaiser. Then in '14 they thought up the quick-change barrel, and we adopted that. Then Thompson came up with his gun, and God, wasn't that useful in Mexico...so the Germans copied that in 9mm last year, and found it was even more *useful for trench fighting. Everyone copies everything these days; isn't Progress grand?*

"Driver, forward to that stone wall two hundred yards northwest. Loader, HE."

Clang again, as the loader worked the lever of the breech and the shell sprang out to clatter with others at the bottom of the turret basket. A fresh wave of sharp-smelling gasses from nitro powder joined the staler previous residues, to a chorus of coughs; that was why you delayed opening the breech after a shot if you could.

Roosevelt kept a mental list of suggestions and wrote it down most evenings unless he was fighting for his life; *some way of keeping fumes out of the turret* went on it now. It had been bad enough with the breeches of a machine-gun and a pom-pom in with you. A real cannon bid fair to choke the crew like poison gas, especially when artillery fire made you keep the hatches closed—that hadn't been a problem in Mexico, where the enemy started with a few guns and kept none after a couple of months.

They halted again by the stone wall, but before he could give the order to fire heavy Stokes mortar rounds began smacking into the place he'd marked as where the German Lewis-gun team had set up, though they were bobbing and weaving between one firing position and another. The finned bombs—those were an American innovation, though Stokes was British—were nearly silent until they arrived; he couldn't hear them at all inside the turret or even the *bampf* of firing.

Then they exploded with a fast *crump-crump-crump*, as fast as the gunner could drop them down the tube, throwing dirt and dirty snow and rock...and probably parts of bodies and weapons...into the air.

He looked back, and saw that another tank—this one a turretless model functioning as a mortar carrier—had come up a few hundred yards back and opened fire, showing commendable initiative. The American army thought highly of that; unfortunately, so did the other side. Two more of the same type accelerated forward as it did; those would each have a squad of dragoon infantry with Thompsons and grenades, ready to hop out over the side and mop up.

He grinned again, the distinctive tooth-baring expression he shared with his father: it was with pride this time. The 2nd Cavalry's motto was *Toujours Prêt*—Always Ready—and they were living up to it. He'd been in the 2nd since 1913 when the Mexican Intervention started, beginning as a captain and moving up to command the regiment as of this spring—and helped them live up to it.

The radio had been clicking for a minute. As they halted, Drowning Bear spoke, "Sir. Orders from Division."

There was a rustle as the loader leaned forward. Glancing down, Roosevelt could just see a big brown hand—Chief was a big man, and about two-thirds Cherokee—extending backward with a page torn off his message pad. His father's famous Rough Rider regiment had included a lot of men of Indian or part-Indian or Mexican blood. The vast volunteer influx in '13 had imitated that, along with much else, and Chief had been among the rush to the colors.

Martinez handed it up to McGregor, who passed it to the commander.

"It's a pretty odd message, sir," he added as the colonel read.

It started: *Orders from GHQ follow*—

Roosevelt's eyebrows went up; that meant Expeditionary Force HQ just outside Marseilles. Regimental commanders didn't usually get directives from that level. From the date-stamp they'd come in during the last half-hour, which meant minimal time taken on coding, something only done for urgent matters that would be over too quickly to make the enemy listening in relevant.

"What the hell?" Roosevelt said as he took in the brief directive. "Chief, you sure of this?"

The 1st Mechanized Division was the point of the spear, though—they'd been brought over despite the logistical problems of feeding their thousand-odd vehicles with gasoline because they could really *move*, four or five times the speed of a conventional infantry outfit even without counting their ability to punch through opposition. The 2nd Cavalry were the very *tip* of the point of the spear, and probably the only coherent American unit close enough to what seemed to be a sudden emergency to have any hope of getting there in time.

American agents with crucial repeat crucial secret enemy device have crashed in captured German airship at your square G-7.

He glanced at his current tactical map; Square G-7 was about six miles away, across territory under Entente control until last Monday and which nobody really controlled at present…According to the French ordnance survey this map was based on there was absolutely nothing there except a large farmhouse or small manor, some outbuildings, a road and woods and fields, the woods thickening towards the north and west.

"All right, this is like something out of *Argosy All-Story*," he muttered.

That was the magazine that published the likes of Edgar Rice Burroughs and A.A. Merritt; at nearly thirty, Roosevelt considered himself beyond his youthful consumption of that sort of thing. Though he had a good friend with a first-class mind only a few years younger who devoured them, interplanetary travel, lost cities, lost races, evil occult masterminds, and mad scientists with secret weapons and all.

"On the other hand, God knows this war has been full of nasty technical surprises," he went on.

"Damn right, sir," McGregor said.

"October 6th for starters, colonel," Drowning Bear added.

Roosevelt read on: *German air and ground forces moving to recapture material. Maximum repeat maximum priority that agents and material be recovered regardless of cost. Proceed with all speed. Air units also moving to support; recognition code in force. Impossible to overstate importance of mission.*

"Well, that's unambiguous, at least," he muttered.

Do it or die trying was about what it amounted to. Experienced soldiers rarely jumped for joy when they got that sort of order from on high.

Then he went on aloud: "Chief, acknowledge, say *will carry out*, then a message to the battalion commanders."

He looked at the map again, thinking rapidly. At least all the battalion and squadron commanders' vehicles had wireless—much more than would be present in an ordinary infantry unit. And they would need some extra transport for whatever-it-was that had the General Staff's knickers in such a painful twist.

"Dispositions as follow—"

* * *

"Well, that's spectacular," Roosevelt said, lowering his binoculars.

The gunner and loader were head-and-shoulders out of their hatches too—the cold damp air was paradise after the choking stinks inside—and were looking up as well.

"It's fucking awesome, sir," McGregor said.

Martinez whistled softly. *"¡Híjole!"* he said.

Which meant roughly the same thing—everyone in this crew could speak fair Spanish, and Roosevelt was quite fluent. He didn't swear much himself but it didn't disturb him the way it did his father, who would walk out of a room if someone started a mildly smutty story.

Then the loader went on in English:

"Many brave men will die very soon now."

There must be eighty or a hundred German airplanes diving from the north, dots swelling into shapes and the insect buzz of their engines growing towards a roar—sleek molded-plywood Albatross V fighting-scouts, the latest German model with twin Maxims. From the south came a similar sound, and an equal number of French Spads and Curtis Pumas—these climbing slightly, since the high overcast was lower there. They must be closing on each other at two hundred and fifty miles an hour combined speed...or better.

"We're not here to watch a football game," he said, as the *tacka-tacka-tacka* of machine-gun fire punctuated the engine-growl. "Here come the scouts."

A guvvie was coming down the frozen ruts of the muddy, tree-lined country road from the north—a little four-wheel-drive Model T in Army colors. It was crowded, with Captain Sanders of the regimental reconnaissance company, one of his men at a pintle-mounted Browning .30, and a scout-sniper team, one man with a scope-sighted variety of the old bolt-action Springfield called a Sharpshooter, and his spotter-partner cradling a Thompson. They wore white-and-brown covers over their winter parkas and helmets, and the rifle was decked out in strips of burlap to break the telltale outlines.

"Report, Corporal," Roosevelt called.

The spotter with the Thompson unwound his lanky height from the guvvie, hopped down, sprang lithely onto the bow of the commander's Lobo and up to the turret. Close-to, his face had a narrow knobby angular look that his hillbilly twang confirmed. Many of the best scouts and snipers came from the southern hill country, and an old Regular Army outfit like the 2nd recruited from all over the country, not just from a single military conscription district.

"Well, we-uns went up the road a ways, Colonel," he said with respect but no particular formality, tracing the north-trending road on the map with a gloved fingertip. "Them lumps unner the snow, they wuz bodies, like you figured."

Roosevelt's eyes went northward for a moment; that was about a thousand yards north and east, not far from the roadside.

"Whose?" he said.

"Frenchies, sir—civilians, a lot of 'em women and kids."

The Tennessean spat over the side of the tank into the snow, which might be an expression of opinion, or just a result of the chaw of tobacco that bulged one lean cheek and had stained his teeth brown, or both.

"Massacred?"

The Intervention in Mexico had been merciless enough, especially in the three years of putting down guerilla-bandit resistance by the likes of Villa and Zapata after the first stand-up battles, but what had happened in France over the last few weeks had set whole new standards in butchery. Equaled only by the Turkish destruction of the Armenians, but in the heart of what had called itself the civilized world and on an immense scale as the whole population of France seemed on the move.

"No, sir. Just…daid. From the looks of 'em, they ran as far an' as fast as they could after what the Boche did to Paris, then just laid down hungry and died in their sleep," the observer continued. "Them hard freezes we been gettin' the last week would do it, with them havin' no food to speak of and bein' city-folk not used to movin' cross-country and not dressed for it neither. There were some fires, burned out. All right pitiful to see, let me tell you."

His finger moved across the printed silk, up the road to the northeast until after it straightened and turned due north.

"Then just like the map says, there's a farmhouse—big place before it burnt, sorta like the one a planter would have down to Nashville way. There's outbuildings west of it, barns and stables 'fore they wuz wrecked up. Now *here*—"

His finger tapped a spot north of the buildings, about a thousand yards.

"Was where that there airboat came down. Crashed, but not too hard an' not burned. Not one of them big 'uns with a frame inside, looks like. Gondola 'bout, oh, fifty, sixty feet long, envelope about five, six times that afore the gas got out and it came down like an ol' wet sock."

Roosevelt nodded. "Semirigid, Naval type. We use similar ones."

Which is because there was mutual copying again.

"We didn't get close 'cause I could see movement east of the house, thousand, two thousand yards out and they'd see *us* if we broke cover, but I'm pretty sure whoever came down in that airboat lived through it an' made tracks for the farmhouse. And there's folks there—I could smell their smoke, cookin' smells like."

Roosevelt looked over his shoulder to the southwest. He could hear the thudding of artillery back there—German whizbangs, something louder that was probably howitzers, and the distinctive sounds of American field artillery too. The 1st Mechanized was mixing it in with whatever the Germans were sending forward, while he'd pushed northeastward at a slant right across the front of the German force with nothing more than some light skirmishing with men shocked and terrified with the unexpected impact of the tanks. They'd moved fast, too; he glanced at his wristwatch, a new fashion for men that the Great War had brought in, and it was still a little shy of 1030.

Such a temptation to hook northwest and take them in the flank, he thought. *But this up ahead must be exactly what the orders from GHQ were talking about. And orders are orders…*

"Chief," he said to the radio operator. "On the regimental push: we're going to rush them, in column up the road and don't deploy until we're under fire. Captain Johnson—"

Who commanded the reinforced company of dragoon infantry and their mortars.

"—is to swing west and take the outbuildings when we're in sight of the objective. Dismounted action and be cautious about fire support, there are friendlies in the farmhouse. Detach one platoon of dragoons to follow the HQ company. Lieutenant Kovacs—"

Which was a Magyar name, and meant…*smith*; some things were apparently universal.

"—is to have his engineers ready for a hasty salvage mission on the crashed airship. Get me confirmations."

Chief did. A year or two ago Roosevelt would have had to take time to get his commanders together and give his orders face-to-face, or risk one-way communication by runner if he was in a real hurry…which was generally the case. Sending things in code made the process far quicker and smoother.

The drawback, of course, was that this still wasn't like being able to talk to someone. Pretty soon wireless radio-telephones would be small and rugged enough to be used for jobs like this, but that day wasn't here yet.

He cocked an eye upward at the melee in the sky. His youngest brother Quentin—at nineteen just barely old enough for field service and with a teenager's conviction of his own immortality—was a fighting-scout pilot. When you combined that natural recklessness with the burden that being called Roosevelt put on a young man...not only from their father and the memory of San Juan Hill, but now from Ted's own Medal of Honor, too...that was a dangerous combination. Quentin might be up above his head right now.

A burning fighting-scout falling in a corkscrew nose-down spin plowed into the ground not two hundred yards to the north and exploded in a ball of flame, throwing bits and pieces all around. The tank commander shook his head; nothing to be done about that. Soldiering wasn't a safe profession.

"Let's go!" he said, waved a hand around his head and chopped it forward.

Before someone can strafe us from the air, he added to himself. *And our flanks are as exposed as a cootch-dancer's, too.*

* * *

A green flare went up from behind the ruined manor; that was Captain Johnson going in, and automatic weapons fire chattered—the typewriter clatter of Thompsons, and something sharper and faster that he didn't realize.

God-dammit, the Germans are inside there too! Roosevelt thought.

Tanks had any amount of punch, but they were an invitation to friendly fire losses if you if you tried to shoot into a hand-to-hand melee. His height gave him a good view of a fight he couldn't intervene in until his infantry came up—they'd dismounted and were running forward, but seconds counted.

"Get those!" he barked to McGregor.

The gunner was already turning the turret, and his first burst walked towards half a dozen Germans running towards the farmhouse, all of them carrying some sort of stubby automatic rifle with a curved high-capacity magazine, one he didn't recognize at all. They very sensibly pivoted in place and started running the other way, towards a creek running northwest-southeast about four hundred yards away.

"Load HE!" Roosevelt barked. "McGregor, let them have it as soon as they're far enough away!"

Behind the waist-high remains of the manor-house wall a deadly drama was unfolding inside the house. A big blond man, helmetless but in a German officer's uniform, smashed an American away, blood flying as the butt of the German's weapon cracked across his face.

A wounded man lying on the floor—also, oddly enough, in German uniform—was trying to shoot him with a Thompson, but it clicked empty.

Behind them in what had probably been a rear room—maybe a kitchen—a short figure in a leather flight-suit struggled to raise a Lewis as a German came at her in a limping but snake-fast rush, with a sharpened entrenching tool raised, his hideously scarred face contorted and pale blue eyes staring. Another American in flight gear fired a Sharpshooter sniper rifle from the hip.

Crack!

The little German's body snapped sideways as the bullet hit the blade of his entrenching shovel, punching through it and at a slant into his belly, the distorted shape of the bullet pinwheeling like a tiny buzz -saw. He screamed and staggered right into a burst from the Lewis gun that sent him flopping backward with most of his torso smashed into fragments of meat and bone. The gunner froze; nobody else was on their feet there, but two women in tattered civilian clothes were bandaging a wounded man in a French uniform that was almost as ravaged.

And out in the burned remnants of barn behind the house a brief savage firefight was raging, American Thompsons against the German whatever-they-were, a couple of grenades, and then a shout in an unmistakable hillbilly rasp:

"All daid, Loo-tenant! Ever'thang clar here!"

CRACK!

The tank rocked, oddly since the turret was turned to one side; Roosevelt darted a quick glance that way and saw most of the fleeing Germans fall, though one man managed to dive into cover. Inside the front room—what had once been an elegant country living-room, with the smashed remnants of a piano still lying in one cor-ner—the flight-suited American dropped the sniper rifle. A knife came up in his—

No, that's her hand—I recognize that knife! Roosevelt thought, as whispers of blasphemous amazement dropped from his lips.

—*her* hand, but her left was pressed to her side and face twisted in a rictus of effort.

The big blond German pulled his rifle free; the point of the bay-onet had struck in the boards of the floor. He saw the knife-wielder.

"¡Híjole!" she blurted, confirming his guess.

He'd known that voice since they were both children; Luz O'Malley—Luz O'Malley Aróstegui, daughter of one of the Rough Rider officers who'd gone to Cuba with his father, and childhood friend.

And Black Chamber agent since 1912. No wonder there's a secret weapon stolen from the Germans! She's the one who handed us Villa!

The German screamed, an endless racking snarl, weapon levelled leveled as he charged in a blur of motion. She left it until the last second, and twisted to her right, sweeping the knife at the rifle. Steel clanged on steel and the German went past her, dodging her backhand cut at his face by going under it with cat-quick grace. Roosevelt's breath caught.

Crack!

The German jerked and fell. The wounded American on the ground in German uniform started to laugh, looking at another ragged woman where she lay flat two paces away with a Luger in a clumsy two-handed grip. A woman...girl, he realized...half-dropped, half-flung a head-sized chunk of rock she was carrying down on the German's wound and slumped backward herself, collapsed against a snag of wall.

And Luz hobbled over and kicked the fallen German in the head, hard enough to make him go limp—but carefully, Roosevelt noted, not hard enough to kill him.

"¡Ay! But I bet that hurt you worse than it did me," she panted.

The one with the Lewis gun came up, sans machine-gun, and Luz leaned a hand on her shoulder—it was yet another woman—as she hobbled to the doorway.

Luz started to smile. The woman she was leaning on buried her head in Luz's neck and sighed, sliding an arm around her waist, and they helped each other out into the open.

"Hola," Luz said, as she closed her navaja and slipped it into the pocket of the flight suit.

Then: "Ted? *Ted?*"

Roosevelt pushed his goggles up onto the leather helmet he wore. He spoke into the cone of the speaking tube in front of him and the engine noise dropped to a ratcheting idle amid a cloud of blackish acrid-smelling exhaust fumes.

"Luz?" he said.

Almost as incredulously now that he was really sure, looking past the flight suit, and the scrapes and dirt and blood. The sharp comely dark features were unmistakable, full-lipped and high in the cheekbones, despite the way she wore a bandana over a head that seemed to lack her usual raven-black bob-cut.

"What the hell are *you* doing here?" he said.

"Spy work," she replied.

Yup, I guessed right, Roosevelt thought.

She pointed to the wreck of the airship to the northwest.

"Secure that, would you? Important ultra-secret German machinery in there. We need to get it back to our lines, pronto, and shipped home."

He called and waved and sent a squad of the dragoons to guard it: the engineers followed, moving their Model T truck—the new model, with four rear wheels—carefully.

"And what are *you* doing here, Ted? Not that I'm not grateful, but…"

He looked around at the wreckage of the farmhouse, and signaled several men with Red Cross armbands forward.

Then he slapped the side of the turret, where the 2nd Cavalry's palmetto leaf and eight-pointed shield were painted in white.

"I'm doing what the cavalry always does, Luz—ride to the rescue!" he said; that was what happened in those lurid tales in *Argosy All-Story* magazine she liked so much.

She laughed, though from the look of it that hurt. Ted Roosevelt joined in, though it jarred his arm and that hurt.

"Old times," he said; they'd been wounded in the same actions before, too. "Old times, Luz."

* * * * *

S.M. Stirling Bio

S.M. Stirling was born in France in 1953, to Canadian parents—although his mother was born in England and grew up in Peru. After that he lived in Europe, Canada, Africa, and the US and visited several other continents. He graduated from law school in Canada but had his dorsal fin surgically removed, and published his first novel (*Snowbrother*) in 1984, going full-time as a writer in 1988, the year of his marriage to Janet Moore of Milford, Massachusetts, who he met, wooed and proposed to at successive World Fantasy Conventions. In 1995, he suddenly realized that they could live anywhere and they decamped from Toronto, that large, cold, gray city on Lake Ontario, and moved to Santa Fe, New Mexico. He became an American citizen in 2004. His latest books are *Theater of Spies* (May 7th, 2019) and *Black Chamber* (July 3rd, 2018), Roc/Penguin Random House, with *Shadows of Annihilation* upcoming (March, 2020). His hobbies mostly involve reading—history, anthropology, archaeology, and travel, besides fiction—but he also cooks and bakes for fun and food. For twenty years he also pursued the martial arts, until hyperextension injuries convinced him he was in danger of becoming the most deadly cripple in human history. Currently he lives with Janet and the compulsory authorial cats.

# # # # #

The Blubber Battle: The First Falklands Campaign

by Joelle Presby & Patrick Doyle

April 1916

"Finally! Let's get off this rust bucket and go blow some shit up!" Lieutenant Marshall said.

The officer's pale skin and dark hair combined with his infectious grin had a recruiting poster polish to it, which was ironic since Navy staffers and political handlers alike had learned to avoid letting him anywhere near officer candidates or voters. His resemblance to his important uncle only intensified the effect.

Lieutenant Marshall threw a grease-stained set of coveralls at me underhand and a grin lit up his face like I hadn't seen on him since we left the Port of Hamburg.

This man will be the death of me. I struggled into the rough cloth, pulling it on over my pressed uniform. I hoped we'd be on land only for a night or two but this entire plan was short on details. Petty Officer Wicklow'd suggested we double the layers in this backwards southern hemisphere weather, and I agreed we'd be grateful for them during the chill nights.

And I'd not mentioned that it'd decrease our chances of being hung as spies if it all went wrong.

The *USS Denver (CL-14)* was a U.S. Navy protected cruiser in fine repair with a history of transporting lots of raiding parties small and large. It almost certainly did not qualify as a rust bucket. I checked the ship's deck for senior officers who might take offense and found none.

Nearly two dozen of the toughest sailors I could find assembled on deck in uniforms stained by years of coal dust shoveling. This lot would fade into the darkness quite as well as our brave rowers back in Port Doula had. Petty Officer Wicklow, with his telltale Boston Irish red hair, had the seventeen others lined up smartly and walked between them checking their packs and their boots. At least our petty officer had served on several raids in the past, even if the lieutenant and I were new to this business. Belatedly, I thought about just what the boss had said.

"We're only to take out the wireless station, sir. Then right back to the ship," I whispered at the lieutenant's ear. It wouldn't do to undermine him in front of the crew. He'd gotten used to some unorthodox ways of doing things in our time abroad.

There'd been that attack on Port Doula where we'd been rather more active as military observers than one would generally expect. And then he'd been sent to Germany with me tagging along to see if the good will from the role he'd had in Afrika might allow him a close view of military aeroplane developments.

It had.

He, and then I, had learned to fly the damned things and then shoot from the damned things. It had gotten bloodier and bloodier from there.

I stood at attention in my very best formal imitation of a solid U.S. Navy chief who hadn't gone tearing after Lieutenant Marshall on all those escapades. He gave me a bear hug and spun me around by one shoulder to leave both of us facing the team.

So much for military discipline.

The seventeen sailors looked on with mixed interest and amusement. Petty Officer Wicklow's eyes twinkled and our boss gave him a slight nod of acknowledgement before raising his voice to be easily heard by all.

"The chief's doing a chief's job reminding me of our narrow orders. But what do you think, boys?" The delight in Lieutenant Marshall's eyes promised nothing the political campaign managers back home were going to like.

Damn it, so what if he's 'unmanageable' and 'a blight on the vice president's political prospects?' Why did they have to tell him that right before shipping us off to be quietly useful?

"Ah, no, I'm to say, 'Gentlemen.' And pretend to be one myself." He gave me an exaggerated wink.

Sir, please don't embarrass yourself. These are regular American servicemen, not sons of the rich playing at aeroplane flying or foreigners accepting of odd ways from strangers.

Lieutenant Marshall executed a disaster of a German court bow, making fun of himself. It was much worse than the much practiced one he'd used when presented to the Kaiser back when he'd thought being amenable was the quickest way to be allowed back into an aeroplane.

"I'm not so good at talking." He shrugged.

Not quite a lie, I agreed with his self-assessment. *If he could talk just a little bit less about the nasty parts of war, he'd be excellent at talking. Instead his talking got us all here.*

"And yeah," my lieutenant continued, "you've probably heard it all already. Yes, the Vice President is my uncle. Yes, President Wilson has still not recovered, and my uncle intends to seek the nomination and ask the country to let him run things officially. But that other stuff in the papers isn't quite right: I only shot down a couple of British warplanes dropping bombs on my friends..."

And learned how to fly Eindeckers and flew one of those first dozen aeroplanes to have Fokker's machine gun on it when actually he was only ordered to tour German bases and learn what he could about military uses of the aeroplane.

It was only my long years of service that allowed me to keep a poker face while several months of memories, more bad than good, flashed through my head.

But sure, boss, we can pretend it was all exactly what Rear Admiral Fiske expected.

"And then," he said, "I got recalled home to write stacks of reports about how to make aeroplanes with guns on them."

"And to make speeches," Petty Officer Wicklow added. "I was at the one in Virginia where you answered that reporter asking after Lieutenant Thompson and how that crash looked and the trouble it was to get the body parts together for the burial."

"Glad we aren't getting into any aeroplanes," Davis, a young sailor in the back, muttered to the general agreement of the group.

Never mind that bullets are quite good enough at making people dead, I added to myself. *Never mind what you're carrying.*

Davis's pack included most of our explosives, and he'd actually volunteered to carry it. He was plenty brave enough walking around on the ground.

"Like I said, I'm not so great at talking," Lieutenant Marshall acknowledged. "They didn't much want me speaking up once they realized I was going to answer the questions about what it was like over there. People die when folks start fighting, and I figure it's only worth doing if there's something important to be fighting each other about.

"So, let's be clear on what we're doing now. On the other side of that." He pointed at the horizon, a dark blue line of South Atlantic Ocean meeting a pale sky of fading light. "Is a collection of little islands filled mostly with sheep and rotting whale carcasses. The Malvinas, or Falklands, if you'd rather. A couple decades now they've been claimed as a British Overseas Territory. Not so polite of them to be taking American lands and we're going to do something about it."

"Um, we are going to take down their wireless station, that's it," I said, with what I hoped was an agreeing sort of expression on my face. I do not look like a recruiting poster.

"So we will." Marshall gave me a jovial shoulder punch. "Tell the fine gents what we know about the locations."

"Um. Right, sir." I hadn't expected to have a speaking role. I hastily pulled from my pack a copy of the coastal chart I'd nabbed from naval records back when I'd first heard whispers of this plan while we were in Virginia. "Uh, this island is the one with most of the people living on it, unfortunately, but it's of course where the wireless antenna is too. Plenty tall and easy to see in daylight, but we're going over in the dark on account of wanting to not get seen ourselves. They've got it high enough and high-powered enough to signal Montevideo in Uruguay and Buenos Aires in Argentina. Both those mainland countries are neutral in the European war just like us, um, of course," I added.

"For however long that lasts," one of the sailors snarked. That was Allen, a sandy-haired broad-shouldered recruit who idolized the lieutenant and spoke out of turn too often, but if even he was paying attention, then everyone in the bunch was listening close.

I ignored the comment but couldn't suppress my own thoughts: *Attacking a Brit territory isn't the way to stay neutral if anyone ever learns who did it.*

"The wireless is here." I tapped a spot on a peninsula where the tower itself was marked as an aid to navigation. Not far to the south of it was a small ridge labeled Sapper Hill that might be useful if it were tall enough. We'd have to scout it, so I moved on rather than mention it now.

"That tower is about two miles away from the town proper. It's a village, really, and the British call it Port Stanley."

Lieutenant Marshall gave me an encouraging nod and beckoned the group to huddle around me.

"So, uh, Stanley is there." I pointed at a couple other aid to navigation marks for a church steeple and a building described in the mariner's notes as 'Governor's House.'

"And maybe we don't even meet up with anybody but a night operator or two, if they bother to have one." A note of hopefulness crept into my voice, so I did my level best to add in what cautious information I'd been able to glean from buying rounds for that one merchant sailor I'd found in a Norfolk dock bar who'd worked as a whaler down this way.

Best money I've ever spent, honestly.

"There's some sort of town watch. Could be a tough group with all the ship repair shops closed. Or, um, nearly so. That is, now that Panama's canal is open and the merchant ships don't make the trip around the Horn anymore."

I gave a pleading look to the lieutenant. I'd never been part of a raiding party before and really wasn't sure what I was supposed to be saying.

Petty Officer Wicklow noticed and stepped up.

"Hundreds of muscle-bound out of work dock workers too buzzed to feel any pain, but lacking sufficient funds to be truly drunk, and with nothing better to do of a night than wander the beaches looking for a fight then," Wicklow summarized, most unhelpfully. The man had a thick Boston accent, but the group had been together too long for me to hope nobody understood him. "And they'll be locals, too, mores the pity. Not really Brits."

I remembered then that his family had lost all they'd had in Ireland before coming over, and he was very much looking forward to getting some licks in against the British. Lots of Americans still liked the idea of letting the continentals have their Great War alone, but not all. Some couldn't wait to join Germany, Austria-Hungry, and Italy in the fight against the Entente powers.

The lieutenant took one look at the mixed expressions of eagerness and fear on the assembled faces and let out a genuine belly laugh.

"Ha! As if they could take you boys!" Marshall's confidence spread through the men and banished the uneasy expressions as even Brown, our smallest sailor, stood taller.

"We will," Marshall admitted, "go in quiet like to avoid waking His Governorship, but don't think it's because we're afraid of some minor militia. My aunt met the governor's wife at an event once when both were in Nova Scotia, and it'd be awkward if we had to shoot her husband." He gave the group a wink.

Quiet? I carefully did not look at the spools of wire and explosive charges we had already loaded onto our small boats.

"Right then." I clapped my hands together. "Everyone check their packs are secure. As soon as dusk falls, the *Denver* will steam in to drop us off. Then we'll have some hard rowing to do, a quick scramble over the beach, watch things for just a bit to get the lay of the island, then we do some good old fashioned destruction."

So, so neutral.

"After that, we scramble back to the *Denny* again."

Allen blinked at me. "Scramble back? But won't the ship just steam into the harbor to pick us up?"

"Did you hear anything Chief said?" Williams, our radio expert, rolled his eyes. "We go in. We take the island's communication rig out, and we come back. Might be a lot of rowing after depending on how far out the *Denver* is and if we miss the tide."

"What if we just took the whole place over though?" Petty Officer Wicklow mused. "That'd sure put paid to these British Overseas Territories, wouldn't it, sir?"

"That it most certainly would." Lieutenant Marshall agreed.

No, sir, don't go thinking like that, I pleaded. *Because that'd put us in the war for certain.*

I looked around the ship's deck to see if the cruiser's captain or any other officer of rank might come over to say a few words and, just maybe straighten things all out. The decks were conspicuously empty besides our almost two dozen man landing party.

"Uh, what do you think, Chief?" the radioman asked.

The lieutenant's political handlers were idiots if they expected someone who routinely went off script on the campaign trail would make a good choice as the leader for a politically-delicate raid, I thought. And a vice president's nephew was a long way from being a deniable link if they wanted to pretend this was an unauthorized attack in the event we all ended up captured or dead. Unless...

Oh shit. Maybe they did want into the war and needed a good reason. Like a dead hero. God help us.

"I think our lieutenant will lead us right in and right out," I lied.

"So, we should leave American soil under British control?" Marshall asked the men.

Hell yes!

"This is South America, sir. Not any sort of part of the United States," I protested.

"Still America," Davis pointed out. The others looked at him and nodded giving me sidelong looks as if I needed to go back and study my geography a bit more.

As if I didn't know more about British Overseas Territories than any self-respecting American ought to.

"Should we leave a place for hostile ships to coal up and restock on ammunition so that they can take their embargoes over to our side of the ocean?" Marshall shook his head. "I'd rather not. But, Chief Hays, if you really think it's in the interest of the people of the United States of America..."

I sighed. The lieutenant had an irritating tendency to be right.

"What the hell, sir. Why not? It's not like these Falkland Islands could have any real strategic importance to the Great War over in

Europe. But your uncle might have you write an apology note to King George V or something after."

Or go ahead and declare war like it seems the political handlers have wanted all along.

"They can trade notes then." Lieutenant Marshall agreed. "It'll make him feel better about all the apologies the British have been making about taking our merchant cargoes."

"This is the first step, boys," Marshall said. "We may only knock over a wireless tower and destroy a few war supplies this time in, but America is done letting the Brits built forts on our shores. Let's go take back America!"

Argentina might have a few things to say about that. I kept my grumbling thoughts off my face while everyone from Seaman Brown to Petty Officer Wicklow cheered.

* * *

Our row boats scraped onto the sand in the dim moonlight. Bleached whale bones, stripped of their lucrative blubber and everything else of any remote value, gleamed in white shards scattered over the sand.

"Whales," Marshall said with a speculative tone in that single word.

The rest of us kept strict silence in case our voices carried across the cove to some garrison or troop manning the port guns.

Petty Officer Wicklow and three others crunched up the sand to near the peak of a seagrass and scrub covered rise. Continuing up on their bellies, Wicklow lifted a glass, ducked down again, peered at his wrinkled map, and repeated the process several more times.

With quick hand gestures, he sent the sailors scrambling over the rise and off in three directions to scout and return.

On a tip from that Norfolk merchant seaman, we'd avoided any coves likely to hold carcasses still being processed. The governor had strict limits on the number of whales allowed to be taken in each season, but the blubber's value kept going up, especially as it proved more and more useful to His Majesty's war effort.

Logistics, I was coming to suspect, *might win wars more than aeroplanes or even battleships. Though in this case maybe logistics could end a war…But probably not.* I paused to kick a whale bone and pulled my boot back in disgust to find it hadn't been picked as clean as it should have been. *We could maybe strangle the supply lines?* I wondered if it'd be possible.

Whale oil typically made soap. But it also produced glycerin as a by-product, which was converted in turn to nitroglycerine, a component of cordite, the oh-so-useful standard propellant for artillery shells and small arms ammunition.

Norwegian captains and Norwegian shipping companies owned most of the whaling fleets, and Norway was neutral in the war. But they used British Overseas Territories as supply ports and sold primarily to the Entente side of the war. When we'd been in Germany, they were so short on glycerin supplies that there were posters in all the portside bars begging fishermen to kill anything at all with blubber, even little seals and dolphins. The United States might need to have something to say about those 'Overseas Territories' that happened to be located in the Americas.

"Not just coal at issue here, huh, sir." I pointed out, keeping my voice as soft as I could manage.

Lieutenant Marshall nodded quiet agreement.

"Several senior officers pulled me aside before we left. They'll all have to deny everything if we don't pull this off. But quite a few men will also be patting themselves on the back for their insight and strategic brilliance as well, if we win."

"When, sir." I corrected.

He smiled wanly. "If we get separated, get as many of the boys off the island as you can. The *Denny's* captain assured me he'll try a pickup no matter what happens."

Oh hell no. Don't imply the ship might abandon us all here if it gets too risky!

"They've only got two shore guns!" I protested. *A ship's a fool to fight a fort,* my mind reminded me. *Even a wimpy fort.* "But sir—"

"And they have a quite reasonably sized militia if they ring up the bells hard enough before we get into position."

"We hold the governor hostage then?" Petty Officer Wicklow suggested. I started. He'd ambled up to us without me hearing him and had both Williams and Allen with him.

"Might work." Williams replied.

"Nah." Lieutenant Marshall shook his head. "My aunt says he's not so popular around here. Keeps limiting the increases on the whaling and elephant sealing."

"But they'll have no work for their sons if they don't cap it down now?" Allen whispered with a note of protest raising his voice enough for Wicklow to shush him.

"Didn't say the governor was wrong to do it," Marshall acknowledged with a softer tone. "Just folks don't necessarily appreciate being stopped from killing their golden geese."

Seaman Davis, lying flat up on the rise, signaled warning and we all went silent and unholstered our rifles.

The sound of feet on sand crunched way too nearby. Then the brush rustled on both our left and right, and I just about had a heart attack until a sheep lifted its head high to blink at me before leaning back down to gnaw on some tender green shoots.

Laughter spread through the group, and I was grateful nobody had shot at any of the sheep now wandering across our beach.

The three scouts returned with nothing useful to share other than the belated information that sheep were wandering freely all around our position.

We divided ourselves into two groups, and in minutes we too were crunching along on seagrass-covered sand away from our hidden boats to circle wide of the herd in case a shepherd came looking to pen them up for the night.

Sweaty and tired with our packs of explosives grown far heavier with the night march, we reached Sapper Hill a few hours before dawn. Petty Officer Wicklow repeated his work with the scouts and then turned the glass over to the boss.

Lieutenant Marshall took a look at our target and with careful thoroughness scanned right all the way to the lighthouse at the point and left to Port Stanley himself. Sliding back down to the indent where I waited, he handed the glass back to Wicklow.

"Chief, I have an idea," he said.

Uh oh.

The most fleeting grin passed over his face despite being quickly suppressed. It was nothing more than a twitch at the corner of his mouth, but I knew the Lieutenant.

Not good. Very, very not good. Whatever this is, he thinks it's a good idea. No, a really good idea. Oh hell. If we survive this, he better be buying my drinks for years.

"Get up there and take a look," he said.

I did.

Looking down the shallow slope we were a mile or two from the port area on the western edge of Port Stanley, where the wealth of the former shipyard stood tall next to empty piers. The line of the inlet's shore curved towards us with a whale carcass and a dotting of storage buildings along the coast. Directly ahead, the radio tower rose high into the sky ahead of us with a small almost shed like building at its base. Off to the right, more scrub grass and rocks meandered along the shoreline all the way to the lighthouse at Cape Pembroke.

The cold ground seeped the warmth out of me and replaced it with damp. With no trees, the ever-present wind howled unabated over the barren landscape of the island. The thick grey clouds raced eastward across the sky above us while intermittently releasing a fine mist to ensure we stayed wet and cold.

I gave Wicklow back the glass. He collapsed it and returned it to a brown leather case as we scooted backwards below the crest of Sapper Hill. Wicklow had three sailors positioned and watching our flanks to ensure we weren't surprised by a wandering islander. Those scouts were far enough away that we could speak without being overheard. The rest of our group huddled back in an upcropping of rocks to stay out of sight while we decided where to lay our explosives.

Lieutenant Marshall huddled over a sketch in the dirt. He'd made a map of the area with a groove in the sand to mark the shoreline, another thin line for the path running from the lighthouse to Port Stanley, and a third for the crest line of Sapper Hill. Rocks marked the lighthouse, the town, and the whale carcass.

"Did you see all those barrels down at the coast?" He pointed at the whale rock.

Uh, those dark splotches behind the rotting bones? I wondered.

"Of course, sir." Wicklow said, "The whalers won't fill their holds with the oil barrels when they're doing the flensing on land and sending the boat right out again to get another one before the season ends."

"Worth a lot, do you think?" Lieutenant Marshall said.

"Yes, sir," Petty Office Wicklow said. "The whale oil's good for lots of things. Soap and lamp oil, it used to be. But these days, mostly cordite and whatnot."

Where are you going with this, boss? We need to have that wireless tower down or a nice thick haze of black smoke around it soon so the Denny *gets the signal to come get us.*

"Exactly. Far too much whatnot, we can't just leave those barrels."

No time for that, sir! I protested mentally. Petty Officer Wicklow leaned in, delighted. "You want we change the objectives, boss?"

"I'm thinking so." He pointed up at the radio tower. "If we take that down, how long do you suppose it'd take them to get the wireless back up and running?"

"At least a couple months," I said, determined to be the voice of reason. "The papers said it was a Marconi crew brought in special that installed it a few years ago, back in 1911. They'd need another one down to repair or rebuild it."

"But they would repair it. Or maybe even decide they didn't need a wireless station here after all." Marshall held up a hand to delay more objections from me, "But, any whale oil we destroy, stays gone."

Stabbing a finger at the map he said, "There is the port and here nearer to us are the barrels." Pointing to another location slightly south of the piers. "If we trot along here and come up from the south, we can get a good look and make sure they aren't just empty and waiting for the next whale or something."

"Won't be empty," Wicklow said with confidence. "The empties will be back with the barrel wright waiting for a ship's purser to buy them."

"Um, sir, we need to signal the *Denny*. The lookouts will be watching the radio tower. We didn't pack enough explosives to take it down and blow up some rotting whale bits."

Wicklow pressed his lips together.

Lieutenant Marshall grinned. "Good thing oil burns on its own then, isn't it, Chief?"

"Ah. Yes, sir," I acknowledged.

We made quick arrangements for Wicklow to take a team in to secure the radio communications shed and wire our explosives to bring it down while the lieutenant and I did our own scouting of the new secondary objective with a couple of the sailors sent along with us to carry a spare detonator, some wire, and a bit of coal to get a nice big fire going.

We jogged along a footpath in the direction of Port Stanley, making good time on the relatively flat path with clear moonlight to guide us. We'd be running back this way after to rejoin Wicklow and the rest of the men, so I kept a keen eye out for anything that might trip us up on the way back.

Two scouts waited for us at a bend in the path with one flat on his belly watching the way to Port Stanley and another down slope, signaling us to keep coming while he watched the other man for any sign to tell us to scamper off the path and take cover on the other side of Sapper Hill.

We reached the beached whale carcass and Lieutenant Marshall gathered us round. I had to stop myself from doing a circuit of the neatly lined barrels myself. The scouts had already checked for guards and found not a soul left behind.

Where the hell is everyone? I wondered.

"Okay boys," Lieutenant Marshall said. "We need to get one of these cracked open and slopped around on the others to be good and sure they all burn. Once the fire gets going here, it'll draw attention and we don't have time to stay and mind the fires." He scratched a quick map of the island in the dirt and pointed out where to go if anything went wrong. "Any questions?"

There were none, but Lieutenant Marshall made eye contact with every man and got a nod of acknowledgment from each anyway. Allen and a couple other sailors produced marlinspikes from their packs and punched holes in the closest barrel. I splayed out the detonator wire to full length and was getting ready to position a secondary charge in an oil-wetted cranny between four barrels, when, CRACK!

I leapt back and spun in a circle looking for attackers.

A couple more spurts of rifle fire rang out and Seaman Allen pointed behind us at the radio tower.

Oh no. "Petty Officer Wicklow's team found trouble," I said.

"We'll show them trouble," said the lieutenant.

He whistled sharply, making no effort to be quiet any longer and we all pulled back from the shoreline. With no time for anything else, I tossed the secondary charge into the middle of the barrels and hoped for the best.

At a nod from the lieutenant, Allen plunged down the detonator and we ran for the wireless station.

A whoomph went up behind us and the fire lit our way through the first bend in the path.

A look over my shoulder showed little flames racing over the tracings of spilled oil and quickly turning back to blackness without the dark red char of the barrels themselves catching fire.

Too late now.

We sprinted and waited in a maddeningly slow leapfrog. The lieutenant and two sailors running to the next bend and stopping to peer ahead while Allen and I watched our rear and then charged on past Lieutenant Marshall's group to the next point while they took our role.

We were almost on top of the disturbingly not-burning radio shed when more shots rang out.

I dove to the ground immediately as the gunfire reverberated over the sound of the wind. At least one of those bullets ricocheted uncomfortable close. I pulled my rifle close to my chest and rolled to the right to get behind some rocks.

A figure stood up from the other side of the rock and bellowed: "Ceasefire! You idiots, ceasefire!"

Petty Officer Wicklow pulled me to my feet and dusted me off. "Sorry, Chief," he whispered. "Everyone's nervous."

Davis peered, white-faced from the side of the radio shed. "Oh! It's you, Lieutenant!" he called out with obvious relief.

"Anyone hit?" Marshall asked in an urgent undertone.

A grumbled murmur of responses came back with a negative.

"Guess it's a good thing the lieutenant didn't ask for any Marines to come along," Seaman Allen said to Wicklow. "Marines probably wouldn't have missed."

The petty officer shrugged.

"Yeah," Seaman Davis said. "But Marines wouldn't've gotten spooked by rats and sheep! I figured they must have had some reasons for not bringing 'em."

Lieutenant Marshall and I exchanged a look.

I had no idea we could've asked for Marines.

His raised eyebrows back seemed to say, *Me either, but I'm glad we aren't dead.*

The sailors with us advanced on Seaman Davis with hands starting to ball into fists.

I cleared my throat, and they paused.

"I, I, I'm...sss," Seaman Davis stammered nervously looking from his fellow sailor's grim faces to mine and Lieutenant Marshall's.

A little late for apologies.

"Forget it," the lieutenant snapped. "We don't have time for a court-martial right now." Turning to me, he said, "Someone may have heard that shot." And then looking at Petty Officer Wicklow, "Or all those other shots."

"Ah. Sir." The petty officer turned a shade of red visible even in the predawn light. "We, um, secured the radio tower and took a prisoner."

"There were guards?" I asked.

"Yes." He shifted back and forth. "We took him prisoner."

"One guard," Lieutenant Marshall noted. "And all those shots were at sheep?" Lieutenant Marshall exchanged another look with me.

What is going on?

"And then some rats came out." Davis volunteered. "Spooked Petty Officer Wicklow something fierce, so he shot at them, and then we all thought we must be under attack, so we shot at things too. Harry freaked out and dropped down onto the floor with his hands over his head and jus' said, 'Don't kill me, don't kill me,' over and over like."

Davis shook his head as if this were a completely unreasonable response. Then he brightened after a moment, remembering one success worth noting.

"And we killed a sheep!" He nodded with pride at a small mound of dirty fleece, I'd not noticed earlier.

"Seaman Williams shot the sheep." Wicklow corrected. "You missed."

Lieutenant Marshall scrubbed his face with his hand.

"Okay," I said. "We've got a tower to bring down."

"But who is Harry?" Marshall said.

"Our prisoner." Petty Officer Wicklow answered as if that were perfectly obvious. "He's been extremely compliant. Seems to think we're likely to shoot him if he even looks at us sideways."

"Can't imagine where he'd get that idea," Lieutenant Marshall said.

Me neither, sir, I thought, not even bothering to hide my annoyance. *Me neither.*

"Right. Petty Officer, let's get everything wired and see to moving the prisoner to somewhere he doesn't get roasted alive, alright?"

Wicklow seized the opportunity to redeem himself and set the sailors to completing our demolition project. The shed itself at the base of the tower was a simple wood thing but a steady damp rain had started to fall and thoroughly soaked the timbers. I wished for a couple barrels of whale oil to get the fire good and smoky in case the tower survived the blast, but I couldn't even see a glow over the rise for the oil barrels anymore. Full dawn had broken and sunlight burned brighter than any flickering flames that might have remained from our attempt at adding a secondary target.

We'd packed charges specifically for this task and wasted some of it, but hopefully we still had enough. Wicklow had three different detonator lines running from charges around the communications shed and at the base of the tower. The wires snaked along the ground over a slight rise up to that very rock outcropping where I'd ducked our welcome bullet volley.

Williams unspooled the third and final wire. Using his knife, he scraped the insulation off and wrapped the bare metal onto a knob on the detonator box.

The lieutenant watched as some of the men made the final preparations while Petty Officer Wicklow checked to make sure Harry stayed back over the next rise a little further down the path with about half of our sailors set to guard him. Mostly I wanted them there to keep any curious sailors from wandering back into the radio shed to check the charges one last time and getting themselves blown up. But I could only use so many for scouts without them getting in each other's way. We had a full circle of lookouts now with everyone being very, very clear on not shooting at our own people, ensuring no more nasty surprises.

"Sir, the charges are all ready to blow," Williams reported to the lieutenant.

I peered back at Wicklow's group. He lifted his head just over the rise and gave me a thumbs up. My lookouts crouched and lay on rises and behind outcroppings all around us in pairs with one looking out and one signaling back to me. Each pair gave me the 'everything fine' sign.

"If you'd like to do the honors, Lieutenant?" Williams finished and gestured to the detonator box with the handle fully extended upward.

Kneeling next to the detonator box, Lieutenant Marshall put both hands on the handle. Looking around at all of us he said, "Everyone down." Williams and I ducked down and covered our ears. When he was satisfied that everyone was behind some cover, Marshall slammed down the handle.

A boom flattened the shed into kindling. The tower still stood.

Williams mouthed something that seemed apologetic. He looked at the two remaining wires, and seemingly at random selected another to attach next.

The western sky flared suddenly bright as a million oil lamps. Then a fraction of a second later, a deep roar of the explosion swept over us, everyone instinctively winced at the deep, reverberating sound. Williams stared in slack-jawed awe at the billowing smoke.

I stayed down and twisted back and forth to check on each of my lookout teams. They caught my glares and turned back to their work.

A steady ringing of church bells echoed over the bay. Port Stanley was awake.

Lieutenant Marshall snatched the wires from Williams' hands and finished unhooking the first set of wires and hooked up the next set to the detonator box. With the new set of wires hooked up, the Lieutenant dropped the handle.

Nothing happened. He looked back at me. I expected another explosion at any moment. He looked at the wires, then, satisfied that they were hooked up correctly, he raised then lowed handle again, and again, nothing.

"Shit!" He exclaimed. Two more tries produced the same lack of results.

Williams grabbed the remaining end and set to switching it out.

A moment later, the church bells stopped. A thick gray streak of smoke poured upwards into the sky.

Williams lifted the detonator box and checked it for any signs of damage. Nothing seemed wrong.

"You try it," said Lieutenant Marshall.

He obeyed and dropped the handle and again, nothing. Out of pure frustration he raised and lowered the handle several more times. Exasperated, he looked at the Lieutenant.

"Sir, should I go back and check the explosives and the wires?" I said. *The first detonation might have broken a wire or dislodged it from the charge. Or any number of things. Forget Marines, why didn't we ask for a couple of petty officers who'd blown things up before and were good enough at it to still have all their fingers?*

Lieutenant Marshall thought a moment, then shook his head. "No, we don't have the time. We've got to go."

Well at least we don't have to worry that the Denny *won't see our signal,* I thought.

Seaman Allen waved his arms wildly to catch my attention and his partner lookout facing outward pointed straight at the path from Port Stanley with a death grip on the back of Allen's coveralls as if afraid we'd withdraw and leave him behind.

"Boss," I interrupted with an urgent warning. "The militia is coming."

At my signal, all the lookouts hid and Marshall, Williams, and I ducked out of sight behind our outcropping.

Almost before we'd gotten behind the rocks, three young boys holding ancient muskets far too big for them came running down the path hollering.

"We're coming for you, Whalers!" This was not going to have been a sneak attack even if our scouts had been blind. They charged straight past us into Petty Officer Wicklow's team. 'The governor's going to—"

The shouts cut off abruptly with some muted grunts. Wicklow's men had them well in hand. *What kind of militia is this?*

Five more armed townsfolk came puffing down the path. The only head not solid gray or near bald with fringes of white was a man in a fine tailored suit with a heavy mustache and expression of fury on his face.

It's the war, I realized. *All the able-bodied men not working the whalers have gone for the war.*

"Damn you all!" the well-dressed man yelled. "So help me, I'll triple the price of your coal and impound your next three whales if you've tried to exceed your quotas again! Fifteen per season it is now, you bloody fools, and it'll starve your own children when there's none left to catch, blast you!"

"What the hell?" Lieutenant Marshall said, as he peaked over the hilltop even while I frantically motioned for him to stay under cover. Some of those older fellows might know a thing or two about sharp-shooting.

Keep your fool head down, boss! Just because some folks in Washington would prefer a dead hero was no reason to give them one!

"What's that you say sir?" I called back at the man leading the militia, wanting very much for any random shots to come my way rather than a dozen feet further to the left at the lieutenant.

"You heard me!" The leader yelled. "Where the bloody hell is your captain? Gone out to harpoon another whale while you lot try to render one down in secret on my own beaches? Not even bothering to do it on one of the other islands anymore, eh? You tell that puss-rotted fool, I'll—"

Lieutenant Marshall stood up, clear in the early morning light. The silver of his collar devices glinted nicely. If the rest of him was rumpled from a night scrambling around with a stained coverall overtop everything, he still stood like an officer.

The man stared.

"I don't believe I've had the honor, sir." Lieutenant Marshall made a short bow, one gentleman to another. "Lieutenant Marshall of the United States Navy. Your islands are under attack."

"Uh, governor?" One of the four aging militia men with Governor Allardyce leaned in and mumbled in a quavering voice not quiet enough to avoid reaching us. "Shouldn't we be hurrying after the boys?"

Governor Allardyce puffed out his chest again. "We're most certainly not under attack! The sheep girls haven't reported seeing a German ship in nearly a year. After Coronel, of course we were concerned, but then there was Port Doula and von Spee's squadron has been up and down the African coast ever since. There's only been that American flagged vessel lurking about."

"I knew it!" Williams whispered at my side, "There must have been people watching those sheep."

"Hush," I growled, keeping my voice down. I'd thought we'd be shooting at somebody and then running away by now. I motioned for everyone to keep their heads down while waiting for the lieutenant to give us some kind of order.

Lieutenant Marshall pointed over his shoulder at the smoke still rising from our sabotage.

Governor Allardyce squinted at it. An older man, who seemed to be some sort of advisor stepped up.

"That's not whale flensing, Gov," he said. "You be able to smell the reek of it from here if'n it was, and besides, the color of the smoke's all wrong too."

"I believe we've already established that I'm not a whaler captain," Lieutenant Marshall said.

Or at all likely to make captain of anything if he singlehandedly starts a war with England, I kept behind my teeth and did not add.

"So." The lieutenant pointed over his shoulder at the still rising smoke. "A stretch of your coastline is burning. We could sack the town and just leave you with wreckage. Or you could surrender the island."

"But the United States is neutral!" Governor Allardyce protested.

Lieutenant Marshall shrugged. "I have my orders."

"To attack Britain? Here?" The governor's advisor's skeptical expression did not look properly receptive for a man with twenty people pointing rifles at him.

I turned the barrel of mine to get ready to turn him into a leaking former advisor. The man saw my motion and jerked to the side to stand in front of the governor. *Damn brave idiots.*

The other three tried to point their own pistols in all directions, not too sure of where all Lieutenant Marshall's men were. They'd have heard American voices from both sides of the track and more tellingly, not heard anything from the three youngsters who'd run on ahead.

Governor Allardyce waved his hat from behind the man. "A truce while we talk?" he called out.

"Ah well, I've got four captives already," Lieutenant Marshall replied. "You might just go ahead and surrender and then we can discuss terms."

Yelps from behind had me jump almost out of my skin.

"Ten!" yelled Petty Officer Wicklow. "Make that an even ten captives now, Lieutenant. The governor had another six of these boys try to sneak up on us."

Another scuffle erupted, and Wicklow's voice dropped to a growl. "Lieutenant, how many of these brats can we shoot?"

The governor paled. "We surrender," he said.

The older gentlemen around him lowered their rifles and a pack of bruised young boys, with their weapons taken away from them, scurried up over the ridge into the arms of their grandfathers.

"Do you suppose the Americans might lower the whaling quotas back to ten as part of the terms?" One of the older men asked the governor while looking hopefully at Lieutenant Marshall.

Governor Allardyce cocked his eyebrow at my boss.

I expected something like, *That'll be for Washington and London to discuss.*' but this was the Vice President's nephew. He said, "Of course, gentlemen. The United States must ensure the freedoms and prosperity of its territories."

* * *

"**L**ieutenant!" The young local scamp bounced on his toes eager to make his report. "Sir, the lookouts have spotted H.M.S. *Invincible!*"

"Oh really?" A broad grin spread across Marshall's face. "What an unfortunate name for a warship."

"Do you think we ought to test the harbor guns, sir?" I suggested. "Just to make sure they are in proper working order, of course."

"But this is ridiculous." Governor Allardyce turned to me to plead, "You don't really want to fire on British vessels. We aren't at war with you!"

"Don't worry," Marshall patted the man on the shoulder. "We'll reimburse the King for the islands. And the ships," he added.

"God help us." Governor Allardyce raised his hands in defeat. "And supposing His Majesty suggests these islands aren't for sale?"

"Funny you should put it that way." Lieutenant Marshall nodded. "Neither were the sixteen American cargos taken in the last month by the Royal Navy in the North Sea, but that seemed to make no difference to anyone. This is only the natural extension." He gave the governor a perfect court bow.

Petty Officer Wicklow looked over at me. "Are the history books going to say the United States entered the Great War today?"

"Could be," I said.

The shore guns boomed a warning shot.

"Do you suppose it'll be called the Battle of the Falkland Islands?" Davis asked me.

"I doubt it," I said. "I don't think anyone much cares what happens down here. How important can one little southern patch of islands be?"

* * * * *

Joelle Presby Bio

Joelle Presby is a former U.S. naval officer who was born in France but not while it was occupied by Germany. She also did not serve during the Great War. She cowrote *The Road to Hell*, in the Multiverse series, with David Weber. She has also published short stories in universes of her own creation, Charles E. Gannon's Terran Republic, and David Weber's Honor Harrington universe. Updates and releases are shared on her website, joellepresby.com, and on social media through MeWe, Facebook, LinkedIn, and Twitter.

https://www.mewe.com/i/joellepresby
https://www.facebook.com/joelle.presby
https://www.linkedin.com/in/joellepresby/
https://twitter.com/JoellePresby

* * *

Patrick Doyle Bio

Patrick Doyle graduated from the University of Minnesota in 1993 with a degree in History, a commission as an Ensign in the U.S. Navy, a love of flying, and no pilot slot. Pat's desire to be a pilot won out, and he left active duty back when peace was breaking out in the mid-90s to eventually become a commercial airline captain at a large regional airline. As a member of the Navy Reserve, and with the downturn in the airline industry in the 2000s, he resumed his Navy career, serving in various active duty assignments. He recently returned to the airlines as a Captain and simulator instructor teaching the next generation of commercial pilots how to throw themselves at the Earth and miss. In his spare time, he writes, travels, and designs games. He currently lives in Minnesota with his wife, Linda, and son, Matthew.

# # # # #

Drang nach Osten
(Drive to the East)
by Christopher G. Nuttall

All the rest was merely the proper application of overwhelming force.
-Winston S. Churchill

Germany, 1919

I t was a bitterly cold day.

Hauptmann Hans Lehmann dug his shovel into the half-frozen ground, produced a lump of earth and dumped it in the pile behind the makeshift trench. It was hard, so hard, to keep himself warm, no matter how strenuously he worked. The cold seemed ommipresent, working its way through the layers of clothing he'd pulled on that morning, into his skin, and seemingly into his very soul. The days when the army had been given everything it needed were long gone. The men under his command could only keep themselves warm—barely—by lighting fires all along the trenches.

Which tells the Tommy aircraft precisely where to drop their bombs, he thought, as he straightened up and looked along the trenchline. *It won't be long now before we find out if they're bluffing or not.*

He allowed his eyes to wander over his men, the scratch unit that had been hastily put together and thrown into the trenches. There were men from a dozen different units, ranging from grizzled army sergeants who'd been fighting since 1914 to a handful of sailors and students who'd been press-ganged into the ranks when the provisional government had started funnelling men and material back to the trenches. The motley crew included a former dispatch rider who'd been badly wounded during a gas attack and only just made it back to the front. Hans scowled as he saw the man lecturing his comrades on the importance of protecting the *Fatherland* from the British and French hordes. Adolf...if he hadn't been so desperate for manpower, he would have sent Adolf back to the hospital. There was no doubting the man's bravery—dispatch riders had a particularly dangerous task—but there was something about the man that bothered Hans. It was as if Adolf never wanted the war to end.

Sergeant Keitel came up behind him. "We were meant to be in Paris by now, weren't we?"

Hans gave him a sharp look. Discipline had been fragmenting since 1918, when the army had been driven out of France by overwhelming firepower. Men who were once trustworthy were now openly spreading defeatism or simply voting with their feet and heading home. Hans had dared to hope, once upon a time, that peace talks would lead to actual *peace*, but...it was starting to look as though the war would continue until everyone was dead. The Allies—the British, French and, despite their protestations, even the Americans—wanted to break Germany into its component pieces, ensuring the *Reich* would never rise again. Or so he'd been told.

"Right now, I'll settle for keeping *them* out of Germany," he said, harshly. He'd heard horror stories about colonial troops from Africa and India. The thought of his mother or sister being…he swallowed hard, unable to even *consider* the prospect. "If we can…"

He looked along the line, trying to keep his face utterly blank. A civilian would see it as an impressive trench, he supposed. A soldier knew it wouldn't last more than a few minutes, when—if—the enemy sent in tanks. They didn't have the concrete or barbed wire or *anything* they needed to make the network impregnable, if that were even possible. The concept of impregnable trenches had died at Cambrai, when the British tanks and artillery has smashed through the lines and crushed the defenders in their trenches. Hans had been there, watching helplessly as the tanks advanced. If the British themselves hadn't been so surprised by their success…they'd learnt from that, hadn't they? The Hindenburg Line had been smashed the following year, leaving the road to the Fatherland open. And he knew, all too well, that *his* trenchline was flimsy by comparison.

We have to make a stand, he told himself, as he heard an airplane buzzing high overhead. Probably British. Or French, or American…it hardly mattered. He hadn't seen a friendly aircraft in the skies for weeks. Rumour had it that the pilots were living the high life in Berlin, while the soldiers sweated on the ground and waited for the grand offensive.

If we can win better terms…

He forced himself to walk along the trenchline, assessing progress. The men had done a remarkable job, given what little time and tools they had. A handful of guns had been carefully sited, backed up by a pair of tanks…he'd been told they were better than the latest British designs, but it hardly mattered. The British had a *lot* of tanks. He'd heard whispers filtering through the lines, reports brought back by scouts who'd crossed No Man's Land and spied on the British positions. There were literally *thousands* of enemy tanks being positioned for the offensive. If the Allies were bluffing, as some rumours claimed, they were doing a very good job.

"This position will be held, *Herr Hauptman*," Adolf assured him as Hans surveyed his section of the trench. The *swinehund* deserved credit for having worked at least as hard as his men. "They will not pass."

That's what the French general said, Hans thought. Back then, he'd thought nothing could stand in their way as they marched towards Paris. The men had already been chatting about the French girls they intended to bed.

And the Frenchman was right, Hans thought. *We didn't pass. Doubt that we will hold nearly as well as they did.*

Hans heard more aircraft, high overhead, as he completed his survey. It sounded ominous, even to him. The Allies had complete freedom of the skies, thanks to the provisional government's desperation to come to *some* kind of agreement, but they'd never sent so many aircraft before. It bothered him, more than he cared to admit. It felt like the calm before the storm.

"I heard a rumour," Keitel said. "They're stockpiling troops and ammunition behind the lines."

"I doubt it," Hans said. That suggested competence, something the provisional government had yet to display. And a willingness to engage in street fighting...he shuddered. Verdun had been terrible. A battle in the streets of Germany itself would be worse. "I think..."

He felt, more than heard, the sound of hundreds of guns opening fire as once. Hans, and every other experienced soldier, threw himself into the nearest trench and braced himself for the impact. The ground shook seconds later, water and mud splashing into the trench and cascading over the hapless defenders. He heard pieces of shrapnel flying through the air and prayed, desperately, that the Allies had not started firing gas shells into the trenches. Half of his men didn't have masks, let alone full-body protections. The Allies could wipe his force out overnight if they used gas. But they'd be wary if they wanted to take the trenches for themselves.

Trenches are defensive, he thought. *I doubt they're worried about ever being on the defence again. But we can hope.*

"I think the negotiations failed," Keitel shouted, as the ground heaved time and time again. The sound of explosions was deafening. "This isn't random shelling."

"I think you're right." Hans cursed as a disembodied head landed next to him. One of the former sailors, apparently. The idiot hadn't had the sense to get down when the shells had started to explode. He'd had a cushy billet on a ship until the fleet had sailed off to England and safety.

"Damn you, damn you all," Hans muttered at the distant gunners, scurrying forward on his hands and knees.

He stayed low, cursing the enemy gunners under his breath. The entire trenchline was starting to collapse. They hadn't had time to secure the trenches properly, let alone keep mud from sliding back into the trenches and driving the inhabitants out. He saw a rat rushing past, the tiny beast maddened by the impact. It would have been dinner, if his men had caught it before the offensive. They'd have had no choice. There was little else to eat, even for officers.

The shelling started to move eastwards.

Now we're in trouble, Hans grimaced, knowing that wasn't a good sign. The enemy would be advancing from the west. He straightened up, careful to keep his head low as he peered into the distance. He could see a handful of shapes, moving up behind a smokescreen. Tanks. British tanks. There was no mistaking the familiar shape of vehicles that had brought so much death and destruction to the army. Or, behind them, the advancing Tommies. The British might lack the gallantry of the French or the pervasive fatalism of the Russians, but they had nerve.

If the British hadn't made their stand in 1914...wait, no point in worrying about it now, Hans told himself. *It doesn't matter.*

Looking down, Hans felt his heart sink as he drew his pistol from his belt, then braced himself and waited. It looked as if the British were hurling *everything* at him and his men. There were hundreds of tanks, pressing against the German lines in a frontal assault; infantrymen flanked them, ready to protect their armoured comrades from grenades and mines. The tactics were far from subtle; no gentle prodding to find a weakness before hurling in the main assault for this offensive. Just overwhelming force, aimed all along the line. There would be a hundred breakthroughs within the hour, if the defenders had the nerve to stand and fight.

Whether HQ is keeping troops back in the hopes of cutting off any breakthroughs before they could be exploited won't matter, Hans thought bitterly. *We might as well have tried to stop the tide by shouting at it.*

"Take aim," he shouted. He suspected that half his men couldn't hear him over the din, but he knew his duty. "Fire!"

With that, he snapped off a shot at a British infantryman. The solider didn't fall. He heard the machine guns open fire, spraying the tanks with bullets. The gunners were new, clearly unaware there was no point in wasting bullets on the tanks.

"Idiots, fire at the soldiers instead!" he screamed. He shouted curses at the men. The scared former sailors complied, and a handful of Tommies fell. The remainder ducked as the tanks aimed their machine guns and opened fire. Hans hit the ground, a second before a stream of bullets tore through the air above him. Then the sponson cannon fired, and the machine gunners were vaporized before they could even shift positions. *I need to get that gun back up*, Hans thought. He started scrambling towards their guns, then realised it was useless. They'd already been disabled, and clearly there was no time to perform a hasty repair.

Keitel caught his arm. "We have to move!"

Hans nodded and followed him into the connecting trench, feeling sweat trickling down his back as the enemy tanks started to crush their way into the forward trenches. The noise was too loud, his ears hurt as shells crashed down in the distance. He could barely hear himself barking orders at what remained of his men, trying to dissuade one man from snatching up a knapsack full of grenades and hurling himself on a tank. Whether in zeal or deafness, the soldier ignore Hans' command.

You fool, Hans thought, ducking away from the blast. The British tank blew up nicely, the screams of its crew dimly audible in the flames. Of course, there were hundreds more behind it. *That man just wasted his life...*

"Fall back," Hans shouted. The retreat was rapidly turning into a rout. He saw one tank get stuck in a trench and felt a moment's hope, only to lose it when three more tanks crunched their way through the trench and fired on the retreating men. "Hurry!"

With that, Hans put his head down and forced himself to run. They had orders to rendezvous at a village a mile or two behind the lines if all hell broke loose, but that seemed pointless. Hans tried not to think about what he'd seen as he collected the remainder of his men and marched them east, towards the next line.

As they moved, the attack seemed to have slacked. Some of the men even remarked on this, but Hans knew better. The Tommies were merely catching their breath and rushing reinforcements forward, before resuming the offensive. They wouldn't give their enemies time to dig more trenches and make a stand, not now. They'd learnt better over the last few years.

A flight of aircraft buzzed over them, a couple dropping low to strafe the retreating soldiers. Hans hit the ground, cursing as Adolf fired on the aircraft...he understood, all too well, but it was just a waste of bullets. There was no real prospect of hitting anything, unless Adolf got very lucky. Hans bit down the reprimand that came to mind. Firing back would give his men a sense they were hitting back, even though they were vastly outnumbered and outgunned. And besides, who knew? Perhaps Adolf *would* hit something.

He heard a rumbling behind him as they finally staggered into what remained of the village. It had been a farming town, only a few short hours ago. Now...enemy shelling and aircraft had worked it over thoroughly, smashing every last building into a pile of rubble. The HQ was burning, flames licking merrily towards the skies. He glanced at Keitel, then looked around. A handful of men were still straggling into the village, but the officers who should have commanded the front were gone. He felt a flash of pure hatred. It was possible they were under the rubble, dead or wishing they were, but he didn't believe it. The cowards had probably taken their drinks cabinets and their mistresses and hotfooted it back to Berlin. He *knew* it. The brave men were dead. Only the cowards survived.

A young man, so young that Hans thought he should still be in school, saluted. "*Herr Hauptman*. What should we do?"

Hans bit down the urge to tell the boy to throw down his weapon, change into something a little more civilian and swear blind he'd never had anything to do with the army. If the child had even a month of training, it evidently hadn't taken. He was so wet behind the ears that he was addressing a senior officer with almost casual informality...Hans shook his head. Right now, there was no point in crying over spilt milk. The rumbling was growing louder, and they *weren't* being shelled. It could only mean one thing. Enemy troops were on their way.

"We retreat, back towards Frankfurt," he ordered, harshly. The city hadn't—yet—been declared a free city. "And we don't look back."

He glanced westwards, cursing as he saw the plumes of smoke rising into the sky. The enemy were pushing forward along a very wide front, taking the time—no doubt—to smash as much of the army as possible before they pushed further into Germany itself. Perhaps they'd waste time dividing the spoils once they crossed the Rhine...he shook his head. They had to get back in touch with higher authority, if they wanted to do anything more than take pot-shots at enemy troops before they got wiped out. And if they had to make a stand...well, then they'd die in place.

The march east rapidly turned into a nightmare. A handful of men from other units joined them, along with a number of civilians who hadn't been evacuated before the enemy offensive began. Hans had expected them to have food, but...they were as deprived as his men. A couple of women begged for food, offering their bodies to anyone who had something they could eat, but...no one took them up on it. There was *no* food and little water. Hans gave the last of his canteen to a little girl, even though he knew the poor child was probably doomed. Perhaps it was for the best. She'd grow up starving and hungry when the war finally came to an end.

He'd hoped to see a couple of friendly aircraft in the skies, but there were none. Enemy aircraft roamed freely, shooting up railway lines and the handful of tanks and lorries on the roads. They walked past a burnt-out column of motor lorries that had been apparently heading east. A dead body—a man in a general's uniform—lay beside the convoy. Hans guessed he'd fled when the shelling started, along with his staff. It hadn't bought him safety.

"Traitor," Adolf hissed.

Hans couldn't disagree. The general, whoever he'd been, hadn't stuck around to lead the defence. And it had killed him…Hans smiled, even though he knew it was a bad sign. The betrayer had been killed before he could do more damage.

Night was falling as they stumbled into Frankfurt and passed their civilians to the local government before reporting to the army HQ. The officers on duty didn't seem to know what to do. One of them was chattering on the phone, giving ludicrously optimistic reports about enemy tanks being destroyed and thousands of enemy soldiers being killed; another was moving imaginary units around an equally imaginary map. Hans had no idea what country's defences were displayed on the map, but it sure as hell wasn't Germany in 1919. The newspaper on the desk, weeks out of date, babbled about the Free Corps in what had once been Russia. Hans snorted, despite himself.

What does the Free Corps matter when the Reich itself was doomed?

The officer in command was fat, wearing a uniform that had clearly never seen action. Hans disliked him on sight. He'd bet whatever remained of his life savings—if the government hadn't already seized them to fund the war—that the officer hadn't seen action either. A strong man in his position could have accomplished much, but instead he appeared to be dithering, his eyes flickering between the imaginary maps and the handful of more realistic reports someone had pinned on the noticeboard. Hans tried not to wince when he read them. If they were accurate, Frankfurt would come under attack in less than a day.

"They'll be coming to our rescue," the officer said, stiffly. "The masses of manoeuvre are on their way."

Hans would have been more impressed if he'd known who *they* were. There were *no* masses of manoeuvre left in Germany, save for distantly unfriendly ones. The idea of the British turning on the French now…the officer babbled on, claiming that the Allies would fall out and start fighting amongst themselves now they had *real* spoils of war. The *Reich* merely had to hold out long enough for them to fall out…Hans shook his head, not bothering to hide his disbelief. The *Reich* had almost nothing left. Even if the British and French *did* start fighting, the *Reich* couldn't take advantage of it.

He stole a packet of cigarettes—French, according to the label— and walked back outside. Frankfurt looked like a hive of activity, even to him, but most of the activity looked distantly unfocused. Soldiers gathered around fires, sharing what little heat they could as they scrabbled over food and drink. Someone had started to loot civilian homes, dragging out hoarded food and opening wine cellars.

Goddammit, this won't end well, Hans thought as he saw soldiers passing out bottles of alcohol, while beating civilians who tried to object. There wasn't a single military policeman in sight. Order was on the verge of breaking down completely. He wanted to try to take control, but he knew it would be futile. The men had been pushed too far, betrayed once too many times. He tried not to look at a body swinging from a lamppost. He didn't want to know.

Keitel and the rest of the unit were waiting for him. Hans shared out the cigarettes, then sat down, too despondent to do anything. He could *still* hear the sound of guns in the distance, as the Allies continued their advance. There were any number of things the Germans could do to slow them, but it looked as though no one was bothering to try. Even Adolf had fallen quiet, lost in his own thoughts. Hans watched the younger man for a long moment, then shrugged and unpacked his blanket. Sleeping in the open would be rough, but he'd slept in worse places.

*At least we're be relatively safe...*he thought as sleep claimed him.

Hans was jarred awake, what felt like seconds later, by shells falling within the city. He glanced around, half-convinced that he was having a nightmare. He'd slept so poorly that it was hard to believe that it was really dawn, that the enemy were bombarding the city itself. Dazed, he staggered to his feet, looking around for water. There was none. A series of rumbles ran through the city as more and more shells crashed down, a handful coming alarmingly close. He saw a building topple and fall, pieces of rubble smashing to the ground. He hoped—desperately—that no one had been inside. The civilians should have had the sense to stay underground.

A messenger ran up to him, looking utterly terrified. "They're attacking from the west!"

"Well, of *course*," Hans snarled. Where *else* would the Allies be attacking from? "Do you know anything *useful*?"

Another volley of shells slammed into the city before the messenger could answer. Hans ducked, cursing as more shrapnel flew through the air. He was too tired and sore to panic, but the messenger turned and fled. Hans opened his mouth to call him back and demand some *real* orders, but it was too late. Far too late. The messenger was in the middle of the streets when the shells fell again. He was knocked to the cobblestones. He didn't get up again.

"Get everyone into position, ready to fall back," Hans snarled to his men. Frankfurt was practically undefended. There were certainly no *modern* defences. The stone walls wouldn't last a minute when the Allies brought tanks and guns to bear on them. "We have to start moving…"

He watched, grimly, as the shellfire began creeping east. The Tommies were definitely coming, the British and French and Americans and God alone knew who else. He could practically smell them, well-fed and well-armed men inching towards a defence line that was pathetically weak. Hans wondered, with a savagery that surprised him, just what had happened to the fat bastard in command. Frederick the Great would have done a much better job. Even Hindenburg and Ludendorff would have done *something* to make the city difficult to take. But the provisional government had dismissed them. That had been a mistake.

A handful of enemy infantrymen appeared, probing through the city. Hans muttered orders, instructing his troops to hold fire until the enemy got closer. There weren't any tanks, as far as he could tell. Tanks wouldn't be so useful in crowded streets. If they just waited…

The sound of aircraft passing overhead caused him to jump. To Hans' pleasant surprise, they aircraft simply roared overhead.

They're not going to drop this close to their troops in a city, he realized. *The fight will be even.* Hans waited, silently counting down the seconds, until dozens of enemy soldiers were within range.

That's the best we're going to do, he thought.

"Fire!"

His men fired as one. A dozen enemy soldiers fell, the remainder scattering and taking cover. Hans snapped more orders, telling his men to run. They didn't have the ammunition or the positions to make a fight of it, not now. Moments later, shells fell on where they'd been. Hans gritted his teeth. One of the bastards who'd survived had a radio, clearly, and enough nerve to risk shelling himself—and his troops—in order to kill the Germans. Hans forced himself to run harder as the defence line shattered.

"Get to the river," someone shouted. "Flee!"

"Stand and fight," Adolf shouted, as they reached another makeshift defence line. "Stand and fight…"

"Don't be a fool," Hans snapped at him. "Run!"

He saw flashes and flickers of moments in the fall of the city as he ran for his life, heading towards a fallback point no one had expected to have to use. Buildings collapsing into rubble, hundreds of civilians running in all directions. A uniformed officer gunned down by his own men, half-drunk on the alcohol they'd liberated the previous night. A woman lying dead on the cobblestones, her head missing; another *frau* screaming her life away as she stared at her missing arms. Hans wanted to help her, but there was nothing he could do. Her arms were gone. Even if someone stanched the bleeding, what sort of life could she expect? The thought was sickening.

A building towered up beside him. He leaned against the stone to catch his breath, feeling everything start to catch up with him. He hadn't eaten properly in days…he hadn't even had anything to *drink*. Despair was yammering at the back of his mind, threatening to overwhelm him. Perhaps life in a POW camp wouldn't be too bad. He'd be fed, at least. The war—his war—would be over.

He heard someone—a woman—whimper and froze, then inched along the side street and peered around a corner. A woman was bent over a metal bin, tears streaming down her face as a half-dressed soldier fucked her from behind. He held her down, even as he ploughed his way in and out of her. Hans knew, beyond a shadow of a doubt, that he was *raping* her. His stomach churned as he reached for his pistol, trying not to look at the girl's blonde hair. She reminded him of his sister.

The rapist smiled at him. "You want a go?"

Hans levelled the pistol at him. "Get away from her!"

"Oh, come on," the rapist said. "Does it *matter* any longer? You can have her after I'm done."

Hans gritted his teeth. Part of him was tempted, even though he *knew* it would be wrong. It had been too long since he'd lain with a woman, too long…he swallowed hard, angrily dismissing the thought. It would be wrong. He pulled the trigger before he could think better of it, putting a bullet though the rapist's head. His body fell backwards and hit the ground. The woman straightened, took one terrified look at Hans and ran for her life. Hans didn't blame her. He just hoped she managed to pull herself together before someone decided to blame her for being raped. Or she ran into someone else who'd thrown civilised behaviour out the window.

He checked the rapist's body, then stood and hurried towards the edge of the city. The sound of firing was getting closer, but…if he was lucky, he might just be able to get out of the city and hurry to the fallback position before the noose closed. He hoped...he joined hundreds of soldiers and thousands of civilians as they headed east, searching for a safety he knew probably didn't exist. Would they eventually retreat all the way to Moscow or Siberia? He wouldn't have ruled it out.

His legs hurt dreadfully by the time he finally stumbled into the fallback position, a mid-sized town that had already been bombed by enemy aircraft. Keitel met him at the HQ, looking surprisingly relieved to see him. Adolf was the only other familiar face, standing in front of a crowd of soldiers and civilians and urging them to fight to the last. Hans looked at his audience and knew the message was falling on deaf ears. The men, soldiers and civilians alike, looked as if they were ready to give up. It was clear that hundreds of men had already deserted.

"We have orders to dig trenches and hold the line," Keitel informed him. "They say they're already talking about a truce."

Hans snorted. He might be an officer, but he hadn't had his brain removed during his promotion ceremony. One couldn't bargain if there was nothing to bargain *with*. The Allies had made enormous gains in two days...and they'd know it. Of *course* they'd know it. Four years of trench warfare, where neither side had managed to gain very much no matter how much blood and treasure they'd thrown into the fire, had taught them how hard it was to push through a determined defence. Now...the only thing slowing them down was their logistics problems. He glanced at the half-ruined town and shook his head as his stomach growled angrily. There were no guns, no tanks, no nothing...not even food. They were thoroughly fucked. He checked his pistol and frowned. Only a handful of rounds left.

He laughed, despite himself.

I should have beaten that rapist to death, not shot him, Hans thought. *I didn't even get any ammunition out of the incident.*

Keitel gave him an odd look. "*Herr Hauptman?*"

"Never mind," Hans said. "We'd better get to work."

He pulled his men back into the trenches, working hard to set a good example. Four years ago, an officer would *never* have dug trenches with the men. Now…he *had* to convince his men that he was sharing their sufferings. Adolf might want to continue the fight, but the rest of his men—most of whom didn't even *know* him—had other ideas. Hans knew he couldn't stop them if they chose to desert. Order and discipline had broken down everywhere.

A snarl ran through the line as a farmer drove his horse and cart into the town. No one said anything, as far as Hans could tell, but the men ran forward as one and snatched the horse. The farmer tried to object and they knocked him down, cutting the beast's throat and butchering it inexpertly before cooking the meat over the fire. Hans knew he couldn't object. The men were starving…they were *all* starving. They'd done their best, but their trench network was pitiful and they knew it. They honestly didn't have the strength to do a proper job. He promised the farmer compensation, a promise he knew he wasn't going to be able to keep, as the meat was shared out. Hans was careful to take only his fair share. He really didn't want the men turning on him.

"We'll stop them," Adolf said. He ate his meat like a dog, holding it in his bare fingers and snapping at it until the bone had been picked clean. "They won't get past us."

Keitel found a radio and turned it on. Hans listened, half-expecting to hear Radio Berlin announcing an armistice—or a surrender. They were whipped. They *knew* they were whipped. But, instead, there was patriotic music and exhortations to hold the line, exhortations his men roundly jeered. Hans groaned, inwardly, as the music played on, without even a single shred of real news. Who was in charge now? Who was running the government? And what were they thinking?

He looked up as he heard a motorcycle approaching from the east. The rider waved to the men as he drove through the town and came to a halt by the HQ. Hans stood and hurried to him, desperate for news. But the rider merely shrugged and hurried into the building. Hans groaned, then waited. It was nearly an hour before the rider and an officer hurried back out into the cold air.

"You have command," the officer said. "I have to go back to HQ."

Hans watched him go, feeling his last shred of hope evaporate. The hordes of enemy tanks were steadily grinding towards him, smashing the Fatherland under their treads. And, above, he could hear hundreds of aircraft flying through the sky. He knew it was only a matter of time before they started to bomb his position. There was no point in trying to hide. The town was an obvious chokepoint. He'd have been more impressed if he'd thought someone higher up the chain of command was knocking down bridges and tearing up roads and doing hundreds of other things to slow the enemy down and buy time.

He looked at his men, gathered in front of the radio and felt an insane urge to cry. He didn't know any of them, apart from Keitel and Adolf. A number seemed to have vanished over the last few hours, abandoning their comrades and heading east. The radio claimed that deserters were being shot, but Hans didn't believe it. The remnants of the once-great army were nowhere near that organised. A man could throw away his uniform and claim to be a civilian in a protected category and…who could say otherwise? The days when a deserter couldn't hope to hide were long gone.

A thunderclap echoed across the town, followed rapidly by another. The enemy had started shelling again, firing ranging shots to check their targets before they fired a full barrage. He heard the sound of tanks advancing in the distance, their crews readying themselves for yet another brief and utterly one-sided encounter. They'd smash his defences with ease…they might not even notice they *had* encountered defences. And the infantry behind them would mop up his men and move on.

"The defenders of the Fatherland are strong," the radio proclaimed. Hans had no idea who was speaking, but the voice was starting to grate. Some pompous ass with good connections, probably some aristocratic brat important enough to be granted a pass from the trenches of the war. "They will not falter."

"Shut up!" Hans shot the radio, then glared at his men. "Take your positions."

He forced himself to wait as the sound of advancing tanks grew louder. The enemy *had* to come through them, unless they wanted to take their tanks cross-country. Perhaps they did. Rumour claimed the French wanted to starve the Germans into submission, even though they'd already won the war. Destroying acres of farmland would make it difficult, if not impossible, to feed the civilian population. Hans believed they'd do if, if they were given a chance. And why not? The Germans had done worse when they'd occupied parts of France, back when they'd been sure they'd win the war.

And now the French will be chasing the ladies of Berlin, he thought, morbidly. *And laughing at us as we starve to death.*

Hans' despair grew as the first enemy tank came into view. It was a monstrous beast, blowing smoke as it ground forward. Others followed, the ground shaking as they advanced on his position. Hans closed his eyes for a long moment, clutching his pistol in one hand. He didn't have a hope in hell of stopping them and he knew it. They knew it too, if they had the slightest idea he was even there. They'd crush his men and move onwards, advancing right into the heart of the Fatherland until they reached Berlin itself.

Surely, he told himself, *the provisional government will see sense long before Berlin itself is taken.*

"Order the men to fire one round and then retreat," Hans told Keitel. There was no point in trying to make a stand. It would just get them all killed. "We can't stop them."

"We can," Adolf insisted. His dark eyes gleamed. "We can hold them…"

The tanks opened fire. Hans crouched in the trench, feeling uncomfortably like he was lying in a grave. Bullets flew over his head, so close he was *certain* they were tearing through his clothes and scratching his bare skin. He knew it was his imagination, he knew it couldn't possibly be real, but the sense of being utterly naked was irresistible. There was no point in returning fire, not with his pistol. He crawled through the trench, back into the town. A couple of the houses had been turned into strongpoints. They'd probably slow the tanks down for a handful of seconds. Who knew? It might just be long enough for him to get the rest of his men out.

"Johan is dead," someone shouted. "They killed him!"

"Move," Keitel snarled. The sergeant caught the younger man and shook him, violently. "Or you'll join him."

The ground shook, time and time again, as shells landed in the rear of the town. It had been a nice place to live, once. Now…Hans shook his head as he took cover behind a house, knowing it might draw fire at any moment. Half the buildings were already on fire, the remainder falling to pieces or sheltering soldiers who'd die the moment their homes were targeted for destruction. He felt his heart turn cold as he saw an enemy tank run over a mine and explode, feeling a flicker of glee a second before it was quenched by *another* tank rumbling past the burning wreckage and pressing onwards. There was nothing glorious in war, not now. There were no heroic cavalry charges, no infantry making brave stands against eastern barbarians and tribesmen. There wasn't even any honour or glory or shared brotherhood between men who fought together during the day and drank together at night. There was just an endless row of machines, crushing men beneath their treads even as they stripped the glory from war.

Hans remembered his father's stories and shuddered. The old man had fought in the *last* war. He'd glossed over a lot, Hans realised now. He'd…lied, perhaps. War wasn't glorious…it had never been glorious. And the men in Berlin, whoever they were, knew they were sending thousands of men to their deaths, for nothing. It was only a matter of time before Berlin fell, if they didn't surrender first. There would be nothing left to fight for. The *Reich* was doomed. It had died when the Kaiser had fled for neutral territory.

"We lost all, but seventeen," Keitel said, as they gathered at the edge of town. The sergeant sounded as though he was at the end of his endurance. The men didn't look any better. A couple looked shell-shocked, as if they'd snapped under the weight of enemy fire; the remainder looked tired, worn and beaten. "I think…"

"Put down your guns," Hans ordered, harshly. He suspected they were effectively out of ammunition. It didn't matter. Even if they had full loads, they didn't have anything that could stop the tanks. "It's time to surrender."

"But we can still win!" Adolf brandished his rifle. "We can stop them."

"We can't." Hans allowed his gaze to move from face to face, silently noting how many agreed with him. All, but two seemed to understand. "Anyone who wants to go can go. Now. The rest of us will walk into a POW camp."

"Treason," Adolf said. He sounded stunned, as if he couldn't believe what he was hearing. "I…"

Hans shot him straight through the chest. Adolf's body hit the ground. The men looked on in shock.

"If anyone wants to leave," Hans repeated, "they can go now. The rest of us will surrender."

He put the pistol down, heedless of the danger. One of his men could put a bullet in his back, if he wished. In truth, Hans no longer cared. He was tired and cold and hungry and he knew he'd been put out on a limb to die. He wanted to march back to Berlin and drag the rats out of their lair, but…he knew it would never happen. He couldn't endure any more. He turned and raised his hands, walking in the open and hoping the tanks realised that he was trying to surrender. If they didn't…at least it would be quick.

Behind him, the body of Adolf Hitler lay in the mud.

* * * * *

Author's Note

If Germany had tried to continue the fight in 1919, she would have encountered a number of serious difficulties. The army knew it had been beaten—the 'stab in the back' myth didn't start until after the war was over—and just about *everything* was in short supply. They had a handful of tanks and aircraft, but the Allies had *more* of everything, including food. Worse, perhaps, the government was not in complete control of the country, let alone the 'independent' forces fighting in the east. An attempt to continue the war, for whatever reason, would have ended very badly. The population would have starved if they hadn't been conquered by the end of 1919.

And yet, it might have worked out better in the long run. If the Germans *knew* they had been beaten in 1919, would they have been so quick to rally behind Hitler in 1939?

Hitler himself served as a dispatch rider in the trenches, until he was wounded in a gas attack and sent to hospital. In this timeline, he leaves hospital in time to join the final defence of the *Reich*—whimsy on my part, I admit, but a world without Adolf Hitler would probably be an objectively better place. But then, no one in that world would know it

* * *

Christopher G. Nuttall Bio

Christopher Nuttall has been planning sci-fi books since he learned to read. Born and raised in Edinburgh, Chris created an alternate history website and eventually graduated to writing full-sized novels. Studying history independently allowed him to develop worlds that hung together and provided a base for storytelling. After graduating from university, Chris started writing full-time. As an indie author, he has published fifty novels and one novella (so far) through Amazon Kindle Direct Publishing.

Professionally, he has published The Royal Sorceress, Bookworm, A Life Less Ordinary, Sufficiently Advanced Technology, The Royal Sorceress II: The Great Game and Bookworm II: The Very Ugly Duckling with Elsewhen Press, and Schooled in Magic through Twilight Times Books.

As a matter of principle, all of Chris's self-published Kindle books are DRM-free.

Chris has a blog where he published updates, snippets and world-building notes at http://chrishanger.wordpress.com/ and a website at http://www.chrishanger.net.

Chris is currently living in Edinburgh with his partner, muse, and critic, Aisha.

# # # # #

Fighting Spirit
by Philip S. Bolger

Supreme Allied Command
Sharm El-Sheikh, Egypt
April 3, 1944

Commander Seth Bailey walked through the door to the planning room, carrying a briefcase full of the Navy's latest plans. The room was converted from some British colonial outpost—the whole place felt vaguely Victorian-meets-Arab. Numerous boards had been set up to track everything from casualties to fuel expenditure rates. Busy men and a few women in American uniforms—Army, Navy, and Marines—hustled by, and the steady click of typewriters generated the background hum of a theater command. He noticed there were a lot of Japanese staff planners, though all of them were wearing Imperial Japanese Navy uniforms—only one was clad in the uniform of the Imperial Japanese Army.

Bailey walked up to the desk of a Marine colonel and saluted.

"Sir, Commander Bailey reporting with the Combined Fleet's Plans."

The colonel returned the salute and had one of his aides take the plans briefcase.

"Take a seat, Bailey," he said. "I'm Colonel Dan Kemp, chief of staff of this whole nightmare. I take it fleet's sent you here as liaison?"

"Yes sir," Bailey said. "That seems to be my job a lot these days."

"It's not glamorous, Bailey, but someone's got to do it. How much landlubber do you speak?"

"If it doesn't involve small arms, none at all," Bailey said.

"Before I put you in front of a bunch of brass," said Kemp, "I'm gonna prime you up on where we are. Since you boys in the Navy kicked Hitler's ass out by the Horn of Africa, we've made some progress. Come with me to the map."

Bailey followed Colonel Kemp to a large map of the Middle East, adorned with symbols for military units.

"In three months," Kemp said, "we managed to thrash Mussolini's boys in Ethiopia. The Free British and Free French, along with the Ethiopians, are driving north from there through Sudan. We've got our 3rd Armored Division with them."

He motioned to the map, pointing at some symbols near the Atlantic coast of Africa.

"On the other end, Operation Torch is a go. This one had to be all-American; too tough to pull Japanese assets from the Pacific here, especially with the turbulence in Indochina and the Middle East. The Krauts' U-boat force did some damage to the invasion force, but Jerry learned the hard way that it's one thing to sink trawlers and another entirely to go after a full fleet invasion force."

Bailey whistled. *Enough escorts to make a submariner's nightmare,* he thought.

"The Vichy haven't put up much resistance," said Kemp. "They saw the writing on the wall from the brush-up in Indochina, and they ain't wild about speaking German, but they're still manning positions. So that leads us to this, the main effort."

He pointed to the map. The Suez Canal was covered with pins, each representing different units.

"We've got the entirety of the Japanese Special Naval Landing Force, as well as two divisions of soldiers they trust."

"I'm sorry, sir, what was that? Trusted divisions?" asked Bailey. "I was just the liaison to Yamamoto, he mentioned nothing like that."

Kemp smiled. "'Course he didn't. The Japanese, they're big on 'face.' Means they don't like to look bad, think John Wayne, but if he could never stop being the guy he is in the pictures. This whole 'trust' thing is incredibly shameful to them, but simply put, they don't trust their army right now, what with the coup and assassination attempts a decade ago, the whole 'let's start a fight with China and force the empire to go along' gambit. When that failed, they had to sideline most of their army, which is why they're pulling garrison duty on Formosa or confined to the home islands. Don't bring it up around the Japanese; they're sensitive, but yes…that's the deal."

He went back to the board.

"Here, just past the Suez, we've got three corps' worth of troops—VI and VIII Corps, plus my old friends from 1st Marine Division from the US and the Japanese Naval Infantry Corps, which also has their army guys. We've got a problem, and that problem is Cairo."

"Right," said Bailey. "Since the real problem is the Suez, and if the Krauts have a bunch of heavy hitters fortified in Cairo, it's one quick movement to jeopardize the canal."

"And if they do that, with Britain currently speaking German, it'll be that much harder to put American boots to Hitler's ass," said Kemp. "This is the main effort. We're up against Erwin Rommel and his Afrika Korps. You ever heard of Rommel, Bailey?"

Bailey nodded. "His name's been in the newsreels."

"And the intel briefs," said Kemp. "He's a tough son of a bitch, and clever. When he realized he was being hit from three sides, he brought all his boys and all their toys into Egypt. Easy to be resupplied from Axis bases in the Med, and a way to contest the canal. Got his armor spread out across the Nile, and his infantry holding the city itself. Gonna be a bitch to dig him out. Intel thinks he's not gonna stay on the defensive forever, so we need to strike fast, before he overwhelms our Sinai forces."

"What's the plan?" asked Bailey. "I can tell you the Navy plans to support throughout the gulf, but presumably, you ground guys have something else going."

"Sure do," Kemp said, grinning. "A two-corps offensive, kicking off tomorrow. First elements into the city will be the 45th Infantry Division. They were green boys six months ago, but since then they've fought in the biggest engagements we've had in this theater. They took the Suez, and they did so with some heavy losses. We've got replacements in, but they're first in the pipe. Immediately following them will be 1 MARDIV, along with the Japanese SNLF Division covering the northern flank. Once this advance secures the outskirts, we'll find out if Rommel has the stomach for a city fight."

"Wait, how much naval infantry do the Japanese have?" asked Bailey, quietly wishing he'd paid more attention to the land-centric intel briefing.

Kemp looked at him. "They've got about a division and a half, plus their loyal army units. Their SNLF, though, they're the real deal. Japanese Marines." Kemp grinned broadly. "So you know they're worth a damn."

"How long do we have to plan?" asked Bailey.

Kemp shrugged. "Not long enough, so let's get to it."

* * *

Sergeant First Class Gary Kurtzhals took another pull on his Lucky Strike. Smoke breaks were his time to relax—a time where he didn't have to worry what his crewmen were doing or what tasking the platoon leader or first sergeant might have. He could just relax, at least as much as he could relax clad in greasy tanker coveralls and sweating under the desert sun.

He stared out at the wastes, all flat sand, with only the silhouettes of his unit's tanks breaking up the endless dunes. Egypt was, as far as he could tell, a really lousy place to live. It wasn't that it was ugly— hell, his home state of Nebraska got made fun of for being flat and boring—but more that it was the site of a war. Kurtzhals was sitting against the ruins of a German Panzer III medium tank. It wasn't one he'd shot—it had been blown to smithereens years ago when the Free British were fighting their rearguard action here.

That was what made Gary think it was such a lousy place to live. To live in Egypt meant to live in a war that didn't show any sign of ending. The Germans had defeated the British, nearly entirely, and looked poised to be the masters of Europe, until the US and Japan entered the war, but none of that should've mattered to Egypt. They were just another battleground between stronger powers.

Gary shook his head. His cigarette was finished. *Time to get back to maintenance*, he thought.

Sergeant Kurtzhals walked back over to where his tank was parked to find Corporal (T/5) Alex Spataro holding court with the rest of the tank crew. Spataro was a tall man, a bit heavyset for a soldier, with a strong Philadelphia accent and brown hair in an army crewcut. He was standing over two of the other tankers, who were conducting a functions check on a .30 caliber machine gun.

"No, you dumbass," said Corporal Spataro. "That's the wrong way to load that."

"Sorry, Corporal," said Private Eugene Matoi. "I, uh, I forgot."

Matoi was much smaller—his tanker's coveralls hung off him with room to spare, and the man's features always reminded Kurtzhals of a small child. The young private was eager to please and prove his worth—good traits in a younger soldier, Kurtzhals thought, but the lack of extensive training prior to his deployment had some other issues. Kurtzhals was always concerned about undisciplined soldiers.

"How the fuck do you remember all those baseball stats and can't remember the right order to load the damn machinegun?" asked Spataro.

Kurtzhals observed. *Looks like Spataro is growing into his NCO role*, Kurtzhals thought. *Suits him. If we keep taking losses, he'll be a tank commander sooner than later. It's Matoi I'm worried about.*

Private Matoi tried again. Spataro watched intently. This time, the young private got it right. Alex clapped, slowly.

"Hey, second time's the charm, I guess," said Alex. "But just remember, the Krauts won't give you a second chance."

"Are they as good as the newsreels say?" asked Matoi.

Kurtzhals groaned internally. The new recruits were all scared of the dreaded Blitzkrieg. The collapse of Britain had led to a flurry of press lionizing the Germans—Kurtzhals was tired of having to dispel those myths. Before the sergeant could open his mouth, Spataro solved the problem for him.

"Nah," said Alex. "They die just like you and me. You put your crosshairs right on the side of their fancy fuckin' Panzers, and they still buy it. Just because they're not invincible don't mean they ain't tough."

"I agree with Corporal Spataro," said Kurtzhals. "The Jerries are still human. They've got good tanks, I'll give the bastards that, but they leak and smoke and explode just like ours."

"Oh, hey Sarge!" said Alex, turning around. "Didn't see you there."

"Don't call me Sarge," said Kurtzhals. "You know damn well it's Sergeant."

"Roger, Sergeant," said Spataro. "We were just going over the .30 cal."

"I heard. You did a good job teaching. Matoi, you used to it yet?"

Matoi nodded. "I think so, Sergeant."

Kurtzhals nodded. "For a guy trained as infantry, you're taking to more honest work real quick."

The sergeant turned to face Alex.

"Where are Fritz and Herrera?"

"Went to go get water, Sergeant," Alex said. "Should be back shortly."

"Is *Grizzly* ready to go?"

Alex nodded enthusiastically. "Sure is. Got our extra fuel reserves, too, in case we get stuck again."

Kurtzhals nodded once. "Yeah, we'll see."

The sergeant climbed up on the tank. *Grizzly* was an M4A2 Sherman, manufactured in July of 1943 at Lima Locomotive works. Painted in an olive green that didn't match the desert environment and a bright white star that Kurtzhals privately thought made a great target reference point for the enemy, *Grizzly* was Kurtzhal's home. The crew had put extra tracks on the side of the turret, to provide a bit more protection from enemy rounds, and Fritz, the driver, had painted a grizzly bear on the side of the hull. Kurtzhals and Spataro had taken *Grizzly* from the Persian Gulf all the way up to Egypt, and the tank was a bit banged up and in need of some depot time. There was blast damage on the front armor from where a Pz IV had smacked them head on, and dings and dents from fragments of artillery. Despite that, as Alex promised, *Grizzly* was ready to go, at least, once the loader and driver got back.

"Matoi," Kurtzhals shouted from inside the tank.

"Sergeant?" Matoi's voice came back.

"Pop quiz—what are the five crew roles on an M4 Sherman tank?"

"Commander, gunner, loader, driver, and assistant driver," Matoi rattled off.

Kurtzhals popped his head out of the tank. "Yeah, you got the names right. What do they do? Start with yours."

"Sergeant, I am *Grizzly's* assistant driver. My primary responsibility is managing the radio, and my secondary responsibility is to man the forward-facing .30 caliber machinegun. In the event the driver is wounded or killed, I am supposed to take over."

"Very good. Driver?"

"The driver is responsible for driving the tank," said Matoi. "He keeps us moving, which Corproal Spataro says keeps us alive."

"That's because Corporal Spataro has seen enough wrecks to know what happens to tanks that stand still. How 'bout the loader?"

"The loader is responsible for loading the 75mm gun, as well as choosing the correct shell to load."

"What types of shells are there?"

"Umm…I'm not sure, Sergeant," said Matoi.

"That's a job you should be training for," said Alex. "When Herrera gets back, ask him."

"Yes, Sergeant," Matoi said.

"Two more positions, Matoi," Kurtzhals said.

"The gunner is responsible for engaging and destroying the enemy, and the commander is responsible for, as you said, Sergeant, keeping this whole shitshow rolling."

"Not the doctrinal answer, but I won't fault you for quoting me," said Kurtzhals. "We'll make a tanker out of you, yet, Matoi."

As Kurtzhals finished, he saw Fritz and Herrera walking up. The two men were accompanied by Lieutenant Haskins, which meant orders were coming.

Private Nate Fritz was relatively new, but had experience on tanks, just not the right kind. He was the sole survivor from an earlier fight with the Germans—his M5 Stuart tank came out on the wrong end of a fight with a German 88. In a lot of respects, it was a miracle Fritz had survived unharmed. Fritz was a lithe, blonde Minnesotan with a friendly disposition and perpetually sunny attitude.

Private Johnny Herrera was an older hand. He wasn't Kurtzhals' original loader, who was killed shortly after landing during an enemy air raid, but he was a good replacement, and had been in every tank-on-tank fight Kurtzhals and Spataro had been in. Herrera stood tall with darker skin and greasy black hair that he had grown out beyond regulations. Kurtzhals tolerated Herrera.

1st Lieutenant Aaron Haskins was Kurtzhals' platoon leader. Kurtzhals didn't know Haskins that well—he was a replacement for Lieutenant McCord, who had been killed a week prior, but the man seemed pretty good, if a bit cocky.

"Sergeant Kurtzhals," said Haskins. "We're having a platoon meeting. Got some new orders. Bring Private Matoi."

Kurtzhals acknowledged, but privately wondered. *Matoi? The newest guy on the tank? Why? Did the infantry finally ask for him back?* But a good NCO didn't question orders unless the lives of his men were at stake, so Kurtzhals kept his concerns private as and called Matoi. The two men followed Haskins back to the center of the camp. The platoon's four tanks were arranged in a rough diamond, and the commanders were all at the center. There had been a fifth tank, but it had been destroyed, all crewmen lost.

Kurtzhals walked up to see a few unfamiliar faces at the meeting—Japanese men in their tan fatigues. Each wore a tan cap as well, with an anchor on it. Their apparent leader stood slightly taller than the others, exuding pride. He carried an American weapon—an M1A1 Thompson submachinegun—but the rest of his kit was strange and foreign, and for some reason, the man had brought a sword. Kurtzhals eyed his brother tank commanders, wondering who was going to ask the question.

"Gents, we've got word from Battalion. We've got a mission," said Aaron. "I'm going to a larger briefing later, but wanted to pass on a warning order. Bottom line is that the entire 753rd Tank Battalion is going to be pieced out, platoon by platoon, to infantry elements as we get closer to Cairo."

Haskins looked right at Kurtzhals.

"And, seeing as we have the only Japanese speaker in the entire battalion, we've been selected to help out the Japanese, hence why Ensign Nakamura is here."

At the mention of his name, the Japanese man saluted, and rattled off a phrase in Japanese.

"Go ahead Matoi, translate," said Haskins.

"He says he's honored to be here, among our tanks," Matoi said.

"Right," said Haskins. "There's more coordination to be done before we go in. I know the Krauts have Cairo sealed down tight, but as long as they've got forces there, we're gonna have trouble holding the Suez. If we can't hold the Suez, we have to go the long way to the Med, and with the German U-boat threat, higher ain't keen about that. Besides, our friends from the Pacific aren't wild about taking that route."

A hand shot up. Staff Sergeant Borawski, one of the other tank commanders.

"Ski?" asked Haskins.

"Yes sir," said Borawski. "Just have a question."

"I've got a lot of questions myself, Ski," said Haskins. "But sure, go ahead."

"Are we getting a replacement tank? For the five tank?"

Haskins shook his head. "No replacements. We have to make do. With that, I'm gonna leave you guys to get acquainted with Ensign Nakamura. I've got to go see the CO and get whatever our orders are gonna be."

The lieutenant jogged off, leaving the American NCOs staring uneasily at the Japanese SNLF contingent.

"So Matoi," said Kurtzhals. "Guess you're our translator. Tell the ensign we're happy he's here."

Nakamura nodded as he translated.

"I'm Sergeant First Class Gary Kurtzhals," Kurtzhals said as he stuck out his hand. Nakamura gripped it, a strong grip. Kurtzhals could respect that. "I'm this platoon's platoon sergeant. Means I'm responsible for these guys."

"I thought the officer was in charge?" asked Nakamura through Matoi.

Kurtzhals shrugged. "Lieutenant Haskins gets the orders and keeps Captain Ramsey happy, but the care and feeding of soldiers, and looking after these tanks, that's all me."

Nakamura nodded once. "I see," he said.

"So you're Japanese army?" asked Kurtzhals.

"No," said Nakamura, tensing up a bit. "Special Naval Landing Force, Sasebo."

He repeated Sasebo, and his men shouted it after him, raising rifles in the air.

"We are Naval Infantry," explained Nakamura. "Japan's finest."

"I see," said Kurtzhals. "Well, we're America's best tankers, so I think we'll get along just fine. What should we call you? Marines?"

Matoi and Nakamura exchanged some words.

"Not Marines. Sailors. Infantry Sailors."

Matoi translated, and Nakamura smiled broadly. Kurtzhals suppressed the urge to raise an eyebrow. *Sailors in the desert*, he thought. *Funny way these guys organize their military.*

"You guys got any combat experience?" asked Borawksi.

"Yes," said Nakamura. "Two tours on Formosa. One in the Philippines. One in Indochina."

"No tanks in those fights," muttered Borawski.

"And all small, counter-rebel affairs," added Altshue.

"You guys know much about tanks?" asked Kurtzhals. Nakamura nodded once.

"A bit, yes. Your Marine Corps advised us how to work with them. We have some at Sasebo, but they are not assigned to our unit."

"So you don't have any tanks?"

Nakamura shook his head.

"Have you ever fought alongside tanks, or was this just in training?" asked Borawski.

Nakamura paused. A man behind him tensed up. Kurtzhals realized they were ashamed of admitting ignorance, but these guys had no idea how to use armored support.

"We know how to fight," came the terse reply.

"Right," said Kurtzhals. "Matoi, keep our guests entertained. Show 'em you know how to load a .30 cal, it'll blow their mind. Borawski, Altshue, we need to have a chat."

The two tank commanders walked over with Kurtzhals.

"Now," Kurtzhals said. "I get that higher wants us to work with these guys, but they don't seem to have any fuckin' clue what the fuck is going on."

"Right?" asked Borawski. "If these crunchies can't keep their shit straight, we're gonna get wrecked out there. Hard enough to fight panzers in the open with maneuver. Harder still to fight worrying about running over our own guys, and now we're finding out, most of 'our own guys' in this case don't speak English. How the hell are we gonna give them orders?"

"Hurts me to say this, but I agree with Borawski," said Altshue.

"We can't teach them how to work with tanks overnight," continued Borawski. "And—"

"No, we can't," injected Kurtzhals. "But we can do something about this. We've got Matoi, and I'll bet some of their guys have been trained in at least basic English. I'd wager it's not much harder to teach Japanese infantry about tanks than it is Americans, just got to figure out the right words. Remember those 1st Infantry Division guys we were working with back near Amman? They didn't know dick about tanks, either. We all know it's our responsibility to keep those knuckle-draggers alive. Besides, since we thrashed the Krauts up in the Sinai, they shouldn't have a lot of armor left. What they do have probably won't be any good."

"Unless it's a Tiger," said Altshue.

The men went silent for a beat.

"Tigers can be killed," said Kurtzhals. "Just gotta be tactical about it and not a bonehead. Flank armor is flank armor."

"Do these crunchies even have any anti-tank?" asked Borawski. "Looked like they were mostly carrying bolt-action rifles and Johnson light machineguns."

"It's what we're stuck with," said Kurtzhals. "Uncle Sam doesn't pay us to bitch, he pays us to figure it out."

"Speak for yourself, Lifer," said Altshue. "I'm paid because a letter in the mail said I had to be here."

Kurtzhals fixed Altshue with his best quit-fuckin'-around gaze, and the younger NCO immediately clammed up.

"That's what I thought," said Kurtzhals. "Now, c'mon, let's go make nice with the Japanese."

The sergeants returned to their tanks, and the Japanese followed. As the hours wore on, Lieutenant Haskins returned, bringing with him the rest of the Japanese SNLF platoon that was supposed to be with them. Matoi hustled from tank to tank, hurriedly translating, trying his best to teach the infantry the basics of how to talk to tanks.

As the sun was setting, Lieutenant Haskins called everyone together again.

"Alright boys," he said. "We've got our orders. I can read you the general's speech if you want, but I think we're here for the particulars, so I'll start there. First, practical matter—Matoi can speak Japanese. The SNLF have two troops who can speak English. So, here's how we're gonna parse out the tanks. Until we get into urban areas, I'll be with Altshue, and Borawski, you'll be with Kurtzhals. Once we get too cannibalized to keep our wingmen, we'll split off. Sergeant Kurtzhals, you'll be with Petty Officer Shimada."

Kurtzhals looked over at the Japanese. The biggest man they had, he stood easily as tall as Kurtzhals, but nearly twice as wide, and all muscle, nodded.

Haskins read out the rest of the assignments.

"Now, our objective is simple—there's a BBC radio station on the north side of town. We think the Krauts are using it as a forward command post or maybe a signal relay station. One way or another, it's got to go. Our company team has been assigned to seize it. Between our tank platoon, the Japanese infantry, and a platoon of troops from the 45th, we have enough manpower. Earlier units should be clearing out most of the paths on the way, but it's possible they've missed something."

"Sir," asked Sergeant Borawski. "Am I correct in saying that higher wants to send tanks…into the largest city in Egypt?"

Haskins shrugged. "We've got an easier mission than some others, Borawski. At least we're in the northern outskirts. We won't be downtown. The Marines drew that straw."

Ensign Nakamura bolted off a rapid sentence in Japanese.

"We have experience in city fighting," Matoi translated. "Manila. Seoul."

"Yeah, but not against tanks," said Borawski, rolling his eyes. "Just because it's dangerous for tanks in a city doesn't mean they're not dangerous against infantry."

Matoi grimaced.

"Don't translate that, Matoi," said Lieutenant Haskins.

"Two of them speak English, anyway," grumbled Altshue.

"Look," Kurtzhals said. "We're not paid to bitch and give up—we're not Italians, for Christ's sake. We've got our orders, they make sense, seize is about as simple of a mission as we can get assigned. So how 'bout we let the lieutenant finish this briefing, then we roll out and crush some Germans?"

The lieutenant smiled and continued the order.

* * *

As Haskins briefed the rest of the order, Spataro was supervising *Grizzly's* crew conducting maintenance.

Private Herrera stopped adjusting one of the tank's roadwheels to observe the Japanese. They were broken off into teams of four, conducting drills.

"Hey, Corporal," asked Herrera. "What's your read on the Japs?"

"It's Japanese," said Spataro. "Matoi says they don't like the abbreviation, says it's a slur, ain't that right, Matoi?"

"Yes, Corporal," said Matoi.

"And, in today's 'modern,' 'new,' army," said Spataro, "that's apparently something we care about." Spataro spat into the sand.

"What kind of weapons are those?" asked Fritz.

"I don't fuckin' know, what am I, a gun encyclopedia?" said Spataro. "Get back to work."

Herrera and Fritz just looked at him. Spataro groaned.

"Oh, so we're not doing any more work until Uncle Alex tells you guys his most valued-fuckin-opinion. I'm a fucking tank gunner, you numbskulls."

"Got it, Corporal," said Herrera. "But what's your read on them?"

"They're infantry," said Spataro. "Same in any language—idiots who carry heavy stuff long distances on foot and think they're elite because of it."

"Think they'll be worth a damn in a fight?" asked Fritz.

Spataro watched as two of the Japanese troops conducted movement drills. The SNLF men were quick and aggressive. They didn't fight like the Americans Spataro had witnessed, nor the Germans he had shot at. In each team of four, three carried bolt-action rifles, while the fourth carried an unusual MG with a side-mounted magazine that Alex didn't recognize.

"I think they need our help, and Sergeant Kurtzhals thinks they need our help, and we've done all the thinking there needs to be on this topic. Now shut up and make sure we've got all our shells onboard."

* * *

The Outskirts of Cairo
April 4, 1944

The movement was quick enough—mostly straight forward travel, through the lines of forward units, the Japanese riding on the back of the tanks, or in borrowed trucks. As the unit passed through the forward line of troops, the Japanese dismounted, and the trucks returned to their other duties. In the distance, Cairo loomed, its visage foreboding in the bright light of midday.

Grizzly rumbled, slowly, into the outer belt of the outskirts, past the final observation post. Kurtzhals nodded professionally to the scout NCO on watch as the tank moved in.

"Alright kids," Kurtzhals said. "We're in the Wild West now. Keep a look out for Jerry."

The tank moved forward, the Japanese SNLF in double file behind it.

"Can you believe the Russkies are fighting this shit all the time?" asked Spataro, his face glued to his periscope. "Up in Stalingrad, Leningrad, Kiev…just all urban combat. What a fuckin' nightmare. Bad guys could be anywhere. Above us, below us, just one Kraut with a bazooka could end our whole fuckin' world."

"Technically, the Kraut bazookas are called 'panzershrecks,'" offered Fritz.

Spataro groaned.

"Shut up and scan your sectors," Kurtzhals called from the commander's hatch. "We can chat when we're all back at the bar after we crush these bastards."

Kurtzhals kept scanning the horizon. The rough desert had given way to the urban sprawl of Cairo—all simple, tan, drab houses, a couple of stories tall, max. In the distance, the sounds of combat echoed. Behind Kurtzhals, the sun was just coming up. *Grizzly* crawled forward slowly, edging toward the enemy.

Matoi talked hurriedly with Petty Officer Shimada on the field phone, exchanging a few sentences in Japanese.

"Sergeant," said Matoi. "Shimada says we are at the RV."

"Yeah?" asked Kurtzhals. "Well somebody fucked up. There's nobody here to rendezvous with."

They pulled up on the edge of a simple town square around a well. It was empty. The Japanese Naval Infantry fanned out, securing vantage points and taking cover. Kurtzhals didn't like this. Something felt rotten.

Suddenly, one of the doors burst open, and a burst of machinegun fire rippled across the square. Kurtzhals dropped down into the tank hatch.

"Fritz, halt," said Kurtzhals. "Let the dismounts circle around outside."

As he said this, the SNLF troops fanned out around the tank. *One of the most dangerous parts of combined arms operations*, Kurtzhals recalled from training. One wrong move, and his tank could kill one, or all, of his dismounted companions. *I just wish I could move around a little, sitting still makes me nervous.*

"Spataro, swivel left, check for that machinegunner," Kurtzhals said, looking back out the tank hatch. It was risky, but it was the best way to make sure his gunner would hit correctly.

Spataro used the turret's power to move, and pulled away from the periscope, checking instead on the Sherman's gunsight. His crosshairs were lined up neatly over the muzzle flash of the MG42 machinegun. Spataro smiled as he depressed the coax, putting suppressive fires on the enemy, as well as making sure he was lined up as well as he hoped.

Outside, Shimada aimed his Thompson and fired. To his right, a pair of Naval Infantry fired rounds from their Arisaka rifles, but the enemy machinegunner kept up, unabated.

Rounds pinged harmlessly off the Sherman.

"Herrera, load high explosive," ordered Kurtzhals.

"Roger!" Herrera shouted. In three rapid movements, Herrera slammed the breach release lever, ejecting the unfired armor-piercing round. He slammed in a fresh HE round.

"Up!" the Californian said as he scurried to secure the loose armor-piercing round in the ammo box.

"Fire," Kurtzhals ordered.

"On the way!" said Spataro.

The round left the barrel off the M4's 75mm gun and flew across the firefight, straight toward the simple home the German machinegunners were in. The machinegun team never registered what happened—a flash of light, a deafening noise, and a fire that consumed them, stopping their fire.

"Up!" said Herrera as he loaded a fresh HE round.

Kurtzhals saw the wreckage of the enemy MG nest. He couldn't see any bodies, but the gun had stopped firing, its barrel pointed skyward.

"That's a kill," Kurtzhals said. "Good shooting, Spataro."

"Easy at this range," said Spataro. "Think they got any friends out there?

"Keep looking," said Kurtzhals. "The Krauts never come alone."

Spataro went back to his periscope, trying to aquire a new target.

The tank crew scanned their sectors. Kurtzhals went to a chest defilade in the turret, allowing himself to see more, though also making himself even more vulnerable. He saw Shimada run toward the back of the tank.

Matoi picked up the field phone, and conversed hurriedly in Japanese.

"Sergeant Kurtzhals," he said. "Shimada reports no losses, thanks you for the work."

Kurtzhals grinned. "Holy shit. Grateful dismounts! I like the Japanese already. Tell Shimada we'll check the map and then head out, and have his boys keep their eyes peeled. This place is a bazooka paradise."

The tank crawled forward. In the distance, the sounds of gunfights echoed. Kurtzhals tuned to the platoon frequency on the radio, and listened in.

"Blue 4, Blue 1, over," came Haskins' voice, crackling.

"Go for 4," said Kurtzhals.

"4, heard some contact down your way, everything ok?"

"Roger, 1, engaged and destroyed enemy dismounts."

"Excellent, 4. 1 and 2 have linked up with our American dismounts. Proceeding on to the objective. See you there. Out."

Kurtzhals pulled out his map. He made a quick note on where they were, and what they'd encountered, in case he needed to report it later.

"Alright, Matoi. Tell the sailors we're moving out. We've still got another mile to go before the objective, and it's looking like the infantry did as good of a job of clearing shit out as they ever do."

Matoi acknowledged and relayed the orders in Japanese.

Grizzly rumbled forward, and the Japanese followed behind in a double file, Petty Officer Shimada checking off his men as they went.

Hours passed as the soldiers advanced through the northern outskirts of Cairo, encountering minimal resistance, though the sounds of gunfire, both small arms and artillery, echoed throughout the city. Kurtzhals returned to the unbuttoned position, keeping watch on every alleyway. As the sun got lower and lower, it was in his eyes.

May as well be blind, Kurtzhals thought.

Four streets west, Kurtzhals found his first real problem.

It looked simple—a dead camel, strewn in the middle of the road, along with a stopped truck with British markings. The intersection was flanked on all sides with simple two-story homes, which appeared to be abandoned. Kurtzhals didn't see movement in any of them, but it was dark inside, and the afternoon light unhelpful. On the far side of the square, over the truck and the dead camel, Kurtzhals could make out a sandbag roadblock—it wouldn't stop *Grizzly*, but it could be problematic for the infantry, and would provide ample cover to any German soldiers behind it. Kurtzhals imagined German AT teams, or SS men with radios, calling in artillery fire.

Kurtzhals shouted back at Shimada. "Phone! Phone!" and made the phone signal with his hands.

The tall sergeant ducked back inside the tank.

"Matoi, tell the Petty Officer we need his men to push forward, check this out. This smells like a trap."

"Fuckin' A, Sarge," said Spataro.

"It's Sergeant," said Kurtzhals. "Scan the second floor of those buildings. If they've got AT, that's where it'll be."

"Roger," acknowledged Spataro.

On the ground, the SNLF men spread out. Shimada's squad was 13-strong—there hadn't been a set size for shore parties prior to 1941, but after training with the USMC, the SNLF had copied their organization—three fire teams and one squad leader. Shimada ordered his first and second teams to either side, the men taking up positions near mailboxes, rubble, and whatever else they could find.

Shimada spotted movement in the truck.

"Enemy spotted!" he said.

His first team confirmed and conducted a recon by fire. From his tank hatch, Kurtzhals watched three riflemen and a Johnson gunner open up on the truck. The truck's door opened, and a man in German camouflage slumped out.

Then all hell broke loose.

From the second story, as predicted, gunfire blazed down on the infantrymen.

"Gunner, HE, second story," ordered Kurtzhals as he slammed the hatch down.

"On the way," growled Spataro as he pulled the trigger. The round streaked toward the second story, but missed the window, exploding outside, showering the street with rubble.

Herrera slammed in another HE round.

"Up!"

"Repeat target. Fire."

Spataro shot again, and this time, the round struck true, blowing out the room.

Outside, Shimada's ears were ringing, but he could see the enemy had stopped shooting from that location, though bullets poured down from the other building across the square, as well as the muzzle flashes of Germans behind the secondary roadblock.

It was then he heard the rumbling—an engine, like *Grizzly*'s, but bigger. Much bigger.

He ran over to the field phone and picked it up.

"*Grizzly, Grizzly*, there is an enemy tank approaching! Unclear what direction."

"Understood," came Matoi's voice. "Use a signal flare if you spot it."

Shimada barked the order in response, getting acknowledgement from his NCOs, in between bursts of gunfire.

The German infantry on the second story paused in fire. Shimada heard something in German, and the enemy tank made its presence known.

The Panzerkampfwagen V "Panther," variant D, bulldozed its way through one of the simple structures to *Grizzly's* right.

Shimada pulled the flare, and threw it, rushing to grab the phone.

"Enemy, 3 o'clock!" Shimada said. "3 o'clock!"

Inside *Grizzly*, Matoi furiously relayed the order.

"Gunner right," said Kurtzhals. "Loader, load armor piercing."

Herrera picked up the ready shell—an M72 Armor piercing round. He slammed it home.

"Up!" he shouted.

There was no time to fire.

The Panther spoke first.

The Panther's gun slewed toward *Grizzly* and fired. The round smacked into the front facing hull armor. The enemy gunner had fired too quickly—the round hit at a nearly 45 degree angle, and pinged off the front, but the hit was right in front of the driver's position.

Fritz screamed in pain.

"Matoi, check Fritz," Kurtzhals said, calmly. Matoi scrambled out of his position to see if Fritz could still drive. The young private wasn't bleeding, but kept screaming, and looking disoriented. Matoi couldn't pull him out of the position, not easily, but Fritz was in no position to drive.

From the commander's position, Kurtzhals was determined to make this count.

"Gunner, AP, tank."

Spataro swiveled the turret, and looked through the sight. At this distance, he could practically read the bumper number on the Panther. He aimed it toward the front side of the hull—the Panther was pivot-turning to put its heavy frontal armor toward *Grizzly*, but rubble stopped it from moving as quickly as it should've. Spataro wasn't about to let that opportunity pass.

"Identified," said Spataro, over Fritz's screams.

"Fire!"

"On the way!"

The round hit the enemy tank on the hull at a better angle than *Grizzly* had received. The AP round penetrated the side armor of the tank, and killed the enemy driver instantly. The Panther ground to a halt, and its hatch opened up. An enemy tank commander, clad in black, was barely visible on top.

Kurtzhals cursed. The enemy tank's turret was still moving. *Maneuver with those sailors around is gonna be hell. Still, I've got to do it.*

He unbuttoned the hatch and pulled himself out. He pulled his M3 "Grease Gun" up with him, just in case, and scanned the tank. He saw Shimada on the field phone.

"Matoi," Kurtzhals shouted down into the tank. "Tell him to clear out, we've got to maneuver!"

Matoi acknowledged, and the big Petty Officer dove for cover. Shimada looked at the enemy Panther.

"Petty Officer Shimada!" one of his team leaders said. "What do we do about that tank?"

Shimada grunted. "Kill that tank commander."

The team leader coordinated, ordering his Johnson gunner to open fire. Shimada himself sighted in his Thompson, spraying rounds. He'd expected the enemy commander to be suppressed, but one of the sailors had gotten lucky—an Arisaka round clipped through the German's head, blowing his brains into the nearby rubble. The commander slumped over.

At the same time, the German infantrymen spotted the American tank commander, and adjusted fire. Rounds pinged off the top of the Sherman just as Kurtzhals closed the hatch.

"The sailors are clear," he said. "Reverse. Spataro, fire again."

Spataro fired a second round at the Panther, but it glanced off the armored glacis.

"You're too far right, Spataro," said Kurtzhals, his voice loud, but calm. "Adjust left, then fire. Fritz, why are we stationary?"

The Panther returned fire. The enemy round banged off Grizzly's front turret armor, but as Spataro moved the power traverse, a hideous creaking sound reached out. From the driver's compartment, Matoi tried to retrieve Fritz.

"Can't reverse!" said Matoi. "Fritz is real fucked up!"

Kurtzhals cursed again as Herrera announced the next round was loaded. Over in the loader's position, Herrera got the second set of rounds ready—five rounds left easily available. A reload of extras into the turret was nearly impossible in a firefight once those initial crates were empty.

Spataro switched to manual traverse and brought the gun to the left. He looked back down his gunner's sight, and had a good side shot on the Panther.

The enemy Panther wasn't firing again—its crew had yet to realize the tank commander had been killed, and was struggling to make gunnery adjustments.

"Fire," said Kurtzhals. This time, Spataro's round struck true. The Panther had heavy armor, but even the heaviest of armor has its weaknesses.

The M72 Armored piercing round was a little high—it cracked the Panther right in its turret ring, fragmenting inside, killing the remaining two crew members. The Panther ground to a full halt.

"I think we got him, Sergeant," said Spataro.

"Fire another for insurance," said Kurtzhals. *Lost too many wingmen to tanks we* knew *were dead,* he thought.

On the ground, Shimada watched as his first team fired down on the Germans. His second team stayed with him, while his third team crossed the street. They didn't make it—a flurry of gunfire from enemies behind the sandbag roadblock cut them down. The four sailors lay dead. Shimada cursed.

In the tank, after putting one more round into the turret, Kurtzhals ordered the vehicle forward. Fritz, still concussed, was rocking back and forth in the assistant gunner's seat. Matoi reversed, awkwardly, back out of the linear danger area. Spataro manually traversed the turret, and fired coax rounds at the enemies behind the sandbag barrier.

From his position, Shimada knew what must be done. His first team continued to suppress the enemies on the other side.

"Sailors! On my mark, move!" he said, gesturing across the danger area. He hoped, for the sake of his men, the enemy was properly suppressed this time.

He gave the signal, and sprinted across with his five men. One, Seaman Yamaguchi, took a round through the leg. Shimada paused and ran back into the fire to drag him out. The simple building had a flimsy door on it. After dropping off the wounded sailor, Shimada motioned for his men to fix bayonets. The three riflemen affixed their blades. Shimada leveled his Thompson. The rifleman kicked open the door, and Shimada fired a burst before the four sailors ran in, screaming. A pair of Germans hustling up the stairs with machinegun ammunition were caught unaware and shot to pieces. The sailors stabbed their corpses to make sure. One of the sailors primed a grenade and ran to the top of the stairs, where a door was cracked. He tossed the grenade and closed the door.

Outside, Kurtzhals, in the open hatch, saw the explosion and watched as the second story fell silent. He heard commands in German and saw movement as the enemy abandoned their roadblock. He wasn't about to let them get away—Kurtzhals acted in a moment of recklessness, hopping out of the turret and manning the Sherman's .50 cal. He fired a burst into the retreating Germans, cutting them down.

Dust settled on the street, and the sounds of violence faded. Kurtzhals, recovering his composure, got back in the tank.

"Sergeant," said Herrera. "I think someone's trying to raise you on the radio."

Kurtzhals picked it up.

"4, this is 1, come in, 1," came Haskins voice.

"1, this is 4, still alive here."

"Thank God for that," said Haskins. "It's not looking good out here."

"Yeah, I hear you, 1," said Kurtzhals. "Fritz's banged up. *Grizzly's* damaged—turret won't traverse right. Sailors on the ground took some losses, too."

"It's just you and me, 4," said Haskins. "Plus whatever dismounts you got left. Can you still meet up at RV Point Charlie?"

Kurtzhals paused, looking at his map.

"Roger; can be there in five."

Grizzly limped forward, along with the surviving sailors. The streets had gone quiet—the destruction of the German platoon had cleared out whoever else might've been lingering.

As the men approached the RV point, a makeshift traffic circle, Kurtzhals heard an engine. Lieutenant Haskins' tank, *Shamrock*, came out into the open, along with four SNLF sailors.

The SNLF men fanned out to secure the area. After a few minutes, Kurtzhals dismounted, heading toward Haskins' tank.

Haskins got out, looking disheveled. The normally dapper lieutenant was battered, with a small cut on his head and his face caked with dust and grime. Kurtzhals noticed *Shamrock* was missing some of the tracks that had been on its right flank in the morning.

"So what happened, sir?" Kurtzhals asked.

"AT gun ambush," said Haskins. "One of those big 88s. Got Borawski and Altshue, plus that SNLF squad that was with them. The American dismounts were pinned down and panicked. We lost track of them a few thousand yards back. Nakamura got taken out by an MG42. I've got four SNLF junior enlisted that don't speak a lick of English following my tank around like lost baby ducks. I'm fixing to call higher and report that the mission failed."

Kurtzhals let the words hang in the air before he responded. He took a good look at the lieutenant—the man's confidence was sapped. *He's not thinking clearly*, thought Kurtzhals. *Time for some NCO business.*

"Can't do that, sir," said Kurtzhals. "You know the stakes. Next unit to get here might take hours."

Haskins sighed. "I know. I got a report back from higher. The radio station's guarded by a pair of Panzer IVs, plus an 88 flak gun. That's a lot of firepower against two wounded Shermans and the remnants of his Imperial Majesty's whatever the fuck, too many fuckin' syllables."

"Sir," Kurtzhals said, stepping closer. "I know shit's rough right now. But these men are gonna be looking to you for leadership. Even the ones that don't speak English, they know what defeat looks like, but they also know how to spot fighting spirit. Now we can sit here and wait for someone else to come along and do this job, or we can push forward. I know, technically, we're combat ineffective, down to just two tanks. I also know that in war, time is everything. If we don't move on this station, right now, and put boots to ass, the

Krauts are gonna double, maybe triple up its defenses. We know they're bloodied; we've got to push on."

Kurtzhals saw Petty Officer Shimada striding over. The big man had been wounded and patched up—blood streaked the left arm of his uniform.

"Decision time, sir," said Kurtzhals.

Haskins nodded. "You're right, Sergeant. I'll call up. We're going in. Enemy's a mile out, right?"

Kurtzhals grinned. "Not far enough away to save them from us."

Shimada strode up.

"I...I have idea. Get Matoi."

* * *

The former BBC radio tower wasn't a tower at all, but a one-story relay, down in an unassuming neighborhood, some British bureaucrat's brilliant idea to save money on real estate cost and perhaps invigorate what passed for the local economy. The ugly brick building was sturdy, and had electronics valuable for command and control. The Germans had fortified it— the 88 gun in a makeshift open-top bunker, facing east, toward the sun, and the advancing enemy. German pioneers had come in and cleared out most of the buildings nearby, establishing fields of fire, but only out to about 200 yards or so, owing to the difficulty of shaping urban terrain. Even the "open" area was covered with rubble and provided ample concealment.

The two Panzer IVs, in their desert camouflage, were bunkered in fighting positions on either side of the 88, facing northeast and southeast. The fighting positions concealed the damage to these salvaged tanks. Around the tanks, Germans moved in scattered pairs, shuffling through patrol routines.

Feldwebel Mark Krueger struggled to stay awake. His men had been on shift for a full day, knowing the Americans were right outside their gates. As the battalion HQ inside lost contact with their forward elements, Krueger and his men struggled. The fatherland demanded vigilance. *Wish I had some of those pills the guys on the Eastern Front get,* he thought. *My gun and these panzers are the only hope this command post has against the Yankee armor.*

He took a swig of his canteen as he heard something odd behind him—it sounded like something being dropped. He hurriedly grabbed his rifle.

"Steiner? Stransky?" he called out. He got silence in return.

He was expecting tanks. He was expecting airplanes.

He was not expecting the small, khaki-clad man who emerged beside him and plunged a bayonet into his throat. As he gargled away the last of his lifeblood, Krueger was at least grateful he could, at last, sleep.

Shimada's infiltrators wreaked havoc on the 88 crew, stabbing and slicing the half-awake Germans. The perimeter sentries, with their throats slit, could not have warned them.

The 88 sat abandoned. Just to be sure, Seaman Tanaka and Seaman Ichiro smashed the optics with the butts of their guns, while Petty Officer Second Class Shiro Kitsurugi put a grenade down the weapon's tube. The explosion tripped off the surviving Germans—something wasn't right.

A pair of staff officers ran out of the command station, pistols drawn—they were cut down by SNLF fire. The entire station erupted into a frenzy of gunfire and confused shouts in German. Taking advantage of the chaos, Shimada motioned for his surviving troops to follow him.

He paused and fired a flare into the air. *Hopefully,* he thought, *the Americans will see this.*

Grizzly and *Shamrock* roared to life from their hide positions and floored it toward the enemy command post.

The two Shermans burst into the open at the same time—each facing their own Panzer. The four tank crews scrambled to engage each other in a deadly race.

The Panzers, aided by their fixed position, fired first. The first round popped straight through *Shamrock*'s hull flank, starting a fire in the engine compartment. Lieutenant Haskins and his crew bailed out, and moved to the cover of the nearby rubble as the tank burned down. The second went high over *Grizzly*'s turret as Matoi jerkily maneuvered the tank.

Grizzly returned fire, knocking an AP round straight through the northeast panzer's turret side. The smoking hole confirmed a kill.

The southeast Panzer fired, and the round smacked through *Grizzly's* left hull. The AP round shredded Matoi and Fritz up front, and blew through Spataro's left leg.

The gunner screamed in pain, but still worked the manual traverse, bringing the gun to lay on the Panzer IV.

"Fuck you!" shouted Spataro as he hit the trigger. The 75mm AP round smacked straight through the side of the hull, destroying the enemy Panzer. Smoke billowed from the ruined tank.

Kurtzhals jumped out on top and looked to see infantry approaching—scattered in ones and twos, as the remnants of the enemy staff hurriedly evacuated the field HQ. He had two dead crewmen and one wounded. In the hatch, Herrera was still dutifully loading an HE round, and Spataro, wheezing in pain, was working the gun.

Kurtzhals did the math. There was at least two squads of Germans outside. They were split up. His HE shell could take one, but then it was a question of math. Barring divine intervention, his tank was done.

Salvation came from his right flank. Shimada's men emerged from an enemy trench, opening fire, catching the enemy soldiers on the move. The Germans stopped and hit the dirt, reacting to the flanking fire.

Big mistake.

The Sherman's gun tracked right over their heads, not 50 yards away.

Spataro didn't wait for the fire command, he just triggered the round. The HE round exploded, killing the suppressed soldiers.

Kurtzhals nearly cheered, only to remember the dead men in the front of his vehicle.

"Play it calm, men," he said. "There still could be more Germans out there."

As the battle calmed down, there was a knock on the turret. From the periscope, Kurtzhals could see it was Shimada.

Kurtzhals opened the hatch and grinned.

The big Japanese Petty Officer grinned back.

"We did it," said Kurtzhals. "We fuckin' did it."

The Japanese Petty Officer just put his hand out.

"Kurtzhals. Sasebo now."

Kurtzhals grinned and shook his hand. The tankers and infantry treated their wounded the best they could, and waited for an enemy counter-attack that never came.

Over the next few hours, follow-on forces moved in. The first rung in controlling Cairo was secure, and the Oahu Pact won the opening salvo of the Battle of Cairo. Over the next two weeks, the battle lines shifted as the Oahu Pact forces encircled Rommel's consolidated Afrika Korps. Dramas like *Grizzly*'s saga replayed themselves over and over again throughout the next two weeks of fighting, and countless lives were lost over objectives big and small, but at the end, the only flags flying over the city were the Stars and Stripes and the Rising Sun.

* * *

Ruins of the Former British Embassy, Cairo
April 18th, 1944

General Douglas MacArthur kicked aside the scrap of the Nazi flag that once adorned Rommel's Afrika Korps command, pausing to take a puff off his corncob pipe and pose for a photo. In the background, Colonel Kemp and Commander Bailey directed aides to set up the new command post.

The flashbulb captured the general in the ruined German command center, triumphant, and, as always, picture-perfect.

"Thank you, Stacy," said MacArthur. "Damned fine photo for a damned fine war. Took our boys weeks to do it, but they did it, by God! Colonel Cleveland, let's have an update."

"Sir," said his aide. "We've confirmed it—Rommel is in full retreat. He can't mass forces to meet us in the open, and he chose to withdraw rather than be encircled. He can't stomach the bleed of any more prolonged city fighting or a siege. And, according to these files we found, we got him just in time."

The aide offered over a set of folders. Written in German, MacArthur just scowled.

"Son, just cut to it—what do they mean?"

"Corps attack, sir, right at our staging areas. Supposed to begin a day after we struck."

MacArthur chuckled. "Yamashita was right."

"It's nice to hear you say that, General," said Tomoyuki Yamashita, doffing his cap as he walked up, flanked by SNLF aides. Mac-

Arthur noted that several of them wore IJA ranks—technically forbidden by the Imperial government at that echelon.

"Admiral, good to see you," said MacArthur.

"I think, in these circumstances, I may be called general," said Yamashita, with just the barest hint of a smile. "Tokyo won't find out, and for an old army hand like myself, in the aftermath of such a battle, the distinction matters. Let's just keep me and my staff out of your pictures."

The man knows the value of image, thought MacArthur. *I can certainly respect that.*

"Your men acquitted themselves well over the past week," said MacArthur.

"As did yours, General. The Germans fancy themselves different than the Filipinos, the Chinese, and the Koreans," said Yamashita. "They are not. Once one understands this, it is simply a matter of applying the lessons we learned against the others."

"How'd you know Rommel was going to attack?" asked MacArthur. "Seems to me like it would've been better to hold out, play the long game."

"Not Rommel's style, General. Not mine either."

"Hmmph," said MacArthur. "I suppose so. We made a great call either way."

Yamashita decided not to correct the general. The American was preening; this was important to him.

"He's like a peacock," muttered one of the Japanese aides as a photographer took another picture.

"Maybe so," said Yamashita. "But we need him."

"That," said his aide. "Is a good description of the Oahu Pact."

Yamashita smiled at that as another flashbulb popped.

* * * * *

Philip S. Bolger Bio

Philip S. Bolger is an army veteran who left active duty service to work as a cog in the Military-Industrial Complex while pursuing his passion for writing. "Fighting Spirit" is his third published short story, and second examining the Oahu Pact timeline. His debut novel, the Urban Fantasy adventure "The Devil's Gunman," was released in January of 2019. In his free time, he enjoys history, wargames, and pen and paper RPGs. He lives in the heart of Northern Virginia with his partner, Victoria, and their two dogs: Robert the Bruce and Francois Guizot. Philip can be reached at philipsbolgerauthor@gmail.com.

# # # # #

An Orderly Withdrawal
by Taylor Anderson

A *Destroyermen* Universe Short Story

Details of all the major battles of the Great War against the Grik, Domin-ion, even the fascist League have been exhaustively recounted in the years since the old Asiatic Fleet "four-stacker" destroyer, USS Walker, *brought me to this "alternate" Earth. However, Allied historians have hardly yet touched upon innumerable other notable actions for various reasons. Most are likely less attrac-tive to chroniclers because they were smaller, somewhat obscure, perhaps less "sig-nificant," though I'm sure they were profoundly important to those who fought and fell in them, not to mention others who unconsciously benefitted from their sacrifice. One stubborn rear-guard action in particular was especially vital to myself, Legate Bekiaa-Sab-At, and perhaps General Kim's entire Army of the Republic, though we were scarcely aware of it at the time. It—and the brave participants—certainly deserve more than a meager footnote or passing reference, so I've taken it upon myself to recount it here.*

Note: I mean no offense, of course, but I've substituted the term "Lemurian" for the more proper "Mi-Anakka" in the interest of clarity, even though members of that species in the Republic of Real People didn't call themselves that at the time, and many still resist it.

Excerpt from Courtney Bradford's *The Worlds I've Wondered*
University of New Glasgow Press, 1956

"They're doing *what?*" demanded Prefect Soli-Kraar of the 7th Legion, Army of the Republic of Real People, her frizzed tail arching incredulously—challengingly—behind her. "Sir," she added hastily, lowering her tail and blinking embarrassment. She'd struggled to cope with a lot over the last few months, advancing (through attrition) all the way from the rank of junior centurion to legion prefect, a post she wasn't remotely prepared for. Now, the heaviest Grik artillery barrage the roughly six hundred survivors of the legion ever faced had put her even more on edge. That was no excuse for her outburst, however. The 7th was depending on her, and so was the human crouching close in the rough, hastily-dug trench.

I must keep it together, she thought.

The human Colonel Zhao, commanding the 7th Legion and acting legate for the entire 11th Division, grimaced sympathetically, implying Soli's tension was entirely understandable. Especially considering what he'd just told her. His first attempt at a reply was annihilated by another flurry of heavy Grik roundshot hammering the hasty brush and earthen breastworks heaped in front of the trench along the southern bank of a dry, rocky riverbed. Dirt and gravel rocketed up around bounding cannonballs, blanketing the area in a choking, pinkish dust haze that already covered the mustard-brown battledress and new "platter" style steel helmets worn on the line. The dust had given every human the same color skin, Lemurians and Gentaa the same color fur, and at a distance all would appear identical if not for the fact about half of them had tails.

Colonel Zhao coughed and wiped reddened eyes with a field scarf as the cracking impacts moved off to either side. "At least they're not using their new exploding shells," he observed in a clinical tone. "Perhaps they haven't any, reserving them to oppose our ally's advance up the Zambezi?"

Prefect Soli hawked and spat gummy, almost blood-colored phlegm before waving a furry hand to the north. When she spoke again, her tone was more level but just as skeptical. "But...but the enemy's *there*, right in front of us! The whole Grik army!"

Colonel Zhao shook his head. "Apparently that's what we were supposed to think. General Kim no longer does. As you know, Legate Bekiaa-Sab-At and her Fifth Division marched to discover the enemy flank to the west. They found it," he stated grimly, "or rather it found them, and now the legate has quite a battle on her hands. Her reports, combined with aerial reconnaissance, convinced General Kim that we face only a—admittedly large—blocking force here, while most of the Grik have been groping for *our* flanks."

Zhao paused while Republic counterbattery fire shrieked overhead and pounded enemy positions barely 500 meters away. Geysers of earth, scrubby brush, and fragments of Grik vomited into the sky. The Grik would always outnumber them, but the Allies had better weapons. The Republic in particular had far superior artillery.

Colonel Zhao's expression hardened. "So General Kim is shifting our army west to support Legate Bekiaa and smash the Grik deploying there. After that?" Zhao shrugged. "Ideally, Kim might take the force across from us in the flank in turn, or even bypass it and leave it floundering behind us." He snorted. "The Grik aren't known for quick and decisive responses to the unexpected."

Neither were we, not long ago, Prefect Soli conceded.

"But what does that mean for us?" she asked. "*We* can't simply form up and march away." She pointed across the dry river again. "*Those* Grik still represent a significant percentage of their army and will attack at once whether they know what we're doing or not. Without some sort of discouraging entanglement to slow them, we'd be destroyed and General Kim's entire redeployment..." She stopped and blinked rapidly, dread creeping into her Lemurian equivalent to human facial expressions. "*We're* the rear guard, the sacrificial 'entanglement,'" she hissed lowly so troops around them couldn't hear.

Zhao nodded uncomfortably. "All three legions of the Eleventh will remain in these works, along with the Second Division to the east. Their right flank should be secured by the closest elements of General Taal-Gaak's cavalry. But we must continue to *seem* to be the entire army for as long as we can."

"And then die," Prefect Soli murmured.

"Possibly," Zhao agreed. He waited until Soli's large yellow eyes met his smaller brown ones. "As acting legate for the Eleventh Division, I may not be with the Seventh Legion as much as I'd like in the…difficult time to come, but I'm confident you'll hold the line as long as anyone possibly could…" He paused and frowned. "And when the time comes," he continued darkly, "as I'm morally certain it will, you'll ensure that the Seventh Legion performs an orderly withdrawal from these works and rejoins the rest of the army intact. If it can be done, you'll do it, Prefect Soli."

Soli gulped involuntarily. She believed she was a good soldier and knew she'd been a better than average optio, then centurion. But casualties had mounted quickly in the battles that brought them here, and she'd become senior centurion, then prefect, in the space of a single day at the Battle of Soala. Despite going through the motions and emulating senior officers she respected, Soli considered herself utterly unqualified to be Zhao's XO, much less to *command the* 7th Legion.

I'll have no idea when *to pull out, much less* how, she thought.

Zhao abruptly turned to move along, but stopped and spoke over his shoulder. "Now I must pass the word to the other legion commanders." He waited while more heavy shot pounded the breastworks, showering him with a small landslide of gravel. "I'll be back as soon as I can," he assured. "*If* I can. Until then, you're in charge." He grinned. "And who knows? Maybe the Grik won't attack, and we can simply leave this position under cover of darkness."

We both know better, she thought.

The dark-bearded Senior Centurion Fannius, now Prefect Soli's acting XO, crept closer as Zhao disappeared around a corner of the zigzag trench. Soli wasn't surprised to see the canvas cover securely fastened over the bolt action of the human's 11mm rifle and suspected every weapon in his entire 1st Century would be similarly protected.

"So that's how it is?" Fannius almost shouted, making it clear he'd heard the exchange. He was just as conscious as Soli how Zhao's news might affect morale, but the renewed thunder of heavy guns made whispering unnecessary. Besides, word would spread regardless, sweeping back from the 19th and 31st Legions as Zhao apprised their leaders. Fannius had proven that people always overheard, and it was better to get ahead of things before rumor made them worse.

"Go to the other centurions," Soli told him. "Explain what's happening, but stress to them *and* their troops that we'll still have plenty of support. All we have to do is delay the Grik long enough for Kim to get out from in front of them—and smash their friends before they know he's coming."

"Support, eh?" Fannius asked dubiously.

"That's right," Soli snapped back, surprised as much by her sudden spike of anger as by Fannius's tone. She'd always thought he was as steady as a rock, ever since their training days.

Maybe the familiarity has bred contempt? she thought, then continued in a still forceful tone.

"Artillery, air, and General Taal's cavalry. The cavalry, at least, will support our withdrawal when the time comes."

"If you say so."

Soli bared her sharp canines. "I do, and so will you if you don't want to be broken to the ranks."

Taken aback by Soli's intensity, Fannius must've done some quick thinking of his own and readily accepted the rebuke. He might've even saluted if such gestures weren't forbidden on the front lines. "Aye, Prefect, at once."

Soli squinted around, catching furtive, dusty glances from nearby troops. "And hurry back," she called after Fannius. "I'll be here with your First Century when you return."

Fannius wasn't gone for long, as there wasn't much "word" to spread. And under steady bombardment, there was little else the legion could do other than deepen their trenches and add to the berm protecting them. Occasional volleys of Grik musket fire pattered loose soil in the vicinity of anyone who showed themselves, however briefly. A Republic soldier would have to be amazingly unlucky, however, for even one out of a hundred balls fired from smoothbore muskets to strike him or her at this distance. The much improved Grik field artillery had a better chance, and even if it seemed excessive to send a nine-pound ball at a single soldier, the Grik were willing. They were going to shoot it anyway.

They might not have exploding shells, but apparently they do not want for powder and roundshot, Soli thought.

The same couldn't be said for the 7th Legion. Plenty of small arms ammunition—and water!—was still coming up through hastily dug communication trenches, but Soli had been wrong about continued artillery and air support. Occasional barrages still fell on the enemy, churning well-known positions and doubtless slaughtering Grik. Far less often, a little Cantet—swift but fragile-looking biplanes that were the Republic's only land-based aircraft so far—swooped over the enemy lines and dropped a couple of small incendiaries. Combined, it wasn't much at all, as the Republic's precious aircraft and most of their long-range artillery was obviously busy to the west.

I hope the lack of support here means things are going well for the 5th Division, Soli thought. The possibility that Kim's redeployment had perhaps run into more than it could handle was too grim to consider for long.

"It's all that bloody foreign female's fault we're in this mess. That 'Legate Bekiaa,'" Senior Centurion Fannius grumped, risking a quick glance over the berm to convince himself the enemy wasn't already sprinting down on them from across the dried-up river.

"How do you mean?" Soli asked.

Fannius glanced at her a little sheepishly as if wondering how Soli would react to criticism of another female infantry officer, regardless of origin. Like virtually every culture entirely or partially composed of Lemurians (or what the rest of the Grand Alliance simply referred to as "Cats"), there was absolute equality of the sexes in the Republic of Real People. They might be a little more...genteel about it than most, but the very idea of discrimination based on sex was preposterous to them—with a couple of exceptions. Human and Lemurian females had never been prohibited from serving in the navy or cavalry, and even female Gentaa occasionally went in the navy. But harkening back millennia to various inter-species conflicts, wars, the unification wars, and the numerous civil wars that followed, females weren't allowed in the infantry or, for that matter, artillery when it first became available.

This was considered sensible for a variety of entirely practical reasons, from the simple necessity to populate the Republic to the nature of infantry warfare and its requisite heavy armor, shields, and weapons. Few females in the Republic could compete with the majority of males in that kind of combat. The earliest large and cumbersome field artillery had posed the same problem. Prohibitions against females in those branches began to dwindle over the last couple of generations, however, as gunpowder weapons became lighter and equally lethal in anyone's hands.

Still, Soli thought, *it took the current war to really start sweeping that old thinking away, and even now I'm likely one of a handful of females my rank. Which only took a lot of misfortune and dead people.*

She looked sharply at Fannius but not for the reason he expected.

"I don't care where she's from, Legate Bekiaa-Sab-At—and Ambassador Bradford—saved this army at Gaughala when everything was falling apart. You don't remember that? How scared we all were? They probably saved it again at Soala by helping us build it into what it is!" Blinking thoughtfully, Soli stared off to the west. There was little to burn in this desolate, rocky waste, so only the smoke of battle and bursting artillery shells could so thickly smudge the heat-shimmered sky a dozen kilometers away. Ironically, probably only the smoke of the immediate, ongoing Grik cannonade kept the enemy from seeing it too, and learning the real battle was shifting elsewhere.

"I'll wager that 'foreign female' is saving our army yet again," Soli said, glaring back at Fannius as she nodded in the direction of the rising smoke. "Whether we live to know it or not."

The hot, dry, choking day went on with little change as the glaring sun seared its way inexorably overhead and scorching iron spheres pummeled their position without pause. The barrage caused relatively few physical casualties but the psychological toll was mounting on the helpless troops, unable to respond. Colonel Zhao requested periodic updates via one of the ingenious battery-powered field telephones their allies in the United Homes had provided, checking on them and ensuring they knew he hadn't forgotten them,

Soli was sure. He only returned once, however, in mid-afternoon, bearing news from a runner that the battle in the west was in the balance, and General Kim had joined it but a number of units were lagging badly. More immediate from their perspective, aerial reconnaissance had confirmed the Grik in front of them were massing for an attack. Zhao then apologetically explained that he felt compelled to return to the 19th Legion to help steady its wobbly commander. Soli understood, and was actually a little flattered, but would've preferred that he stay and "steady" her. It never occurred to her that Zhao's absence did more to bolster her confidence than his presence ever could.

Surprisingly, the Grik never attacked that day. Perhaps they heard about the battle in the west themselves, or maybe they were just waiting for the heat of the day to pass. In any event, they seemed content merely to maintain the daylong, galling bombardment that jarred the berm above the trench and showered troops with dust, grit, and the occasional wounding stone. Troops that were exhausted, afraid, but also now somewhat complacent, hunkered beneath their helmets with scarfs around their faces. That all changed shortly before dark when the Grik on the north side of the desiccated river bed finally revealed they possessed exploding shells for their artillery after all.

A brief lull teased the shattered, breathless air in the open space between the armies, during which Soli, Fannius, and quite a few others raised their heads to watch the last rays of the dying sun flare red-gold across the top of the gunsmoke cloud before winking out entirely. Then flashes erupted deep in the cloud as the cannonade resumed, redoubled, and the curious spectators quickly ducked. A thunderous rumble of what seemed like a hundred guns reached them just as sputtering shells cracked and flashed amid dirty rags of smoke almost directly overhead. Jagged iron slashed up irregular ovals of dust and sparking, shattering stones. Shrieks of pain and terror rose, mainly to the rear in the communication trenches, but the next salvo would probably burst right into them. The Grik had finally begun to learn the art of artillery from their enemies, and if their cannon were still exclusively muzzle-loaders, (most of the Republic's allies would have to say the same), and their ammunition remained somewhat crude, the skill of their gunners had improved disconcertingly.

"Get down! Everyone against the north side of the trench!" Soli roared, her warning repeated by officers and NCOs up and down the line. Grik guns began firing independently, about half the fuses on their shells set for best effect, and hot iron churned the trench itself. It seemed everyone was yelling and screaming now, and Soli wasn't sure she wasn't one of them. A shell dropped directly in the trench barely thirty meters to the left, blasting men and Lemurians up and out, to lie dead or moaning in the open. Only the zigzag nature of the trench protected Soli and those around her. Stunned or terrified, a trooper tried to bolt to the rear and Centurion Fannius tackled him and slapped him on the back of the head when his helmet rolled away. "You idiot!" he roared over the stunning cacophony of explosions and whirling fragments. "Are you trying to get yourself killed? Your only chance is to see this through!" Yanking the man up, he flung him back against the north side of the trench. A shell snapped just to the front, most of its force flailing the berm, but a single shard slashed down and through the top of the frightened trooper's unprotected head. He collapsed to the bottom of the trench and writhed as soundless and senseless as a worm. "Well, shit!" Fannius seethed.

"You tried," Soli consoled him.

Fannius blinked at her in the way of her people, conveying disgust. "I tried to save him so he could fight, and maybe keep *me* alive!" He glared at the corpse. "Useless bastard!"

The savage barrage continued unabated for forty minutes or so, until it was completely dark, and the bright yellow-red flashes blinded, deafened, and filled the air with sharp, lethal shapes. Soli and the Seventh Legion had no artillery on the line, and even if their light mortar crews could ply their weapons without being slaughtered, the Republic variety barely had the range, and they needed to save their ammunition for the inevitable assault. At present all they could do was lay as flat as they could and take it.

Some cracked, like the first man, and simply disappeared. Most of those were probably cut down by slashing iron in the open. More vanished in a welter of gore with handfuls of comrades when the trench confined and concentrated a direct hit, proving it mattered little what they did at that point and survival was as much a result of luck—or divine providence—as anything. Many a voice was loudly raised in frantic prayer to various deities reflecting the diverse origins of Republic citizens.

Then, when the shelling finally—suddenly—stopped, there came an almost silence. Most had been sufficiently deafened by the constant blasts they could hardly hear the high-pitched shrieks of the wounded. Only low-frequency sound could reach them now, and that's why they clearly heard the rumbling, thrumming roar of the bellows-driven war horns of the Grik.

"That's it!" Soli shouted. "Up! Up and make ready! They'll be coming now!"

"Action covers off! Fix bayonets!" Fannius shouted, tearing the canvas cover off his own weapon and wiping at the dust that had filtered past it. Long-bladed bayonets clacked and clattered as they were latched in place. Repeated orders spread swiftly, buglers in the communication sections blowing 'stand-to, action front.' Men and Lemurians readied themselves on the forward slope of the trench. Even a few Gentaa, who'd been carrying crates of ammunition, snatched up weapons no longer of use to the dead and prepared to fight as well. Soli was surprised by that. Gentaa resembled both Lemurians and humans—with their fur and tails, but otherwise more human features and bearing—closely enough to inspire legends (uncomfortable to all concerned) that they were hybrids. Most knew that was ridiculous, and Gentaa were an entirely different species, yet the...delicacy with which they'd always been treated allowed them to establish a clannish, lucrative, and somewhat separate culture within the Republic, and they were very particular about the roles they played in its society. Fighting wasn't generally one of them. Under the circumstances, these Gentaa seemed ready to make an exception.

Half a kilometer away, fierce Grik voices, rising in anticipation, smothered the strident moan of the horns.

"Runner!" Soli shouted, voice a little higher than usual, "have the comm section ask the corps artillery reserve to resume firing in our support."

"Yes, Prefect!" cried a frightened young Lemurian, bolting to the right.

Fannius leaned over and spoke in her ear. "*If* the communication lines haven't been chopped up by the barrage, and *if*..." The young soldier was already back, led by a signaler with an optio's rank device.

"There *is* no corps artillery reserve, Prefect Soli!" the optio cried, desperately trying to keep the terror from his voice.

"They already pulled it out and started moving it west," Fannius guessed. "There's nothing left?" he demanded.

The optio shook his head. "Even our own few batteries close behind have pulled back, out from under the barrage." His voice rose. "They know we're going to be overrun and want to save the guns!"

"Silence, fool. Get hold of yourself!" Fannius scolded, but Soli figured the optio was right.

What does that leave us? Soli wondered. During the army's reformation after the Battle of Gaughala, legions had been standardized at ten centuries—roughly a thousand troops. *The 7ᵗʰ has been whittled down to half that number, and so has the 19ᵗʰ. The 31ˢᵗ has seen little action, so it's probably close to strength. The Maker knows how badly the enemy artillery hurt us, but I doubt the entire 11ᵗʰ Division has two thousand effectives left. The 2ⁿᵈ Division in line to our right probably suffered similar losses in the current offensive. So, figure four thousand effectives with breechloading rifles, probably a couple of hundred close range mortars, and forty or fifty Maxim-style machine guns—with limited ammunition.* (The Maxims had been made to fire the same 7.93x57mm cartridge as the weapon that inspired them, and though the factories were now turning out more of them than even the 11x60mm standard infantry round, Maxims really gobbled them up. *Not much against…how many thousands of Grik? Way too many.*

The tone of the horns abruptly changed to a deeper, ominous, *brapping* drone, and the Grik attackers roared in response. Soli couldn't see that far in the hazy darkness but knew the Grik were swarming out of their own defenses now, starting across the space between them like a great black tide of death.

"Mortars, commence firing! Three rounds each at four hundred meters, then drop fifty for each set of three after that!" Mortars started firing immediately; the three-inch "drop and pop" design they'd also been gifted by their Union allies. They were shorter-ranged than the ones they copied, intended for very close support. With the Republic's superior long-range artillery, the adaptation had made sense at the time. Tracers already arced out from Maxims down the line and mortars exploded along the leading edge of the oncoming swarm. The lurid glimpses the flashing mortars gave Soli of the enemy was enough to chill her blood, even in this climate.

Grik were terrifying enemies, taller than Lemurians and as heavy as a human man. They carried vicious claws on their hands and feet and nightmare teeth in long, narrow jaws. Adults had impressive tail plumage and bristly crests on their heads, (under helmets, now), but all were covered by downy, feathery fur, generally dull brown with black highlights and washed-out stripes. Lethal as they were, Grik didn't rely on their natural weapons. They'd recovered and copied smoothbore muskets with socket bayonets like the Union used early in the war, and primitive as they remained compared to what most of the Allies now had, they were deadlier at a distance and fired much faster than traditional Grik crossbows ever had. They wore armor, too; gray leather covered with rectangular iron plates. That wouldn't save them from the 7th Legion's bullets, but it made things tougher when fighting got intimate.

Details such as those were only clear in Soli's mind, at present, since all she could see in the rippling flashes was a seething wall of ravenous monsters rushing directly at her. Just for an instant, she froze.

"Machine guns and rifles, set your sights at three hundred! Commence independent fire!" Fannius bellowed.

A lot more troops than Soli thought survived the artillery had risen from the bottom of the trench to cover its forward slope, and the front erupted in stabbing muzzle-flashes and choking smoke. Bright tracers from a Maxim crew to the right swept back and forth, disappearing in the growing fogbank of gunsmoke that quickly hid the enemy again. Soldiers, *Soli's* soldiers, frantically worked their bolts, inserting single cartridges, firing into the growing thunder of the invisible horde.

We should've had repeating, magazine rifles by now, Soli railed inwardly. *They were supposed to send conversion stocks already cut for box magazines...* She shook her head angrily, furious at herself, blinking quick appreciation at Fannius. He only shrugged, and now that he saw she was present again, trotted to the left, around one of the zigzag curves.

Soli looked up and down the line. *More than I thought I had*, she conceded, *but still far too few in the face of what's coming.* "Adjust your sights," she called in that curious way Lemurians have of making their voices carry. "I know you can't see anything, but I'd rather you miss low and bounce a bullet into the bastards. Mortars will cease dropping the range at two hundred meters and expend all remaining rounds at that distance." Theoretically, the small three-inch mortars could drop their bombs much closer, but dull flashes in the smoke only gave the slightest hint of where they were falling now. They'd keep killing Grik, but any closer and they might accidentally drop one on themselves. "All mortar crews will destroy their weapons when they're out of ammunition and join the firing line," she concluded grimly. Turning to one of her Lemurian messengers, she spoke directly in her ear. "Have the communications section send to…" She shrugged. "Anyone still on the other end of the line, that whatever they're doing they better get on with it. They won't hear any more from *this* position. Not without a wireless set," she added a little bitterly. "Then have the comm section pack their equipment and retire through the communications trenches. Set up and tie back into the line at the corps—*former* corps HQ—if they can."

The messenger regarded her with wide, amber eyes. "Are we going to be overrun?"

"Of course we are," Soli told her, then blinked reassurance. "At least this position will be, and there's nothing we can do but make it cost the Grik more than they'll wish they paid. But I don't intend for the Seventh Legion to be *in* the trench when the Grik roll over it. Go." Soli suddenly, finally, began to relax and feel more like the soldier she'd been before her promotion. Any part of the legion beyond her view would soon be past her control. She'd be lucky to keep a pair of centuries under her direct command when everything fell apart.

The mortar fire was beginning to slack but the machine gun and rifle fire intensified when blocks of running shapes began emerging from the haze.

"Pour it into them!" Soli roared, pacing behind the firing line in spite of the growing crackle of Grik musketry and the rising storm of musket balls whizzing past. "Kill them!" she shouted. "Tear them apart! Bugler, walk with me, but keep low. I'm going to need you." All buglers were human since Lemurian lips didn't do bugles well, and humans were almost always taller than Lemurians. This very dark-skinned man was even taller than most, and he responded wryly. "I appreciate your concern, but perhaps the prefect might heed her own advice. We might need *her* before this is done as well."

Soli looked at him, then laughed. She couldn't help it. And it wasn't a hysterical laugh, but one of genuine, tension-shattering amusement. Even while men and Lemurians fired their rifles and died around her, and countless Grik rampaged down on them, Prefect Soli laughed—and it was probably her most important contribution to the battle to that point. Troops around her seemed to take heart and fight even harder, and those who were shaky firmed up a bit. The mood spread outward from there. Everyone was desperate and afraid—no normal person wouldn't be—but just as Soli had doubted herself, her troops had doubted her too. Now, simply because she'd laughed at a private soldier's wisecrack, she was deemed fit to command.

The Grik were clearly visible now, slowing in the face of withering fire as entire layers of them were ground away, but they had the weight of an avalanche behind them and though they slowed, they didn't stop. Worse, Soli should've received orders of some sort by now, regarding how to pull the 7th Legion out when the time came, as it surely must very soon. They *couldn't* get caught in the trench under that wave of Grik.

For just an instant, Soli considered sending another messenger to seek guidance from Colonel Zhao. *But if he's still with the 31ˢᵗ Legion—and alive—he could be half a kilometer to the right. The messenger will never get there and back before the Grik are in the trench.* She tore her eyes from the enemy, muskets flashing, teeth gnashing, and glanced to the right. *Maybe orders will come from the 19ᵗʰ Legion? Colonel Mbili is certainly senior to me.* She gauged the approaching Grik. *But there's been no word from Mbili either, and there isn't even time to send a messenger to him.*

"All right," Soli shouted, "pass the word; all machine gun crews close enough to a communication trench will pull their weapons out of line and take positions to the rear. The rest will wreck their guns in place and retreat with the rest of us. Listen for the bugle calls. They'll tell you what to do. Hopefully they'll help other legions coordinate with us," she added.

"We're pulling out?" Senior Centurion Fannius asked, trotting up to her. There was blood all over his tunic and his left arm flapped loosely at his side.

"That's right. I see no choice."

"No." Fannius gestured to their front. "And you better make it quick. We're murdering them, but they smell blood. They're going to make a rush."

"Especially when they see us climb out of here—and it'll be rough in the open."

"Better than in this hole with them firing down on us."

Soli once more gauged the distance between her trench and the leading edge of Grik. The enemy line was ragged, made more so as warriors died and others started to sprint, rapidly closing the gap. She had to time this exactly right—it wasn't something they'd trained for—and some of the enemy would get in the trench with her people no matter what she did. "It's time—and may the Maker help me," she told Fannius. "Bugler," she cried, and the tall man poised his instrument. "Sound, 'back ten paces and resume firing' until I tell you to stop!'"

There was no bugle call for bailing out of a ditch into the open, reforming, and continuing to fight. The one she specified would have to do. It wasn't even a long call, consisting of only five notes, ordinarily preceded by other calls preparing troops for a fighting advance or retirement. Soli hoped it would be self-explanatory now, since her soldiers had to climb out the back of the trench to retreat the required ten paces.

The bugler blew, loud and sharp, over and over. To Soli's gratification, most of her troops responded at once. The need was obvious. Actually doing it was a slightly other matter, however. Though it wouldn't much longer, the trench still afforded some protection from musket fire. It wasn't as heavy as it might've been since most of the closest Grik had already fired their weapons, and it was particularly difficult for them to load muskets on the run. Still, enough Republic troops were struck in the back as they turned to claw their way out of the trench that a discouraging number hesitated, still frantically shooting.

"Come on!" Soli shouted. "Pull back, damn you! Form up to the rear. We're not finished yet!"

More finally heeded her words and made it out. Others might have, with a few more seconds, and maybe a few even deliberately stayed to cover the rest, but far too many were caught when the Grik spilled over the edge. For a few tragic, precious moments, the firing directed at the erratically coalescing formation mere meters away dwindled to nearly nothing as the leading Grik leaped in the trench and slaughtered the remaining defenders in a gleeful orgy of blood. Furious, Soli joined the ragged line, splitting into two ranks, as

NCOs shoved troops where they wanted them and packed the gaps with people.

"Stand your ground!" Fannius yelled, echoed by five or six centurions and optios. Gazing around her, Soli feared—yet should probably be grateful—she might have as many as four hundred troops. Granted, many were wounded, but all could stand. None who couldn't had made it out. Soli looked at the abattoir directly in front of her, practically all firing having ceased while triumphant Grik paused to gorge themselves on the fallen. Those behind them pressed tightly forward, blocked from shooting—or eating.

"Look!" Fannius cried, gesturing to the right. The 19th Legion was falling back too, exactly as they had. Not that Soli had left them a choice. Part of the 19th where it touched the 7th had probably pulled out with them.

"We better get back in the fight," Soli growled, blinking at the Grik in front of them. "Keep them disorganized and hesitant to cross the trench. Besides, our friends on the right might need a little encouragement."

"And an example," Fannius agreed. "With your permission?"

"By all means," Soli told him, but she was gazing farther to the right where the 31st Legion—and Colonel Zhao—should be. The moon was rising, painting the dark land a hazy, sickly gray, and she saw figures streaming to the rear but no formation assembling behind the line. Her heart collapsed within her as she realized Colonel Zhao must be dead. He never would've allowed the entire legion to be overrun and slaughtered. Never would've left the other two legions to essentially fend for themselves. *He must've died in the bombardment and nobody even bothered to tell us*, Soli now realized.

"Let's give them some volleys! They'll like that!" Fannius roared. "First rank, present! Fire! *Crash!* A swathe of Grik, some starting to look at them now, preparing to pursue, tumbled back into the trench.

"Five paces to the rear and reload!" Fannius continued. "Second rank, present! Fire!" *Crash!*

"Messenger!" Soli called.

"Prefect?"

Soli pointed about two hundred meters beyond the 7th's battered right where the 19th was spitting fitful volleys of its own while doing its best to sort itself out. "Run over there as fast as you can. Find out who's in charge and tell..." Soli paused. "*Suggest* that we quickly join our lines and eliminate the gap between us. They also need to be ready to refuse their right flank, as it seems the 31st Legion has collapsed. The Maker knows what's become of the Second Division beyond. Go!"

Somehow, the remains of the 11th Division managed to coalesce into a creditable line as it withdrew, even accumulating half a hundred stragglers from the 31st while the Grik milled about in the corpse-choked trench, feasting on their enemies as well as their own. They'd taken their objective, probably beyond expectations, and likely fulfilled the extent of their orders. Without further instruction which would only come when their leaders came up to join them, they seemed hesitant to advance into the increasingly crisp volleys of their receding foes. If the defenders had simply broken and fled, it would've triggered a "chase" instinct even if these Grik were no longer the mindless Uul that had composed all Grik armies, (led by "elevated" Hij generals), since the beginning of time. This war had shown that Grik warriors must be permitted to live long enough for their minds to mature sufficiently to operate sophisticated weapons and obey more complicated commands. Along with that blossoming intelligence however, came unprecedented and irrepressible notions among even the lowliest Grik, such as a vague conception that life is good, and this prey they hunted deserved respect because they were *very* good at ending Grik lives.

Battered as it was, Soli's remnant of the 11th Division didn't run, and its painful, deadly mode of retreat appealed more to the "leave it alone" instinct often refined in more sensible predators. Follow-on waves of Grik kept stacking up behind the first ones, resulting in more confusion, even violence in the ranks. This gave the survivors of the 11th, now all apparently under Soli's command, precious time to gain distance from the enemy.

"We're getting low on ammunition. We have to stop firing," gasped the human Centurion Hanno, limping up to Soli supported by a Lemurian trooper. Hanno was the 19th's senior surviving officer. Like Fannius, he'd been painfully wounded, but obviously wasn't ready to quit.

"We're astride one of our communications trenches and are re-covering ammunition from it," Sori told him. "I'll see that it's distributed." She gazed off in the darkness, but blinded by the firing of her own troops, couldn't see much. There was still a loud commotion in the vicinity of the trench, now a kilometer away, but the Grik weren't firing back and the enemy artillery remained silent. "But you're right," Soli told Hanno. "We've been shooting to discourage pursuit, but I doubt we're hitting much anymore and we're only marking our position." She snorted. "It may not seem so at the moment, but we've been very lucky on this campaign, often winning battles we shouldn't. And the fact remains, every time we face the Grik we're a little more experienced and they're always new, untried troops. Their leaders don't have much practice at exploiting 'victories' such as they achieved tonight, and might be as disarrayed as if we'd repulsed them. But they *will* reorganize, and they *will* charge into our concentrated fire in the same old way once they do." She took a breath. "Senior Centurion Fannius! Cease firing and continue our retreat—in line, and at the quickstep," she stressed, knowing how hard that would be in the dark, "back in the direction of General Kim's former HQ."

"Yes, Prefect Soli!" Fannius barked, calling on the bugler to sound 'cease firing.' "Skirmishers to the rear," he added.

The shooting stopped after a final volley, and officers and NCOs directed the troops to turn about and advance to the rear at a brisk walk. "How far to Kim's HQ, do you suppose?" Hanno asked. Sori blinked concern at his labored gait. He was having trouble, even with assistance. A few small ammunition carts were being hauled up out of the comm trench and some of their machine guns on their awkward little two-wheeled carriages had joined them now, but there was nothing but stretchers for the wounded. Sori was suddenly horrified by the realization that stretcher bearers couldn't fight. If they were pressed, they'd have to leave their wounded. For the first time, Sori's sadness over Colonel Zhao's death transformed into a sharp resentment that the man had left *her* to make such dreadful decisions.

"Only about five kilometers," Sori assured the wounded senior centurion. "Perhaps less. I've never been there, you know. We moved directly into position from the southeast, and General Kim hasn't gotten around to inviting me to dine."

Hanno chuckled at her attempt at a joke, then paused, staring intently ahead. "I believe it must be less than that," he told her, nodding forward. "But you tell me. Your eyes are better."

A great fire was rapidly growing just a little south of east, and there was no doubt it was General Kim's HQ. The communications trench angled directly toward it, and even this far away Soli could see a virtual city of tents and huge mounds of supplies the main army would never be able to pack along, all going up in flames. Most disconcerting, since the ground in that direction was unusually flat, Sori didn't see any formations of friendly troops silhouetted between them and their burning objective. She'd half suspected Kim's redeployment would still be underway, still lagging, with several divisions strung out on the march as they crossed from east to west behind the lines. Kim would be furious, of course, but such foul-ups were normal. She supposed she should be proud the army she was a part of had managed such a professional movement, but it wasn't much consolation.

"Yes, much closer," she told Hanno absently, "though it doesn't look like it will help."

A pair of signalers from the communications section scampered to intercept them. "Prefect Sori!" one called.

"Over here. Were you able to patch into the line and keep...someone apprised of our situation? Anyone?"

"Yes, Prefect." The man gestured behind where other members of his section were disassembling and boxing the field telephone and its heavy batteries. The trench had abruptly ended, out of Grik artillery range, and a heavily trodden path visibly continued on. A lot of equipment was scattered along it, including a number of light freight wagons, Soli noted with a little relief, though there were no horses or suikas to pull them.

"So? Report!" Sori demanded. "Where will we meet relief? There must be another rear guard."

The signalman hesitated, matching her stride as the long, wavy line pressed on. "My report was acknowledged," he temporized, "by a junior officer in General Taal's cavalry, detailed to destroy the camp and all the equipment they couldn't carry." His eyes went wide. "The enemy in the west, perhaps a third of the army facing us, was routed. The Army of the Republic is abandoning its supply line to sweep north at once. General Kim hopes to bash directly through to our allies on the Zambezi!"

A bold stroke, Sori thought. *Too bold? There's no way to know. But what does that leave us? Have we been forgotten?* She asked the signalman.

"The officer I spoke to said the last infantry legion passed his position shortly before…"

"Obviously not the *last* legion," Hanno inserted dryly, eliciting a few dark, tired chuckles.

"No sir, but if we hurry, we can catch up."

"You mean hurry faster than we are?" Sori asked. Her people were already tired and many were hurt. They couldn't maintain their current pace for long under ordinary circumstances. And they'd have to stop entirely to face the Grik once the enemy caught up, and no one doubted that would happen.

"How long ago was that?" Sori asked.

"Just before they fired the camp. The cavalry officer was going to destroy the communications equipment himself. He did say he'd inform his superiors of our predicament. I got the impression he was surprised any of us were alive."

"So, we're alone *and* abandoned," Hanno growled.

"Enough of that," Sori scolded, and he sheepishly nodded. "Though essentially correct," Sori added lower. She fixed the signalman with her gaze, large yellow eyes almost glowing in the dark. "Nothing else at all?"

The signalman hesitated. "The officer I spoke to said nothing about it, but the bulk of General Taal's cavalry was supposed to sweep up the rear. It hasn't passed or I would've seen it—heard it—myself, from here."

"If he's just as sure we're lost, he probably came around further to the south," Hanno said, maintaining the gloomy persona Soli was beginning to expect from him.

"Perhaps not," she objected, thinking hard. "I don't flatter myself he remembers me, but I've made Taal's acquaintance. He struck me as a courageous and conscientious commander. He'd aid us if he was aware of our situation." She paused, unsure whether to continue, but did so. "I also have it on greater authority than rumor that he's...entranced by Legate Bekiaa-Sab-At. I suspect that if he knew she was in action and was told to support her he'd take the straightest route."

"Bringing him close to us," Senior Centurion Fannius concluded. "A weak hook to hang our hopes on. One of only two, I suppose." Soli looked questioningly at the man, and he grinned. "Either love will bring the cavalry to our rescue—mortifying but survivable—or the Grik will lose us in the dark, and we'll join the tail of our army before it leaves us entirely behind."

Soli lowered her voice and whispered to her XO. "Neither sounds likely when you put it like that."

"No, but we did survive being overrun, and brought out nearly a thousand troops counting those from the Nineteenth and Thirty-First. How likely was that?"

Before Soli could answer, a stutter of rifle fire crackled, and bright orange muzzle-flashes stabbed the night behind them. The Grik were here.

"I guess it's up to love after all," Fannius said disgustedly. Skirmishers were shooting almost continuously now, falling back slowly at first, then hurrying to rejoin the ranks. Hundreds of musket flashes flared and sparkled close on their heels, nearer than Soli would've hoped, followed by the staccato thumping of their reports and lead balls warbling past. A few struck flesh with a sound like a broom whacking a rug. Then there were the screams.

"Sound 'Halt! Action to the rear!'" Soli called to the bugler. Sharp notes stopped the retreat and began turning the troops around. Soli cast her gaze at Fannius. "Take charge of the Nineteenth Legion. I'll rely on Centurion Hanno as my second here." Fannius nodded, and without a word, hefted his rifle and dashed off. A clutch of runners chased him. Soli turned to Hanno, his clouded expression revealed by the rippling fire. Then, to her surprise, he smiled and shrugged. "You're right, of course. Crippled as I am, I'll never get back where I belong before we're fully involved." He looked toward what had been the rear and was rapidly becoming the front again. The initial maneuver required only seconds, but it was taking longer to re-form what had become a very ragged line in the darkness. "Not that it much matters," he added, his tone turning dark once more. Skirmishers were sprinting through now, gasping and taking their place to the rear, ready to become a reserve after they caught their breath—if there was time. The Grik were barely two hundred meters behind them, the progress of what looked like a shapeless mob marked and lit by diminishing musket fire. The leading edge of the swarm had largely emptied their weapons again and those behind couldn't shoot. Still, though it was impossible to tell how many there were, it was obvious Soli's mangled division was desperately outnumbered.

"It matters," Soli snapped at the centurion, possibly realizing it herself for the very first time as her eyes cast about, judging how solid the long, double-rank line appeared. The troops weren't standing shoulder to shoulder, not yet—though it might come to that— and the front rank maintained a roughly two-meter separation. The second rank filled the gaps behind them, prepared to commence an almost un-interrupted fire—as long as the ammunition held out. Only six machine gun crews remained, and Soli wondered if some had just kept going when they retreated. She looked back to the front and saw all the skirmishers were in. "It *always* matters," she told Hanno, "even if it's only how we die—and nobody ever knows but us." Raising her voice, she cried to the bugler. "Sound 'commence firing by volleys!'"

The first volley was always the best, and even in the current rush and confusion, five hundred rifles spoke almost as one down a kilometer-long line. Seconds later, five hundred more rifles slashed at the tightly-packed mob of Grik, each heavy 11mm bullet potentially smashing through the leaders and one or two Grik behind. Hundreds fell dead or shrieking in pain, and despite inevitable misses, more Grik were probably hit than there were bullets in the air. The machine guns opened on the flanks, sweeping tracers across the tumbling, faltering horde. And the volleys kept coming, heaping a ghastly wall of corpses and writhing wounded in the dark.

Regardless how well-trained these Grik might be, they'd lost the cohesion and relative discipline with which they initially attacked—on the heels of a terrifying artillery barrage—and the troops opposing them hadn't broken. No doubt there were other large groups of Grik fanning out in pursuit, possibly shifting this way even now, but this one surged forward in the age-old way, its commander perhaps overconfident after the victory at the trench. For whatever reason, the result was quite different, and the charge was battered to a wailing, frustrated standstill.

Soli was feeling the first delicate touch of triumph caress her, light as a feather, when a markedly less gloomy Hanno reminded, "Ammunition," and she blinked and flicked her tail in agreement. "Yes. We'll start backing away again," she told him. "The enemy fire is increasing. They use their dead as breastworks to load behind and smoothbores or not, their muskets are taking a toll." The trickle of wounded moving to the wagons was growing by the minute. Those who could walk would have to pull and push the wagons loaded with those who couldn't. "We'll retire by volleys once again, but this time each rank will move fifty paces to the rear before turning, ready to fire. That'll pick up the pace and lengthen the interval between volleys, conserving ammunition. We'll cease firing altogether at three hundred meters. Hopefully, we'll have bloodied them enough that they'll let us break contact."

The Grik that had stuck their snouts in the 11th Division's grinder probably would've been happy to oblige by themselves, but Soli suddenly became aware of rapid, independent fire on the far right flank to the east, southeast, and felt a sick, swirling sensation in her gut. A Lemurian trooper almost crashed into her, huffing from exertion, eyes wide, blinking fear. "More Grik, Prefect Soli! Thousands of them!" the trooper managed to gasp. "They almost got behind us, but Senior Centurion Fannius pulled the Nineteenth Legion back to refuse our flank."

Soli and Hanno whipped their heads to the left in response to a vicious escalation of cries and shots from that direction, and one of the machine guns fired a short burst before it went silent, probably out of ammunition. "Their ancient tactic," Soli ground out. "Whether the Grik we've been fighting knew it or not, they served only to hold our attention while two other hordes—probably their equivalent of divisions, came at us from the sides!"

"They couldn't have known where we were to plan it in advance!" Hanno protested.

"They didn't have to!" Soli replied with disgust at herself. "All they had to do was come to the battle we illuminated for them and then revert to instinct!" She took a deep breath. "My fault. I waited too long. Just a slightly quicker," she snorted, "less 'orderly' withdrawal might've gotten us past them. Now...?"

Hanno's voice hardened, now scolding, not morose. "Then do something! It seems they've fooled us—and not only you—but to paraphrase what you said earlier, if we're going to die, I won't die like a fool!"

Soli nodded, suddenly wearier than she'd ever been. "Bugler," she called, "sound 'form square." The tall man hesitated, then nodded, and the eleven clear notes rose above the growing roar of battle. Soli could imagine the chaos that ensued even if the details came to her only as bellowed commands, near panicky cries, and a kaleido-scopic blur of flashing motion. Moving from line into square was something every century and legion practiced. The defensive square had almost been the Republic's default combat formation before the current war, not to mention the more lethal weapons that came with it. But doubling portions of *two* shaky legions from a kilometer-long front into a square a hundred and twenty five meters to a side, in the dark, under attack, resulted in a frenzied tumult unlike anything Soli ever saw—short of bailing out of the trench, at least, and the hellish bombardment before that…She was experiencing an awful lot for the very first, and likely last, time.

She forced herself not to watch, gazing intently at Hanno instead. The repositioning would succeed or not. They'd live to fight a while longer or they'd be dead in minutes. There was nothing she could do about that, so she focused on preparing to fight. "Centurion Hanno, have the skirmishers help move all the wagons and remaining am-munition to the center as the square forms—*if* it does—and take charge there. Use the skirmishers as a reaction force to fill gaps or bolster the lines as you see fit, but you and the wounded will be our final reserve as the square…contracts upon you."

"Where will you be?

Two Gentaa were dragging a wounded man from the line where Grik musket balls vrooped and warbled, smashing flesh and shatter-ing bones with an almost frantically growing intensity. Soli took the man's rifle and ammunition belt off the shoulder of one of the Gentaa, then gestured around at the messengers, even the bugler. "We'll form a reaction force of our own," she said.

"But…you must command!" Hanno objected.

Soli laughed grimly. "Everyone in the division will soon be close enough to hear my orders, though I doubt they'll need them by then."

Still partially supported by a surprisingly stoic Lemurian whose blinking and tail posture revealed almost nothing about his thoughts, Centurion Hanno saluted Prefect Soli-Kraar—no one would see in the disorienting flashes, gunsmoke and darkness—and allowed himself to be helped back to where the wagons were gathering. Soli looked at the men and Lemurians around her, sighed, then opened the breech of her weapon to see if it was loaded. She was better with a rifle than the pistol and sword at her side. It was hard to tell, but the square actually seemed to be assembling, muzzle flashes now booming out in nearly every direction. Of course, the sparkier, more red-orange flares of Grik muskets were all around them now as well, and the clattering, screeching, thundering roar of battle redoubled to a frenzy when the Grik smashed into the desperately solidifying square and bayonets took over most of the killing.

"Maker protect you," Soli cried to her comrades, raising her rifle and taking aim, but the crash and roar of battle was so loud by then, they probably didn't hear.

* * *

General Taal-Gaak had grown increasingly frustrated as the dreadful day, then night, wore on. He'd learned via the wireless cart accompanying his cavalry that General Kim had smashed the Grik army in front of Legate Bekiaa-Sab-At and broken out to the west, but also that Bekiaa was wounded. Cherishing a more than professional interest in the extraordinary officer from the United Homes, Taal was anxious to join her—and the rest of the army, of course—but it took longer to assemble his far-flung scouts in the east than he'd hoped. Making matters worse, all communication with the divisions blocking the Grik in the north had been lost, likely severed by the unprecedented bombardment lavished upon them. Rumor had it the troops in the trenches had been overrun and scattered, so Taal waited to consolidate his entire force before attempting to bash through what might be hordes of marauding Grik. Moving at last, his caution seemed vindicated when his cavalry started running into exhausted, terrified survivors of those broken divisions in the dark. Most were alone, or sometimes in pairs. A few squads had managed to stay together. All agreed the line had shattered, and the Grik were loose all around them. That appeared to be true. Taal's cavalry encountered clumps of Grik numbering from a few score to a few hundred as it hastened on, but they were just as disorganized and confused as the Republic fugitives they seemed fixated on hunting. All were easily swept aside or slaughtered by brisk, mounted assaults. Grik had nothing like cavalry and had always hated and feared it, particularly that of the Republic's Union allies who rode swift, vicious monsters called 'me-naaks,' but Taal's horse cavalry was just as effective at routing disoriented and unsupported packs of Grik in the dark.

"A damnable mess and a tragic waste," General Taal remarked bitterly, tail swishing rapidly behind him. "Perhaps if we'd come quicker..." Clouds were moving to block the setting moon, but there was sufficient light to see innumerable dark mounds of Grik and Republic corpses all around. Occasional shots in the distance alerted screening squads of riders to another desperate straggler, or possibly a few isolated enemies stumbling upon each other in the gloom, and they clattered off to rescue a comrade or butcher more wandering Grik.

The human Prefect Kirham, commanding the 4th Cohort and riding alongside Taal, blinked denial in the Lemurian way. "We came as fast as we could," he said. "And costly as it appears to have been, the blocking force accomplished its task. Victorious here or not, these Grik have spent themselves as an immediate threat to General Kim's rear."

"So it would seem. But almost all of them are gone. Where did they go?"

Kirham shrugged. "Who knows? If they outran their orders, they may still be racing south toward nothing but desolation and thirst."

A pair of riders galloped in from the front. Spotting Taal's flag, its limp shape vaguely discernable, they whirled around in a cloud of dust and trotted up alongside. "General Taal! Beg to report. Decurion Snis-Ala and her squadron are observing what looks like a few centuries of our infantry, in square, under assault by a sizable enemy force. The square is rapidly shrinking, however, and she doubts it can endure for long."

Taal and Kirham exchanged quick glances, realizing the mystery of where many of the Grik had gone was solved. "Where? How far?" Taal demanded, even as Kirham asked, "How many Grik?"

The trooper pointed west, northwest. "Beyond that low ridge, six kilometers. As to numbers, the decurion estimated two or three thousands. It's impossible to say, and whoever is fighting them has killed a great many more."

Though Kim was now advancing through plenty of hills and gullies to the west, the ridge—actually a long, flat-topped peak—was the only feature here that might've hidden a fight that close. Taal now thought he heard firing as well, though it was badly muffled and almost obscured by the clattering noise of his column. He glanced behind at the eastern sky, detecting the slightest hint of gray.

"It will be dawn before we reach them, even at a gallop, and the horses will be blown," Kirham cautioned.

"Regardless," Taal barked, brooking no argument. "Runner!" he shouted aside. "Inform Prefect Diola of the Fifteenth that he's in charge of the column. He'll press forward quickly, but without tiring his mounts! Bugler! Sound 'advance the Third and the Ninth at the canter.'" He looked at Kirham as the high notes blared. "That infantry must've been at it all night, and *anyone* still fighting after this fiasco deserves saving at almost any cost."

The horses were lathered and huffing hard by the time the 3rd and 9th Cohorts galloped around the rocky, southern foot of the hill with the rising sun behind them, yet they seamlessly deployed from column into line less than three hundred meters from what looked more like the top of a writhing anthill than a battle. Taal found it difficult to believe anyone might still be resisting down in the middle of that. Yet they certainly *had* been. A glance at the plain around the final melee made it clear there were far more dead Grik than live ones left for his cavalry to face. And they didn't really have to "face" them. Except for those in closest combat, possibly sensing victory after the long bloody night, Grik began peeling away and fleeing from the cavalry even before it finished shaking out.

General Taal raised his voice in a belligerent roar. "The Third Cohort will drive the charge home, securing our people and destroying any Grik that remain. The Ninth will pursue those that flee, but no farther than two kilometers. Keep your cohesion, don't overstress your animals, and you'll shoot plenty of Grik in the back today!"

He was right. As soon as the tired horses began trotting forward again, in what must appear to the desperate Grik as a solid, impenetrable wall of death, almost all the rest of them bolted. Just a few hundred stayed to fight, likely because they had no choice. The same mushy, nearly solid ring of bloody carrion that actually started Kirham's cavalry balking and rearing before it penetrated more than halfway to the enemy, trapped the panicking Grik as well. The beleaguered defenders, probably long out of ammunition, never stopped killing them with their bayonets, and cavalry troopers leaped from reluctant mounts and waded through the corpses with long-bladed spathas and pistols.

General Taal-Gaak himself was one of these, firing a couple shots from his 11mm revolver, but it was all over before he got close enough to swing his sword. Pushing onward through countless bodies, he finally saw what couldn't have been more than a single century of bloody, blinking, dazed-looking survivors still on their feet, tightly ringing a cluster of bullet-riddled wagons full of desperately wounded troops. There was no cheering as the pitiful defenders began to realize their ordeal might somehow be over, there was only a kind of stupefied silence as nearly all simply dropped to their knees in abject exhaustion.

Taal was appalled and anguished by the scene, yet simultaneously so filled with a fierce pride and love for these troops who'd obviously endured so much that he didn't know if the tears in his eyes were born of grief or thankfulness that at least a few survived. Probably both. Shots came from the Ninth Cohort, killing running Grik, but the only sounds around him came from moaning, crying, (sometimes gurgling Grik) wounded, and the neighing of still nervous horses. He cleared his throat and called behind. "Every squadron medicus to the front, at once! Prefect Kirham, details to clear a path through these bodies and get those wagons out. And have our own ambulance wagons brought forward!" He lowered his voice and addressed a kneeling Lemurian, staring at him with wide, unblinking eyes. "Who commands here," he asked gently. The trooper blinked meaninglessly and just kept staring.

"Down here, General," came a gruff, weak voice from under one of the wagons.

Stepping over more bodies, Taal patted the insensible trooper on the shoulder as he moved to squat by the musket ball-splintered spoke of a wheel. There were almost as many wounded under the wagon as on it, but Taal saw a Senior Centurion leaning against the inside of the right rear wheel staring intently back. His dark beard and hair were wild and matted with blood, and more blood stained the mustard brown cloth of his tunic around a large hole in his upper right chest. Leaning on him in turn, almost lying in his lap, was a female Lemurian with large yellow eyes and a Prefect's rank tabs. There were only a few female infantry prefects so Taal recognized her at once, shuddering to note she bore even more wounds than the senior centurion, but her striking eyes were clear and bright.

"Prefect Soli-Kraar," Taal said, smiling and blinking respect.

"You remember me!" she murmured softly, wetly, but her pleasure was clear.

"Of course I do! And I'm not the least surprised to find you, of all people, still holding your ground."

She blinked regret. "I...attempted an orderly withdrawal, as ordered by Legate Zhao, but that became impossible. I fear I've squandered an entire division."

"Nonsense!" Taal assured her, then looked at the senior centurion. "You are?"

"Fannius, General. Centurion Hanno was with her most of the night, but he caught a ball with his head."

"You had elements of two legions with you?"

"Three. What was left of the Thirty-First fell in with us while we pulled back."

"Most of a division," Soli lamented again.

Taal glanced around, taking in the survivors—perhaps a bit more than a century still in one piece—who knew how many wounded, but alive, and the absolutely *stunning* number of Grik heaped around them. All accomplished by this young female and her sturdy XO *after* they'd been driven from their position. The ability to inspire that kind of loyalty and confidence simply couldn't be lost. "Medicus!" Taal called insistently. "I need a medicus here *now*, damn you all!" He looked back at Soli. "You kept your head when older, presumably more experienced commanders lost theirs, and diminished though it might be, you *did* save your division, and kept it fighting until relieved. The Second Division disintegrated entirely." He didn't mention they'd probably picked up twice as many survivors from the legions of the 2ⁿᵈ in the night, but they'd been useless, doing nothing but running while the 11ᵗʰ fought—incidentally making itself the focus of all the semi-organized Grik left in the area. "Your action here might well have prevented the Grik from organizing sufficiently to hamper General Kim's movement to the west. You lost a lot of people, Prefect," he acknowledged, "but I've no doubt you saved many, many more."

"Thank you, General," Soli whispered. "I hope you're right. I feared I'd let so many die because I wasn't ready to lead."

Taal harrumphed. "'Ready' or not, I wish more of our commanders could lead so well," he assured. "And after last night, I suspect you're better qualified to do so than anyone else in the Army of the Republic, General Kim included." He smiled. "But let's keep *that* between us, shall we?" Locking eyes with Fannius, Taal nodded significantly at the man, then stood to allow a Gentaa medicus room to crawl under the wagon.

Looking around, Taal took in the activity. Bodies were being cleared and wounded tended, while the ambulances drew up behind their blowing teams. Squadrons of the 9ᵗʰ Cohort were filtering back, and Kirham was sending squadrons of the 5ᵗʰ out to scout. They'd be here a while, getting everything sorted out. Stepping briskly down the growing, blood-muddy path that members of the 5ᵗʰ were making, he called for a runner. "Ride back to the column and tell Prefect Diola to hurry along, and send the remaining ambulances ahead." He paused, glancing back toward where another medicus had joined the first, frantically working on Soli. "Go to the comm-cart when you get there," he added, "and have them send a message to General Kim from me. Tell him I hope his sudden change of strategy was worth the cost." Taal actually suspected it was, coming at the insistence of Courtney Bradford and Bekiaa-Sa-At, after all. "But I also want him to know that, worth it or not, it's likely that only the magnificent, orderly, fighting withdrawal Prefect Soli-Kraar and her Eleventh Division performed, prevented the Grik from crawling up his army's arse."

The Lemurian runner hesitated, blinking incredulously. "Sir...You want me to say...to *General Kim?*"

"Those exact words," Taal growled, tail whipping, as he turned to look back under the wagon where the battered heart of the 11th lay bleeding on the ground.

* * * * *

Taylor Anderson Bio

Taylor Anderson is the New York Times bestselling author of the Alternate History/Military Sci-fi DESTROYERMEN Series. He's a gun-maker, forensic ballistic archeologist, and technical/historical consultant for movies and documentaries. He has a Master's Degree in History and has taught at Tarleton State University in Stephenville, Texas.

Facebook https://www.facebook.com/TaylorAndersonAuthor/
Website http://taylorandersonauthor.com/

# # # # #

Mr. Dewey's Tank Corps
by James Young

Chapter 1: Words Have Meaning

TF McPeak
0830 Local
1 July 1950

"**I**f you use that word to describe *any* of my men again, you best either make sure your deputy can perform your duties or learn how to give orders with sign language," Lieutenant Colonel Leonard Kraven, commander of the 72nd Armored Battalion, spat. Unsurprisingly given his martial profession, Kraven was a short, squat block of a man hailing from upstate New York. As he looked at his opposite number, Kraven could feel the bottom half of his face, horribly marked by a pattern of burn scars, starting to throb.

I could give less of a fuck that I look like some freak show right now, he thought angrily, well aware that the flesh tended to outline in stark white against his flushed face. It seemed to have a salutary effect on three of the officers standing on the other side of the terrain model in front of him, as the trio of company commanders took a seemingly involuntary step back.

Their commander, on the other hand, simply raised an eyebrow at Kraven's comment, his face serene as if he were unconcerned. A tall, slender man, Lieutenant Colonel Ramsey McPeak had seen combat as an infantry platoon leader, then company commander, during the Second World War. Unlike Kraven, however, it had been in Europe, a fact which gave him a much different perspective on "colored" troops it seemed. Which was why the commander of the 24th Infantry Battalion had felt so comfortable using a racial slur in reference to his imminent reinforcements.

Freakin' cake walks make it easy to be a bigot, Kraven thought. *Russians did most of the killing for you idiots once that bomb saw off Hitler. Hell, when we killed Hirohito it made things* worse.

"My point remains," McPeak said, his accent growing thicker as he began to drum on the map board. "Ni…*Negro* troops are unreliable, and I respectfully request that you reconsider your order of movement."

Unreliable? Kraven thought, his mind's eye turning back to a night of absolute madness. The screaming waves of Japanese soldiers, their faces contorted with rage as they swarmed towards his tank. The women and children bearing improvised Molotov cocktails, spears, and even rocks as they ran with their men. The flames of Tokyo burning all around his platoon and the company of armored infantrymen desperately holding onto a crossroads…

"Sir," his S-3, Major Andy Klein said as he grabbed Kraven's shoulder. The touch and familiar voice brought Kraven out of the fugue state he'd slipped into while taking a step forward. Kraven noted McPeak's slightly shaking hand had drifted down to the bayonet on his belt during his brief mental flashback.

I think my S-3 just saved your life, asshole, Kraven thought angrily. *Too bad your S-3 decided it was a good idea to try and reconnoiter north in an unarmed liaison plane. Having met you in person now, I can see why such idiocy would be acceptable in your unit.* The North Koreans had been demonstrating their anti-aircraft prowess against aircraft far superior to a Piper *Grasshopper.*

I'd sooner have Demon company at my back than your whole battalion. Dog Company, 758th Anti-Tank battalion, was not technically part of Kraven's unit. However, the "Demons," as the last Japanese hold-outs had taken to naming the M18 *Hellcat* company, had been assigned to 72nd Armored when the latter had shipped to Korea in order to "deter aggression." Which, it seemed, had now morphed into "stopping" the same.

"Lieutenant Colonel McPeak," a third voice interjected from the tent entrance, "it would be extremely entertaining to watch "Mad Dog" Kraven forcibly sodomize you with that bayonet you're foolishly thinking of using. However, I remind *both* of you that the North Koreans are a more pressing issue."

The gathered officers all came to attention as Brigadier General Jeffrey Watson, Military Advisory Command-Korea (MAC-K) stepped further into the tent. Like McPeak, Brigadier General Watson looked the part of a stereotypical Southern gentleman, with a patrician face, blue eyes, and graying cropped hair.

"If you don't want to have Lieutenant Colonel Kraven's men supporting you, Lieutenant Colonel McPeak, then I strongly suggest you do *your* men a favor and go stick a .45 in your mouth," Watson spat, completely erasing any thoughts the gathered men might have about 'Southern solidarity.' Whipping the walking stick he carried up in one savage motion, Watson speared the map that was between the two men.

"Major General Paek informs me that his men, quite possibly the last one thousand good men the ROKs have, are giving way as you are busy here complaining about having to actually work with colored troops," Watson continued angrily, his voice savage. "If you cannot bring yourself to close with the enemy regardless of who is beside you, take off that damn rank and tell me which one of your company commanders has fighting spirit."

McPeak drew himself up to his full height.

"I will…"

"You will *what*?" Watson cut the man off angrily.

I'd choose your next words carefully, Kraven thought, feeling bemused as he looked over at Klein. There was a long pause as McPeak's Adam's apple moved several times before he looked down at the map.

"Sir, I will integrate Lieutenant Colonel Kraven's men into my defenses," McPeak said, his voice just above a whisper.

The brigadier general turned to Kraven. The sound of distant artillery made the senior officer's lips purse. The explosions were carried by the strong wind out of the north, but Kraven could tell the North Korean People's Army (NKPA) forces would likely be through Suwon by that afternoon.

"Lieutenant Colonel Kraven, how soon until your company of *Hellcats* can be here?"

"Captain Gibson's M18s can get here in another two hours," Kraven replied. "The rest of my battalion will likely take another hour beyond that."

Watson scowled at the report.

"Well, hopefully the North Koreans will have to take a pause when they get through clearing Suwon," Watson said worriedly. "Lieutenant Colonel McPeak's men will have lanes marked for the M18s when they arrive."

The brigadier general gave the infantry commander a hard look.

"Let me know if they're not, Lieutenant Colonel Kraven," he finished. "I'm sure Major Klein would like a chance to get promoted."

"Sir, are my orders to defend or delay?" Lieutenant Colonel McPeak asked stiffly. "*Major* General Dean…"

"Major General Dean has placed me in command of all American forces north of Taegu," Watson replied, well aware of what McPeak had been trying to infer. "Your orders are to punch the North Koreans in the face until you can't punch anymore. Do you need any additional guidance?"

"Sir, words have meaning," Lieutenant Colonel McPeak replied angrily. "I do not want to be accused of cowardice if I judge it prudent to leave my position…"

It was not Lieutenant Colonel McPeak's day to finish a sentence.

"Lieutenant Colonel Kraven?" Watson asked.

"Yes, sir?" Kraven asked.

"You may order the general retreat when you feel that the position has become untenable here north of Osan," Watson replied. "Lieutenant Colonel McPeak's surviving forces will ride on your tanks if you are forced to retreat, and he has no remaining transportation."

Holy shit, Kraven thought.

"Understood, sir," Kraven replied, watching as McPeak's jaw moved in frustration.

"And *where*, pray tell, will you be, sir?" Lieutenant Colonel McPeak asked. The implication and belligerency in his question were clear.

"In Osan with my damn .45 to the head of the ROK engineer lieutenant," Watson snapped. "His charges are currently on the bridge over the river," Watson replied.

Kraven winced at that.

If that bridge drops, we'll have a long way to go to find another bridge.

"I'll be damned if the only armored battalion for at least a thousand miles is going to end up on the wrong side of a dropped bridge," Watson snapped. "Happened to those poor ROK bastards in Seoul a couple days ago when the Han River bridges got blown.

Fat lot of good giving Rhee an armored regiment last year did at that point."

Watson looked at the map, then at Kraven and McPeak. Just as he was about to speak, he was interrupted by the snarl of several piston engines flying close overhead.

Sounds like Navy birds, Kraven thought. The Marines had just finished establishing airfields around Pusan when the North Koreans had struck.

"I guess we can't get lucky and have one of those guys carrying Oppenheimer's Firecracker, can we?" one of the captains asked nervously, referring to the name the newspapers had given to the new bomb tested just the previous June. The redheaded officer's comment drew a hard look from Lieutenant Colonel McPeak.

"Captain, I'm pretty sure the first one of those will be going to Moscow if they've got one ready," Kraven replied. "Be nice if a couple of those had been available in '45 when we could have used them."

"If wishes were horses, we'd all ride," Brigadier General Watson said. Once more, the general met the eyes of every man around the room.

"We can hope for wonder weapons all we want, gentlemen," he stated. "The fact of the matter is, with China gone red, you are standing on the last piece of free ground between the Sea of Japan and Siam. If you don't want our children and their children to curse our names, we have to stop the damn Reds here in Korea."

If we can stop them, Kraven thought, sharing a look with Klein.

"Your role in this is to slow them down long enough for more help to get here and for defenses to be prepared," Watson continued. "You have your orders. Godspeed."

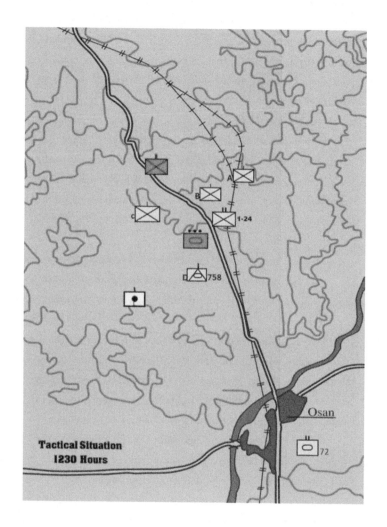

**Tactical Situation
1230 Hours**

Dotty III
1230 Local

Sweet mercy, what the hell do they have in these fields? Captain Jeremiah Gibson thought, holding onto the ring mount that enclosed the commander's position on his M18 *Hellcat*. The tank destroyer was going north from Osan as fast as its driver, Private Schiller, could force it. Unfortunately, given the vehicle's open turret and the wind coming from the north, that had the effect of forcing the rice paddies' stench into Jeremiah's face as well as that of the loader, SPC Washington.

I feel like I'm in the middle of a manure tornado, Jeremiah thought glumly, looking to his left over the M18's side. Unlike American tanks, the *Hellcat's* commander and gunner sat to the left of the vehicle's 76mm gun, its loader on the right. While it made feeding the main gun difficult, Jeremiah had to admit he liked sitting on the same side of the vehicle's turret as he had while driving his father's fruit truck back home.

Although I'm pretty sure if I drove this into town back home people would be...upset. Before he could continue that thought, the sound of piston engines brought his eyes upward, and he saw four dots rushing down from the north.

Oh my word, he thought for a brief second, his hand tightening on the butterfly grips of the *Hellcat's* .50-caliber machine gun. As the shapes grew closer, he immediately relaxed at their familiar gull-shaped wings, then shook his head grimly as he noted the trail fighter was streaming thin smoke behind it.

"Oh shit!" his loader, Specialist Washington, shouted and grabbed his arm. He snapped his gaze down just in time to see the ox cart enter the road from a hidden entrance off to his left.

"Schiller, right!" he shouted into the intercom, gripping the turret edge as the poor farmer, farmer's wife, and five children riding on the cart's back all looked at their onrushing doom. Private First Class Schiller, *Dotty III's* driver, and his assistant, Private Downs, both worked the controls to throw the nimble M18 into a hard right turn. Unfortunately, the raised road they were on was not used to that sort of abuse from pivoting tracks, and Jeremiah felt it start to crumble under the tank destroyer's weight. Washington, lacking a platform, tumbled down onto the turret's floor with a surprised cry.

Hold on, dammit, hold on! Jeremiah thought, hearing the right track threatening to slip off its sprockets. With several audible pops the tread remained where it was supposed to, and Jackson turned around to make sure the next *Hellcat* in line saw the farmer. To his relief, D32's commander was on the ball, his evasion far less violent than that of his company commander's.

Those poor bastards, Jeremiah thought, turning to give the man a wave. The ROKs had managed to start gaining control of their refugees compared to even a few short days before, but the clog of humanity streaming out of Osan had still considerably slowed the Americans' movement north. Jeremiah couldn't help but be sympathetic and understanding of the people's fear and anguish as the Communists struck south.

Like a damn Klan convention rolling down the road towards a town of Freedmen, he thought. As the son of dirt poor Alabama sharecroppers, Jeremiah knew exactly what his fellow man was capable of. Burying his lynched uncle in a closed casket, the sickly sweet smell of burned flesh filling the church, had been his first introduction to man's inhumanity to man. Being a platoon leader during the final weeks of the Battle of Tokyo had just further cemented it.

"Sir!" Washington, shouted, slapping his arm. He looked to where the man was pointing, squinted his eyes, and saw nothing.

"I saw a tank!" Washington said, his eyes wide. "Just crossing that ridge over yonder."

Jeremiah checked his map. The sound of artillery opening off somewhere to his right, followed by an eruption of small arms, bazookas, and the crack of several tank main guns told him more than his loader's warning did.

Looks like the North Koreans got out of Suwon quicker than Lieutenant Colonel Kraven thought they would, Jeremiah thought grimly.

"Schiller, there's a railroad cut fifty yards in front of us! Take it and find us a hull down, now!"

"Yes sir!"

As *Dotty III* made the turn, Jeremiah quickly whipped his binoculars up. With the diesel suddenly quieted, the sounds of warfare were much louder. He estimated that the fighting was just on the other side of the low rise roughly five hundred yards in front of him. Jeremiah watched as mortar rounds began impacting on that ridge and instinctively knew that's where the friendly infantry they were supposed to be linking up with had been.

"Demons, we have armor to our front," he said after switching the microphone to radio. There was nothing but static.

Of all the times to have problems, he thought angrily, looking over at the device. It was half out of its mount, clearly thrown off in the hard turn.

"Washington, fix the radio!" he snapped. Looking over *Dotty III*'s rear, he saw that his 3rd Platoon was already deploying towards a nearby hill, the lighter M18s fighting their way up towards the top. His 2nd Platoon was just starting to round the ox cart, the farmer having somehow managed to overturn the vehicle while cutting across to a paddy trail. Inexplicably, D24 had stopped, its crew starting to dismount to help the South Korean family.

Should have let 1st Platoon lead! he chastised himself. *Ignorant officers or not!* Major Klein's hurried briefing as the Demons left Osan hadn't given Jeremiah much confidence in 1/24 IN's leadership. Which was the reason why the Demons had changed their usual march order from 1-2-3 to 3-2-1. His 1st Platoon Leader, 2nd Lieutenant Collins, was a mouthy college kid from Chicago. It hadn't struck Jeremiah as a good idea to bring him into contact with some racist wearing oak leaves.

"Wash, what's in the breech?!" Sergeant Mullock, his gunner asked.

"HVAP!" Washington replied, referring to the High Velocity, Armor Piercing rounds that were the M18s primary tank killer. Jeremiah looked at the five ready rounds next to the gun.

Here's hoping we can shoot straight, he thought. *Also, that the intelligence idiots are right about them working against the North Korean tanks.* One advantage the M18s had over their armored brethren had been their ability to cross most of Japan's remaining bridges and thus find areas to train in. The 758th's former battalion commander had been a stickler about gunnery, even in the resource-strapped Truman years. Jeremiah had taken the man's teachings about training to heart, even as his men had grown dismayed at their fellows slowly rotating home.

All that time away from the whorehouses is about to pay off, I hope, Jeremiah thought. *Even if the men thought I was just making sure if I wasn't getting laid, neither were they.* His eyes briefly turned towards the picture taped on the front of his ring mount.

Dorothy, I'll see you soon I hope.

"Sir, I don't see a thing!" Sergeant Mullock stated, scanning to their front.

"Four tanks came over a hill and then down into a valley," Jeremiah responded. "They're going to be coming at our eleven…"

An artillery piece opening fire to his left front interrupted Jeremiah. Whatever it was shooting at was just behind the slight rise roughly six hundred yards to their front, just below the ridgeline. The shot was a hit, however, as the artillery shell ricocheted up towards the heavy clouds that seemed to be reaching ever lower above them.

Well clearly that wasn't effective, Jeremiah had time to think. Then suddenly a dark green tank, red star prominent on its prow, was hauling over the hill. The vehicle's turret was traversing right towards the offending artillery piece, and the tank stopped suddenly.

"Tank!" Jeremiah barked.

"Identified!" Mullock replied.

The North Korean vehicle's 85mm gun belched fire towards the artillery position.

Well at least that confirms he's hostile!

"Fire!"

"On the way!"

The 76mm gun had originally been designed to equip the ubiquitous M4 *Sherman*s fighting across Europe. The M18, the bastard child of the tank destroyer corps, was at best half the *Sherman*'s weight, and *Dotty III* rocked backwards like a toy truck nudged by a clumsy St. Bernard. Jeremiah held onto the ring mount as the muzzle blast washed back over the vehicle's open turret in an unpleasant stench of gunpowder, fertilizer, and singed dust.

The HVAP round would have had more than enough power to punch through the T-34/85's front turret at 500 yards. Hitting the much thinner side armor, the tungsten penetrator hardly slowed down before passing first through the ready ammunition, then the loader and commander, and out the structure's other side before the 85mm rounds began exploding. The eruption of flames from the North Korean tank's turret hatches served to signal the transition from fighting vehicle to crematorium, but not quickly enough to prevent 3rd platoon putting two more HVAP rounds into its front hull.

Oh man, that rain needs to just start falling, Jeremiah thought, his eyes burning. Reaching upwards, he dropped his goggles as first 3rd, then

2nd platoons engaged the next four North Korean tanks to come over the rise.

"Driver back up, seek alternate," he managed to croak out as Washington slammed another HVAP into the 76mm gun's breech.

Now I see why they said the company commander riding his own Hellcat *might be a bad idea,* Jeremiah thought. The muzzle blast had completely obscured things to his front, and he was no more coordinating the company's fire than the man on the moon.

A round impacting in front of the reversing *Dotty III* highlighted another danger, the spray of dirt clods washing over the M18's front. The offending T-34/85 did not live long enough to try and correct, two rounds knocking it out. Its three surviving crewmen attempted to bail out, only to die in a hail of .50-caliber fire.

At least we seem to have justified our reorganization, he thought. Originally Delta Company had had only two four-vehicle platoons rather than its current 13-vehicle organization. In less than two minutes, it appeared the Demons had killed five T-34/85s, and no more North Korean tanks were trying to rush down the road. A single T-34/85 was attempting to turn away from the Demons, misses throwing up dirt as smoke poured from the tank's diesel.

"…get that bastard trying to pass east of the road!"

The radio traffic in his headphones told him Washington had worked magic with the electronics. The Demons' net was a bedlam of crosstalk as 1st platoon joined the fray with three solid hits to the lone remaining tank. The Russian-made vehicle burst into flames.

"Clear the damn net!" he shouted into the microphone, then waited for the chaos to simmer down some.

The sound of machine gun fire and mortars to the north told Jeremiah that some sort of fight was still going on, and as he tried to get his bearings, he saw men running south roughly five hundred yards to his right front. Bringing up his binoculars, Jeremiah focused in on the group even as he heard 2nd Lieutenant Collins call out a warning about infantry sneaking around the Demons' right flank. The distinctive rhythm from at least two M2 machine guns told Jeremiah others had sighted the dismounts.

Holy shit, has 1/24 been overrun? Jeremiah thought, focusing. What he saw through the lenses caused a wash of nausea. The men diving into the muck wore olive green uniforms and steel pot helmets.

"Cease fire! Cease fire! The infantry are friendly!" Jeremiah shouted into his radio. Even as he received acknowledgments, he saw one of group of men bowled over by an accurate burst.

"Schiller, get us over this railroad and follow the paddy trail," Jeremiah said, hoping his voice wasn't as shaken as he felt. Third Platoon, with its elevated vantage point, was continuing to lob desultory rounds at some distant target.

"Third Platoon, what are you shooting at?" Jeremiah asked over the radio as Schiller pulled them onto the narrow dirt roads leading towards the infantry positions. There was a long pause, then 2LT Hamm's belated answer.

"There's some infantry huddling under an enemy tank, Demon Six," Hamm replied, his voice apprehensive. In his mind's eye, Jeremiah could see the skinny, bookish lieutenant standing in his M18 turret. The sole white officer in the Demons, Hamm had never given Jeremiah an ounce of trouble despite being from Birmingham, Alabama.

"Let the mortars and artillery take care of them," Jeremiah said. "We need to save that ammo for the next bunch. Cover Red and White while we all get moved up."

Fifteen minutes later, Jeremiah was grabbing his Thompson submachine gun from its makeshift scabbard within the turret and preparing to dismount. 1/24 IN had dug in on a low ridgeline through which the Osan-Suwon road passed. To Jeremiah's quick glance as he'd directed Schiller into position, the North Korean probing force had apparently come hell for leather down the road towards the American infantry positions.

Infantry riding tanks always seems like a good idea…and then the artillery arrives, Jeremiah thought, gazing over the clumps of mustard brown bodies lining the road. *Of course, artillery doesn't do a damn thing to actual tanks.*

A lone T-34/85 sat off the side of the Osan-Suwon road, looking from all appearances like it had thrown a track. The vehicle's crew had bailed out and, along with some of their infantry brethren, taken shelter near their vehicle. 1/24's mortars had made Jeremiah a prophet, a quick barrage quickly killing most of the hiding North Koreans.

"Captain Gibson!" a man shouted from roughly 50 yards away. "Captain Gibson, you need to get over here *right now.*"

Looking over at the tall, Caucasian officer, Jeremiah had a feeling he knew who the man was. That guess was reinforced by the numerous NCOs and enlisted nearby trying to be inconspicuous in paying attention to the two men's interaction.

"Sir, I have to see to the platoons' sector," Jeremiah called back, gesturing to where 1st and 2nd platoons were arranging their vehicles then holding up his radio microphone.

"Goddammit, boy, I didn't *ask* you, I said *come here,*" Lieutenant Colonel McPeak shouted, starting to come out of his foxhole.

Jeremiah set his microphone down and looked at 1/24's battalion commander.

I will not be summoned like some cur, he thought.

"Don't get yourself shot, sir," SPC Washington muttered from beside him.

"I think if anyone's going to get shot, it's going to be that asshole if he's not careful," Sergeant Mullock muttered.

Then again, I can't expect my men to have discipline if I'm going to ignore a superior officer, Jeremiah thought angrily.

"Both of you, hush," Jeremiah snapped. He pulled his Thompson submachine gun out of its traveling scabbard just below the ring mount. Moving just the right side of glacial, he started clambering down the M18's front.

Stupid son-of-a...

Jeremiah did not hear the initial shells of the artillery barrage. One moment he was getting ready to jump down off the M18. The next he was face down in the Korean dirt, struggling to breath from the blast that had knocked the wind out of him.

CRUMP! CRUMP! CRUMP!

As the world heaved beneath him, he finally began to hear the tearing canvas sound that signified incoming artillery. That was almost as much a relief as the dull, throbbing pain in his left shoulder, as experience told him both meant he was not in shock from a severe injury. Rolling over, he slithered underneath *Dotty III* as the bombardment shook the ridge.

Dammit, dammit, dammit, Jeremiah thought, dragging in a shuddering breath. He looked down and was strangely unsurprised to see he'd literally had the piss knocked out of him. The front of his body felt like a giant bruise, and even as the M18 rocked above him Jeremiah did a quick check to make sure he actually hadn't caught some shrapnel.

Thank God, he thought. The bombardment stopped almost as suddenly as it began, the explosions stilling causing Jeremiah's ears to ring. As his hearing gradually returned, he realized two things. First, as if the shells had pierced the clouds and opened them, a hard rain was starting to fall. Second, a high-pitched, terrible screaming told him that someone close by had been hit.

Oh damn, please not one of the crew, he thought, adrenaline suddenly giving him a snake's alacrity as he slithered out from under *Dotty III.*

"…get out and check the damn track!" Sergeant Mullock said.

"Someone shut that fucker up!" an infantryman was yelling, hopping out of the foxholes to *Dotty III's* front. Jeremiah saw the chevrons and rockers of a platoon sergeant, the NCO's eyes wild and darting. From the way the man was holding his pistol in the deluge, Jeremiah had a feeling the sergeant didn't intend to render first aid.

This is profoundly not good, he thought, slowly sliding the Thompson off his shoulder as he also moved towards the screams. Men were running around in the chaos, attempting to treat the wounded and prepare weapons for an assault that could be right behind the artillery barrage. Looking to either side, Jeremiah felt bile rise in his throat as he spotted at least two of his M18s ablaze.

Damn open turrets, he thought. *That had to be heavy guns.*

"Holy Christ…" the NCO muttered in front of Jeremiah. The man was stopped stock still at the edge of an impact crater, looking down at what was within. The man who had been screaming slumped at the bottom. Jeremiah, upon stepping up to the crater, realized why the NCO had stopped dead in his tracks. While the ruin that had been a healthy human being not two minutes before was startling in and of itself, it was not the half severed right arm or savaged lower abdomen and groin that had stopped the sergeant and made him fall to his knees.

Well, looks like we get to find out who the senior captain in 1/24 is, Jeremiah thought, seeing the decapitated body just beyond Lieutenant Colonel McPeak's mortal remains. It was hard to tell in the rain, but given McPeak's lieutenant colonel's rank was visible on his helmet, Jeremiah could only assume the headless body's oak leaves were gold, not silver. Which meant that 1/24 had, ironically, also been decapitated.

"Sergeant, you need to go grab your company commander," Jeremiah stated. The man turned to look at Jeremiah, and the black officer could see the moment of hesitation.

No time for that shit.

"Now, Sergeant!" Jeremiah shouted.

The man shook himself out of his moment of near insubordination and hurried off. Jeremiah looked south, then north.

"Lieutenant Colonel Kraven, you need to hurry the hell up."

* * *

Chapter 2: Jabs

Crusader 66
1345 Local
1 mile north of Osan

"You have got to be kidding me," Lieutenant Colonel Kraven shouted.

"Sir, I wish I was," Major Klein said, looking anxiously south back towards Osan. The rain was pouring down on both men, making it hard to see the city edge behind them. "But that bridge is fucked, and Apache 33 is at the bottom of the damn river."

It never fails, Kraven thought. *Just when you need something to go right, the world is going to punch you in the head.*

"How many got out?" he asked.

"Just the tank commander" Klein replied, clearly shaken. "Major Donahue is trying to scare up a pontoon boat as we speak, and that ROK lieutenant thinks he can make repairs over a couple of hours.

We can *try* that rail bridge or to find a ford site, but that won't be quick."

Two companies north of the bridge, Kraven thought. *If we want to stop the North Koreans for a couple of hours, we're going to have to give them a good, hard punch in the head to make them think about things.*

Kraven looked north, the pounding rain dampening any sounds of combat that might have drifted backwards. It was hard to tell if the rolling, deep sounds he heard were thunder or artillery. Kraven sincerely hoped the former, as if it were the latter, then the North Koreans were pounding the shit out of TF McPeak and Demon Company.

"Still no freakin' radio contact?" he asked Klein. "What in the hell happened to Demon 6?"

"We lost contact with them just after they reported the North Koreans attacked again," Klein answered. "I don't know if they're being jammed or there's something wrong with their radios."

Six in one hand, half dozen in the other, Kraven thought.

"I'm headed north, Andy," Kraven said. "We'll try to buy some time with Baker and Charlie Companies."

"Roger sir," Klein replied. "I'll try to get that bridge fixed. What do you…"

There was the sound of a truck engine and honking horn between them and Osan. Turning to look beyond Klein, Kraven watched as a jeep followed by two 5-ton trucks proceeded up the road towards *Crusader 66*. He recognized a mud-spattered Brigadier General Watson in the jeep seat.

"Wonder what in the hell he wants?" Klein muttered, drawing a hard look from Kraven.

"Sorry sir," Klein stated. The jeep stopped rolling a couple minutes later, and Kraven noticed that the third man in the jeep was a ROK lieutenant colonel who was covered from head to toe in mud

404 | KENNEDY & YOUNG

and what looked like straw. The man's arm was in a sling and as he got closer Kraven realized some of the dark spatters were not mud, but that didn't seem to detract from the South Korean's intensity.

"Lieutenant Colonel Kraven, I present to you Lieutenant Colonel Sung, Republic of Korea Army," Brigadier General Watson said. "His men are what's left of 3rd battalion, 1st ROK Infantry Regiment."

There's barely two platoons in those trucks, Kraven thought.

"My men and I are here to help you, Lieutenant Colonel Kraven," Sung said, his accent indicating he'd been taught the King's English rather than American. "We have limited equipment, but I have one hundred anti-tank mines and men who know how to emplace them."

This time the rumbling from the north was clearly man made. Kraven looked at the Scout Platoon heading north at their best speed, the little M24 *Chaffees* throwing up mud as they accelerated.

"Hold that thought, Lieutenant Colonel Sung," Kraven said grimly. "It appears Round 2 of this match has just begun. If TF McPeak gets knocked out, we might be making a stand here."

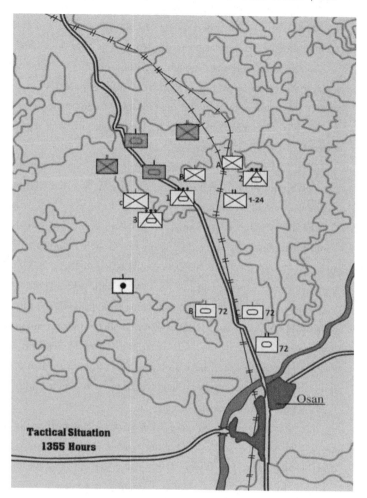

Dotty III

1355 Local

"Over, reengage!" Jeremiah shouted, angry as the 76mm round passed just above the T-34/85s turret. The North Korean tank's last minute zig had closed the range just enough. The vehicle's commander whipped around and saw *Dotty III* just as Jeremiah depressed his butterfly trigger. The burst ricocheted off the turret all around the

North Korean commander, but miraculously none of the slugs struck home before Jeremiah's target dropped into his open hatch.

Lucky bastard! Jeremiah thought, fighting the urge to order Schiller to back up in order not to ruin SGT Mullock's shot. It was no matter, his gunner putting the next round just in front of the T-34/85 as their target braked hard, then began to slew its turret around.

We're dead, Jeremiah thought, even as Washington desperately grabbed another HVAP out of the ready rack. At less than 300 yards, the tank was unlikely to miss.

"Clear!" Washington shouted as the 85mm gun lay onto them. From Jeremiah's perspective, the main gun looked as big as a drainage pipe. Jeremiah closed his eyes...only to open them as a Super Bazooka rocket exploded against the turret's right side.

Thank you, Jesus! The 85mm gun remained stopped, the infantry rocket's HEAT warhead having obviously halted whatever intentions the North Korean crew had with regards to *Dotty III*. Sergeant Mullock's next round turned hesitation into detonation less than a second later, hitting just below the turret ring before going into the ready ammo with spectacular effects.

These things burn worse than the Japanese tanks, Jeremiah thought crazily as the North Korean commander started to clamber out of his now-blazing track. The effect of the heavy rain dousing the man's garments in a wreath of smoke and steam was strangely hypnotizing...

"Sir, look out!" Washington screamed, clawing for his pistol. The *ping* and whine of a bullet glancing off *Dotty III*'s left side armor told Jeremiah that *Dotty III* had enemy infantry close at hand. An object sailed past him trailing a streamer from left to right, slamming into the ground and exploding. Gazing in the direction it came from even while ducking below the lip of the turret, Jeremiah saw the offending North Korean reaching for another anti-tank grenade.

How in the Hell did they get on top of us? he thought, reaching desperately for his Thompson. Even as his hand grasped the SMG, the snarling grin on the North Korean's face and those of his comrades raising their own submachine guns let him know that it was going to be far too late. In seeming slow motion, the man pulled the pin on his next anti-tank grenade even as the other two men's fire drove Jeremiah to the turret floor. Specialist Washington grunted and slumped to the turret floor himself, curling up around his abdomen.

Instead of the roar of the anti-tank grenade penetrating *Dotty III*'s hull, Jeremiah heard the dull *thump!* of a 75mm cannon. This was followed almost immediately by the hail-on-steel-roof sound of canister balls bouncing off of *Dotty III*'s flank and the detonation of the North Korean anti-tank team's ordnance. Popping up, Jeremiah saw all three men converted into red smears, the charging silhouette of a 72nd Battalion M24 *Chaffee* with its 75mm gun roughly 150 yards beyond them.

That was entirely too close, he thought while trying to assess what was around him in the smoke, rain, and chaos. Jeremiah's hand shook as he gripped the Thompson, not seeing any more North Korean infantry sneaking up towards him. The M24 pivot steered to the left and its machine guns began to chatter. The fire cut down several other men in mustard brown uniforms as they approached the two vehicles from *Dotty III's* west.

Jeremiah popped up into his turret and swung the M2 around towards what appeared to be at least thirty charging North Koreans. Depressing the trigger, he fired short bursts, bowling over at least ten men even as the screaming soldiers' return fire pinged off of his turret.

They're all over us, inside the perimeter, Jeremiah thought angrily as the machine gun ran through its box.

"Schiller back up!" Sergeant Mullock shouted, grabbing the hand mike from Jeremiah's station. "Straight back, down the ridge!"

The M18 surged backwards from where it had been in the center of 1/24's positions. Something very, very bad had obviously happened to C/1/24 out on the TF McPeak's left, and Jeremiah could see three of his M18s engulfed in flames in that direction. The radio was dead, and the rain made it difficult to know what was truly happening over there. However, what Jeremiah saw after he switched his box of ammunition looked to be a confusing mix of olive green and mustard brown uniforms at two hundred yards' distance.

"Bandits! Bandits on me!" one of the infantry company commanders was yelling. Rallying one of his platoons towards him, the man screamed for bayonets then set off towards C/1/24's position.

"Sir, Washington's dead," Sergeant Mullock said grimly. Jeremiah turned around in shock, then looked down towards where his loader lay impossibly still.

"Goddammit," Jeremiah said, fighting back a surge of rage and helplessness. The distant sound of bugles jerked him out of his state just as quickly as he'd gone into it, and he belatedly realized the North Koreans were retreating. In moments, most of the enemy had melted back into the pelting rain from which they'd come, chased by machine gun fire and mortar fire.

Okay, if the mortars are that accurate, the radio problem is in this vehicle.

"What the hell happened?" 1LT Reese, the Scout Platoon leader asked as he brought his M24 aside *Dotty III.* Jeremiah took a moment to process the man's question.

"Sorry, sir," Reese said, misunderstanding the reason for Jeremiah's silence.

"They waited until the damn rain got really bad, then tried to bumrush right up the road," Jeremiah said, waving off the correction. "Twenty tanks, looks like two battalions of—"

The sound of incoming artillery fire caused both men to drop into their respective turrets. Thankfully, the initial North Korean salvo was long, landing roughly half a mile behind the 1/24 ridge. The next was similarly off, at least if the target was 1/24's defensive positions. After one more salvo, wildly inaccurate in azimuth, thundered down the North Korean barrage ceased.

Dammit, Jeremiah thought, feeling momentarily helpless. Fighting the emotion away, he forced himself to stand up in the turret.

"Is your radio down, sir?!" 1LT Reese called over. "Crusader 6 has been trying to reach you for the last thirty minutes."

Jeremiah looked over at the radio set.

"Get SPC Washington out of the turret," Jeremiah said. "I'm going to go talk to LTC Kraven on 1LT Reese's radio."

* * *

Ten minutes later, Jeremiah felt as if his time could have been better spent on consolidation than talking to LTC Kraven. As *Crusader 66* pulled up beside *Dotty III*, Jeremiah was still getting a tally of just how badly the Demons had suffered. The news was not good, as there were only eight serviceable *Hellcats* left. The crews of D13 and D25 were working feverishly to repair their vehicles, but Jeremiah had the feeling the North Koreans weren't going to give them much more of a respite.

Certainly not enough time to replace a busted sprocket and service a holed engine, Jeremiah thought.

"...then you'll split your men and hold that damn position!" LTC Kraven was shouting at a hapless infantry company commander as Jeremiah walked up. "Do you understand?"

The junior officer mumbled something, unable to meet LTC Kraven's eyes.

"Well I could swear that dead son-of-a-bitch who was your commander was going on and on about how he had the finest troops in the Army and didn't want to be supported by some 'colored' troops."

Kraven jabbed towards where Jeremiah was standing. "Well I don't see Captain Gibson whining like some whipped child about how bad his losses are," Kraven said. "So you need to get with your fellow captains and cross attach infantrymen, as we're going to hold the bastards at least one more time."

Jeremiah saw the captain glance over at him and met the man's gaze.

Sure I'm a glorified platoon leader right now, but if it helps LTC Kraven rally the damn infantry then I'll do what I can, he thought.

The infantry captain gulped, turned back to the 72nd battalion commander, then nodded.

"I'll get the men together, sir," he drawled. To Jeremiah's surprise, the officer turned and nodded in his direction before speaking.

"I'd serve with you any time, Captain Gibson," the man continued, his voice raw. "You saved our lives today. I hate to think what would have happened without your *Hellcats* being here."

Well, I guess Jesus is coming soon, Jeremiah thought.

"Thank you, Captain Larson," he replied.

With that, the man moved off, shouting to a nearby group of soldiers from HHC, 1/24. Jeremiah turned back to LTC Kraven.

"We can't stay here, Captain Gibson," Kraven said, shocking Jeremiah, then nodded towards Suwon. "Eventually someone up there is going to realize our flanks are just hanging out in the air and try to bypass us. Probably after the next attack."

Jeremiah nodded, glancing as a platoon of *Pershings* moved by them. He noticed all the M26s were staying below the ridgeline, but were also having to carefully pick their paths across the paddy trails.

"So far, I don't think any of the North Koreans have seen our tanks," Kraven said. "Besides the Scout Platoon, that is. So we're going to try something a little different this next time."

"Sir?" Jeremiah asked.

"I need your *Hellcats* to move from place to place," Kraven said. "I want the North Koreans to commit fully to the attack and try to rush down this road, where those ROKs are about to put down some anti-tank mines."

Jeremiah looked at where the South Koreans were placing the mines on the surface.

"Sir, are those..." he started to ask.

"Yes, they're old Japanese mines," Kraven replied. "Should still be good enough for blowing off a track."

"Roger, sir," Jeremiah said, glad he wasn't the one messing with the old explosives.

"I don't need you to be heroes," Kraven said, jerking his attention back to the present. "Don't stay above the ridge line, and if you lose another track I want you to very obviously turn and run for it."

"Sir?" Jeremiah questioned. Kraven raised an eyebrow.

"Sir, it's just the infantry..." he started, then made sure no one was in earshot. "The infantry are probably just about ready to run for it. They lost LTC McPeak and their XO to artillery, and I'm not sure if we run if that won't start a general panic."

"Let the infantry company commanders worry about a panic," Kraven said. "If I have to, we'll fire over their heads to stop it."

Jeremiah's eyes widened at his commander's ruthlessness.

"I didn't cross the Sea of Japan to die on some damn ridgeline because the infantry can't keep it together," Kraven said. "You familiar with Joshua Chamberlain, Captain Gibson?"

"Yes, sir," Jeremiah responded.

"Well, this ain't Pennsylvania, but it's the same principle," Kraven said. "When they get within five hundred yards, I'm going to have Charlie pop up and hit them hard. Then we're going to counterattack."

"Sir?" Jeremiah asked, shocked.

"I'm going to roll those bastards back to Suwon," Kraven stated, looking determinedly past the ridge. "We're going to shoot up the first things we come to, convince them I'm coming off this hill with murder on my mind. I imagine that's going to cause some consternation with the enemy's higher headquarters, and they may dig in."

Jeremiah remained silent as Kraven looked around at the infantry redigging their positions.

"After that happens, *then* we're going to fall back off this ridge."

I'm not sure that's the best idea anyone's ever had, Jeremiah thought. *But I guess it beats sitting here waiting to get kicked in the head again.*

"Sir, how are you going to get back through that minefield?" Jeremiah asked.

"I suspect the North Koreans are going to set off most of the mines," Kraven replied. "The big point of them is to make them stop on the ridge just before we kick them in the head."

Jeremiah looked back to where the first T-34/85 the Demons had killed still sat smoldering.

"Well, we've given them plenty of reason to be cautious," he stated, then looked in surprise as a ROK officer came up behind Kraven.

"We are dug in to the north end of your line and have coordinated with your infantry company," Sung said. "We will guard your flank as best we can."

"Thank you, Lieutenant Colonel Sung," Kraven said. "Gentlemen, let's go make history."

* * *

Chapter 3: Kraven's Right Hook

Dotty III
1555 Local
TF McPeak Defensive Positions

"How many rounds of HVAP do we have, PFC Caine?"

Jeremiah shook his head sadly as he stood relieving himself behind *Dotty III*. It was the NCO's polite, but firm, way of telling the private to wake up and pay attention. That the man had had to ask it six times in the last hour or so reflected the brutal post-combat fatigue that was seemingly sweeping over the entire position.

"The same number as there were last time, Sergeant," Caine replied.

Well shit, Jeremiah thought, quickly tucking himself back in and turning towards the track.

"What the fuck did you say, Private?!"

"You heard me, dammit," Caine said, his voice rising. "I don't need you…"

Jeremiah was halfway up *Dotty III*'s back deck when he heard the sound of a helmet thudding off the turret side, then another blow being struck and a cry of pain.

So help me, if you make me have to go get another loader, I'll have a stripe, Jeremiah thought angrily.

"Is there a *problem?*!" he asked, poking his head over the turret ring. SGT Mullock had the scared private pinned against the turret wall with his hand around Cain's throat, the enlisted man clearly stunned from the first two blows. Seeing the look on his lieutenant's face, SGT Mullock quickly let Caine go. The young private took a shuddering breath, coughing and retching as he slumped.

"Caine, maybe you need to get some fresh..."

Jeremiah never got a chance to finish, the all too familiar sound of incoming indirect fire sending him diving into the turret. He reached the bottom at the same time the shells reached the American defensive positions. For the second time that day, Jeremiah felt himself barely hanging onto his sanity as the M18 pitched and shook like a cork in a storm-tossed sea. The barrage was a short, savage thing, moving over the position like a hurricane once, then back again.

In the long silence that followed, with the acrid smell of gunpowder clogging his nose, Jeremiah had a few moments to think about his life choices. Joining the Army. Fighting for his country in the Pacific. Not simply refusing to return to the airport in Mobile when his all too short postwar leave had been up. He thought of his daughter, and how she'd screamed blue bloody murder when the strange man at the airport had scooped her up back in '46. Of the son he'd never met, almost certainly as a casual "Fuck off..." from the senior officers who'd been open about their thoughts the 758th's troops were a bit "uppity." Briefly, Jeremiah thought about just staying on the M18's hull floor, of no longer fighting for an Army that made sure he was forever aware of his second-class status.

Then the moment passed, and he recalled that he was a damned commissioned officer...and some North Koreans were about to pay.

"Tanks! Tanks coming down the road!" one of the infantrymen was screaming from fifty yards in front of *Dotty III*.

I hope that damn radio is truly fixed, Jeremiah thought. *Or that whatever the hell heavy artillery the North Koreans just dropped on us didn't break it again.* The commo section had found where either an artillery fragment or the Scout Platoon's canister round had severed an antenna wire. To his great surprise, he plugged in in time to hear 2LT Collins calmly counting down the range from where *Darkchild*, his M18, was in a turret down position at the northernmost edge of TF McPeak's infantry positions.

I can't say I argue with Captain Larson's decision to basically concede the center of the line, Jeremiah thought. In effect, C/1-24 had ceased to exist when the North Korean infantry battalion had managed to fall upon it. While the ROKs had placed anti-personnel mines across the small draw that had allowed the North Koreans to advance without being seen, Jeremiah kept casting nervous glances in that direction.

"Wait a second…" Collins reported. "Those tanks are stopping."

"Red One, what do you mean they're stopping?" Jeremiah asked, looking towards the ridge lip three hundred yards ahead of him.

"They're stopping at twelve hundred yards or thereabouts," Collins said. "Shit. Demon 6, I've got many, many more tanks coming out of Suwon!"

There was a long pause, then Collins reported with much more excitement.

"They're *heavy* tanks, Demon 6! Looking like some of those damn *Stalin* tanks the boys from Europe kept talking about."

Well this is bad, Jeremiah thought. He was about to inquire as to what the first group of tanks were doing when the ridgeline erupted with shell impacts and machine gun fire in front of him.

So much for letting them charge in, he thought.

"Up and at them, Demons," he said. "We've got to take care of those tanks that are stopped."

Reaching down, he switched to the 72nd Armored radio net.

We didn't make sure the infantry had our frequencies, he thought stupidly. *Shit.*

"Crusader 6, we have heavy tanks coming out of Suwon," he said, then quickly brought Kraven up on what he'd seen. He'd barely stopped talking when the artillery battery located to their rear began firing, followed by both the 72nd Armored and 24th Infantry mortars.

"Two battalions of infantry trying to work to the west also," LTC Kraven replied. "Looks like that two-hour pause was the enemy bringing up reinforcements. Charlie, Baker, stand by to attack. Demon, I need you to get those tanks sitting still shooting up the ridge."

"Roger, sir, we're on it."

The cracks of 76mm guns were swiftly answered by more distant booms and shells passing over the swiftly shifting Demon M18s. As *Dotty III* pulled up, Jeremiah began seeking targets.

"Tank, eleven o—"

Captain Jeremiah Gibson, son of a grocer and teacher, husband to a devoted wife, never even realized he'd been targeted by two platoons of the advancing *Stalin* tanks. Even if he had, at a range of just over 1200 yards there would not have been enough time for him to react to the incoming fire. In any event, the two 122mm rounds that hit *Dotty III's* hull ripped completely through the M18's front and detonated inside the vehicle's turret. None of the five-man crew were alive to feel the secondary detonations.

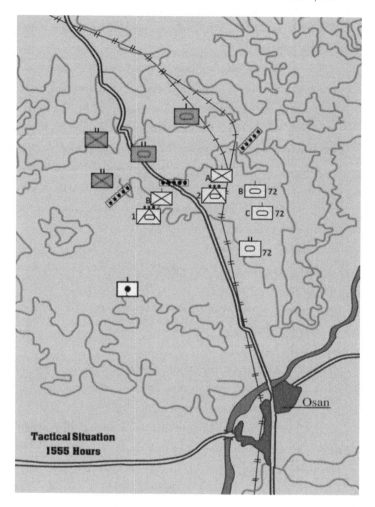

**Tactical Situation
1555 Hours**

Crusader 66

1620 Local

"Those which the gods wish to punish, they first make proud," LTC Kraven muttered bitterly to himself as he watched *Dotty III* burn in front of him. His hands were shaking in rage as *Crusader 66* sat in its firing position, the newly arrived Able Company coming on line with his track.

Ten more damn minutes, he thought. *If only the North Koreans had waited ten more damn minutes.* Able had hauled ass up from Osan, maintaining radio silence the entire way. Now, just as the Demons were falling back off the hill as planned, Kraven stood up in his turret and extended his hands horizontally. The thirteen M26's of Able came on line with his vehicle, their turrets sighted in on the ridgeline.

The infantry is holding, he thought, pleased to see that there were no masses of olive drab breaking and running from the ridge.

"Baker is in position."

"Charlie is in position."

Kraven watched as the remaining M18s passed back through Able then pivoted to find positions. Then his eyes were back to the front as the first massive *Stalin* tank came storming over the ridge.

"Gunner, fire!"

"On the way!"

Kraven was certain the North Korean commander had a moment to realize his danger, as the *Stalin* was attempting to stop just before *Crusader 66*'s 90mm gun slung its HVAP round at it. At just over 500 yards, the round penetrated the front hull, decapitated the driver, then burst into the turret in a cloud of spall and deformed penetrator. Lacking the energy to pass back out the other side, the heavy core ricocheted twice around the turret, turning the crew to ruined flesh as their vehicle caromed to a halt.

The next four minutes were a one-sided slaughter, as Baker and Charlie pressed to the top of TF McPeak's defensive position at its north as Able continued to pummel the tanks from the front. While not nearly as well-trained in gunnery as the Demons had been, due to the difficulty of moving *Pershings* to and from the range, at under 1,000 yards, the Crusaders did not need to be experts. Unlike the lightly armored M18s, the *Pershings* had little to fear from the T-34/85s attempting to lend distant fire support from their stationary position. As the IS-2s attempted to turn to retreat, Baker company quickly taught those North Korean tankers the error of their way, picking off six of the offending vehicles before those tanks also turned to retreat back into Suwon.

"Driver move forward," Kraven ordered as the Crusader's cannonade slowly came to an end. He consciously did not look at the shaking, shuddering wreckage that was *Dotty III* continuing to burn as his *Pershing* skirted the minefield and a knocked out IS-2 that had indeed lost its track trying to push forward through it.

Well at least something *went as planned*, he thought angrily, bringing his binoculars up to look towards Suwon.

"Crusader 6, Baker 6," his radio crackled. "Do you want me to continue the advance?"

For a long moment, Lieutenant Colonel Kraven considered his options.

You got lucky, Lenny, he thought to himself. Once more he looked over at *Dotty III*'s wreckage, then considered the fact he could still hear and see the infantry to the west engaging North Korean forces.

"Negative Baker, hold your position," he said. "Able, head on over there to the west and lend the Scout Platoon and the infantry a hand. Charlie, stand by to help cover the infantry's movement south."

Kraven took a long second as he considered his next words.

"I think we've done enough punching for one day, gentlemen," he said. "We're not throwing in the towel, just finding a better gym to kick our opponents' ass in."

* * *

Epilogue

Osan AFB
1000 Local
1 July 1990

"*. . . a*nd it was here that my father, an American who could not even eat at the same officer club back in Tokyo, gave his last full measure for the Republic."

Lieutenant General (retired) Leonard Kraven gripped his cane at that statement, feeling the same old anger and disgust at his fellow officers' bigotry and ignorance he always had.

All of us should have fought that bullshit a lot harder than we did, he thought, looking at the small boy next to him with a familiar face. The child was regarding Leonard with the intense curiosity only three-year-olds could muster, even as his grandmother was listening to her brother speak.

"Thankfully, his sacrifices were not in vain," Brigadier General Custis Gibson II continued, his eyes meeting Kraven's. "The 72nd Armored gave the North Koreans pause. That pause, in turn, gave the 24th and 101st Infantry Divisions time to dig in. More importantly, it gave the Air Force time to plan."

Kraven fought the urge to smile at that.

Here come the usual Zoomie talking points, he thought.

"That fiery July night, when the nascent SAC rained atomic ruin on Pyongyang, brought the war to a screeching halt," Gibson finished. "While it would not be a lasting peace, and our nation's resolve would be tested twice more on this peninsula before the specter of Communism was finally ended, it was enough of a pause for the surviving men of Delta Company, 758th Anti-Tank Battalion to be finally returned back to their loved ones."

Brigadier General Gibson paused, and Kraven could see several conflicting emotions pass over his face.

"When…" the man began, then took a moment to gather himself. "When then Lieutenant Colonel Kraven came to visit my mother, I will never forget what he said to me."

"Mommy, why is that man crying?" Kraven heard the young boy ask, his voice suddenly clear as a bell in the silence as everyone turned to look at him. In the total quiet, to the horror of the boy's relatives and family in earshot, Jeremiah Gibson III continued.

"Is it because his face is all burnt up?"

There was a collective intake of breath at that. Kraven saw the boy's grandmother recoil in horror, then start to open her mouth. He waved his hand at her, smiling.

"No son, I'm crying because I miss your grandma's daddy," Kraven replied evenly. "He was very brave, just like your great uncle."

"Ohhh," Jeremiah said. The boy looked like he was going to ask another question, but was quickly "embraced" from behind by his grandmother. Brigadier General Gibson, recognizing the fiasco that was unfolding, had quickly continued with his prepared remarks.

Your father was just as quick on his feet, Kraven thought with melancholy.

"…this memorial to the 'Delta Demons.'"

With Gibson's gesture, the cloth covering was drawn back with a flourish to reveal a full scale sculpture of an M18 *Hellcat*. A group of four men stood in front of it, their gazes raised northward. As he gazed at the statues, Kraven had to fight back a laugh.

Oh McPeak, looks like some artist had the last damn laugh, Kraven thought. The statue's left arm was resting on the Gibson statue's left shoulder, his right arm extended as if he were pointing at something in the far distance.

How fitting that after all that, the racist son-of-a-bitch will be standing shoulder to shoulder with Gibson for eternity, Kraven thought. Looking up, he saw Brigadier General Gibson regarding him with a smile as the gathered group applauded.

Looks like Mr. Dewey's Tank Corps did a good job after all, Kraven thought with a smile.

* * * * *

Dedication

To the men of Task Force Smith. Outgunned, outnumbered, and undeservedly forced into being a cautionary tale.

* * * * *

Author's Note

Astute readers will note that this is a continuation of the "Lightnings and the Cactus" (found in To Slip the Surly Bonds) timeline. With an earlier than historical victory in the Pacific coupled with a successful Operation Valkyrie (and resultant Nazi collapse), this story assumes most of the Manhattan Project's funding would have slipped away even before a misfire at Trinity. Add on the brutal bloodletting of a May 1945 invasion of Japan and…well, you get Harry Truman called the Butcher of Honshu and Thomas Dewey victorious in 1948. The rest, as they say, is (alternate) history.

* * *

James Young Bio

James Young holds a doctorate in U.S. History from Kansas State University and is a graduate of the United States Military Academy. Fiction is James' first writing love, but he's also dabbled in nonfiction with articles in the *Journal of Military History* and *Proceedings* to his credit. His next alternate history, *Against the Tide Imperial*, is the third novel in his *Usurper's War* series set during World War II and will be published in 1st Quarter 2019. You can find more information on the series and James's Comic Con schedule on his FB Page (https://www.facebook.com/ColfaxDen/), Twitter (@Youngblai), or by signing up for his mailing list on the front page of his blog (https://vergassy.com/).

# # # # #

Soldiers of the Republic
by Justin Watson

J ack Beasley struggled to appear calm and unfatigued even as the altitude, heat and humidity of central Vietnam at mid-day conspired to steal the air from his lungs and drain life out through his pores. From his position traveling between 2nd and 3rd squads he could see ten to twelve guys of the forty man platoon of the Viet Minh—*Free Vietnamese Army*—Jack corrected himself mentally. They marched single file along a narrow footpath on a hillside winding between thick stands of bamboo and growths of dagger-edged elephant grass.

A soft *thunk* drew Jack's eyes away from scanning the verdant landscape for threats to the rear of the column. One of the Vietnamese troops, a short rifleman carrying an M1 carbine bent to pick something up from the ground; a curved magazine. A sheepish expression was apparent on the Vietnamese soldier's face, and he kept his almond-shaped eyes downcast as Jack stormed towards him. Jack's interpreter, Corporal Dong, followed close on his heels. Slinging his own Garand rifle on his shoulder as he walked, Jack snatched the lighter weapon and magazine away from the shamefaced young trooper.

It was the third time on this patrol that one of the Vietnamese had dropped a magazine from their weapon unintentionally. Instead of tearing into the hapless private, Jack snapped in French, "Who is this man's squad leader?" Dong repeated the question in the sing-song Vietnamese language.

An older man turned from his place in the column in response. Unlike the soldier who had dropped his magazine to the ground, the FVA sergeant approaching Jack looked more annoyed than intimidated. This man was tall, for a Vietnamese, only surrendering two inches to Jack, and the ease with which he crossed the jungle floor and the faint burn scars on his right cheek bespoke experience.

"Sergeant," Jack said in French. "I know we talked about this when we got the new thirty-round magazines. They do not fit in the old M1 Carbines, only the M2 Carbines, the ones that can fire fully automatic. I know they look the same, but they are different."

As Dong translated, Beasley held up the curved, 30-round magazine in one hand and shook the M1 in the other, then shook his head vigorously side to side.

The FVA sergeant's nostrils flared, and he exhaled sharply before he turned to Dong and started chittering away. Jack, who had drawn this assignment in part due to his knack for picking up languages, hated the sound of Vietnamese. It pitched up and down too fast and too sharply. Much as he tried, Jack couldn't get a grounding in it like he had Tagalog, Korean, Japanese, French and Spanish.

"Sergeant," Dong said in French to Jack. "He says that his men are trading them out because they don't want to run out of ammunition before their friends do. He says they think you're playing favorites with who gets them."

"Jesus H. Donovan Christ," Jack said, English profanity slipping into his French. "I'm not playing fucking favorites. You see here—"

Jack flipped the carbine in his hand upside down so the magazine well was facing up.

"It doesn't have the right latch," Jack said. "The M2 does, but if you use a thirty-round mag instead of the fifteen-round mag in an

M1, the fucking magazine falls out of the fucking gun, and some Franco-Fascist sonofabitch turns you into Swiss cheese while you're fumbling for it. I don't know how to explain it any goddamn simpler than that."

Dong struggled to keep up with the rapid fire, profanity-laced rant.

"Sergeant Beasley, a word." A calm voice from behind Jack said.

Jack took a deep breath before turning around, knowing who wanted a word. The words were English, but the man's accent made his name and rank sound like, "Sar-zhaun Beez-lee." Jack thrust the carbine back at the soldier and the magazine at the NCO, then turned to face his commanding officer.

Captain Rapicault was shorter than Jack, with dark eyes that never seemed surprised at anything. He wore the same uniform as Beasley and the Vietnamese, save the captain's bars on his collar and the black stenciled USMC and Eagle, Globe and Anchor insignia on his breast. He carried a radio in his ruck sack and a Thompson sub-machine gun held at the low ready in his hands. Rapicault's posture was relaxed and his perpetually amused expression pissed Jack off every time he looked at him.

"Yes, Captain," Jack said. "How can I help you?"

Instead of annoyance, Rapicault smirked at Jack's avoidance of the word, "sir." The Gallic nonchalance only pissed Jack off worse.

Bad enough I'm humping a ruck through a goddamn jungle...again...but I had to pull a CO who is a frog and a fucking jarhead on top of that.

Military Assistance Command-Vietnam wasn't run by the War Department, but by the OSS. Jack, Captain Rapicault, and all the other American ground personnel were on detached duty from their parent units to serve as advisors to the Viet Minh. Their detachments were mixed, Marines and Army, willy-nilly.

In Jack's case, a short, bespectacled man named Feldman had shown up with orders pulling him away from his platoon in the 10th Mountain Division. He'd been on year one of an accompanied tour with his wife and kids in the comfort of Pyongyang. Six years after the end of the Japanese War, Korea was booming economically. Better yet, an American sergeant's paycheck was more than enough for a family of five to live very comfortably.

Instead I'm here, in the crotch of the Orient, where the country smells like shit, half our "friends" are goddamned Reds and the other half are cavemen who haven't learned to wipe their asses.

"Sergeant, you have some experience working with foreign troops, no?" Rapicault said.

"Yes, Captain," Jack said.

It was true, he had worked with both Philippino and Korean troops in war and peace, respectively. But he *liked* Phillipinos, brave little brown bastards, and he *liked* Koreans, who were open, friendly, and industrious to a fault.

"Then you know," Rapicault said, "or you should know, that how you communicate information is easily as important as the information itself."

Jack paused, passing a sleeve over his sweat-drenched face before answering. If he did not like Vietnam, or the Vietnamese, he liked turncoat French officers telling him how to do his job even less.

"That's true," Jack said, keeping his voice even. "But given how aggressive your countrymen have been lately, I think by now these troops should understand how to put the right magazine in the right weapon, Captain."

Rapicault's brow furrowed in irritation for a moment, gratifying Jack.

Their team was responsible for advising the 1st Battalion of the 112th Regiment of the FVA. Unfortunately, the 1st of the 112th had been rushed to the contested Central Highlands of Vietnam a mere week after receiving its basic loadout of American equipment and their advisors. Other FVA units had spent a month to six weeks with their American advisor teams training in relative security near Hanoi or Saigon.

"My *former* countrymen, Sergeant," Rapicault corrected, sardonic half-smile back in place. "Despite my mellifluous accent, I have been a US Marine since 1943, and an American citizen since 1944. Regardless, if my *former* countrymen decide to take Vietnam back by overt force, and if you were to be wounded in the ensuing battles, how likely are our little yellow friends to haul your overfed American ass up and down these mountains when you've been treating them like dogshit for weeks?"

Jack frowned, but didn't respond. Rapicault nodded at his silence.

"And while you're pondering that question, Sergeant, you might also ask yourself how long you're going to sulk before you start discharging your duties like a professional," Rapicault continued sharply. "Perhaps it is different in the Army, but Marine sergeants don't generally pick and choose which missions they will accomplish and which they won't."

His fatigue forgotten, Jack's spine stiffened, and he opened his mouth to respond furiously, but Rapicault had already turned away to address the column.

"*Không sao đâu, trung úy,*" Rapicault said, issuing the Vietnamese song-speech without apparent effort. "*Chúng ta có thể tiếp tục di chuyển.*"

No more magazines fell on the return march, nor did the platoon make contact with the enemy. All Jack had to take his mind off the oppressive climate was the knowledge that, whatever he thought of Rapicault, he'd earned that ass-chewing.

* * *

From his hide position in the tall, sharp elephant grass, Adjutant Jean-Baptiste Vanderburgh of the Groupement de Commandos Mixtes Aéroportés saw and heard the entire altercation between the Americans. He'd followed the French and Vietnamese conversation easily, but then the American sergeant and captain had switched to English, of which he didn't speak a word. He could tell they were not happy with one another, though.

Though he lay mere meters away from dozens of the enemy with only one comrade beside him, Vanderburgh was unafraid. He was renowned for his ability to blend with the countryside. He had spent his boyhood stalking game in the Alsatian countryside, then the subsequent decades stalking men everywhere from the woods of the Low Countries, to the burning deserts of Algeria, all the way here, to the sweltering jungles of Indochina.

The American officer turned more towards Vanderburgh, giving him a straight-on view of his face for a moment. Vanderburgh's breath caught in his throat, and his eyes grew wide.

Lieutenant Rapicault? No, it can't be…

It was. It was Pierre Rapicault, a comrade he'd thought long dead in a Japanese prison camp.

Obviously he escaped and linked up with the Americans. Jesus Christ, has he been here in Indochina the whole time?

Rapicault finished his conversation with the American sergeant abruptly, then switched back to Vietnamese and ordered the platoon to move out. Foom and Vanderburgh waited long minutes after the soft tread of the FVA rear guard was no longer audible before they moved, each rising like a strange jungle denizen, cloaked in layers of vegetation and dirt to obscure their bipedal forms.

"Something troubles you, sir?" Foom asked in a low voice as they made their way west, toward the rest of Foom's company. Although Foom was a captain and technically outranked Vanderburgh, a warrant officer, it was understood that Vanderburgh retained command over not just this GCMA company, but also their parent battalion.

"I know their officer," Vanderburgh said. "He was my platoon commander before the Japanese occupied Indochina."

"A Frenchman fights for the Viet Minh?" Foom said, aghast.

"Many of my countrymen still resent France's position in the Greater Reich," Vandeburgh said. "I knew some of them had defected to America. I didn't know they were being used here."

Foom shook his head. In the Hmong's captain's devout Catholic mind, the Viet Minh forces were comprised of nothing but godless, communist butchers and their brainwashed slave soldiers. Rebranding themselves the "Free Vietnamese Army" meant nothing. The idea that any Christian, much less a Frenchman, fought alongside the Viet Minh was anathema to him.

For his part, Vanderburgh understood why de Gaulle's fanatics fought. He too hated German hegemony over France. But siding with the Viet Minh to rob France of one of her rightful colonies? How would that hurt the Germans? France's economy would falter as money from Indochinese rubber, rice, and opiate exports lined foreign pockets instead of French ones. It would degrade France's already diminished status as a power in the world without thwarting Hitler one whit. The so-called Free French were cutting off their nose to spite their face.

"So, Foom," Vanderburgh said, putting the thought out of mind. "What did you think of our erstwhile opponents?"

"Definitely a new regiment. City boys, most of them," Foom said, his tone clinical. "But they are trained well enough; they seemed alert and motivated despite their shoddy treatment by the big white sergeant. They will not be easily defeated in the defense."

Vanderburgh nodded.

"The 3rd Foreign Legion regiment will attack the base camp," Vanderburgh said. "Our part will be to cut up any outlying patrols, then delay any relief force from the main base at Plei Mrong."

"Yes, sir," Foom said. "How long before we begin?"

"Not long. Most of the light forces are in their assembly areas," Vanderburgh said. "They haven't moved de Castries' armor into place yet. Once they do, we'll have to move fast or lose the element of surprise. I think our friends back there have about a week to live, at the most."

* * *

Jack squeezed the trigger on an M1 carbine. The recoil drove the butt of the weapon into his shoulder and, as he'd intended, his magazine hit the ground for the third time. He carefully safed the weapon and placed it on a plywood stand pointed down range. Then, with comically exaggerated movements, he scratched his head underneath his helmet, then bent over, looking back at his audience between his knees, allowing his helmet to fall off. The Vietnamese troops sitting in a half-circle on the ground watching him howled with laughter. Seeing the wayward magazine, Jack snatched it up and stared at it, eyebrows quirked quizzically to more laughter.

"Corporal Dong," Jack said, his French pronunciation artificially deep and gruff. "What is wrong with my magazine?"

Dong trotted up to him with an M2 carbine in his hands. The weapon was physically identical to the M1 in outward appearance. He didn't bother translating Beasley's French for the non-Francophones in the audience, but he spoke in Vietnamese himself. Having rehearsed this, Jack knew he was saying, essentially, "Sergeant, the magazine isn't the problem, you're just using the wrong weapon, here—"

Jack took the proffered weapon while Dong delivered a string of Vietnamese narrative on the features of the M2 and in particular how the 30-round magazine only worked with it. Jack waited for him to finish, then, nodding appreciatively, he rocked the magazine into the M2's well, pulled the bolt back and let it fly forward to chamber a round, flipped the selector switch near the trigger assembly from SAFE past SEMI straight to AUTO and pulled the carbine's stock into his shoulder.

BRADADA...BRADADA...BRADADA

Aligning the sites at the right hip of the silhouette, Jack methodically treated each target in turn to a short, staccato burst of automatic fire. Then, still careful to keep the muzzle pointed away from his audience, he held the carbine so that the audience could see the thirty-round magazine was still firmly in the M2's magazine well.

"So, you can see," Jack said in French as he ejected the magazine and cleared the carbine's chamber. "The thirty-round magazine is very useful *if* your weapon has the automatic function. Otherwise, it's just going to end up on the ground."

As Dong took up a running translation, Jack saw Captain Rapicault step around one of the sandbag embankments at the rear of the range complex. Rapicault gestured with his chin for Jack to join him. Turning the class over to Dong, Jack followed Rapicault to the other side of the sandbags and up wooden steps to the platform of the observation tower. Rapicault told the sentry on duty there to take a break.

The firebase encompassed a lakeside fishing village of no name and was just large enough to accommodate one rifle company from the 112th on a rotational basis. This week it was 2nd Company of 1st Battalion. The range where Jack had been training the men on the M2 was on the southern side, oriented toward the lake to the south, southwest and southeast. To the north, northeast and northwest, the battalion had cleared the vegetation away from the perimeter for five hundred meters. The camp's defensive engagement area was defined by the treeline on the far side, and by multiple rows of triple-strand razorwire on the near side, punctuated by anti-personnel minefields.

The perimeter fighting positions themselves were well dug in and carefully laid out to create interlocking fields of fire and eliminate dead space. But Jack frowned at their overhead cover. They'd done the best they could with bamboo, earth and those cypress trunks they'd been able to harvest from lower altitudes. Jack wasn't confident they'd withstand concentrated mortar fire. He *knew* a well-placed artillery barrage would collapse most of them, even the heftier machine gun nests and command dugouts.

Jack knew that Rapicault sent weekly requests for engineer support to further harden their defenses, but thus far those requests had gone unanswered. Even the company command post and the advisors' own operations centers were just Quonset huts surrounded by sandbag walls.

"The classes seem to be going well," Rapicault said, tapping a cigarette out of a pack and holding it out to Jack.

Jack took the proffered cigarette, his brow furrowed. Rapicault's tone betrayed no hint of I-told-you-so, but maybe the Frog sonofabitch was just being subtle. Jack decided to take the observation at face value.

"Yes, Captain," Jack said. "They seem to be dropping fewer magazines lately."

Rapicault lit his cigarette then passed his zippo to Jack. After he got the cherry on his cig glowing, Jack heard the crack and rattle of small arms fire as the range went hot. He glanced over his shoulder and saw that the platoon he'd left in Dong's care was going about the range in good order, firers standing at the line engaging targets, their mates queued up nicely a safe distance behind them.

"The balloon is going up, Sergeant. We have reconnaissance photographs of 1st and 3rd Moroccan Spahis staging near Xayden and the 1st Foreign Cavalry at Pak Nhai," Rapicault said without further preamble. "What's more, Colonel Huu tells me that his intelligence people may have underestimated the number of infiltrated French units. There may be as many as a regiment of French Colonial Regulars in the Plei Mrong area already."

The Spahis were units of armored cavalry comprised of Panzer IIIN light tanks and Stug self-propelled assault guns. The 1st Foreign Cavalry was a lighter force comprised mainly of Sonderkraftfahrzeug 234 Armored Cars. Each unit, fully manned, amounted to roughly two thirds the strength of an American regiment of similar function.

The French armored forces were indeed formidable. Taken together, they were unquestionably the most powerful ground combat force in Southeast Asia, but Jack wasn't worried about them.

Plei Mrong, their area of operations, was several kilometers of dense jungle away from Colonial Routes 9 and 14, the only paved roadways in the area. It was possible that the French, through determined effort, might bring their armor to bear on Plei Mrong by moving it cross country. It would take them days, perhaps weeks to do so due to the combination of dense vegetation, steep elevations and water obstacles. Thus Jack's *immediate* problem was the possibility of a couple thousand regular infantry already within striking distance.

"What the fuck?" Jack said, cigarette dangling from his lip. "How the hell did we miss a regiment of fucking Frenchmen?"

Rapicault shook his head.

"Very little about the French Army is French nowadays, Sergeant. German weapons, colonial troops," Rapicault said. "Can you tell the difference between a Thai or a Laotian and a Vietnamese? I grew up here, and I can't until they start talking. The locals could, but the Viet Minh have never been popular here in the Highlands, nor is the, 'new,' FVA. Not that the locals love the French either, but until they figure out who is more likely to win, most of them aren't going to go out of their way to help either side. Safer for them to keep their mouths shut, no?"

"Shit."

"Indeed," Rapicault extinguished his cigarette. "*Merde.* They will move soon, they cannot keep that many soldiers concealed and supplied for long."

The two men stood in uncomfortable silence, looking out at the camp and the mostly green troops who defended it. Jack had found, once he stopped feeling sorry for himself and started acting like a sergeant again, that they weren't bad soldiers at all. Some of the NCOs were hard core bastards, as their senior guys had fought the Japs during the war and the French off and on ever since. But he didn't know if they were enough to stop a regiment of professionals, equipped and trained by the most successful Army in human history, Hitler's Wehrmacht.

Jack *did* know that he didn't want to die here. Fighting the Japanese had been one thing. They had started a war with the United States. The reason they had to be stopped, had to be forced into *abject surrender*, was abundantly clear. Breaking Japan down so they never threatened America again was imperative.

The French, on the other hand, had never done anything to him. Even the Nazis who pulled France's strings had done nothing to him, personally, or to his country. He'd heard they were evil, murderous bastards, but the world was full of evil, murderous bastards. Was it America's responsibility to fight every last one of them?

Jack stole a glance at Rapicault's impassive face.

If I don't like this situation, what is he thinking?

"Captain, I'm going to ask a rude question," Jack said.

Rapicault chuckled.

"I am shocked," he said. "You've been the soul of tact thus far."

Jack smiled sheepishly.

"Right, well," Jack said. "Look, you were right, I needed to get my shit together and do the job."

"Yes," Rapicault said, still smiling. "I'm glad we agree on that. Now ask your rude question."

Jack exhaled sharply before he spoke, trying to phrase the question in a way that wasn't a flat-out challenge to Rapicault.

Oh, fuck it.

"Captain, if I don't want to be here," Jack said, "and, frankly, I don't; doesn't it bother you to be here? I know you renounced your French citizenship, but doesn't it bother you fight your old countrymen?"

Rapicault didn't answer for long moments, staring out at the tree line of the jungle, his perpetually amused expression having given way to something more pensive.

"Sergeant, if a man broke into your house, killed your father, raped your mother at gunpoint and declared himself your father, would you go along with the fiction?" Rapicault said. "Would the fact that your siblings accepted the tragic, murderous farce as reality change your mind?"

Jack's eyes widened.

"That's a hell of a way to think about it, Captain," Jack said.

"It's the way I see it, Sergeant," Rapicault said. "My great-great-great grandfather fell at Valmy in 1792. My great-great grandfather manned the barricades to restore the Republic in 1832. He lived, but was imprisoned. His *son*, however, fell in the revolt of 1848. His son, my grandfather, lost an arm and an eye to Prussian shells at Sedan. My father...he's buried, for certain values of buried, somewhere near Verdun. Every man of my line for more than a century has served the republic. For me there is only one credible republic left on Earth, and if it is not the republic of my birth, it is at least more worthy of my service than a cabal of Nazi puppets."

The silence lingered as heavily as the midday humidity between them. Jack chewed on Rapicault's pronouncement until his concentration was broken by the staccato cracks of distant small arms fire—too distant to be on the range behind them. Jack made eye contact with Rapicault, wordlessly both men snatched up binoculars from a shelf and began scanning the jungle.

There—Jack saw three dull gray clouds rising above the treetops. *Fuck. Someone is pitching grenades.*

"Captain, one o'clock, three thousand yards," Jack gave the distance and direction to the explosions.

"I see them," Rapicault said, turning and taking the stairs down the tower two at a time. Jack followed close behind.

* * *

The American advisory team maintained their own operations center in a Quonset hut right next to 2nd Company's command post. It was to this semi-cylindrical structure that Jack and Captain Rapicault sprinted. Corporal McClung, their radio operator, already had the advisor with the platoon in contact on the horn by the time they barreled through the door. Over the speaker, audible even among explosions and the constant roar and rattle of concentrated small arms fire, Jack could hear Sergeant Carabastas' Puerto Rican accent.

"Negative Ajax-One," Carabastas said. "We are under intense fire; I can't get a good count. We've had visual contact with at least two battalions; we are currently engaged with two or more company's worth."

Rapicault gestured for McClung to give him the hand microphone for the radio.

"Ajax-One-Red, this is Ajax One-Six," Rapicault said. "We're spinning up a reaction force to come get you. What else can you tell me about the enemy and your situation?"

"Sir, they've get a ton of automatic weapons," Carabastas said. "Machine guns and automatic rifles. No mortars or artillery yet. These aren't raggedy-ass locals, sir. They're regulars in camo-pattern and fritz helmets."

"Roger, Red," Rapicault said. "Hold out, we're coming for you."

"One-Six, I don't think we're going to last," Carabastas said, his voice shook slightly, but he maintained his composure. "We're down to one squad of effectives. They're pressing hard. We'll kill as many as we can, but you should get ready—"

The transmission ended abruptly. From outside, the sounds of battle began to fade.

"Red, this is Six," Rapicault said, not shouting, but with unmistakable urgency. "Red, Six, acknowledge...Red, this is Six, do you copy? Damn it."

Rapicault stood up, handing the mic back to McClung.

"I'm going to head next door," he said. "Sergeant Beasley, you and McClung report to Ajax Main, relay our situation and request air support—"

A high-pitched, whistling shriek filled Jack's ears.

"DOWN!" Jack and Rapicault screamed in unison, each grabbing one of McClung's arms and flattening themselves to the floor. A brief flash of heat rolled over him and Jack felt his guts undulate from a wave of concussive force. Sheets of fragmentation penetrated the thin, tin walls of the operations center hut, shredding equipment but, miraculously, missing Jack's vulnerable skin.

Well, now we know what they were saving their mortars for...

Lifting his head, Jack saw the room was well and truly shredded from frag. His ears were ringing as he staggered to his feet, and it sounded as if all the noises around him were coming from the far end of a metal funnel. Rapicault was shouting something.

"Grab weapons and radios, we have to move!"

Jack lurched to comply, still punch drunk from the nearby blast. Stumbling through the smoke filled hut to the weapons rack, he grabbed McClung's carbine and tossed it to him, followed by a ruck sack with a radio. Then he secured his own Garand and another ruck with a radio in it. Rapicault already held his own Thompson and was slinging another radio onto his back, headed out. Jack followed, pushing McClung ahead of him through the door, now swinging wildly ajar.

The first sight that greeted Jack as he stepped outside was the smoking ruin of 2nd Company's CP. Looking around, he saw dozens of FVA troops milling about, unsure of what to do. Another whistling shriek split the air.

Rapicault was screaming in Vietnamese, Jack himself screamed, "*Descendre!*" as he dove for the muddy ground of the camp.

Once again he was rocked to his innards from the detonation, and he felt mud, dirt, and harder particulate matter clatter against his steel helmet before he looked back up. He saw a boot, somehow still upright, with the bloody, jagged remains of a human foot in it, but no sign of the victim. A few feet away, one of the FVA troops was clutching his stomach as dark, almost black blood pouring through his fingers while he screamed his agony to the heavens. The rest of the soldiers he saw stood, crouched, or lay where they were, unmoving, clearly in shock.

"New plan," Rapicault said, slightly more rapid speech the only crack in his characteristic aplomb. "You two get to a fighting position and check in with Ajax Main. I'll organize the defense."

Without waiting for an answer, Rapicault sprang to his feet and began issuing orders to the Vietnamese troops, gesturing emphatically toward the camp's defensive line to the north, then to the wounded and to the sand-bagged dugout that was the Camp's aid station. In short order, Vietnamese NCOs and officers began herding their men per Rapicault's direction. Most ran toward the line; a few carried or dragged the wounded to the aid station.

A sound like a half-dozen buzz saws roaring into operation drew Jack's eyes north just in time to see several streams of tracers emerging from the tree-line, across the engagement area and toward the battalion's fighting positions.

"Come on, McClung," Jack said, grabbing the kid by the arm and running toward one of the platoon command dug outs. "You heard the man."

* * *

Spotting a radio antenna sprouting from behind a rock in the middle of the kill zone, Foom settled his elbows into the soft jungle floor and pressed the select-fire toggle on his STG-46 to E for *Eisenfeurer*, "Single Shot." He lined up the hooded front sight post on the dome of the green enemy helmet just below the antenna. Even as grenades detonated nearby, and rifle and machine gun fire cracked, stuttered, and buzzed around him like a cavalcade of malicious, deadly insects, Foom took a deep breath and then exhaled, squeezing the trigger steadily so that the rifle recoiled into his shoulder with a sharp, sonic crack at the bottom of his natural pause.

Foom was rewarded with an audible metallic CLINK and a puff of pink as the helmet flew several feet away from his victim. Foom allowed himself a grunt of satisfaction.

The FVA platoon was dying with a whimper. They'd fought bravely, but Foom's ambush had caught them completely unaware. Rather than having to assault through their position, Foom and his men walked through the kill zone, treating every corpse in the wrong uniform to a burst of fire.

Foom found the corpse of the radio operator he had killed slumped against the rock. The upper left quadrant of the man's face was a grisly ruin, the exit wound of Foom's shot having blown out the man's eye socket, cheek bone and half his nose. Foom noted the chevrons and rockers on the dead man's fatigues; an American sergeant despite his darker skin. And in his ruck sack—

His radio!

Foom stripped the pack off the corpse's back and put the radio hand mic to his ear. His pulse jumped; the Americans were still talking on this frequency. He couldn't understand a word of it, but they were definitely still sending traffic over the net. Foom motioned for his own radio operator.

"Adjutant, this is Foom," he said when he got Vanderburgh on the net. "We have an intact American radio, and they are still transmitting on its frequency."

* * *

Jack's Garand barked twice in quick succession, and a camouflage-clad enemy fell to his knees and then face first into a razor wire obstacle. One of the dead man's comrades stepped on the corpse and hurtled the wire, a long tube, at least fifteen feet in length, in his hands. Jack acquired the new target and fired, but his enemy had dropped to the prone, out of Jack's sight picture. Jack tried to reacquire and fire again but his empty clip ejected from the rifle's chamber with a quiet *ping!*

As Jack thumbed another eight round clip into the Garand, the *THROOM* of an explosion split the humid jungle air, followed by several smaller blasts as the enemy's Bangalore set off a dozen sympathetic detonations. A linear fountain of dirt twenty feet high erupted straight through the minefield.

Jack's hand slipped and the bolt of the Garand kept a tiny scrap of Jack's thumb as it rammed forward, chambering another round.

"Damn it," Jack hissed. In moments, the two nearest .30 caliber machine gun positions altered their sectors of fire to rake the newly opened lane through their minefield with bursts of automatic fire. Four enemy soldiers jerked and fell in the breach, but more hurtled past them, rising and falling, crawling, then sprinting, inexorably toward the 2nd company's main position. From the mixture of black, white, and brown faces advancing toward them, Jack assumed that it was a Foreign Legion unit they faced.

We're slowing them, but we're not stopping them.

Rapicault did a credible baseball slide into the company command dugout. He was speaking Vietnamese into his radio. As he finished speaking, a volley of artillery shells impacted in the tree line five hundred meters in front of them. Three orange-black detonations shredded tree and man alike and the flow of enemy infantry out of the jungle slowed just a bit.

"Just three tubes?" Jack shouted over the din of battle.

"Every one of the outposts is getting hit," Rapicault said. "And at least three regiments are converging on the main base at Plei Mrong. I was lucky to get an arty platoon in direct support."

"Three regiments? They missed a fucking division?!" Jack shouted as a burst of enemy machine gun fire kicked up a row of mud fountains right in front of his sandbags. "What the hell have the intel assholes been doing? Diddling each other over their typewriters?"

"What did MAC-V-Air say about air support?" Rapicault said, ignoring Jack's outburst.

"Major Jordan told me they would scramble what they could," Jack said, gesturing to his pack on the floor of the dugout. "I couldn't reach Pleiku, so the regimental advisory team is relaying to MAC-V-Air. Maybe your railroad tracks will get them moving faster."

Rapicault nodded, taking Jack's hand mic and keying it.

"Ajax Main, Ajax Main, this is Ajax One-Six," Rapicault said. "We are under attack by a reinforced regiment. We will be overrun in less than one hour without support. What's the status of our air, over?"

"Ajax Main, this is Tiger Four checking in." Before Ajax-Main could answer, a deep, smoothly modulated southern voice announced its presence on the net.

"Glad to hear it, Tiger Four," Major Jordan's voice from Plei Mrong sounded as relived as Jack felt. "Stand by for the advisor on the scene. Ajax One-Six, we have air, over."

"Roger, Ajax Main," Rapicault said. "Tiger Four, this is Ajax One-Six, recommend you make your run northeast to southwest, parallel to our position, initial point on or north of Zebra-Baker Zero-One-Zero, One-Five-Two. That pattern should keep you clear of the gun-target line from the artillery at Ajax Main."

"Ajax One-Six, roger," The southern gentleman in the plane answered. "You have sixteen P-80s with two thousand-pound bombs each. We can't see shit through the canopy, can you mark your forward position and the enemy's approximate center of mass."

Rapicault smiled and Jack grinned, too. Sixteen jets; maybe MAC-V cared if they lived or died after all.

"Roger, Tiger," Rapicault said, motioning for Jack to throw a smoke grenade. "Marking our forward position first."

Jack found the first smoke grenade on his gear, a green one, pulled the pin and threw it in between the command dugout and the nearest fighting position so as not to obscure 2nd Company's field of fire.

"One-Six, I see green smoke," Tiger Four drawled. "Confirm green smoke, over."

Rapicault was on the other radio, speaking rapidly in Vietnamese for a few seconds before he took the hand mic back to talk to the jets. Even over the constant cacophony of artillery, mortars and gunfire, Jack could hear the big American jet engines now.

"Roger, Tiger," Rapicault said. "Green smoke, stand by for enemy center of mass."

Another volley of artillery landed, two orang-black detonations sent frag raining upon the enemy, but the third round, in the center of the sheaf, plumed into a white cloud.

"Ajax One-Six, I tally white smoke," Tiger Four said. "I say again, white smoke. Be advised target mark is well within danger close of your position."

"Roger, Tiger Four," Rapicault said. "I confirm white smoke on the target, acknowledge danger-close."

"I have visual on friendly markings, I tally target marking," Tiger Four said, and Jack could hear the eagerness in his voice. "I am at the IP now. Four-ship in the initial pass."

"Roger, Tiger Four, you are cleared hot," Rapicault said.

"Get small, Ajax," Tiger Four said. "This is going to be close."

There—Jack saw four silvery winged shapes diving out of the sky like avenging angels, their engines drowning out the rifles and machine guns below. They were low enough that Jack could make out the shark's teeth on the nose jet intake and bright red tail paint.

As they slowed and leveled, a finned cylinder dropped from each of the plane's bellies, falling gracefully until they hit the jungle floor and detonated. Each bomb contained the explosive force of ten artillery rounds. Jack was rocked back in the dugout by a wave of heat and concussion, his ears popping with the sudden, violent pressure change.

Pulling himself back up, Jack returned to the dugout's firing position and scanned the battlefield. He saw dozens more broken bodies and four great craters in the soft, muddy ground. Seeing a cluster of the enemy staggering as if punch-drunk, Jack had the presence of mind to bring his Garand up and engage them. His shots seemed to wake the rest of 2nd Company from some sort of trance, and those FVA soldiers still standing raked the dazed Legionnaires with rifle and machine gun fire.

"Good drop," Rapicault said, shaking his own head to clear it. "Keep laying it on."

"Alright, Benny, you head to thirty-thousand feet and keep an eye out," A new voice, this one a Texan drawl, said over the radio. "Robin, head for the IP."

Another flight of jet-propelled birds of prey swept down upon the enemy, incinerating dozens more with their bombs and sending the remainder to their bellies to avoid obliterating death. Finally, it seemed, they had stalled the enemy's advance.

"We have to be ready to move," Rapicault said. "We have one chance to break out. According to the 112th staff, the enemy's main axis of advance is east of the lake. So we will end run round the lake to the west, keeping the water obstacle between us and them, and force march south to link up with the rest of the regiment."

Jack thought about the plan. There were a lot of things that could go wrong. They would have to carry their wounded on litters for at least ten kilometers. Even with the enemy suppressed by bombs and artillery, their chances of outrunning them were small. Still, their minefields were breached, their wire obstacles were largely shredded, this outpost was no longer a tenable position.

"Alright, sir," Jack said. "We'll be ready."

The last four jets finished their run. After the thunder of their bombs and the roar of their engines had receded, the staccato cacophony of rifles and machine guns resumed, but at a much slower tempo.

"Much obliged Tigers," Rapicault said. "We're still taking fire, but we've got some breathing room."

"Can you make it back to friendly lines, One-Six?" the Texan pilot asked.

"We're certainly going to try, Tiger," Rapicault said. "We've got a lot of wounded, though."

"Stand by," a feminine voice interjected. "This is Angel Three-Five. We are a flight of three Ravens. Meet me at the clearing on the riverbank one hundred meters south by southeast of your green smoke. My rotor cone will fit there. I can take your wounded first, then drop my litters and ferry the rest of your men on the skids."

"Helicopters?" Jack asked.

"That's right," Rapicault said. "We're about to get a lift from the famous flying lady-doctor of Vietnam."

Jack had heard of her, of course, everyone in MAC-V had heard of the beautiful French doctor who flew helicopters, plucking men from the battlefield like an angel of mercy. He'd never thought he'd meet her, though, much less get his ass pulled out of the fire by her.

"Roger, Angel Three-Five," Rapicault said into the hand mic, his smile much broader, and far less ironic than usual. "Thanks a lot, both of you. I take back every unkind word I've ever said about flyboys."

* * *

Vanderburgh recognized the voice coming out of the radio even though he couldn't understand the language. He'd never seen a need to learn English. He'd enlisted at sixteen expecting to fight the Germans, the Algerians, or perhaps the Thais and Vietnamese, but not Americans.

And certainly not other Frenchmen. God damn you, Rapicault.

Vanderburgh and Captain Foom were standing in the operations center of the 3rd *Regiment Etranger Infantrie.* The regimental commander, a big burly colonel named Faucher, and his operations officer stood on the other side of a folding table, a young lieutenant sat between them at the captured American radio, listening intently. When the radio went silent for a moment, the lieutenant looked up.

"Sir, they're going to try to use helicopters to evacuate across the lake," the lieutenant said.

Faucher looked at the map.

"*Merde,*" he said in a gravelly voice. "We don't have anything that can reach in time. Major, can we finish this business before they escape?"

Major Grenault, the operations chief for 3rd REI shook his head.

"No, sir," he said. "2nd Battalion was mauled by those jets. We're moving 3rd Battalion forward, but it will take time to complete the forward passage of lines since we're still taking artillery and mortars."

At that moment an American jet dove on the treeline, fire spewing from six fifty-caliber machine guns in its nose. The pilot had to be firing blind through the thick green jungle canopy, but it still sent men running for cover.

"And strafing runs," the intelligence lieutenant added lamely.

Vanderburgh studied the map for a moment, then exchanged a look with Foom, who nodded agreement.

"Sir," Vanderburgh said. "We can make it to their LZ in time. Captain Foom's men travel light and we know the terrain."

Faucher considered that for a moment.

"You'll be on your own, too far for us to reinforce or even to support with mortars if something goes wrong," he said.

"With all respect, *mon Colonel,*" Vanderburgh said. "What else is new?"

A harried-looking captain pushed a tent flap aside, jogged up to Colonel Faucher, and handed him a piece of paper.

"Sir, from General Cogny regarding the air situation," the captain said, then he saluted and left the tent as rapidly as he'd come.

Faucher's eyes scanned the paper for several seconds, then he grinned.

"Our friends in the Air Force have a surprise for the American mercenary pilots," he said. He scratched his chin for a moment, then nodded. "Alright, Vanderburgh. You're clear. Get moving."

* * *

The late afternoon sun cast the nameless fishing village in dappled gold as the last lift of 2nd Company boarded their helicopters. Several dozen stone-faced civilians stood, watching them embark. Jack felt a twinge of conscience, but quickly dismissed it.

The French probably won't fuck with them. Besides, the enemy had pretty accurate targeting data on the command post and ops center. Likely a lot of these fuckers are working for them.

The *thwapthwapthwapthwapthwap* of the Hiller H-23's rotor blades drowned out Jack's thoughts and hot rotor wash threatened to blow away anything not tied down. Jack looked dubiously at the insectile metal airframe of the unnatural aircraft as it settled on its skids. He leaned over, putting his lips practically to the captain's ear and screamed to be heard.

"Sir, are you sure about this?" he shouted.

Rapicault shouted his answer in Jack's ear.

"You may swim if you'd rather, Sergeant!"

Jack shot the Marine a baleful look, but Rapicault only grinned at him. Without another word, he slung his Thompson, and ran forward at a crouch under the rotors. Rapicault grabbed a hold of the skids and the side of the cockpit. McClung joined him on the other side. Growling under his breath, Jack followed suit, running at a crouch to the next helicopter, a Vietnamese squad leader, the highest ranking NCO left in 2nd Company, took the opposite skid.

I'd rather fucking swim.

A set of dazzling white teeth and full lips smiled up at him from under a flight helmet when Jack looked in the cockpit. Despite his terror, Jack tightened his grip on the helicopters and smiled back, giving the famous flying lady-doctor a thumbs up.

Jack's stomach lurched as the bird gained a few feet of altitude and started to fly slowly southward over the green water of the lake. They were so close to the water, closer than the high dive board of the pool back at the YMCA. The urge to jump off and swim the rest of the trip was strong, but he resisted. Duty aside, there wasn't a body of water in Vietnam that didn't have leeches and other parasites floating about in it.

Without warning, the leftmost helicopter disintegrated, its skeletal metallic frame crumpling like a crushed beer can. The helicopter burst into flame as its fuel stores ignited, and then the ruined bird crashed into the muddy water with a *SPLOOSH.* Jack's heart hammered as a stream of tracers passed in front of his face, missing him and tearing into the mud and vegetation of their intended landing zone.

Jack's eyes snapped left, to the helicopter's six o'clock. He saw a swept wing jet closing on them fast. Instead of speeding up, the helicopter slowed. Jack looked incredulously at the pilot only to see her jerk her head to the side; motioning for him to jump.

Don't have to tell me twice!

Jack took a deep breath, let go of the helicopter and fell into the water with splash. He fought instinctive panic and let himself sink to the bottom, knowing they'd been near the shore when he'd bailed.

Sure enough, his feet hit the muck long before he ran out of breath. Squatting down, Jack dumped his ruck, knowing his radio wouldn't have survived the submersion anyway, then kicked back up to the surface, and took another deep breath before re-immersing himself in the lake, not wanting to stay a target for longer than necessary.

The murky seconds it took to reach shore seemed like an eternity, and his muscles and lungs burned as he kicked his way through the lake. Finally his boots hit mud and Jack dragged himself onto shore, rifle at the ready. Looking up he saw the swept wing jets and the American P-80s turning and diving on one another.

Godspeed, Tigers.

Jack had no idea where the rest of 2nd Company was other than that they were somewhere on this side of the lake. A few meters to his right he spotted the FVA NCO wading out of the lake as well. He realized it was the scar-faced sergeant he'd yelled at over the M2 magazines six days and a lifetime ago. Looking back south he saw, to his surprise and relief, that their helicopter had managed to land more or less intact among sharp blades of the elephant grass.

Jack turned back to scar-face, pointed a thumb into his own chest then pointed to the helicopter. Then he pointed at Scar-face and scanned the horizon with his rifle to indicate the FVA sergeant should cover him. Scar-face nodded, running out of the water to a bamboo copse and where he kneeled and scanned the area with his rifle shouldered.

Cover set, Jack sprinted forward to the H-23's cockpit.

He was greeted with the muzzle of a Colt 1911 pistol in his face.

"Whoa, doc!" Jack shouted. "Friendly!"

The lady doctor looked at him for a second, nodded, and put down her weapon.

"Sorry, can't be too careful," she said. "Help me out of here, would you? My buckles are bent."

"Are you hurt?" Jack asked as he took out his bayonet and began sawing on her restraints.

"Bumps and bruises," she said, and Jack noted her French accent. Another expat like Rapicault. "My name is Durand."

"Jack Beasley, ma'am," Jack said.

Just as he severed the last restraint, Jack heard voices in French followed by two gunshots.

"Into the grass," Jack hissed as he pulled Durand out of the cockpit. Smart woman, Durand did not question or complain, but followed him down into the dagger sharp elephant grass. As he dove, a bright green grass blade ripped a gash across Jack's left forearm, leaving a bright trail of blood on his fatigues.

As he lay in the grass, barely daring to breath, the French voices became more distinct. Jack could make out one in particular:

"*Abandonnez-vous, Lieutenant Rapicault! Ne me force pas à te tuer, Pierre.*"

* * *

Vanderburgh saw the man stumbling away from the burning wreckage of a helicopter and he knew, he *knew*. The man started to reach for an American Thompson sub-machine gun lying on the ground. Vanderburgh fired two shots into a bamboo tree a few feet away from the man.

"Surrender, Lieutenant Rapicault!" Vanderburgh shouted. When the man paused, he continued. "Don't make me kill you, Pierre."

Rapicault straightened, spared a glance for the three other men with Vanderburgh, then looked Vanderburgh in the eye.

"It's actually Captain, now, Jean-Baptiste," Rapicault said. "And congratulations on your promotion as well, Adjutant."

"Forgive me, sir," Vanderburgh said, suddenly furious with his old friend, a lieutenant he'd mentored from a teenager into an outstanding young officer. A friend who'd betrayed his country. "I had difficulty discerning your rank since you seem to be in the wrong uniform."

Rapicault snorted.

"Indeed," Rapicault said, glancing meaningfully at Vanderburgh's camouflage fatigues. "It was very reasonable of the Nazis to allow you to keep French rank insignia when they put you in their uniform. Then again, the Americans don't make me hand over children for them to gas or vivisect."

"Is that how you justify betraying your country to the Viet Minh?" Vanderburgh said, stepping closer to Rapicault, STG-46 trained on his chest. "American propaganda about the Jews?"

"It's not propaganda, Jean-Baptiste, and you know it. I would've happily died for France," Rapicault said, uncowed despite the automatic rifle leveled at him. "But I will kill every last one of you before I let the Reich have the world."

Vanderburgh's jaws clamped shut on his next words.

There is no point to this. He is a prisoner of war, and we have fucked around long enough.

"You won't be killing anyone, *Captain*," Vanderburgh said. "The war is over for you, Pierre. For what it's worth, I hope they treat you like an American POW and don't hang you."

* * *

Jack risked whispering his plan in Durand's ear.

"I'm going to throw this grenade, pin still in it, and shout, 'grenade,'" he said, voice barely a breath. "When they scatter, I will shoot any of them I see, you grab the captain and start heading that way. Once you're back in the grass, low crawl. I'll cover you. Move out quick, because after the bluff, I'll be throwing the real thing."

She rolled slightly away from him, met his eyes, and nodded. Her expression was stern, her gaze steady. He didn't know what had happened to make this woman born again hard, but he had no doubt he was dealing with someone just as accustomed to killing as himself.

He didn't have time to communicate with Scar-face, but he hoped the FVA sergeant would have the initiative to provide covering fire from the bamboo copse once the ruckus started and the marksmanship not to kill any friendlies while he was at it.

Jack risked another peek at the spot where Captain Rapicault stood, hands in the air, surrounded by a Frenchman and three native troops with weapons trained on him. From the prone, Jack tossed the grenade into their midst.

"GRENADE!" He screamed.

As he'd predicted, all five men scattered, diving for cover in different directions. He cranked off a shot at the Frenchman and missed as the big man circled behind a cypress tree trunk with surprising agility. He shifted fire and put a round through one of the native troop's neck, sending a spray of bright arterial blood into the air.

Durand closed the distance in two seconds. One commando was getting back to his feet, his STG-46 coming up to his shoulder. Durand, one hand on Rapicault's arm, leveled her .45 in her other hand and put a round right through that man's eye socket with a loud CRACK, emptying his cranial cavity onto the elephant grass behind him.

Rapicault quickly snatched the dead enemy's weapon and fired a few quick bursts, splintering bark off cypress trunks and kicking up great clods of dirt before turning and running alongside Durand south toward Jack's position.

Jack cranked off a few more shots to keep the enemy's heads down. From across the clearing Scar-face's M2 joined the hail of gunfire, allowing Jack the chance to move south himself.

Regrouping in the grass, they systemized their retreat. Durand and one man at a time peeled back, with the other two men firing north to keep their pursuers honest. Durand argued that she should provide covering fire too, but Rapicault quickly tore that argument apart.

"Doctor Durand, your courage is already beyond doubt," he said. "But given that you have only a pistol, and that a helicopter-flying surgeon is unquestionably more valuable to the war than three mere grunts, kindly do as I order you."

They ran and traded fire with their pursuers for agonizing minutes as elephant grass cut them, vines pulled at their feet, and the persistent heat pulled life sustaining water from their bodies at a frightening rate. Finally, as they cleared a rise, several blasts of machine gun fire flew over their heads toward their pursuers.

Jack and his companions hit the ground.

"*Kết bạn sắp ra! Kết bạn sắp ra!*" Scar-face and Rapicault both shouted at the top of their lungs. The fire slackened long enough for the four of them to sprint into the midst of 2nd Company's defensive lines, then the jungle erupted with carbine, rifle, and machine gun fire.

Despite its ordeal, 2nd Company still stood at more than three quarters its original strength combat effective. Faced with such a force in good order on terrain of its choosing, the pursuing GCMA commandos chose the better part of valor and retired from the field. The sound of gunfire faded as the setting sun bathed the jungle in pink and orange light.

Rapicault's radio crackled to life. Jack was surprised to hear the same modulated southern voice that had coordinated the bombing runs with them. But he sounded worried, almost frightened rather than the calm, collected fighter ace.

"Angel Three-Five, Angel Three-Five, do you read? Margot? Do you read?"

Durand stood from where she'd been resting, stumbling over in her haste to reach the radio. Rapicault handed her the mic without comment.

"Benny, I'm alright," Margot said. "I'm walking out with the boys. I'll see you back home."

"Roger," Tiger Four, *Benny*, croaked. "Be safe."

"Whoever this Benny is," Rapicault said, grinning as he accepted the hand mic back. "He is a most fortunate man. I have never met anyone quite like you."

"Second that, Doc," Jack added.

"You are both too kind," she said, favoring them with a dazzling smile. "It has been quite the experience, but if you would be kind enough to escort me to the nearest airfield, I believe I have had enough of this infantry bullshit for one war."

Jack and Rapicault both laughed.

"Of course, *mademoiselle*," Rapicault said. "If you'll follow me, your airliner is just a few kilometers down this mountain."

* * *

The FVA base at Plei Mrong fell a week behind schedule, and only after the Americans airlifted most of the materiel out and the 112th Regiment escaped into the hinterlands with approximately seventy-five percent of its personnel strength. Already the armored force under de Castries was being slowed by anti-armor ambushes along Colonial Routes 14 and 19.

Thus, Adjutant Vanderburgh stepped into the Central Command headquarters with trepidation. As a warrant officer, he was normally far too junior to be the whipping boy for such a military setback. Protocol demanded a general, or at least a senior colonel take the fall for such a catastrophe. Given the importance of the GCMA's part in this operation, though, perhaps he was the sacrificial lamb this time.

The main operations center was a bustle of activity. Vanderburgh saw not just French and colonial officers and NCOs, but two Wehrmacht and one Luftwaffe officer meandering through the operations center, offering comment on occasion, but mostly radiating smug superiority to their French, "allies."

Asking one of the French staff NCOs for directions, Vanderburgh was gestured to a quiet corner of the operations center. Vanderburgh was surprised to see General Trinquier, the commander of all GCMA forces in Indochina, waiting for him there. Trinquier was a tall man with close cropped gray hair, overly prominent and pointed ears, and a hard-edged face.

Young for his rank at forty-two, Trinquier's theories on how to deal with guerilla and terrorist forces were in vogue, not just in the French Army but in the upper echelons of the Greater Reich itself. Additionally, unlike many of France's effective combat commanders, Roger Trinquier was unsullied by any association with de Gaulle whatsoever. Vanderburgh had served under Trinquier in some capacity for a large chunk of his career, first in Algeria, then in Indochina both before and after World War II.

"Sir," Vanderburgh saluted crisply. "Adjutant Vanderburgh, reporting as ordered."

Trinquier returned the salute casually.

"Hello, Jean-Baptiste," Trinquier said. "I've heard from the regular Army, now I want your thoughts on the operation."

Vanderburgh spent the next hour recounting his part in the mission. Trinquier interrupted rarely, only asking a few questions for the sake of clarity. When Vanderburgh finished, Trinquier stood quiet and still for a full minute.

"I am convinced you did as well as anyone in your position could have done, Adjutant," Trinquier said. "You will retain command of your GCMA battalion."

"Thank you, sir."

Trinquier nodded. Another silence ensued for several seconds, then Trinquier shook his head sadly.

"He really was such a promising young officer," Trinquier said. "If it were not you reporting it, I could not bring myself to believe he had turned coat."

There was no need to clarify who, "he," was. Vanderburgh's glance flicked to the three Germans taking up space in a French Army operations center. Days of prolonged battle and exhaustion loosened his tongue.

"Who hasn't these days?"

Trinquier's eyes snapped over to Vanderburgh, then to the Germans, then back to Vanderburgh.

"Ours isn't to set policy, Adjutant," Trinquier said, his voice low and furious. "We are sworn to obedience. Dislike of our allies is no excuse for treason."

Vanderburgh stiffened to attention.

"Of course not, sir," Vanderburgh said.

Trinquier glared at him for another long moment, then turned and walked away.

"Return to your command, Vanderburgh," Trinquier said without looking back.

Vanderburgh exhaled and made his retreat from the operations center with all possible haste, his mind churning.

No excuse at all, sir. Then again, if there's an excuse for any of us, it's lost on me.

* * * * *

Justin Watson Bio

Justin Watson grew up an Army brat, living in Germany, Alabama, Texas, Korea, Colorado, and Alaska while being fed a steady diet of X-Men, Star Trek, Robert Heinlein, DragonLance, and Babylon 5. While attending West Point, he met his future wife, Michele, on an airplane, and soon began writing in earnest with her encouragement. In 2005, he graduated from West Point and served as a field artillery officer, completing combat tours in Iraq and Afghanistan, and earning the Bronze Star, Purple Heart, and the Combat Action Badge. Medically retired from the Army in 2015, Justin settled in Houston with Michele, their four children, and an excessively friendly Old English Sheepdog.

# # # # #

Unintended Consequences
by Peter Grant

Southern Angola, 1986

The four-man Reconnaissance Regiment stick moved slowly and carefully along the half-overgrown footpath through the African bush. Few people still used it after several years of warfare between the Angolan government's FAPLA forces and their Cuban supporters on the one hand, and UNITA guerrillas and their South African allies on the other. Most of the villagers in or near the fluid, ever-shifting combat zone, with its unpredictable troop movements that could transform an area from tranquil to terrifying without warning, had long since fled.

The point man brushed sweat from his eyebrows yet again, waving away the flies that buzzed around his head, trying to drink it. He began to repeat the gesture, then stopped dead in his tracks and sank to his haunches, making a sign that the others understood. *Enemy ahead.*

First Lieutenant Viljoen moved up beside him, eyes flickering left and right. The brush ended abruptly ahead of them at the edge of an open area, probably a former cornfield, now covered with low vegetation as the African bush reclaimed it. On the far side were a few broken-down mud huts, between which at least a dozen dark olive

Soviet military trucks could be seen. A bulldozer was parked at the edge of an eighty-by two-hundred-foot patch it had cleared and leveled in the field. Well over half of it was already covered with a layer of concrete, two to four inches thick.

"What the hell is FAPLA doing here, Hannes?" the officer murmured to the scout. "This is just a transit route for troops and supplies. They've never had a base here—there's no need for one."

"*Ja,* sir, but maybe they've changed their minds. There's a waterhole nearby, and that looks like a foundation slab."

"It's not thick enough for that, and there's no rebar or wire frame—although both might be because it's a slipshod, half-done job of work, which would be nothing new for Angolans. Whatever it is, the brass will want to know more."

The patrol took up observation positions along the edge of the field, staying hidden in the thick brush as they observed the Angolan troops. Several of them were unloading cement sacks from the back of a truck, while others worked on the engine of a portable cement-mixer. Idlers lounged around, not making any real effort to maintain security over the area. The smell of cooking rose from a line of fires over to one side, where the evening meal was being prepared.

As the sun dipped towards the horizon, the engine of the cement-mixer finally spluttered to life, and its drum began to revolve. The troops standing around it gave a cheer, then looked towards an officer for instructions. He began to shout orders. Some of the troops began to mix more concrete, while others lined up with wheelbarrows to take it to the next section of the slab to be laid. The officer hurried over there, to ensure that the planks placed around it were still in position, to hold the concrete until it had dried enough to remain in place without support. He summoned a soldier with a can of paint and had him mark a big black X equidistant from the three concrete edges on the finished portion of the pad.

"It's already late afternoon, but they're still working. Whatever this is, they're in a hurry," a Recce corporal muttered.

"You're right, Boeta," the patrol commander agreed. "They don't usually work this hard or this late." He thought for a moment. "Remember that intel we got last month, about the helicopters?"

The other nodded thoughtfully. Another Recce patrol had spent a week infiltrating the port of Namibe, watching Soviet cargo vessels unloading materials to be ferried to the battlefront hundreds of miles to the east. They'd noted a major transport bottleneck, with warehouses overflowing into immense stacks of supplies exposed to wind and weather. Some ships were forced to wait at anchor in the bay, because there was no room to unload their cargoes. Shortly before they left Namibe, the patrol had reported the arrival of a squadron of Mil Mi-8 transport helicopters, flown by Angolan and Cuban pilots. The squadron had established its base at the rundown airport south of Namibe and had begun flying covering missions for road convoys. However, the Mi-8's carried no weapons. The Angolans had Mi-24 gunships, so why were they misusing unarmed transports for a job that might well lead to combat?

"Those choppers don't have the range to ferry supplies all the way from Namibe to the battlefront," the lieutenant pointed out, "but if they built a refueling point, they could. That cleared area's the right size, and we're halfway between Namibe and Cuito Cuanavale—just the right place for it. That big X is a give-away. A second, on the other side of the pad, will make this a two-helicopter landing pad, with plenty of space between them for their rotors to turn."

"And there's two fuel tankers in that convoy," Sergeant Bothma commented, pointing at the vehicles in question. "Thing is, why use concrete? Why not just bare earth?"

"Could be so the rotors will throw up less dust and dirt. That'll make visibility very poor during landing and takeoff. Also, during the rainy season, the ground gets so muddy it's like a swamp. I think we should discourage them. I'm going to call this in."

His encrypted message, sent on a frequency-hopping tropospheric-scatter radio system, caused a flurry of activity in an Operations Center in northern South West Africa. Approval for the patrol's proposed course of action was transmitted within the hour, along with instructions for a nearby UNITA patrol to rendezvous with the Recces the following day.

* * *

The same evening, an Antonov An-24 twin-engined transport aircraft of the Angolan Air Force landed at the airport south of Namibe. It taxied to the terminal building in the last of the sunlight, where a guard of honor had been hastily assembled. Its members—local levies unfamiliar with drill of any sort, let alone an honor guard—shambled to a ragged semblance of attention and falteringly presented arms as a man disembarked, wearing a major-general's uniform of the Soviet Union. Tabs identified him as an officer of the Strategic Rocket Forces.

An East German major stood to one side. He came forward, snapped to attention, and saluted stiffly. "Welcome to Namibe, General Shpagin! It is an honor for us to receive a visit from so senior an officer."

The new arrival peered at his name tag. "Not that much of an honor, Major Brinkerhoff. I was at loose ends between postings. That's why Moscow sent me to investigate this logistics mess—I just happened to be the most senior officer available. I wasn't impressed to see stacks of supplies all over the place as we came in to land. Lobito looked no better as we overflew it on the way down here from Luanda. Why haven't both ports been better organized? Why is it taking so long to clear this bottleneck?"

"I can't speak with any authority, sir, as I'm not involved in port operations or military logistics. Local officers will brief you in the morning." He lowered his voice to a confidential murmur. "If you ask me, sir, it's largely because they're incompetent and bone idle. In the Warsaw Pact, we'd be shot if we worked this way!"

The general eyed him carefully. Brinkerhoff was a professional like himself. As such, his judgment was probably as accurate as it was damning. *"Hmpfh!* We'll see about that. Take me to the visiting officers' quarters, Major. I need a bath, a good meal, and a night's sleep."

His aide followed with the general's suitcase as his boss strode to a waiting utility vehicle.

Next morning, General Shpagin's invective blistered the hides of the staff as they tried to make excuses for the logistics bottleneck. He pointed out acidly, "The Soviet Union has generously provided thousands of trucks to Angola, free of charge, yet you claim you don't have enough vehicles to move these supplies. *Where are they, then?"* As to claims that the roads weren't good enough, he noted bluntly that South Africa appeared to have few difficulties supplying UNITA rebels with material support over a much greater distance, through terrain that often had no roads at all. "If they can do it, why can't you? Your inefficiency is causing weeks of delay to valuable ships that are needed elsewhere. This must stop!"

Nor would he give credence to claims of the mass destruction of transport vehicles by South African forces. "We know beyond doubt, through satellite reconnaissance and other intelligence sources, that South Africa currently has only a few hundred troops north of the South West African border. You have thousands of Cuban troops, fighting alongside tens of thousands of Angolan soldiers—far more than enough to defend against such a small number, no matter how skilled or well-equipped they may be."

A timid Angolan Air Force officer offered what he hoped would be good news. "S-sir, our new helicopter route will open within a day or two. We're building a refueling pad halfway between here and Cuito Cuanavale, so that Mi-8's can fly there with a full four-ton cargo of urgently needed materials. If Moscow gives us the heavy-lift Mi-26's we have asked for, we will be able to lift twenty tons on every flight!"

Shpagin's eyebrows rose. "That will help, although it'll be much more expensive than road transport. When's the first mission?"

"In three days' time, sir."

"Book seats on it for myself and my aide. I want to see this refueling pad for myself, and inspect the cargo handling facilities at Cuito Cuanavale too."

That evening over supper, his aide tried to remonstrate. "But, sir, the Defense Ministry's instructions were clear. You were not to enter the combat zone or expose yourself to danger."

"*Pshaw!* They sent me here to investigate a problem and solve it. The only way I can do that properly is to see everything for myself. UNITA and the South Africans don't know I'm here, and they can't possibly be aware of the new helicopter route. It hasn't even been used yet! As for the combat zone, there's no major fighting going on right now. All anyone's doing is local patrolling. I don't think there'll be any risk."

* * *

As the two Soviet officers finished their meal, Lieutenant Viljoen welcomed a UNITA officer to the camp the patrol had set up, half a mile from the Angolan work site. The two shook hands, and got down to business without preamble.

"The signal said to deliver to you all our explosives," the UNITA man began. "We have four TM-46 anti-vehicle land mines."

"That's great! Just what we need. Here, let me show you what's going on." The South African officer drew a quick map in the dirt using a stick. "The enemy is here. On a circle surrounding their positions, we're here. I'd like you to place your patrol in an arc behind their positions, a third of the way around the circle from where we are. That way we won't shoot at each other through them. I'm guessing the helicopter pad will be ready in the next two days—the first half is already dry. As soon as it's complete, I reckon they'll send out a proving mission, to make sure everything's as it should be. I want to hit them when they come in."

"How can you be sure they'll land on the mines? The pressure plates won't work unless they have enough weight on them."

"We'll make sure they go off. I want your people to stay quiet until they blow, then shoot the hell out of the Angolan vehicles and positions for two minutes, no more. As soon as two minutes are up, get out of here. The main convoy route isn't far away, so the Angolans may be able to get a reaction force here quickly. We aren't strong enough to take them on."

"All right. You head south and we'll head east, to divide any enemy attempt to follow us."

"Agreed. Use anti-tracking, too, to make it as difficult as possible for them."

The twenty-man UNITA patrol headed into the bush to work their way around the enemy's position. The lieutenant laid out the four big steel landmines in a row, and started removing their pressure plates.

"What's the idea, sir?" Sergeant Piet Bothma asked as he knelt down to help.

"We have to make sure these blow, even if the chopper doesn't land right on top of them," the officer explained. "We're going to replace their pressure plates with plastic explosive and a command detonator. We'll connect them all to a firing position at the edge of the bush, and let the enemy lay concrete over them."

"Will they have enough blast to take out a chopper through concrete, sir?" another asked.

"Four TM-46's have as much explosive between them as a couple of 155mm artillery shells. I think that'll be more than enough."

The questioner winced. "That's headache city all right!"

After midnight, when all the Angolan soldiers were asleep—including the sentries, because what possible threat could there be so deep in the bush, and so far from the battlefront?—the South Africans crept out into the cleared area. The lieutenant estimated where the second X marker for a landing helicopter would most likely be painted, then dug holes for the four mines close together around that point. The others covered them, then led the detonator wire to and beyond the edge of the cleared area, burying it. They patted down and smoothed the disturbed earth, then brushed it with leafy branches as they withdrew, removing all signs that they'd been there.

As the sun rose and the Angolans began to pour more concrete, covering the mines, the Recces settled down to wait.

* * *

Antennae all over the operational area, and up and down the coast, fed their intercepted harvest to the South African electronic warfare station at Rooikop, near Walvis Bay in South West Africa, eight hundred miles to the south. In the underground operations center, the signals were analyzed, decrypted if possible, then forwarded to interested parties for further action.

Late the following night, an operator called the Officer of the Watch to come to his station. "Sir, a visiting general is making life difficult at Namibe. The Angolans are complaining to their HQ in Luanda that he's 'insensitive to the difficulties of operating in a war zone.'"

"Awww, my heart bleeds for them," the OOW joked as he began to read the signal. "Hey, that's not a Cuban or East German name. 'Shpagin'—that sounds Russian. Have we seen it before?"

"Nothing in the database, sir."

"Then let's get this off to the Ops Room at Defense HQ in Pretoria. They may know who he is."

They didn't, but the Operations Room knew who would. By early the following morning, the CIA in Langley, Virginia confirmed to their representative in the United States Embassy in Pretoria that a major-general in the Soviet Union's Strategic Rocket Forces bore the same name. What would a man of that rank and importance be doing in an out-of-the-way place like Angola? Questions flashed from Langley to the U.S. Embassy in Moscow, but the answers didn't satisfy anyone.

"Why the hell would they send a senior strategic missile commander to untangle logistics snarl-ups in the third world?" an American analyst demanded. "That makes no sense. They've got to be up to something!"

South African Defense HQ duly ordered Rooikop and other facilities to be on the lookout for any further mention of Shpagin's name and mission, while interested eyes in America sharpened their focus on southern Africa. Cuba was the main Soviet surrogate in the region, after all, and Angola's ally. Could the general's visit be the first move in a new Cuban missile crisis, more than two decades after the last one?

* * *

The day of the first helicopter resupply mission dawned fine and clear. General Shpagin dressed carefully, the rows of award ribbons on his chest making a colorful display. He inspected his boots with displeasure, and insisted that his Angolan servant polish them again.

"Wouldn't it be better to wear battledress, like the Cuban officers do, sir?" his aide asked.

Shpagin shook his head disapprovingly. "They're playing at being fighting soldiers. They aren't even in the combat zone, yet they all look casual and sloppy. Let's show them what it means to be proud of one's uniform!"

"As you say, sir."

Sighing inwardly, the aide resigned himself to another day of tugging at his tight collar, while sweating buckets beneath his heavy jacket.

Why is it, he wondered, *that generals can go through the whole day looking as fresh as a daisy, while their underlings wilt? Must go with the rank.*

A utility vehicle took them to two Mi-8 helicopters parked on the airport hardstand. They were already loaded with urgently needed supplies, strapped down in their cabins. An officer motioned the general and his aide towards the first helicopter, but Shpagin held up a hand.

"Captain, you go in the second helicopter. Nothing's likely to happen, but let's travel separately, just in case. If anything goes wrong, one of us must survive to submit a report to Moscow, and you already know what I plan to say to them."

"Yes, sir."

The crew chief pulled down a folding chair against the bulkhead. General Shpagin strapped himself into it, frowning at the memory of many uncomfortable hours spent in similar transports. At least, here in the southern African heat, he wouldn't freeze his ass off.

"What's our flight time?" he asked the crew chief.

"Two hours, ten minutes to the refueling point, sir, then another two hours, twenty minutes to Cuito Cuanavale."

The general grimaced, already regretting his second cup of coffee over breakfast. "I'll need a pee break very badly by the time we land to refuel."

The Cuban NCO guffawed as he handed him a set of headphones with a boom microphone.

"Just don't piss out the open door as we fly, sir," the man stated, his tone turning morose as he continued. "The rotor wash will blow it back all over you, and everyone else in here. Ask me how I know that."

Shpagin had to laugh as he nodded in response.

The helicopters lifted off with a snarling clatter of rotors, and turned west, staying low over the trees and bushes. A few minutes later the An-24 transport also took off, to fly high overhead and serve as a communications relay if required. A routine signal was dispatched to the Angolan air defense network at Cuito Cuanavale, to confirm that the flights had departed. The identity of the VIP passenger was emphasized, to ensure that no missiles were launched at him in error. Their Soviet benefactors would not be amused by such a mistake.

The routine signal was duly intercepted at Rooikop, and General Shpagin's name noted. Within minutes a message was on its way to Pretoria.

* * *

The concrete had dried quickly under the hot African sun, and the Angolans clearly weren't going to waste any time putting the landing pad into service. The fuel tankers had been driven closer to the edge of the pad, and the encampment had been tidied up. The construction crew were dressing in clean uniforms, while their NCO's marked out parade positions for them.

Lieutenant Viljoen ordered everyone to pack their gear and be ready to move out on the run.

"If they come this morning, and we blow them up, they're not going to be very pleased with us," he pointed out with a grin. "We'll have to get away before they can get organized. I'll be on the detonator. Hannes, we don't have anyone else to spare, so the two of us will have to be a quick-and-dirty snatch party. If we see an opportunity to take a prisoner, let's grab him during the confusion when UNITA joins in. He can answer questions later. Boeta, you're on the missile." He nodded to the team's sole SA-14 shoulder-launched ground-to-air missile, captured from the Angolans like all their weapons and equipment.

"Give them a chance to land," Viljoen emphasized. "If one doesn't, and you get a clear shot, take it down. Piet, you provide covering fire for the snatch team if we need it, then take point when we leave. Head back down the footpath we used to get here. As soon as we've broken contact we'll change direction and start using anti-tracking to stop them following us."

They waited in the thick brush as the sun rose higher, and the heat began to grow oppressive. At last, shortly after ten, the distant sound of helicopter rotors intruded on the silence and began to grow louder. "They're coming!" the lieutenant exclaimed, his face lighting up. "Packs on, weapons ready, and stand by!"

Two familiar silhouettes appeared over the bushes and trees. The leading helicopter slanted down towards the pad in a curving approach, while the second circled above the clearing, obviously looking for any signs of danger. They ignored it. By now, camouflaging their positions against aerial observation was second nature to them. Boeta picked up the SA-14 launch tube, trying to get a clear view of the second helicopter.

The lead helicopter settled almost exactly where Lieutenant Viljoen had anticipated it would. His finger trembled on the detonator switch as he waited, hoping for the second aircraft to land, so that blast and fragments from the mines might damage it as well. Instead, as the engines of the first helicopter began to shut down, a smartly uniformed figure jumped down from it and hurried directly towards them, ducking beneath the rotor blades, one hand holding his cap on, the other fumbling with the fly of his trousers.

"Holy shit, boss, he's coming right for us!" Hannes whispered urgently.

"Stand by to grab him!"

Viljoen waited until the new arrival had almost reached the bush behind which he was concealed, then hit the switch. With a colossal blast, the four landmines blew up beneath the concrete, sending fragments flying in all directions, including into the fuselage and fuel tanks of the helicopter above them. It came apart, erupting in flames as its undercarriage collapsed.

Instantly, chaos broke out. The UNITA patrol opened up with AK-47's, RPK light machine-guns, RPG-7 rockets, and hand grenades. Both tanker trucks exploded, one after the other, in massive orange-red fireballs and billowing smoke, spraying burning fuel and debris in every direction. Many of the Angolan soldiers, who'd been drawn up in formation to honor the new arrivals, were mown down as if by a scythe. The survivors scattered in panic.

In the confusion, Hannes leapt to his feet and tackled the man who'd run towards them, clouting him a mighty blow on the jaw that knocked him out. His cap came off. Hannes picked it up, staring at it, then at his victim.

"Lieutenant! This guy isn't Angolan or Cuban! It's a white man, and he's wearing a shitload of medal ribbons and what look like general's stars. Who *is* this fucker?"

"I don't know, but he's got to be important. Come on! Let's grab him and get out of here!"

* * *

In the second Mi-8, the pilot was screaming into his microphone. *"Emergency! Emergency!* The refueling pad is under attack! The lead helicopter has crashed and blown up! General Shpagin has been captured by the enemy—I saw them tackle him and bring him down! For God's sake, somebody help us!"

Looking out of the open side door, Shpagin's aide saw a trail of smoke erupt from a clump of bushes and head straight towards the helicopter. There was a loud explosion over his head, and pieces of the rotor blades flew in all directions. The aircraft dropped like a stone. The last thing he saw was the whirling ground coming up very fast before his eyes as the helicopter spun in.

High in the sky, the An-24 radio relay plane saw and heard it all. Even as its pilots hauled the plane around and clawed for more altitude, to put as much distance as possible between themselves and any other ground-to-air missiles, its radio operator passed the news to Namibe. From there, a message was broadcast at full power across southern Angola, in clear, to all FAPLA and Cuban forces. "General Shpagin has been captured in an enemy ambush at the new refueling pad! All available forces are to converge on that location and rescue him!" Map coordinates were provided. MiG fighters and Sukhoi strike aircraft scrambled, and helicopters launched to carry responding forces to the scene at top speed.

Almost as fast as the message spread through the Angolan armed forces, it reached South African Defense Force HQ in Pretoria via the Rooikop listening station. The initial reaction was one of shocked incredulity. Who could have launched such an attack, against such a high-value target? It didn't take long for the Special Forces liaison officer to inform the Operations Room about Lieutenant Viljoen's patrol, and his intention to take out the first helicopter to use the landing pad they had discovered. Was that what the Angolans were talking about?

"Send a signal to Viljoen at once!"

"We can't, sir. He won't be listening—in fact, if that was him, he'll be running like hell to get clear before reaction forces arrive. His next scheduled communications window is tonight."

"And until then, we'll have the top brass jumping down our throats, demanding to know what's going on. What are we going to tell them?"

* * *

The patrol had covered only a few hundred yards, dragging their unconscious prisoner with them, when they heard the roar of an overstressed engine drawing nearer from behind them. They scattered to either side of the narrow footpath as a Soviet ZIL-131 six-by-six military truck appeared, gears whining in low ratio, wheels churning in the thick soft sand, bashing through the bushes on either side of the track, its fear-crazed driver intent only on escape from the carnage behind him.

Sergeant Bothma spun in his tracks, shouldered his AK-47, and squeezed off a pair of snap shots that went through the door and killed the driver instantly. His foot came off the accelerator and the truck slowed to a standstill, jerking as its engine cut out. Bothma ran after it, pulling open the door to check on the driver.

"Well done, Piet!" Viljoen called breathlessly. "Throw him in the back, so he won't be found, and take his place. I'll join you. The rest of you, get in the back with the prisoner."

Within moments, the truck was bouncing down the track again. Viljoen consulted his map. "This footpath comes out at the main east-west trail in about two clicks. When we get there, turn west towards the coast."

"*West,* sir? But that's closer to the enemy!"

"Yes, it is, but if our prisoner's as important as he looks, they're going to be after us with everything they've got. They'll expect us to head east and south, towards our own forces. Let's throw them off the scent by doing what they won't expect. The truck's wheels will leave ruts in the sandy soil, but you can't tell from the rut which direction it was moving. Once we hit the main trail, they won't know which way we went. We'll abandon this truck somewhere convenient, and head south from there."

"OK, sir. That guy's uniform and insignia looked different from anything we've seen before. He may be Soviet. If he is, they'll be flying in search parties from all directions. Moscow will be baying for our blood."

"If you're right, we've got less than an hour before aircraft will be overhead, looking for us. A truck moving alone will stick out like a sore thumb. Remember that convoy the Air Force hit two months ago, just east of here?"

"Yessir! The Angolans dragged all the wrecked trucks off to the side of the road, and abandoned them." He sniggered. "The Air Force uses them as a navigational landmark now."

"That's right. It's about thirty clicks from here. Let's park this truck with them. I reckon no-one will bother to count, to see if there's one more vehicle than there was before. That'll buy us time to get away clean."

"Great idea, sir!"

It took them thirty-seven agonizing minutes to reach the trucks, peering out of the windows all the while to spot any other vehicles or a fast-moving aircraft coming towards them. At last they reached the place. The lieutenant pointed. "Take us around the back there, into the bush, on the far side of the wrecks. That'll put this one furthest away from passing traffic, so they're less likely to notice it's not damaged like the others."

They parked the truck, then Viljoen hurried around to the rear while the sergeant started to knock the valve stems out of every tire. The prisoner had regained consciousness, and was sitting nursing his jaw, looking around balefully.

The lieutenant tried his meager, halting Spanish, learned in case he needed to interrogate Cuban prisoners. *"¿Quién eres tú? ¿Cuál es su nombre?"* No response. He switched to English. "Who are you? What is your name?"

"I am Major-General Shpagin of the Soviet armed forces. That is all I shall tell you."

"What the hell are you doing out here in the middle of bloody Africa?" Silence. "Are you attached to the Angolan armed forces?" Silence. "What is your mission?" Silence.

"We can't waste time making him talk, sir," Boeta warned. "Listen!" They cocked their heads. Faintly, but growing louder, they heard the sound of jet engines at high altitude.

"Those will be MiGs, looking for us," Lieutenant Viljoen agreed. He looked back at the general. "Sir, you're a prisoner of war of the Republic of South Africa's armed forces. We're going to take to the bush and head south until we can arrange to be picked up. If you don't make trouble, we'll allow you to walk unrestrained. If you make trouble or try to escape, we'll tie your hands, put a tether round your neck, and bring you with us the hard way. Understand me?"

"I understand." Another baleful glare.

"Right. Everyone, fill your canteens." Viljoen gestured to the drum of water tied down in the load bed. "When you've done that, drink as much as you can, then we'll drain the rest of the water. Take what you need from that box of ration packs. They're Angolan, so they won't be very tasty, but they're better than nothing. We'll carry seven days' food per man. Empty that backpack." He pointed to what had presumably been the personal gear of the late driver. "Fill it with ration packs and the driver's canteens. General, you'll carry it. If you refuse, you'll have nothing to eat or drink, so don't argue. Hannes, make sure he's unarmed—no dinky little officer's pistol concealed anywhere. The rest of you, take the canvas cover off the truck, fold it a few times, and lay it in the load bed over the driver's body. From the road or a low-flying chopper, this truck's got to look like just another abandoned wreck."

"Not going to booby-trap it, sir?" the sergeant asked as he straightened from removing a valve stem.

"No. If it explodes or burns, the Angolans will wonder why."

Within ten minutes, the patrol moved out in single file, heading south, sticking to the cover of the trees and bushes, moving slowly and carefully, covering or disguising their tracks whenever possible. Their prisoner walked in the center of the formation. General Shpagin seethed inwardly, but made no trouble. South African troops had a well-earned reputation for violence towards anyone who resisted them. He had no doubt that any attempt at obstruction or escape would have extremely painful consequences.

* * *

The atmosphere in the meeting room at Soviet military headquarters in Moscow seethed and roiled with barely suppressed tension. The Defense Minister glared at the assembled senior officers. "How do you know it was the South Africans who got him? It could have been UNITA!"

"Minister, the reaction forces captured two UNITA guerrillas, part of a larger force trying to escape after the ambush. Under separate interrogation, both said their unit was ordered to join a South African Reconnaissance Regiment patrol, to help them attack the refueling pad. UNITA took no prisoners during the attack, so General Shpagin must be in South African hands."

"And who the hell thought it was a good idea to send a Strategic Rocket Forces general to Angola in the first place? He knows our nuclear target lists for every NATO country! If the South Africans get him back to their base, the Americans will give their eye teeth and sell their own mothers to interrogate him!"

"H-he was just...available, Minister," a hapless official stammered. "The Foreign Ministry said they wanted someone senior enough to impress the Angolans. General Shpagin had just returned from a period of leave. He said he was tired of sitting around, waiting for his predecessor to depart so he could take up his new post, and volunteered for the Angolan inspection mission in the interim. No one even thought about his branch of service."

A wordless glare from the Minister promised retribution for so grievous an error of judgment. "What do you propose, Marshal?" he demanded, turning to the Commanding Officer of the Strategic Rocket Forces.

"Three things, Minister. First, I want the Air Force to send a couple dozen of their best pilots to Angola at once, by the fastest available means. Some good maintenance technicians would also be useful. They can take over some of the Angolan Air Force's MiG-23's to fly top cover, and some Mi-8 and Mi-24 helicopters. They'll assume primary responsibility for stopping the South Africans from interfering, and, if we locate Shpagin, they can land troops to rescue him. Second, I want a Spetsnaz air assault unit sent to Angola, also by the fastest available means. They'll mount the rescue mission if we find Shpagin. Finally, we need to send a very strong signal to South Africa that they've gone too far. I suggest ordering a Guards Air Assault Division to prepare for immediate deployment to Angola."

"You're crazy!" the Minister exclaimed. "The Politburo would never permit that! The Americans would regard it as an intolerable provocation!"

"We don't have to send them, Minister—just order them to get ready to go, and let it slip that they're preparing. The South Africans will get the message. If we don't get Shpagin back quickly, their war in Angola is going to turn a lot hotter than they bargained for."

"And if they respond by calling up their own reinforcements?"

"Then let's send the division. The South Africans can see how they like facing a real enemy, not third-rate Africans or second-rate Cubans. They won't enjoy it."

The Minister shook his head. "I doubt that'll be approved. Remember, Secretary Gorbachev is putting a lot of emphasis on *glasnost,* reconciliation with the West. He won't want to jeopardize that."

"That's a political consideration, Minister. We're military men. We deal with military solutions."

The Minister managed, not without some difficulty, to restrain himself from pointing out that those same military men had caused the problem in the first place, by sending General Shpagin where he should never have gone.

"Very well, Marshal. On my authority, get the aircrew and Spetsnaz unit moving. Tell the Air Force I want them to assign sufficient jet transports to get them to Angola as fast as possible, along with any equipment they need. They can arrange to refuel in Libya if necessary. Have the Foreign Ministry clear that with Gaddafi, and tell them not to take 'No' for an answer. Hold off on the Air Assault division for now. That'll have to be discussed by the Politburo. Have the relevant agencies see to it—discreetly, of course—that the Americans and South Africans learn of these steps, but try to avoid the news spreading more widely."

* * *

General Shpagin nibbled at a ration pack cracker, nursing his still-painful jaw, washing down the crumbs with water from a canteen as he watched Lieutenant Viljoen, forehead creased in concentration, compose and encrypt a message. At last, the officer sighed, pressed a button, and sat back. "There. That's saved for transmission later." He reached for his ration pack.

"Are you telling them you've captured me?" the prisoner asked.

Viljoen laughed. "I reckon they already know, General. You saw and heard all those aircraft flying around today. They were looking for you. I'm sure there's signals all over the place about you, and I reckon our people will have intercepted some of them. We've thrown the searchers off the trail for a while, but sooner or later they'll realize they're looking in the wrong place. I hope we'll have you across the border by then."

"How will you do that?"

"I don't suppose I'm betraying any secrets when I tell you I'm going to ask for a helicopter pickup. That's far and away the fastest method. Otherwise, it'll be a three- to four-week walk through the bush. That'll be no fun for any of us."

"But you have only enough rations for a week."

"We'll live off the land, General. We're used to that."

"So you are like our Spetsnaz, then? Special Forces?"

"Yes. We're Reconnaissance Commandos." The pride in Viljoen's voice was evident.

"I have heard something about you, yes." The general hesitated a moment. "How can you fight for a government that denies the humanity of so many of its people, because of the color of their skin?"

"You mean the policy of *apartheid?*" Shpagin nodded, and Viljoen sighed. "I'm not saying South Africa's perfect, General. We've got at least as many problems as any other nation, maybe more than most. What we're doing, the four of us and others like us, is buying time for our country to sort out its own problems in peace. Have you ever seen what happens when a terrorist landmine goes off underneath a trailer full of kids on their way to school?"

"I...no, I never have."

"I have. I still wake up screaming sometimes when I remember picking up the pieces of those kids...feet...hands...fingers...half a head that had come right off a little girl. She must have been pretty, once."

The younger man's eyes were far away, filled with remembered pain.

"That's what we're fighting to keep out of our land, General, for long enough that those bastards won't dictate the solution to our problems out of the barrels of their guns." He looked up. "I might as well ask why you serve a government that arms the terrorists who do such things, and that starved millions to death, and sent millions more to the gulag, and invaded Afghanistan. Doesn't that make you just as bad as I am, General?"

Shpagin grunted. "A point to you, Lieutenant. I, too, want to make my country a better place. Perhaps we are not so different, you and I."

"I don't think military professionals are all that different, sir. I've met soldiers from Britain, the United States, and Israel. They're all a lot like us, under the skin."

"Yet, despite those similarities, you would shoot me without hesitation if I tried to escape."

"Uh-huh, just like you'd shoot me if that was the only way you could escape."

* * *

VIPs crowded a conference room in Defense HQ in Pretoria. When Lieutenant Viljoen's signal reached them shortly after midnight, mingled jubilation and concern swept through the gathering. The Chief of the Defense Force swiftly called them to order.

"They've moved beyond our normal operational area. Can the Air Force get a Puma helicopter up there to collect them?"

The Chief of the Air Force frowned. "We have long-range tanks we can install in the cabin, sir. Trouble is, they're all down here, for use during maritime rescue missions. We'll have to take one—no, two, in case one goes wrong—out of choppers at the coast, fly them up to Grootfontein, and install them in helicopters there. That'll take a full day, longer if there are technical issues. Meanwhile, you can bet the Angolans will be looking for our patrol with everything they've got."

"Not just the Angolans. We heard from the Americans a short while ago. The Soviets are sending in their own pilots to take over some Angolan planes, and bringing a Spetsnaz air assault unit with them. If they can find and fix our people, they'll lead the attack."

"When will they get there, sir?"

"They left Moscow aboard Ilyushin-76 transports a few hours ago. They'll have to refuel somewhere, but you can assume they'll be in the operational area within 36 hours from now."

"We'll only just have finished installing the tanks by then, and test-flown the helicopters, sir. I can't guarantee success if we have to infiltrate defenses manned by front-line Soviet pilots and technicians, particularly if they bring more advanced weapons with them—better air-to-air missiles, electronic warfare pods, that sort of thing."

"We may have no choice but to try. What fighters do we have up there?"

"Half a dozen Mirage F1's, sir, but they're 'A' models, configured for ground attack rather than air-to-air."

"Get some of the 'C' models up there right away, armed with the new Python-3 air-to-air missiles we bought from Israel. If our helicopters have to go in, the fighters will have to keep the MiGs off their backs while they pick up our people. Fortunately, the Angolans and Cubans don't yet know we have Pythons. They'll be a nice surprise for them, and the Soviets too."

"Yes, sir. Will the Cabinet authorize us to engage Soviet forces?"

"Let me worry about that." The Chief of the Defense Force turned to the Special Forces representative. "Danie, send a big 'Well done!' to Lieutenant Viljoen and his team from me personally; then tell them to crawl into a hole and pull the top in after them until we can sort out this mess. We've got their backs, and we won't abandon them, but we have to avoid this thing getting any hotter than it is already. Right now, it's like we're all sitting around an open gunpowder keg, tossing lighted matches at it. If we're not bloody careful, things are going to take on a momentum of their own—and then where will we be?"

"Won't the United States back us against the Soviets, sir? They'll have to, won't they?"

"Why don't you ask South Vietnam how well relying on America worked out for them?"

"Ah…I take your point, sir."

* * *

Major Brinkerhoff was at Namibe airport to welcome the Spetsnaz assault team when it landed. He saluted the colonel in command. "Sir, I've put up tented accommodation for your unit behind that hangar. A field kitchen is ready to serve you a meal right away. It's good food—I tasted it myself. When you've eaten, I'm ready to give you a briefing on local conditions, including a video of the action, and provide a current situation report."

Colonel Voronezh looked at him with approval. "Major, you're the most professional soldier I've run into since we landed in Angola! Thank you for making those arrangements. We'll look forward to your briefing in half an hour."

Some still chewing, the Spetsnaz officers and senior NCO's assembled in a tent used as a briefing room and listened closely as the

East German officer walked them through the events of the past few days. He showed them on a large-scale map of Southern Angola where various units were searching, and the patrol patterns they were using.

"What have the South Africans been doing?" Voronezh asked.

"They've brought up more Mirage fighters, but they haven't flown across the border into Angola yet. Moscow signaled a short while ago that satellite imagery shows the newly arrived Mirages are carrying Israeli Python-3 air-to-air missiles. That's a type our forces hadn't seen on South African aircraft before. They're extremely effective heat-seekers."

"That's not good news," the Colonel grunted. "What about their helicopters?"

"Satellite reconnaissance showed two Puma helicopters being worked on outside a hangar, sir. It looked like they were installing long-range tanks in the cabins. They may be going to try for a pickup."

"But they didn't have them already fitted with the tanks, ready to go? That means they were surprised by General Shpagin's presence. They can't have expected to capture him."

"I suppose not, sir."

"Hmmm…As a military professional with local knowledge, Major, what's your opinion of the South African special forces—these Reconnaissance Regiments, as they call them?"

"They're as good as you can get, sir, within their scope. Let me explain. You Spetsnaz, and the American SEALs and Green Berets, and the British SAS, train to operate anywhere. You can jump into the Arctic, or into the Amazon jungle, and be equally at home. The Reconnaissance Regiments are different. Their selection standards are as rigorous as any other Special Forces unit, anywhere in the world, but they train to operate in an African environment. You may spend three months training in Arctic warfare, then three months in the jungle, then three months mountaineering, and so on. They'll spend all those months training just as hard, but focused solely on sub-Saharan African operations. That concentration of effort means that, man for man, on their home turf, they're the best there is."

The Spetsnaz officers looked thoughtfully at one another. They understood the professional evaluation for what it was, a sober reflection of reality. This was not going to be easy.

"So," Voronezh said slowly, "if it comes to a fight, you're saying we'll have our work cut out for us, even though we'll probably outnumber their small ambush team many times over."

"Sir, if it comes to a fight, some of you won't be coming back. Guaranteed. Even if you kill them all, they'll bleed you first."

"And the general?"

"I don't know what their orders are, sir. If they've been instructed not to let him get away, you won't recover him alive. They'll make sure of that."

"Thank you, Major. I'm going to make that point to Moscow when I speak to them in half an hour. They need to take that into account."

* * *

When the recording of the colonel's conversation with his superiors was played back to the Politburo, the shock on the faces of some of its members showed that they hadn't considered that possibility.

"How can we ensure General Shpagin is not killed out of hand?" one demanded.

"If this comes down to a combat operation, we can't," the Defense Minister replied bluntly.

"Then we must make sure it doesn't come down to a combat operation," Secretary Gorbachev said quietly. "I think we'll try extreme diplomatic pressure, and see what that can achieve."

"But we don't have diplomatic relations with South Africa," another member objected.

"True—but the United States does."

* * *

As the moon rose over the African bush, the Recce patrol settled down in a dense clump of trees and bushes. Two sentries kept watch at all times, one over the surrounding area, the other over their prisoner. The general hadn't given any trouble, but that didn't mean he might not do so if he got the chance. They were too professional to take that risk.

"May I ask a question?" the general asked as he ate his meager rations next to Lieutenant Viljoen.

"Sure, go ahead, sir."

"Why have the Angolans not found us yet?"

"They're probably still convinced we're heading east and south, to get closer to our own forces or the border, sir. That would be our logical direction of movement, after all. We haven't seen or heard many aircraft or helicopters over the past couple of days. They're all searching over there trying to stop us getting through, while we're sitting over here, not even trying to reach the border."

"Why aren't you trying?"

"Orders, sir. I reckon the brass have something in mind. They've been clear that we're to take no chances, just sit tight and remain undiscovered until they get back to us. It grates, but they're in charge."

"I suppose so. It must be as frustrating for you as it is for me, just sitting here in the bush."

"Yes, sir, but that's what they pay us for." Viljoen cocked his head, listening. "There's a jet up there, very high. I reckon it'll be carrying a reconnaissance pod. It'll be looking for fires, heat signatures, things like that."

"Is that why you don't have fires at night?"

"Yes, sir. The glow is visible from a long way off, and their heat signature shows up on infrared like a flashlight in a dark room. So do vehicle engines. That's why we dumped the truck, rather than use it to move at night."

General Shpagin snorted. "And I suppose that's why you took my lighter and cigars."

"Yes, sir. We couldn't risk you starting a fire. It wasn't because we wanted them as souvenirs!"

"Why don't the Angolans look at lower altitude with infrared sensors on helicopters?"

"Because they lose aircraft when they do that, sir. We shot down your second helicopter using a captured SA-14 missile. We don't have any more with us, but the Angolans don't know that. UNITA has American Stinger missiles. We've captured dozens of your old SA-7's, a couple of SA-9 vehicle-mounted systems, a few SA-14's, and recently we've started to come across your new SA-16's." He snickered. "You copied or stole so much American technology for it that we call it the 'Stingerski.' It's a good missile—better than the

Stinger in some ways, according to our comparative tests. Anyway, thanks to all those missiles, Cuban and Angolan aircraft generally don't fly below fifteen thousand feet in the operational area, unless they're flying nap-of-the-earth."

"So, to put it bluntly, my country is one of your arms suppliers, whether we like it or not?"

Viljoen laughed.

"I'm not giving away any secrets by saying this, sir, because it's either been publicized in South Africa, or the Angolans and Cubans know all about it from fighting us. We've captured literally tens of thousands of your infantry weapons over the years—SKS rifles, AK-47 assault rifles, grenades, land mines, and so on. We Recces carry them almost all the time."

"Why?" Shpagin demanded. "Why not use your own weapons?"

"Oh, come on, General! If we left South African cartridge cases and other evidence lying around, it'd be obvious we'd been there. This way, the Angolans can't tell that, since our debris looks the same as theirs or UNITA's. South Africa has some of your T-34, T-55, T-62 and PT-76 tanks, against which we test and assess our own vehicles and tactics."

Shpagin seethed as the South African officer continued.

"Our Army's standard-issue rocket-propelled grenade launcher is your RPG-7, and we make better rockets for it. We have plenty of captured Soviet equipment in storage—heavy machine guns, mortars, anti-aircraft guns, cannon and rocket artillery, armored personnel carriers, and trucks. We gave a lot of our captured stocks to UNITA, and they've taken a lot themselves. Every time we beat FAPLA or the Cubans, we hand over more to UNITA, unless it's something advanced like missiles we want for ourselves. In reality, the Soviet Union is arming both sides in this war and has been for years."

The general's mouth twisted bitterly.

When I return, certain people are going to hear about this in no uncertain terms, he thought angrily. *That my aide died as the target of a Soviet missile is a disgrace! I cannot shoot the men responsible, but I can try to see to it that we stop arming the very people acting against our interests!*

* * *

A gathering in Washington D.C. the following afternoon was, if anything, even more tense than the South African cabinet meeting under way at the same time. A CIA representative was ebullient. "We've lined up an interrogation team to head for South Africa the instant we're notified that General Shpagin is there. He must know every Soviet nuclear target in NATO, and what weapons are aimed at it. That'll reveal just how much they know about us. It'll be the biggest intelligence coup of the decade!"

"But will South Africa let us have access to him?" a State Department advisor wondered.

"They'd better, if they want us to continue with constructive engagement in any form at all! We can throw them a bone or two—sell them some spares for their old C-130 Hercules transports, or turn a blind eye while they buy more missiles from Israel or West German fire control system components for their new armored vehicles, or something like that."

The State Department man was about to reply when the telephone on the sideboard rang. An aide answered, listened briefly, and turned to him. "It's for you, sir—the Secretary."

The advisor walked over to the sideboard, took the phone, and listened for a long moment. "Yes, sir...but are they serious?...I see...yes, sir. I'll tell them. Thank you, sir." He replaced the phone in its cradle, took a deep breath, and turned back to the conference table.

"There's been a new development. Secretary Gorbachev has just spoken with President Reagan on the hot line." A rustle of surprise ran around the room. "He's made it clear that unless General Shpagin is returned at once, unharmed, the Soviet Union will withdraw from further negotiations on the Intermediate-Range Nuclear Forces Treaty."

There was a stunned silence. At last the CIA man said, clearly astonished, "They can't be serious! They've been working on that with us for years. Why would their diplomats call it off over a simple general?"

The State Department observer shook his head. "It's not only the diplomats who have a say. Their military knows we'd love to learn all he can tell us, and they're bound and determined to make sure that doesn't happen. Gorbachev's still settling into power after Chernenko's death. He's not yet secure in his position, and he can't afford to ignore them. If he has to, he'll strengthen his domestic position by going along with them, even at the expense of his most cherished diplomatic project."

"What did the President say?"

"He's called in the Secretary of State, and they've summoned the South African Ambassador. We're to stand by until further notice."

* * *

The Commanding Officer, Special Forces of the South African Defense Force put down the phone, and breathed a long, slow sigh of relief. He consulted a map, scribbled some notes, then picked up the phone again and dialed a number.

"Signal to Lieutenant Viljoen, flash priority. He's to take his prisoner and his patrol to map reference..."

* * *

That evening, Lieutenant Viljoen decoded the latest message, read it three times, and swore loudly.

"What is it, sir?" Sergeant Bothma asked.

"Pack up, everybody. We've got to be at a rendezvous by dawn."

They marched through the night, taking all the usual precautions against being spotted, but they saw no sign of enemy movement. Even the usual faint sound of high-altitude jet engines was absent. By shortly before dawn, they were concealed in a clump of bushes on the north side of a large grassy clearing in the brush, almost a quarter of a mile across.

"What now, sir?" Bothma asked.

"We wait."

It didn't take long before they heard two aircraft approaching from the south. As they came into view in the early half-light, the South Africans recognized the familiar silhouettes of Puma helicopters; but they didn't land. Instead, they circled just south of the clearing, as if waiting for others to arrive.

Sure enough, within minutes more engines were heard, this time approaching from the north-west. Two Angolan Mi-8 helicopters appeared, circling to the north of the clearing. After a few minutes, probably consumed in establishing radio communication, one Puma and one Mi-8 landed in the center of the clearing, next to each other, facing north. Their pilots kept the engines running and the rotors turning as two figures disembarked from each chopper. They came together, exchanged salutes and handshakes, and moved out ahead of the aircraft. One of them, a South African officer, raised his hand and made a pumping gesture with his fist.

"That's our cue," Lieutenant Viljoen said, standing up. His team stared in shock as their officer abandoned any attempt at cover or concealment, then slowly, reluctantly followed his example. "General, you're going home in that Mi-8 over there. We're taking the Puma back to our base."

"But…how? Why?"

"I've no idea, sir. I guess we may never be told all the details. Put it this way. We didn't expect to find you aboard that chopper we blew up, and we didn't know what to do with you once we'd captured you. I suppose the situation caused so many complications for so many people that they decided to cut their losses like this. I can't say I'm sorry about that, sir. It'll be good to get a shower and a cold beer, instead of a dust bath and sun-heated water from a canteen."

"On that, we agree." General Shpagin hesitated, then held out his hand. "I won't say it's been a pleasure, but this has been an experience I'll never forget."

Viljoen shook his hand. "We won't, either, sir. Here, you'd better take these." He held out the general's cigar case and lighter. "You can enjoy one when you land."

Shpagin laughed. "Please keep them as a souvenir, lieutenant. There are four cigars, one for each of you, and you can have the lighter and cigar case. I shall drink a toast to you and your men in some good Russian vodka as soon as I'm back in Moscow."

"And we'll do the same for you in South African brandy, sir, as we smoke your cigars."

The two groups climbed aboard their respective aircraft, which took off and headed back to their bases. Within minutes, the only evidence that they'd ever been there was the drifting haze of dust thrown up by the helicopters' rotors. Soon, even that was gone.

* * * * *

Peter Grant Bio

Peter Grant was born and raised in Cape Town, South Africa. Between military service, the IT industry and humanitarian involvement, he traveled throughout sub-Saharan Africa before being ordained as a pastor. He later emigrated to the USA, where he worked as a pastor and prison chaplain until an injury forced his retirement. He is now a full-time writer, and married to a pilot from Alaska. They currently live in Texas.

# # # # #

Nemo Me Impune Lacessit

Motto of the Royal Scots Dragoon Guards (Carabiniers and Greys)

by Jan Niemczyk

15ᵗʰ May 2005. Outside Elze, West Germany.

The Royal Scots Dragoon Guards and its antecedents have served the Crown faithfully for over three hundred years. In that time, they have ridden with Marlborough and charged Napoleon at Waterloo and the Russians at Balaclava. They fought the armies of the Kaiser and Hitler, and more recently those of Saddam Hussein.

However, after 1945 the main preoccupation of the regiment was preparing for The War—World War Three. Spending much of its time based in West Germany. That war was to come in April 2005 and was to prove to be one of the toughest tests the regiment had faced.' Extract from *'Second to None—The Royal Scots Dragoon Guards in Peace and War'* by Major General Richard Stevenson, M.C (Edinburgh 2018).

* * *

"How many rounds do we have left, Angus?" Lieutenant Tom 'Sherman' Potter asked his loader.

499

"We're down to three sabot and a couple of HESH, Boss," Trooper Angus Malcolm replied.

"Christ," Potter muttered under his breath. The sabot rounds were their most effective rounds against tanks. The high explosive squash head (HESH) might work in a pinch, but Potter was loathe to try them.

There should have been a resupply well before now, but it seemed that the vehicles carrying fresh ammunition had gotten delayed somewhere in the chaos of 1 (British) Corps' rear area. Or perhaps there was no resupply?

"Here they come again; time for us to earn our pay again." The voice of the Officer Commanding A Squadron said over the radio. Oddly, the voice was not the one Potter was expecting, but it was familiar somehow.

Too tired to care, not sure it matters, he thought.

Putting his doubts aside, Potter scanned the ground ahead of his Challenger 2—there they were! Dozens of Soviet T-80s and BMPs were rapidly advancing on his position. He selected a tank with additional aerials, which marked it out as a command tank.

"Sabot! One eight hundred! Tank! On!"

"Loaded!" Trooper Malcolm reported, confirming that a discarding sabot round and separate charge were loaded, and that he was clear of the breech.

"On!" Lance-Corporal Gregor Blamey, the tank's gunner, said, confirming he could see the target.

"Fire!" Potter ordered.

"Firing now!"

'KABOOM!'

The Challenger's big 120mm gun spoke, throwing the sabot round at the T-80. The depleted uranium dart struck the Soviet tank on the turret ring, burrowing through to the crew compartment. Less than a second later, the T-80's ammunition exploded, sending its turret into the air.

"Target!" Potter barked. "Next target right!"

The next few minutes were a blur as Potter and his crew fired off their remaining sabot rounds, before switching to HESH to try and kill the lightly armoured BMPs.

"Last round, Boss…oh, Jesus! It's not a HESH…it's cannister!" Malcolm said in horror.

"What!" Potter exclaimed.

"Oh, shite, we're *goanna* to die!" Blamey said, with an uncharacteristic hint of panic in his voice.

"We need to get out of here! Driver reverse!"

"What, Sir?" Trooper Ilivia 'Mac' Macawai, the driver asked. "I don't understand."

"Back! We need to go back!" Potter yelled, panicking now as he could see a T-80 bearing down on them.

"Reverse, 'Mac' you fucking fanny, or we're all dead!" Blamey yelled.

"What? I don't understand?" Macawi repeated.

Potter saw the flash of the T-80's 125mm gun. This was it.

'WHANG!'

* * *

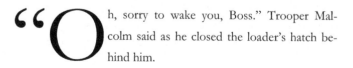

"Oh, sorry to wake you, Boss." Trooper Malcolm said as he closed the loader's hatch behind him.

"What?" Potter said, sitting bolt upright with surprise. "I wasn't asleep, was I?"

"Aye, you've been out for a while," Malcolm confirmed. "Gregor said we should leave you be."

"Yeah, thanks, I think, Angus," Potter replied, rubbing his forehead before pinching the top of his nose, thankful that it had all been a nightmare.

"Boss!" Blamey called down from outside the tank. "The O.C. is on the prowl!"

"Okay, thanks, I'll get myself cleaned up."

Potter grabbed his crewman's helmet and ran his right hand over his face. There was a day's growth of stubble, but it was too late to shave before his superior arrived.

* * *

"Morning, Boss," Sergeant Stephen Miller, the Troop Sergeant of 1 Troop, A Squadron, Royal Scots Dragoon Guards (Carabiners and Greys) said in greeting as the Officer Commanding A Squadron arrived. "How are you?"

"I'm fine thanks, Sergeant," Captain Alison Currie replied. "Mr. Potter about?"

"Think he was having a kip, Boss; he really needed it," Miller replied.

Currie nodded, she understood all too well. She too could feel the fatigue that no amount of sleep could get rid of. It came with command, and even if technically she should not have been in charge of an armoured squadron group, that particular perk had come with the job.

Oh, if all those chauvinists could see me now, Currie thought. One of the first women qualified for combatant positions, Currie had initially only been allowed to serve with a Home Defence Yeomanry regiment, and she'd commanded a company before transferring to the Scots as a Media Operations Officer. The opening of the war had seen her supervising a group of journalists visiting the regiment; initial attrition had led to Scots' commanding officer effectively conscripting her to replace A Squadron's second in command. Forty-eight hours later, a T-80's main gun had simultaneously disabled the squadron commander's tank and given her a battlefield promotion.

I guess it's unlikely the Queen's going to insist a woman can't properly be in charge of forces in combat, regardless of what her regulations might say, Currie thought wryly. *Indeed, if rumours are true, she's already gently prodded the PM to amend those documents*. Currie was one of a number of women who had, by chance, either found themselves leading a combat unit, or fighting on the front-line, regardless of the alleged illegality of such events.

"I think we all need a kip, Sergeant," Currie said with a weak smile.

Currie especially wanted to check up on 1 Troop because it had recently taken on the one remaining tank from 3 Troop, making it four vehicles strong, rather than three. There had been promises that at least one replacement tank and crew would arrive soon to reconstitute the Troop. But, it had yet to appear, and Currie had begun to doubt that it ever would.

* * *

"Good morning, Mr. Potter, I trust you've had a good rest?" Currie said by way of greeting when she reached Potter's tank.

"Ah, yes, thank you, Ma'am," he answered slightly sheepishly.

Currie smiled inside at the subaltern's apparent guilt.

"Don't feel guilty, Lieutenant; commanders need to be properly rested if they are to remain effective."

God, do I feel like a fake, giving advice to a junior officer with more combat experience than me!

"Anyway, how are things? Corporal Campbell and his crew settled in okay?"

Potter nodded.

"Yes, Ma'am. They're a good crew, but I'm keeping my eye, or rather Sergeant Miller is keeping *his* eye on them."

"Good; they may well need a bit of extra TLC. Any other news?"

Potter shook his head, deciding not to share the nightmare.

"Any news on when we'll be getting back into action, or if we'll get any new tanks, Ma'am?" he asked instead.

Currie shook her head.

"Nothing yet, but as soon as I know, you'll know."

Captain Currie spent half an hour inspecting Potter's troop, speaking to the men and checking on the tanks, before heading off back to Squadron H.Q. As he watched her leave, Potter realised who the voice had been in his dream—it had been his father. He wondered what Freud would have made of that.

* * *

16th May. Outside Elze, West Germany.

"**G**ood morning, gentlemen…and lady," Lieutenant Colonel Richard Stevenson, the regiment's Commanding Officer, said to the assembled

'O' Group. "I think I may have some good news for you. Brigade have told me that we are to expect some replacements in the next few hours, so, Alison, you'll be able to reconstitute 3 Troop, and Roger, you'll be able to bring your 3 Platoon back up to strength."

Major Roger Carter, the Officer Commanding, A Company, 1st Battalion, The Black Watch, nodded and looked pleased. The attached infantry had taken quite a few casualties.

"I'm assuming, Colonel, that there's a catch?" Major Ian Anderson, the regiment's Second-in-Command, asked.

Stevenson nodded.

"You've got it in one, Ian. Corps has not decided to release men and vehicles from what reserve it has left to us, and the other battle groups, from the goodness of its heart. We are going to be crossing the Leine...again."

The SCOTS DG Battle Group, and indeed the rest of 1st Armoured Division, had already made two crossings of the Leine River. The first had been a withdrawal, as part of wrong-footing the Soviet 3rd Shock Army. The second had been a follow-up to that—an assault crossing to relieve the airborne troops of the Parachute Regiment Group, who had been defending the city of Hildesheim. The operation had given the 3rd Shock Army a bloody nose and allowed 1 (Br) Corps to pull back to a strong defensive line unmolested. It had also given the British breathing space to rest and refit.

"This time, however, I think that we will be going for good," Stevenson continued. "As you know, the fighting going on as part of efforts to relieve Hamburg has been pretty heavy. The Soviets have been shifting their reserves up there to try and blunt our attacks. As a consequence, 3rd Shock Army has not been significantly reinforced.

The only new troops reported were what the Paras thought looked like penal battalions."

There was a low murmur at that, and Stevenson gave a feral smile as he continued.

"There is one bit of real good news before I move on: Since we've once again given the 3rd Shock a good kicking, they have apparently been stripped of their honorifics and are now just the plain old 3rd Combined Arms Army."

That brought a round of hearty laughter from the gathered group.

"Couldn't happen to a nicer bunch, Colonel," Major Carter commented.

"Quite," Stevenson agreed. "And we are going to be the ones who make sure that they don't get them back."

Stevenson turned to a map-board. The fingers of his right hand rested on the Leine.

"The operation we will be taking part in has been codenamed CONDOR, your guess is as good as mine why. At least the *Septics* are not getting to choose the names, or we'd have something like Operation OBVIOUS NAME.

"We will cross the Leine here, before swinging south of Hildesheim. The Soviets are still clearing a route through the city—the PRG and the West German engineers left one hell of a mess for them. Their armour is on this side of the city, but they can't get their supporting vehicles through, which is why they have not attacked us yet."

Stevenson looked to make sure his officers were understanding what he was saying.

"Our initial objective will be Schellerten," he continued, indicating the West German village with his right index finger. "Depending on how things go, we will then push on Braunschweig."

"Do we have a final objective, Colonel?" Captain Currie asked.

"Helmstedt," Stevenson said simply.

There was silence for a moment.

"That's ambitious, Colonel," Major Anderson commented, breaking the silence.

Stevenson nodded.

"I know," he agreed. "Now, this is for your ears only—the Brigadier let me know that American reinforcements from their I Corps started landing in French ports during the night. That's at least four big, armoured and mechanised divisions, plus an armoured cavalry regiment and a great deal of artillery. It's still going to be at least 72 hours before any of those units arrives in theatre, but SACEUR is willing to take a risk and mount a major counter-offensive all along the line. Quite what form that will take, outside of our part, I don't know, but I would not be surprised if there will be a major push for the border."

That's got their attention, Stevenson thought, seeing several apprehensive looks.

"The Soviets still have a lot of troops heading our way; the Byelorussian Tank Army Group, for example, is still transiting across Poland, and this will be a good chance for us to spoil any potential new Soviet offensive."

"Any chance we'll be allowed to cross the border?" Major Carter wondered.

"That's supposed to be a political decision, but the informal order is not to stop pursuit of the enemy just because you reach the inter-German border," Stevenson said. "If it was up to me, I'd not stop until we reach Poland. But it's not up to me."

He waited a long ten count, scanning the group.

"Well, if there are no further questions, get back to your troops and brief your own command teams. We've got 24 hours before the kick-off, so make the best of the time you've got."

* * *

17th May.

Lieutenant Potter watched from the turret of his Challenger 2 as Royal Engineers finished off the bridge. In the early hours of the morning the 'Toms' of 4th (Volunteer) Battalion, Parachute Regiment, had been inserted by helicopter to secure the eastern bank of the Leine River. The plan was for the paratroopers to clear space for 7th Armoured Brigade, the spearhead of 1st Armoured Division, to cross unmolested.

So far, so good, Haig thought. M3 amphibious rigs had been used to carry the 9th / 12th Royal Lancers, the division's reconnaissance regiment, across. They'd been closely followed by a squadron of The Queen's Royal Irish Hussars and the Royal Scots Dragoon Guard's Recce Troop. However, the engineers were now finishing off a pair of more permanent general support bridges to allow the rest of the brigade to cross more smoothly.

With the engineers apparently finished, a Royal Military Police 'Redcap' motioned to Potter that his troop should cross.

"Keep it down to twenty kays while you're crossing, Sir," the RMP Sergeant said, as Potter's Challenger drew level with him.

"Otherwise the Wedgeheads get upset that you might break their bridge."

"Right, oh, Sergeant. Don't want to upset the Engineers."

"Good luck, Sir, and give 'em one from the Monkeys."

"Don't worry, Sergeant, we certainly will," Potter replied before ordering his driver to proceed.

* * *

'*P*ARP!'

The sound of someone in the troop compartment of the Warrior Infantry Fighting Vehicle was clearly audible in the turret. The smell of the noxious emission arrived a few seconds later.

"God all mighty, what have you lot been eating? *Stinkin'* up my track like that, ah think I'll put on *ma* respirator!" Corporal Andrew Lonnie, the section and vehicle commander complained.

"You think it's bad up there? Try sitting down here!" Lance Corporal Paul MacConachie, the second in command of the section, and commander of the second fire team, replied. "I blame those '*Boxhead*' rations Deeky 'obtained' for us."

"You never complained when I got them at the time," Private Derek 'Deeky' Wilson said defensively. "Anyway, it *wisnae* me; smelt it dealt it!"

"Well, don't look at me," Private David 'Jock' Stein, one of the section light machine gun gunners, said. "I think it was *defo* Deeky!"

"Man, that smell is *boggin.*'" Private Robert 'Robbie' Robertson complained. "Can we no' open a hatch? If the Russians get a whiff of that, they'll think we're trying to gas them!"

The other three men of the section and the Warrior's gunner all also vociferously denied that they had been responsible for polluting the air inside the vehicle.

"*Awwfirfucksake*, we're a couple of minutes away from assaulting a Ruskie position and all you lot can argue about is who's farted," Lonnie said finally, putting an end to the argument. "Anyway, those of you who have got them, fix bayonets."

Private Wilson, the guilty party, despite his protestations, reached down, drew his bayonet and fixed it to the barrel of his rifle.

Well, this is about to get serious, he thought. *To think that we've paid tons of money for a fighting vehicle, and it's still going to come down to 'stick them with the steel' like we're fighting the Zulus, or something.* Each member of the section went through a ritual of checking that he could reach his spare magazines and grenades easily enough, that his helmet and body armour were properly fitted and the straps secured, and that their comms were working. Wilson watched as Stein double checked the LMG's ammunition belt again, the nervous action clearly a comfort. On the other side, Robertson loaded his grenade launcher and then affixed his own bayonet.

Even worse that there's only two of us with the pig stickers, even if the LMG and underslung grenade launchers add to our firepower, Wilson thought. Before the war, he'd remembered his section sergeant complaining loudly about the new section and squad organization's "deficient in cold steel."

I guess there's a point to all—

The Warrior halting interrupted his thoughts. The rear door opened as the IFV's 30mm RARDEN cannon engaged some unseen target.

"Troops out!" Corporal Lonnie ordered.

Wilson, Stein, Robertson, McConachie and the other three men of the infantry section sans Corporal Lonnie spilled out of the vehicle's back. Lonnie remained aboard the Warrior for the moment, the vehicle's optics and radio allowing him to better control the action and co-ordinate their fire support. The reason for this decision became readily apparent as Wilson sprinted forward, as the wood A Company had been assigned to assault was still dark. Smoke from phosphorous rounds was drifting through the trees, further reducing visibility.

Private Wilson saw a few shadowy figures ahead of him through the swirling smoke, and their helmets looked 'wrong.'

Soviets! He charged forward, screaming to release the tension, firing a few shots as he did. The rest of the section was similarly engaged, and a few of the figures dropped. The shock caused the majority of the others to turn and run. One Soviet stood still, either planning to stand his ground, or rooted to the spot by fear. Wilson did not care either way, as he was upon the man before the Soviet could really make any decisions. The British soldier plunged his bayonet into the man, then twisted his rifle to the right as his victim screamed. Operating purely on muscle memory, Wilson withdrew the weapon as his section and squad continued after the fleeing enemy. Looking down as the Soviet soldier twitched then went still, Private Wilson wiped off some of the blood that had spattered onto his face.

Well, guess we're in it, he thought, striding to keep up with the rest of his squad. To his shock, Private Wilson was not scared any more.

Lieutenant Potter watched the infantry assault progress against the Soviet anti-tank gun battery. The battery, equipped with the

125mm towed 2A45M Sprut-B, had hoped to ambush the SCOTS DG battle group as it crossed at the expected ford site to the north.

Good thing these idiots didn't understand thermal camouflage, Potter thought. The guns had stuck out like a sore thumb to the reconnaissance vehicles, and the battle group's fire support officer had brought down a mortar barrage on the battery and its supporting infantry company. That had allowed the Black Watch to get on top of the position before the Soviets had a chance to dust themselves off.

Oh no, that won't do, Potter thought, watching as one of the guns attempted to reposition so that it could engage the friendly infantry. *He's probably got flechette or HE loaded.*

"HESH! One six hundred! Anti-tank gun! On!" Potter barked.

"Loaded!" Trooper Malcom reported a few seconds later.

"On!" Lance-Corporal Blamey confirmed.

"Fire!"

"Firing now!"

'BOOM!' The L30 120mm gun fired, kicking up a huge dust cloud as it sent the HESH round down range. The shell slammed into the anti-tank gun and exploded, almost obliterating it and bowling over all of its crew.

"Target stop!" Potter ordered.

The rest of the assault was over in minutes. With the anti-tank battery and infantry company eliminated, there was now no significant Soviet formation between the SCOTS DG battle group and Schellerten. Soviet forces in Hildesheim were now horribly vulnerable to being cut-off.

* * *

Hildesheim.

A cting Major Pavel Krylov held a cloth over the lower part of his face as he surveyed the rubble that was once a city. A platoon commander at the start of the war, Krylov was now a veteran soldier who had seen his unit rebuilt several times. Each time, he'd taken great pains to properly incorporate the survivors of other, shattered, units. Now for the first time, as the new commander of the 243rd Motor Rifle Regiment's new 4th Battalion, Krylov wondered if his task was beyond him.

At least No. I Company is solid, he thought. No. I Company was formed from the survivors of his old unit, reinforced by some newly arrived reservists, Numbers II to V Companies, however, were formed from a mix of soldiers who were regarded as having 'failed,' mainly political prisoners and common criminals. No. VI Company was made up of MVD personnel, all experienced prison guards, along with a platoon from a KGB 'Security Battalion.'

Allegedly the last is to keep the prisoners 'honest,' but it fills me with dread, Krylov_thought. The appearance of the KGB unit, combined with penal soldiers, was a sign of the Kremlin's increasing impatience with the Soviet Army. No longer would discipline be the sole province of the Commandant's Service (the military police) and the GRU. The KGB had been given near *carte blanche* to do whatever it felt was necessary.

Which means this stench will surely get worse before long. Although Krylov had smelled death a great deal since the start of the war, he had never grown used to it, hence the cloth. The stench was especially bad as his battalion, or at least the 'penal' portions of it, had been assigned the task of clearing a route for vehicles through part of Hildesheim. That had resulted in uncovering decomposing bodies that had been buried by rubble. Krylov had been saddened to see that by far the majority of the bodies wore Soviet uniforms.

'BOOM!'

Krylov ducked reflexively as a booby-trap left by West German *Wallmeister* pioneers exploded. Small pieces of rubble and 'other' material spattered the Soviet major, fortunately not causing him any injury.

Why do those idiots not listen to the warnings? Krylov brushed himself down, noticing to his disgust that there was a piece of intestine on his left boot. He shook it off and tried not to think about the fact that some carrion creature would probably soon be eating it.

"Comrade Major! Comrade Major! Are you all right!"

Krylov turned, seeing his orderly jogging over. The man was a re-servist old enough to be the major's father. Like all the other replacements, Krylov had not bothered to learn his full name, just knowing that he was called Boris.

"I am fine, Boris," he replied. "Which is not something I can say for those clots over there."

"I am glad you are well, Comrade Major. As for those men…" Boris shrugged, evidently indifferent to his fellow soldiers' fate. Krylov regarded the man coolly.

"I have a message from headquarters," Boris added, remembering the reason he had been looking for his commander. The older man handed over a message slip.

'British forces have cut Autobahn 7, south-east of Hildesheim and Bundesstraße 1 at Schellerten. Enemy forces also reported to south of Sarstedt, near Bundesstraße 6. You are to prepare your battalion for road movement and counter-attack.'

Krylov could see that the message had been signed by the Regimental Commander, Colonel Ivanov. Evidently the message had been regarded as too sensitive to risk passing by radio, even though the major was accompanied by a radioman wherever he went.

The major opened a case containing a rare and secret item in the Soviet Army: a map. It showed Hildesheim and the surrounding area as he unfolded it. Casting about for a flat surface, Krylov finally beckoned Boris across so that he could use the orderly's back to support it.

"Damn," he muttered on seeing where the locations on the map were. Enemy forces were now to the rear of Hildesheim and would not have to make much more of an advance to surround the city.

They have effectively done to us what we have done to their paratroopers, like a python eating a barn snake that is swallowing a rat.

"Come on, Boris, time to get back to H.Q.; I have some proper work to do."

Boris enthusiastically hurried off ahead of Krylov, who marvelled at the energy a man of his age had. The orderly opened up quite a gap between himself and the major. This proved fortuitous for Krylov, as after a short distance Boris unwittingly caught his foot in a trip wire connected to the pin of a grenade. The resultant explosion, while not as impressive as the most recent one Krylov had experienced, was still sufficient to strike him with organic debris.

Well, looks like I am going to need a new orderly, Krylov thought with equal parts annoyance and apathy.

* * *

Schellerten.

The Royal Scots Dragoon Guards Battle Group had halted just to the east of the village to allow its vehicle to refuel and replenish ammunition. Its men would also take the opportunity to rush a quick meal.

Lt. Colonel Stevenson was finishing up eating in the turret of his Challenger 2 when he was interrupted by the Regiment's Adjutant, Captain Thomas Young.

"Got the Brigadier on the line for you, Colonel." Young informed him.

"Damnation." Stevenson muttered, putting the plate of curry aside and climbing out onto the roof of the turret, before following Young across to the Sultan Armoured Command Vehicle.

"Stevenson here," he said once he had put the radio headset on.

"*Hello Dick, got a bit of a change of mission for you,*" the voice of Brigadier Harris said. His voice sounded a bit like a Dalek over the scrambled radio link, and the comparison was an apt description of the short, powerfully built officer. From the tone of voice, Stevenson could tell that the impending mission was going to be a tough one.

"*The Soviets are beginning to react, a little faster than we'd hoped in fact,*" Harris said, the distortion forcing Stevenson to pay much more attention. "*While the bulk of their forces to the west of Hildesheim have been pinned in place, a motor rifle regiment in the city itself is moving towards where you are. Division needs you to re-orientate to the west and halt that regiment before they threaten the bridgehead. While you hold them, the Queen's Dragoon Guards Battle Group will hit them from the left flank.*"

"I'll need as much support as you can give me, sir," Stevenson replied. A MRR wasn't far off from a British brigade. Stopping one of those would have been a tough task for his unit at full strength, never mind its current state.

"You'll get it. Corps is going to give your battle group priority for artillery and air support. When your Forward Observer and Forward Air Controller ask for support, they will be at the front of the queue."

Stevenson grew worried at that.

That assumes there's anything in the queue to answer the call, he thought.

"Dick, I can't emphasise how important it is that you stop this Soviet regiment. If they get past you, they'll be in a position to disrupt our advance on Helmstedt. The Black Watch and the Queen's Royal Irish are practically at Braunschweig. I'd have to turn them around, never mind what other units would have to stop. I imagine that General O'Connor would be seriously displeased if CONDOR is messed up," Harris said.

The corps commander can be as upset as he wants, Stevenson thought. *Fact is, that's a lot of combat power I've got to stonewall for this to work.* While a gulag or business end of a Makarov were unlikely for a British officer, O'Connor had developed a reputation for being fond of 'sacking' people.

Of course, have to be alive to get sacked.

"Don't worry, sir," Stevenson replied. "If that regiment gets past us, it will be because none of us are left standing."

* * *

651 Squadron, Army Air Corps. Forward Arming and Refuelling Point.

Captain Rachel 'Firekitten' White carried out a 'walk-around' check of her Apache AH.1 attack helicopter before climbing up into the rear cockpit. She took a moment to reflect on the irony that the current FARP was only a few miles away from the squadron's peacetime home—Tofrek Barracks in Hildesheim.

I hope the Paras or the Soviets haven't wrecked grandma's china, she thought unhappily. *Mum will never let me hear the end of it.*

White shook her head at the memory of her mother fussing at her about 'a bloody war likely breaking out' as she finished pre-flight.

"Ready to rock and roll, Dav?" White asked her Gunner, Staff Sergeant David 'Dav' Jones.

While White's nickname was a slight mystery—it had come with her to the squadron—Jones' was quite the opposite. It had originated from an army form that had left off the 'id' of his first name, and from them on he had been known as 'Dav.'

"Certainly am, Rach," Jones replied.

White glanced to her right to check on the other Apache that would be flying tonight's mission, flown by Warrant Officer Cliff 'Spooky' Budden, Canadian exchange pilot, and Sergeant John 'Jack' Newton. Budden gave her a 'thumbs up' from the other aircraft's pilot's seat.

"Okay, I'm firing up No.1," White said, pressing the button to start one of the Apache's RTM322 engines.

* * *

Half an hour later, the pair of helicopters were over the battlefield heading towards their first target. The airspace at low-level had proven to be almost totally lethal for helicopters and fast jets during the day, so both now preferred to operate at night. Even so, it was still a very dangerous environment. Other than the standard 30mm cannon, each Apache was armed with eight Brimstone missiles and two

CRV7 rocket pods under their stubby wings, while four Starstreak missiles adorned the wingtips.

Both Apaches slowed to the hover behind a small wood, and White slowly climbed until the Longbow on top of the rotor hub was exposed. She briefly illuminated the radar, which scanned the ground ahead of them.

"Looks like we've got some customers ahead." White remarked as she studied the CRT display showing the Longbow data.

* * *

The 243rd Motor Rifle Regiment's sole tank battalion had started the war with forty T-90A tanks. In twenty-three days of conflict it had already gone through that complement one and a half times. It had recently been brought back up to strength, but the replacement tanks were older T-72Bs from reserve stocks.

While a single platoon of four tanks had been detached to the Regiment's Advance Guard, the remainder were following the BMP-2s of No.2 Battalion. Unfortunately, none of the regiment's four 2K22 Tunguska (SA-19 'Grisson') anti-aircraft vehicles were in a position to protect the tanks from what was about to happen. For that matter, no one had even passed a warning so that the tanks might attempt to protect themselves.

* * *

"One away! Two away!" White announced as she fired two Brimstones.

Both helicopters ducked down behind the woods after firing a pair of missiles and rapidly relocated to a new firing point. Not staying in one position too long was a lesson learned by both NATO and Warsaw Pact attack helicopter crews. Even when an enemy formation had no dedicated anti-aircraft systems, tanks had proven quite capable of shooting down helicopters with their main guns.

In an engagement that lasted only around five minutes White and Budden fired sixteen Brimstone missiles at the tank battalion, destroying ten tanks outright and disabling two more. They finished off their attack by subjecting the surviving tanks to several salvos of rockets, a mix of Semi-Armoured-Piercing High-Explosive Incendiary and Flechette Anti-Tank, from their CRV-7 pods.

As the two Apaches departed, they left a scene of total chaos. The tank battalion had been reduced to eighteen operational tanks and found that its route of advance was blocked by burning vehicles. As a parting gift, White requested a fire mission from a Royal Artillery battery equipped with GMLRs, which would drop AT-2 anti-tank mines ahead of the battalion, which would further slow it down.

* * *

18th May. East of Schellerten.

Captain Currie lowered her binoculars and lowered herself down into the commander's seat, shutting the hatch above her head. Despite the best efforts of the Army Air Corps, the Royal Artillery, and the RAF, just under two-thirds of the 243rd Motor Rifle Regiment had made it through. While the enemy might now be short of tanks, they still had approximately sixty to seventy BMP-2s and a dozen 2S1 *Gvozdika* 122mm howitzers in support. It was still going to be a close-run thing.

"Who are those poor bastards riding in what look like trucks ahead of the main Sov force?" Currie's gunner, Corporal David 'Gearbox' Brown, wondered.

Currie too had noticed the rather odd-looking formation, following close behind the Soviet Advanced Guard. There were a few BTRs mixed in, but that group was otherwise made up of URAL trucks.

"Could be they want to use light infantry to take and hold the village." Currie replied. "Or…" She left the thought hanging for a moment.

"It's one of those Penal battalions we've heard about?" Brown wondered. "Poor sods will get shot to pieces when the '*Dropshorts*' open up."

"Well, I guess that's their problem and not ours, David." Currie replied. Part of her recoiled in horror at how casually she dismissed the suffering that was about to be inflicted on men being forced to advance against their will.

When did I start to lose my humanity?

* * *

Private Wilson peeped out of the downstairs window of the West German home his section had occupied. While the majority of the battle group had been positioned to the east of Schellerten, a single infantry platoon had been sent to contest control of the village. It was not expected to hold, but to simply delay the enemy. The platoon had been joined by a party of four Royal Engineers, who had been busy preparing demolitions and other 'surprises' for the approaching Soviets. The unit's Warriors and engineers' single Spartan APC were hidden a short distance away, engines running in preparation of evacuation.

Well there the poor sods are, he thought, spotting the approaching URALs and BTRs.

"Here they come!" he called out as the approaching enemy column halted, and its troops start to debus.

"Hold your fire until the boss gives the word," Corporal Lonnie told his section. "I'll shoot *yous* myself if someone opens up too early!"

Being a well-trained and experienced infantryman, Wilson was not impressed with their attackers' tactics.

Like drunks coming home on a Friday night, he thought as the Soviets milled in his general direction.

"Who are these stupid pricks, Robbie?" he asked his 'Oppo.' "*Dae* they *aw hiv* a death wish, or something?"

"Fuck knows, Deeky," Private Robertson replied with a shrug. "Makes the pricks easier to shoot if they *dinnae* take cover."

The scream of incoming artillery made the men of the section flinch. It was only when the first 155 mm shells exploded amongst the Soviet troops that they realised it was 'friendly.'

"Well makes a change from shelling us, I suppose. So nice one, '*Dropshorts*,'" Private Stein remarked with a wide grin.

"Now! Now! Now! Open fire!" Corporal Lonnie ordered. "Shoot the stupid fuckers!"

Wilson pulled the trigger on his L85A2 rifle in quick succession, aiming at shadowy targets, not really seeing how many of them he hit, if any. To his left, Private Robertson alternated between firing his rifle and launching grenades from the UGL fitted to it. To his right, Private Stein fired short bursts from his LMG

The artillery fire lifted as the AS90 howitzers relocated to avoid any counter-battery fire. Barely had the barrage ceased when the air was again rent by the sound of shell fire. This time it was not friendly.

"Incoming!" Stein yelled, dropping to the floor of the house.

122 mm shells from the Soviet regiment's *Gvozdika* howitzers began to methodically smash up the village. The house that Lonnie's section was sheltering in shook as the shells crept ever closer.

This is it, Wilson had a moment to think.

* * *

Unbeknownst to any of the artillerymen, the Soviet artillery battalion had thrown the proverbial 'one shell too many.' British counterbattery radars, their lobes queued to provide coverage over the village's position, quickly determined the *Gvozdika*s' locations. Mid-salvo, the counterfire from the GMLRs of 39th Heavy Regiment, Royal Artillery, arrived with their typical precision and savagery. Two of the dozen *Gvozdika* survived the steel rain unleashed on them, their crews shaken by the cluster munitions and secondary explosions signifying their comrades' deaths.

* * *

"Well that was short," Stein said picking himself back up. "Looks like we were pretty lucky...*aww naw*, shite. Paul's *deid*."

While the house had not been hit directly, a near miss had caused a roof beam to collapse. Unfortunately for him, Lance-Corporal Paul MacConachie had been directly underneath it.

"*Aww*, shite!" Lonnie exclaimed. "Get his ammo, gat, grenades and tags."

"Robby, you're acting assistant section commander until I hear different."

"Well here's to bloody wars and…" Wilson began to say, quoting a well-known saying.

"Shut the fuck up, *Private Wilson!*" Lonnie snapped. "Paul's not even cold, and you're making jokes. Show some fucking respect!"

"Sorry, Corporal," a contrite Wilson said as he searched through the late MacConachie's ammunition pouches, taking the spare magazines he found, along with some ration bars.

"It's no' me you should be apologising to, *ya bam!*" Lonnie growled.

"I hate to interrupt, lads," Stein remarked from the window. "But we've got infantry at the edge of the village."

"Well, shoot the silly bastards then!" Lonnie replied, crossing to one of the other windows.

* * *

Acting Major Krylov had watched with horror as the British artillery barrage cut the leading two companies of his battalion to pieces. Thankfully, as far as he was concerned at least, they had been Penal companies and not his old unit. He cursed the British gunners for not managing to hit the Guard Company; he would have settled for the KGB platoon.

I cannot depend on anyone these days, he thought angrily. *Not even the enemy.*

The survivors of II and III Companies, piteously few though they were, had simply dropped into cover, until IV and V Companies had reached them. The survivors had been incorporated into these units and the advance continued. No. I Company was now close enough to the village to begin to use its BMP-2s as direct fire support. Annoyingly, the British were not using tracer fire, making it difficult to locate them.

The snarl of machine gun fire from the Guard Company caused him to look to his right. A few small groups from the Penal Companies had started to drift back from the murderous British defensive fire, and the Guards had provided a sharp remainder which way they should be moving.

Well, at least they put that first burst over their head, Krylov thought. *It would have been a double waste if they'd actually shot some of them.* His battalion wasn't short of machine gun ammunition yet, but he knew how quickly that could change in the offense.

"Comrade Major, the IV and V companies have reached the village," his new orderly stated. Krylov smiled as he heard the sounds of the initial assault.

The British might be better trained, but we certainly have many, many more troops, he thought.

* * *

"*H*ello *all call-signs, this is Sunray, time to go, repeat, time to go. Off*," Lieutenant Gary Beaumont, the platoon leader, said over every member of the platoon's Personal Role Radio.

The platoon's four Warriors and engineers' Spartan roared into the village, taking cover and then opening their rear hatches. The survivors of the platoon broke out of their buildings and sprinted towards the vehicles as the Warriors laid down suppressive fire. As he ran, Wilson saw one 'Jock' from another section get hit and go down, wounded.

That poor bastard, Wilson thought, ducking behind some rubble in preparation of laying down covering fire. To his shock, a RAMC medic dashed out of one of the Warriors and grabbed the man.

Bloody hell, Private Norris is stronger than I thought she was, he thought, watching the slight woman drag the man towards safety.

"Come on Wilson, shift your arse!" someone shouted. Wilson shook himself and started dashing for his own Warrior just as BMP-2s rounded the far intersection corner. There was a short, intense exchange of 30 mm fire between the platoon's Warriors and the oncoming Soviet vehicles. Wilson's Warrior was untouched, while another Warrior in the platoon was damaged but not penetrated due to its heavy armour. Unfortunately for the engineer section and their Soviet counterparts, neither the Spartan nor the three BMP-2s were nearly as lucky, their burning wrecks contributing to the general pall starting to surround the area.

* * *

Battle Group H.Q. (Main).

The Sultan ACV from which Lt. Colonel Stevenson was controlling the battle shook as an artillery shell exploded nearby. Waiting to see if it was the start of a barrage, Stevenson was pleasantly surprised to see it was just a stray. Turning, he regarded his staff as they all came back to their feet.

"D Squadron is getting hit pretty hard," he noted. "They're down to seven operational tanks and three Warriors; it looks like my counterpart has concentrated all of his tanks and now his reserve on our left flank. How bad are things there now?"

"Pretty bad, Colonel," Captain Young reported, his face pale as he listened to a radio report. "Their squadron H.Q. just got hit by artillery."

The man paused.

"Sir, Major Mollison and Captain Baxter are out of action," Young said quickly. "Major Mollison is dead, I'm afraid."

Stevenson swallowed.

I've known Brian since Sandhurst, he thought. *My god, will there be any of us left when this is over?* Getting a mental grip on his emotions, Stevenson put those thoughts aside.

Not if you don't save that for later, you idiot.

"Who is in charge down there now?" Stevenson asked, his voice harsher than he wished.

"Lieutenant Patel; he commands the attached Black Watch platoon."

With the pressure D Squadron was under, he needed an experienced officer in charge, not an infantry subaltern.

"Right, I'm going to head down there myself." Stevenson declared, deciding that he needed to resolve the crisis himself. "Captain Young, get onto Major Anderson at Forward H.Q. and tell him he's in charge for the moment. You take command here."

* * *

As Lieutenant Colonel Stevenson's Challenger 2 crested a small rise, he could see why D Squadron had been badly mauled. At least a company of Soviet T-72s were only a few hundred meters away from the British positions, and at that range even the Challenger's heavy armour was vulnerable to penetration from their 125mm guns.

"Right, time to make ourselves look like a whole tank squadron," Stevenson told his crew. "Heyman, find your targets while I get a hold of this situation."

As his gunner, Sergeant Charlie Heyman, followed orders, Stevenson got onto the D Squadron command net, informed the unit he was taking command, and what his instructions were. Heyman, like all good command tank gunners, was able to control the Challenger 2 effectively from his position. By the time Stevenson was done, his tank had fired four times, all from separate positions. As the second T-72's turret flew into the air, the Soviets quickly became convinced that another armoured squadron was falling upon their left flank.

"Uh, oh, Boss," Heyman remarked. "Looks like we've pissed them off!"

"And we're a *wee* bit short of ammo now," the loader, Lance-Corporal Nick White commented.

So, this is how it ends, Stevenson thought, the first volley of 125mm shells going over his head. Anderson tried to think of something inspiring to say, a text message on his Bowman radio terminal saved him.

"The Queen's Dancing Girls are hitting the enemy's right flank!" he said exultantly, referring to the 1st The Queen's Dragoon Guards Battle Group. "I'd say we've done it!"

Stevenson was right, starting with the attack on D Squadron, the enemy found themselves caught between the hammer of the QDG battle group advancing from the south, and the anvil of the SCOTS DG.

The 243rd Motor Rifle Regiment's attack broke down and shortly after that, the regiment itself began to fall apart. Both British battle groups now pursued a beaten enemy, which was also subjected to near constant attack by attack helicopters and fast-jets, now that its air defence vehicles had either been destroyed or were out of ammunition.

Flying a rare daytime mission, Captain White and her wingman, Staff Sergeant Jones, joined the chase in their Apaches, picking off fleeing enemy vehicles with relative ease. She was only brought up short when she realised that she had started to target individual soldiers on foot.

* * *

19th May. SCOTS DG battle group.

"That was a great bit of work, Colonel," Brigadier Harris told Stevenson. "Well done to you and your men. But I don't want to see you playing at squadron commander next time."

"Thank you, sir, and I certainly don't want to have to do that again," Stevenson replied. He was happy that Harris had taken the time to come down and see the battle group personally.

Shows he's not just a mad sacker, Stevenson thought.

"The divisional commander and General O'Connor also pass along their own congratulations," Harris continued happily. "If that Soviet regiment had gotten past you, there's no end of trouble it could have caused. As things are, the Black Watch reached Helmstedt in the early hours of this morning. Other battle groups from our division and the other divisions, from what I hear, have reached the border in several places."

The man paused for a moment, and a shadow of doubt crossed his face.

"The only fly in the ointment is Braunschweig—there are still Soviets troops in the city," Harris said grimly. "They're mainly rear area types, but they'll need dealing with. I'm told that one of the infantry brigades from 2 Division is being brought up to handle that particular problem."

Glad I'm not the poor bastard who gets to go with them, Stevenson thought, then looked worriedly at Harris.

"And the rest of 3rd Shock...I mean the 3rd Combined thingy, well you know who I mean, Sir."

"We've started to have surrenders from the units pocketed to the west of Hildesheim," Harris said. "They have run out of fuel, are low on ammo, and are now running out of food."

Captain Young stuck his head into the Sultan. He was holding a copy of the previous day's *Guardian* newspaper.

Enterprising lad to get a hold of a daily that quickly, Stevenson thought. *No end to the surprises with that one, as usually they're days late.*

"Got some news that I thought you would be interested in seeing, gentlemen," the officer said.

"Holy hell, they've passed the National Service Bill," Harris stated, reading the banner headline.

"Looks like we're planning on the long-term, Sir," Stevenson remarked.

"Not that story, Sir, the one below," Young remarked, jabbing his finger at the paper.

'Revolts break out in Poland and Czechoslovakia.'

Stevenson and the Brigadier smiled.

"To paraphrase Churchill, I think this could be the end of the beginning," Harris remarked.

* * *

20th May. Near Schellerten.

A cting Major Krylov was tired, dirty, and hungry. He had been on the run for nearly two days now. He had been very lucky to escape the destruction of his BMP-2K command vehicle when British tanks had overrun his headquarters. It had been sheer luck that he'd stepped out to relieve himself shortly before a 120mm HESH round had knocked on the vehicle's flank with explosive results. Krylov had been able to escape into the night, but without rations and armed with nothing more than a pistol. He had decided to start to head east, hoping to run into friendly forces.

For the last two hours, he had been hidden in a ditch beside a road as convoy after convoy of British vehicles rumbled past. On seeing a gap, he got up and began to sprint across.

"Halt!" a female voice yelled. "Halt, or I shoot!"

Krylov started running as fast as he could, his legs burning and his chest feeling like it was going to burst.

I will never surrender, he thought. *How could I—*

Krylov was suddenly surprised to find himself face down on the ground, with two sharp *crack*s seeming to come an eternity later.

I've been shot, he thought stupidly. Strangely, he could not get any of his limbs to move, and breathing seemed to be a struggle. There was the crunch of gravel behind him, but he just couldn't make himself roll over.

"Stupid sod just wouldn't stop," the same female voice observed.

"Well, he won't make that mistake again," a second woman observed just before it all went black.

* * *

21st May. The Inner German Border, East of Helmstedt.

'WELCOME TO EAST GERMANY— COURTESY OF 21 ENGINEER REGIMENT, ROYAL ENGINEERS'

The sign, marking the point at which West became East, was in large scarlet letters. Captain, no *Acting Major* Currie (she had to remember that) smiled as her Challenger 2 rumbled over a Medium Girder Bridge that the engineers had laid across a crater in the autobahn. It reminded her of pictures of similar signs she had seen from the Korean War.

Well, time to finish putting a stake in beast, she thought.

British troops had captured the Helmstedt-Marienborn border crossing and pushed on for four kilometres into East Germany before halting and digging in. Going any further was considered both militarily and politically unwise—for the moment. The Scots were far from the only NATO troops to have crossed into the East—American, Dutch, and Belgian, but not West German, troops had all crossed the IGB. To their south, French and Canadian forces had crossed into Czechoslovakia.

We'll see what the Pact gets up to now, she thought. The enemy had initially retreated in good order. However, NATO forces had started to advance quicker than the Warsaw Pact could retreat. The well-ordered retreat had unravelled quickly, becoming a rout in many places. Now only a relatively small area of West Germany, bordered by the Elbe to the southeast of Hamburg and by *Bundesstraße 207* to Lübeck, was still under enemy occupation. Hamburg itself had also been relieved, although it was now very much on the frontline. Someone on the other side had finally stopped the operational bleeding, but Currie couldn't shake the sense that there was only a matter of time and reinforcements before NATO got the next lick in.

Of course, that's if the politicians let us get on with it, she thought grimly. *In any case, not my problem for a couple of days.*

What NATO should do next was something that was currently being discussed in Brussels and in capital cities across the alliance. Some countries wanted to continue to push east, liberate the nations of Eastern Europe, and finish the job. Others counselled caution and pointed out that there was still friendly territory, including the Danish capital, Copenhagen, under Soviet occupation. The latter members' logic ran that friendly territory should be liberated first before other nations were freed from the Soviet yoke.

"Okay lads," she said into her intercom, seeing the Squadron assembly area up ahead, "let's get this old girl into position so we can get some rest and refit done."

"It'll be about time," the gunner muttered. "At least we don't have as much work to do as those poor bastards in D Squadron."

Currie winced at that. After the action at Schelerton, the battle group's casualties had been fairly low thanks to the Challengers' and Warriors' protective capabilities. Still, around fifty men had been killed or wounded. While four of seven of D Squadron's knocked out Challengers and its damaged Warrior had already been returned to service, the crews had suffered roughly half casualties. The three remaining Challengers had taken major damage, with one a total loss and the other two a return to the factory. None of the twelve men inside had survived.

"No, that we don't," Currie said. She saw that the refuelling tankers were busy with C Squadron, and realized it was going to be another fifteen minutes at least.

"I'm going to get a quick catnap," she said as they pulled into their hasty hide. "Wake me up only if the Queen or Kremlin calls."

* * *

"Captain! Cap...I mean, Major! Have you heard?" Lieutenant Potter called out as he saw Major Currie's tank halt by the refuelling tanker.

Why are you not on your vehicle? Currie almost screamed, but figured it would be better to deliver that sentiment in relative private.

"I'm hopping off," she called down to her gunner. She quickly swung down and began hurrying over to Potter.

"What is it?" Currie asked as she approached. The tone did nothing to diminish Potter's smile, and for a moment she wondered if the man had finally cracked.

"It's the Soviets, Ma'am. They've declared a ceasefire! It's over! It's over!"

"Calm down a minute, Mr. Potter. What are our orders regarding them?" she asked, ever cautious.

"Um…orders from SHAPE to all NATO forces are to not engage Warsaw Pact forces, unless they approach within one kilometre," Potter said, holding up a message flimsy. "If they do that, they are first to be warned before being fired on."

"Thank you, Lieutenant," Currie said, taking the flimsy and reading it.

"I hate to burst your bubble, but I'm not sure that it's over quite yet," she stated, handing over the paper. Potter looked exactly like a puppy whose master had strong footed it like a soccer ball.

"But perhaps now it is out of our hands and in the hands of the politicians," she observed, then smiled. "Ask the Sergeant-Major if he still has any of that whisky that he thinks has remained hidden from me. I think this may call for a small celebration."

Potter's infectious grin returned, and she found her own expression broadening.

"But remind everybody we are in hostile territory, so keep alert. No one wants to be the answer to a future trivia question."

* * *

Despite Major Currie's pessimism, the ceasefire stuck. All across Europe and eastern Turkey, wherever NATO and Warsaw Pact forces met fighting sputtered to a halt. NATO forces dug in, while those of the Warsaw Pact pulled back a few kilometres before doing the same. Within two days, the Warsaw Pact opened negotiations in Geneva with their NATO counterparts. With revolution spreading, the former were understandably far more motivated to strike a deal than the latter.

* * * * *

Maps

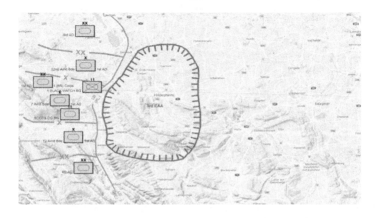

1.   Situation before the launch of Operation CONDOR.

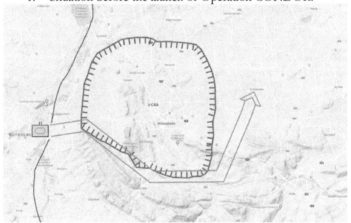

2.   Royal Scots Dragoon Guards Battle Group plan of advance.

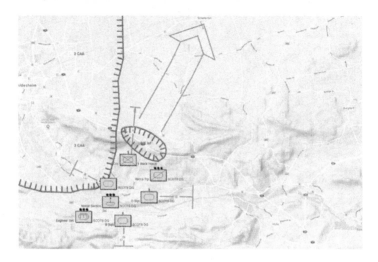

3. A Company, The Black Watch, in action again Soviet anti-tank guns and infantry

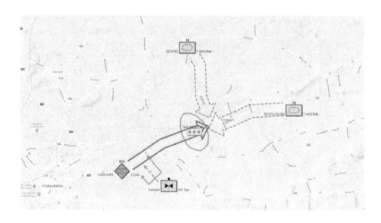

4. Soviet counter-attack east of Hildesheim and the British response.

* * * * *

Author's Note:

Readers who have read my web novel, *The Last War*, will notice that this story shares the general scenario and some characters from that work. However, as I said in relation to my last story, *Per Ardua ad Astra* (in *To Slip the Surly Bonds*) it is not a TLW story, but from a very close parallel universe.

Again, I want to thank all of those who have helped to make my work better. And I want to thank all those who have read my stories in the past. You make it all worthwhile.

I also have special thanks to my German *kamerad*, Henrik Löhr, who drew the maps, using the www.map.army website (used with permission). He is, as he has put it a 'former German Navy officer (a fish-head doing grunt work, go figure) and occasional contributor to "Mr Niemczyk's online magnum opus."

* * * * *

Jan Niemczyk Bio

Jan Niemczyk was born and brought up in Scotland, where he currently lives. He has long had an interest in military history, aviation, naval warfare, cats and horses. He also has an interest in the Cold War. He is still amazed that anything he has written has appeared in an actual proper book.

Mr Niemczyk is the author of the web novel *The Last War*, an alternative history where the USSR has survived into the early 21st Century. He is currently employed in the public sector. He would also like to thank all those who have read his work, helped to make it better and who have bought the first two books in this series.

\# \# \# \# \#

About the Editors

A Webster Award winner and three-time Dragon Award finalist, Chris Kennedy is a Science Fiction/Fantasy/Young Adult author, speaker, and small-press publisher who has written over 20 books and published more than 100 others. Chris' stories include the "Occupied Seattle" military fiction duology, "The Theogony" and "Codex Regius" science fiction trilogies, stories in the "Four Horsemen" and "In Revolution Born" universes and the "War for Dominance" fantasy trilogy. Get his free book, "Shattered Crucible," at his website, https://chriskennedypublishing.com.

Called "fantastic" and "a great speaker," he has coached hundreds of beginning authors and budding novelists on how to self-publish their stories at a variety of conferences, conventions and writing guild presentations. He is the author of the award-winning #1 bestseller, "Self-Publishing for Profit: How to Get Your Book Out of Your Head and Into the Stores," as well as the leadership training book, "Leadership from the Darkside."

Chris lives in Virginia Beach, Virginia, with his wife, and is the holder of a doctorate in educational leadership and master's degrees in both business and public administration. Follow Chris on Facebook at https://facebook.com/chriskennedypublishing.biz..

James Young holds a doctorate in U.S. History from Kansas State University and is a graduate of the United States Military Academy. Fiction is James' first writing love, but he's also dabbled in non-fiction with articles in the *Journal of Military History* and *Proceedings* to his credit. His next alternate history, *Against the Tide Imperial*, is the third novel in his *Usurper's War* series set during World War II and will be published in 1st Quarter 2019. You can find more information on the series and James's Comic Con schedule on his FB Page (https://www.facebook.com/ColfaxDen/), Twitter (@Youngblai), or by signing up for his mailing list on the front page of his blog (https://vergassy.com/).

* * * * *

The following is an
Excerpt from Book One of The Psyche of War:

Minds of Men

Kacey Ezell

Available from Theogony Books

eBook, Paperback, and Audio

Excerpt from "Minds of Men:"

"Look sharp, everyone," Carl said after a while. Evelyn couldn't have said whether they'd been droning for minutes or hours in the cold, dense white of the cloud cover. "We should be overhead the French coast in about thirty seconds."

The men all reacted to this announcement with varying degrees of excitement and terror. Sean got up from his seat and came back to her, holding an awkward looking arrangement of fabric and straps.

Put this on, he thought to her. *It's your flak jacket. And your parachute is just there,* he said, pointing. *If the captain gives the order to bail out, you go, clip this piece into your 'chute, and jump out the biggest hole you can find. Do you understand? You do, don't you. This psychic thing certainly makes explaining things easier,* he finished with a grin.

Evelyn gave him what she hoped was a brave smile and took the flak jacket from him. It was deceptively heavy, and she struggled a bit with getting it on. Sean gave her a smile and a thumbs up, and then headed back to his station.

The other men were checking in and charging their weapons. A short time later, Evelyn saw through Rico's eyes as the tail gunner watched their fighter escort waggle their wings at the formation and depart. They didn't have the long-range fuel capability to continue all the way to the target.

Someday, that long-range fighter escort we were promised will materialize, Carl thought. His mind felt determinedly positive, like he was trying to be strong for the crew and not let them see his fear. That, of course, was an impossibility, but the crew took it well. After all, they were afraid, too. Especially as the formation had begun its descent to the attack altitude of 20,000 feet. Evelyn became gradually aware of the way the men's collective tension ratcheted up with every hundred feet of descent. They were entering enemy fighter territory.

Yeah, and someday Veronica Lake will...ah. Never mind. Sorry, Evie. That was Les. Evelyn could feel the waist gunner's not-quite-repentant grin. She had to suppress a grin of her own, but Les' irreverence was the perfect tension breaker.

Boys will be boys, she sent, projecting a sense of tolerance. *But real men keep their private lives private.* She added this last with a bit of smug superiority and felt the rest of the crew's appreciative flare of humor at her jab. Even Les laughed, shaking his head. A warmth that had nothing to do with her electric suit enfolded Evelyn, and she started to feel like, maybe, she just might become part of the crew yet.

Fighters! Twelve o'clock high!

The call came from Alice. If she craned her neck to look around Sean's body, Evelyn could just see the terrifying rain of tracer fire coming from the dark, diving silhouette of an enemy fighter. She let the call echo down her own channels and felt her men respond, turning their own weapons to cover *Teacher's Pet*'s flanks. Adrenaline surges spiked through all of them, causing Evelyn's heart to race in turn. She took a deep breath and reached out to tie her crew in closer to the Forts around them.

She looked through Sean's eyes as he fired from the top turret, tracking his line of bullets just in front of the attacking aircraft. His mind was oddly calm and terribly focused...as, indeed, they all were. Even young Lieutenant Bob was zeroed in on his task of keeping a tight position and making it that much harder to penetrate the deadly crossing fire of the Flying Fortress.

Fighters! Three o'clock low!

That was Logan in the ball turret. Evelyn felt him as he spun his turret around and began to fire the twin Browning AN/M2 .50 caliber machine guns at the sinister dark shapes rising up to meet them with fire.

Got 'em, Bobby Fritsche replied, from his position in the right waist. He, too, opened up with his own .50 caliber machine gun, tracking the barrel forward of the nose of the fighter formation, in order to "lead" their flight and not shoot behind them.

Evelyn blinked, then hastily relayed the call to the other girls in the formation net. She felt their acknowledgement, though it was almost an absentminded thing as each of the girls were focusing mostly on the communication between the men in their individual crews.

Got you, you Kraut sonofabitch! Logan exulted. Evelyn looked through his eyes and couldn't help but feel a twist of pity for the pilot of the German fighter as he spiraled toward the ground, one wing completely gone. She carefully kept that emotion from Logan, however, as he was concentrating on trying to take out the other three fighters who'd been in the initial attacking wedge. One fell victim to Bobby's relentless fire as he threw out a curtain of lead that couldn't be avoided.

Two back to you, tail, Bobby said, his mind carrying an even calm, devoid of Logan's adrenaline-fueled exultation.

Yup, Rico Martinez answered as he visually acquired the two remaining targets and opened fire. He was aided by fire from the aircraft flying off their right wing, the *Nagging Natasha.* She fired from her left waist and tail, and the two remaining fighters faltered and tumbled through the resulting crossfire. Evelyn watched through Rico's eyes as the ugly black smoke trailed the wreckage down.

Fighters! Twelve high!

Fighters! Two high!

The calls were simultaneous, coming from Sean in his top turret and Les on the left side. Evelyn took a deep breath and did her best to split her attention between the two of them, keeping the net strong and open. Sean and Les opened fire, their respective weapons adding a cacophony of pops to the ever-present thrum of the engines.

Flak! That was Carl, up front. Evelyn felt him take hold of the controls, helping the lieutenant to maintain his position in the formation as the Nazi anti-aircraft guns began to send up 20mm shells that blossomed into dark clouds that pocked the sky. One exploded right in front of *Pretty Cass'* nose. Evelyn felt the bottom drop out of her stomach as the aircraft heaved first up and then down. She held on grimly and passed on the wordless knowledge the pilots had no choice but to fly through the debris and shrapnel that resulted.

In the meantime, the gunners continued their rapid fire response to the enemy fighters' attempt to break up the formation. Evelyn took that knowledge—that the Luftwaffe was trying to isolate one of the Forts, make her vulnerable—and passed it along the looser formation net.

Shit! They got Liberty Belle! Logan called out then, from his view in the ball turret. Evelyn looked through his angry eyes, feeling his sudden spike of despair as they watched the crippled Fort fall back, two of her four engines smoking. Instantly, the enemy fighters swarmed like so many insects, and Evelyn watched as the aircraft yawed over and began to spin down and out of control.

A few agonizing heartbeats later, first one, then three more parachutes fluttered open far below. Evelyn felt Logan's bitter knowledge that there had been six other men on board that aircraft. *Liberty Belle* was one of the few birds flying without a psychic on board, and Evelyn suppressed a small, wicked feeling of relief that she hadn't just lost one of her friends.

Fighters! Twelve o'clock level!

* * * * *

Get "Minds of Men" now at:

https://www.amazon.com/dp/B0778SPKQV

Find out more about Kacey Ezell and "Minds of Men" at:

https://chriskennedypublishing.com

* * * * *

The following is an

Excerpt from Book One of the Salvage Title Trilogy:

Salvage Title

Kevin Steverson

Available Now from Theogony Books

eBook, Paperback, and Audio Book

Excerpt from "Salvage Title:"

The first thing Clip did was get power to the door and the access panel. Two of his power cells did the trick once he had them wired to the container. He then pulled out his slate and connected it. It lit up, and his fingers flew across it. It took him a few minutes to establish a link, then he programmed it to search for the combination to the access panel.

"Is it from a human ship?" Harmon asked, curious.

"I don't think so, but it doesn't matter; ones and zeros are still ones and zeros when it comes to computers. It's universal. I mean, there are some things you have to know to get other races' computers to run right, but it's not that hard," Clip said.

Harmon shook his head. *Riiigghht,* he thought. He knew better. Clip's intelligence test results were completely off the charts. Clip opted to go to work at Rinto's right after secondary school because there was nothing for him to learn at the colleges and universities on either Tretra or Joth. He could have received academic scholarships for advanced degrees on a number of nearby systems. He could have even gone all the way to Earth and attended the University of Georgia if he wanted. The problem was getting there. The schools would have provided free tuition if he could just have paid to get there.

Secondary school had been rough on Clip. He was a small guy that made excellent grades without trying. It would have been worse if Harmon hadn't let everyone know that Clip was his brother. They lived in the same foster center, so it was mostly true. The first day of school, Harmon had laid down the law—if you messed with Clip, you messed up.

At the age of fourteen, he beat three seniors senseless for attempting to put Clip in a trash container. One of them was a Yalteen, a member of a race of large humanoids from two systems over. It wasn't a fair fight—they should have brought more people with them. Harmon hated bullies.

After the suspension ended, the school's Warball coach came to see him. He started that season as a freshman and worked on using it to earn a scholarship to the academy. By the time he graduated, he was six feet two inches with two hundred and twenty pounds of muscle. He got the scholarship and a shot at going into space. It was the longest time he'd ever spent away from his foster brother, but he couldn't turn it down.

Clip stayed on Joth and went to work for Rinto. He figured it was a job that would get him access to all kinds of technical stuff, servos, motors, and maybe even some alien computers. The first week he was there, he tweaked the equipment and increased the plant's recycled steel production by 12 percent. Rinto was eternally grateful, as it put him solidly into the profit column instead of toeing the line between profit and loss. When Harmon came back to the planet after the academy, Rinto hired him on the spot on Clip's recommendation. After he saw Harmon operate the grappler and got to know him, he was glad he did.

A steady beeping brought Harmon back to the present. Clip's program had succeeded in unlocking the container. "Right on!" Clip exclaimed. He was always using expressions hundreds or more years out of style. "Let's see what we have; I hope this one isn't empty, too." Last month they'd come across a smaller vault, but it had been empty.

Harmon stepped up and wedged his hands into the small opening the door had made when it disengaged the locks. There wasn't enough power in the small cells Clip used to open it any further. He put his weight into it, and the door opened enough for them to get inside. Before they went in, Harmon placed a piece of pipe in the doorway so it couldn't close and lock on them, baking them alive before anyone realized they were missing.

Daylight shone in through the doorway, and they both froze in place; the weapons vault was full.

* * * * *

Get "Salvage Title" now at:

https://www.amazon.com/dp/B07H8Q3HBV.

Find out more about Kevin Steverson and "Salvage Title" at:

http://chriskennedypublishing.com/.

* * * * *

The following is an

Excerpt from Book One of the Revelations Cycle:

Cartwright's Cavaliers

Mark Wandrey

Available Now from Seventh Seal Press

eBook, Paperback, and Audio Book

Excerpt from "Cartwright's Cavaliers:"

The last two operational tanks were trapped on their chosen path. Faced with destroyed vehicles front and back, they cut sideways to the edge of the dry river bed they'd been moving along and found several large boulders to maneuver around that allowed them to present a hull-down defensive position. Their troopers rallied on that position. It was starting to look like they'd dig in when Phoenix 1 screamed over and strafed them with dual streams of railgun rounds. A split second later, Phoenix 2 followed on a parallel path. Jim was just cheering the air attack when he saw it. The sixth damned tank, and it was a heavy.

"I got that last tank," Jim said over the command net.

"Observe and stand by," Murdock said.

"We'll have these in hand shortly," Buddha agreed, his transmission interspersed with the thudding of his CASPer firing its magnet accelerator. "We can be there in a few minutes."

Jim examined his battlespace. The tank was massive. It had to be one of the fusion-powered beasts he'd read about. Which meant shields and energy weapons. It was heading down the same gap the APC had taken, so it was heading toward Second Squad, and fast.

"Shit," he said.

"Jim," Hargrave said, "we're in position. What are you doing?"

"Leading," Jim said as he jumped out from the rock wall.

* * * * *

Get "Cartwright's Cavaliers" now at:
https://www.amazon.com/dp/B01MRZKM95

Find out more about Mark Wandrey and the Four Horsemen Universe at:

https://chriskennedypublishing.com/the-four-horsemen-books/

* * * * *

Made in the USA
Monee, IL
17 October 2020